Many Roads to Travel

True Colours: Book Two

Karen Surtees
and
Nann Dunne

Yellow Rose Books

Nederland, Texas

ISBN 978-1-932300-55-0
(Formerly 1-930928-34-3)

Second Edition

Revised, Re-edited, Reformatted in 2006

First Printing 2006

9 8 7 6 5 4 3 2 1

Cover design by Donna Pawlowski

Published by:

Regal Crest Enterprises, LLC
4700 Highway 365, Suite A, PMB 210
Port Arthur, Texas 77642-8025

Find us on the World Wide Web at
http://www.regalcrest.biz

Printed in the United States of America

ACKNOWLEDGMENTS

Thank you to Cathy LeNoir of RCE, artist Donna Pawlowski, and editors Lori L. Lake and Jane Vollbrecht for making this new edition possible.

A big hug to my best buddy, Nann, who despite long delays from me managed to persevere and stick with the story and me. A big thank you also has to go to several computer techs (who have no idea who they are) who fixed my laptop and managed to get it back to me in the middle of the Indian Ocean within six weeks. To my friends and family both in England and the USA who put up with my tantrums and hair pulling when things weren't going well. Lastly but not least to every single one of you that have emailed both Nann and I for your support and appreciation.

— Karen Surtees

To Karen (Kas), as always, who nourishes the tree of my dreams with her generous, loving, and unselfish spirit. The depth of pleasure that writing with her has brought me cannot be measured. Her support has been a true reflection of the adage, "A friend in need is a friend indeed."

Also, to my friends and family and especially my parents; and to all who continue to offer me encouragement, particularly Laney, Sue, Boots (Lou), and her pal Snoopy. You are immensely appreciated.

— Nann Dunne

All of life you travel
On many a winding road,
Walking, wheeling, hobbling,
Or pushed or tripped or towed.
You learn to just keep moving
No matter what your load.
Some roads lead to soul mates
And some, you're all alone.
Good luck, bad luck, hard luck
Everywhere you roam,
With many roads to travel
Before you know you're home.

Chapter
One

PAULA TANNER SHIFTED on the office couch as her partner, Erin Scott, helped move her cast leg into a more comfortable position. "Why don't you sit down for a while?" Paula said to their veterinarian friend, Dr. Mare Gillespie. "You've been pacing back and forth for hours."

"I feel better when I'm moving." Mare's tension was clearly evident in her voice. "How can you two sit there so calmly when TJ's being operated on?"

"You know we care." Erin ran her hand through her tight blonde curls. "But we've been in this situation before, remember? No matter how upset we get, it doesn't help TJ."

"Doesn't seem fair, does it?" Paula said. "TJ gets shot and paralyzed in a mugging, spends nearly two years trying to adjust to that, then winds up being seriously injured when those idiots forced the van off the road."

The accident Paula spoke of had happened a week ago. She had suffered a broken leg, and Erin a broken wrist, while Mare had escaped with only scrapes and bruises. But Mare's partner, TJ Meridian, hadn't been so lucky. Bullet fragments from the mugging had remained next to TJ's spine, and the van accident had caused them to shift. Mare's newly-found father, Dr. Michael Gillis, was operating in an attempt to remove them.

The thick plush carpets of the comfortable hospital office muffled the repetitive sound of Mare's footsteps from her incessant pacing. Not even the view from the window that covered one whole wall had interrupted her trek for more than a few seconds. Every now and then, she would stop and stare at the muted closed-circuit television monitor, then quickly look away. Unable to watch TJ's operation for any period of time, she let her anxious eyes linger just long enough to reassure herself that everything was okay.

Paula understood why Mare found the wait unnerving. It wasn't every day your own father operated on your soul mate.

Despite the fact that Michael had said the procedure wasn't very complicated, a lot was riding on the outcome of this operation.

The three women had originally chosen to be in the waiting room outside the operating theater. Michael had offered the use of his office, but Mare wanted to remain close by. Every five minutes, however, she had asked Erin to check the monitor in the office. Eventually, they had all moved into the office, so they could keep an eye on the proceedings.

Erin and Paula found the couch much more comfortable than the chairs in the waiting room. In here, Paula could keep her broken leg elevated. Although more than a week had passed since the accident, the leg still pained her if she used it too much.

The two-hour trip from the Meridian ranch to the hospital this morning had added to her discomfort. Since neither woman could manage the long drive, Burt, one of the ranch hands, had chauffeured them in the Land Rover and another hand had followed in a ranch truck to take Burt back, leaving the Rover for Mare's use. But Paula hadn't been able to get situated properly during the ride to give relief to her leg. Their decision to stay overnight at a hotel was looking better and better. And Erin, with her usual foresight, had brought her laptop and a duffel bag with extra clothing and other necessities, giving them the flexibility to stay as long as needed.

Erin sat behind Paula on the couch, arms wrapped closely around her body. Her blonde head rested on Paula's dark one, but her eyes were fixed to the television monitor while Paula's eyes followed Mare.

Paula had tried restraining herself, but she couldn't keep quiet any longer. "By the time the operation's over, you'll be exhausted and absolutely no good to TJ if she needs you. Now, sit down." This came out a little more forcefully than she had intended, but it had the desired effect. Mare finally sat down.

Within a couple of seconds, though, Mare was tapping her foot on the floor and her fingers on the arm of the chair. Paula sighed and turned to Erin. "I'm going to take her out for a while or she's going to explode."

"Okay, love," Erin whispered. "Don't go too far. I'll come get you if anything happens." She kissed Paula on the forehead, helped her to her feet, and handed her the crutches.

Paula hobbled across to Mare. "Come on, let's get out of here for a few minutes. Erin will keep an eye on what's happening."

"Sorry, I know I'm being a pain," Mare said as she got to her feet.

"Hey, no problem. You're concerned. We all are. But things

are going okay, and there isn't any point in getting wound up."
Paula patted Mare on the shoulder. "Believe me, there are going to
be more than enough occasions for that in the next few months.
Come on, we can grab some coffee in the cafeteria."

Mare held the door as Paula shuffled through, then she
followed.

As soon as the door closed, Erin grabbed the remote control
and turned the volume up. Mare had lowered it, unable to listen
to her father's calm voice talking about what type of incision he
was going to use on TJ's back and how he would resect the
previous scar tissue in the area.

Michael had a brilliant setup in the operating room. Cameras
and microphones were located in strategic places. By choosing a
different channel, you could see a different view. More important
to Erin, Michael kept up a running commentary throughout the
procedure, fully explaining every decision and action. This
enabled her to follow what was happening, and with the volume
turned up, she could hear Michael's authoritative voice. His
words were precise, clinical, and direct. Anyone not associated
with TJ's case would be hard-pressed to tell that he had a personal
relationship to the patient. The resultant videotapes would be
used for teaching.

Already the surgeons had run into problems: TJ had more scar
tissue around her old injury than had been anticipated. They spent
longer than the time planned removing it, while taking care not to
transect any buried nerves. And for some unknown reason, TJ's
blood pressure kept dropping. She was stable at the moment, but
Erin could tell from Michael's voice that he was concerned.

"You're right, Dr. Morton, there's a substantial amount of
damage in the area." Michael pointed to a section of TJ's spine. "If
you look closely, you can see that the bullet caused damage not
only to the T-11 area but also to the adjacent T-10 and T-12 areas.
Our patient was lucky. If the damage at T-10 had been more severe,
her subsequent level of mobility and control would have been much
less. You can see here," Michael said as he pointed with a probe,
"where the bullet fragmented on impact. The small bone fragments
you see are from T-11 and T-10. At the time of the original injury,
these fragments were inaccessible, and over time, they've calcified.
The patient's recent vehicle accident has shifted those fragments
enough that we can now attempt to remove them."

A nurse's hand came into view as she slipped a retractor into
the incision in TJ's back. The nurse then moved back, allowing a
clearer view. Erin's stomach turned, and her gaze slid away. It
was easy to watch this sort of thing on a TV program, but it was
another matter when you knew the person on the operating table.

She forced her eyes back to the monitor as Michael, always the teacher, continued speaking.

"Dr. Morton, from the MRI scan we've been able to determine that the spinal cord wasn't actually transected, but compressed. What type of complications can we expect?"

Erin leaned forward, fascinated despite her unease.

"Well, classically, compression injuries don't recover well after a period of time. With the amount of time that has passed since the original injury, it's unlikely that this patient will ever be able to walk unaided. On the positive side, considering the advancement in steroidal treatments, we may expect a degree of sensation to return. On the negative side, however, we run the risk of actually severing the cord ourselves. The fragments causing the compression may have calcified around the cord, and by attempting to remove the fragments, we may cause further damage."

"Is there anything else that might cause us concern?" Michael asked. His hands carefully lifted pieces of bone away and removed tissue from the area. There was a deafening silence as his co-surgeon pondered his question. "What about post-op recovery?" Michael said.

"Hmm...well, there may be some problems when return of sensation occurs."

"Such as?"

"Usually, return of sensation is accompanied by pain. Pain control is essential for good recovery."

"Excellent, Jack. What type of analgesia would you use?" Michael asked, relaxing his manner now that Dr. Morton had passed muster on his questions.

"A morphine derivative is indicated, though we would have to monitor the patient's condition closely. It's easy to push a physically disabled person into respiratory arrest. I'd also be inclined to give medication through a PCA—a patient-controlled analgesia pump—at least initially."

"Okay, people," Michael said. "Let's get some extra light in here and try to get the bigger fragments, now that we've cleared the smaller debris." The scene became brighter as more lights were directed at the operation site. Then Michael's head entered the picture and blocked Erin's view. With a quick flick through the various channels, she found a clearer picture, allowing her a different angle.

MARE AND PAULA slowly plodded down the well-lit, carpeted hallway.

"I didn't realize this would be so hard," Mare said.

"It's always this hard when it's someone you love, sweetheart. And I hate to say this to you yet again, but this is only the beginning."

"I know." Mare stopped walking. "I think my major problem at the moment is not being able to be with her. If I could reach out and touch her hand or give her a hug, I'd be okay. Sounds stupid, doesn't it?"

Paula nudged Mare back into a slow walk. "Anything but, in fact. Over the last few months, you and TJ have become extremely close. I never thought I'd see anyone closer than Erin and I, but you and TJ are made for each other. And if you think you've got it bad, you should have seen her whenever she knew you were coming to the house."

They reached the end of the hall where it turned and ran along the outer edge of the building. Chairs and couches faced the windowed walls that provided patients and visitors with a view of the manicured lawns just outside. "She was impossible." Paula slid onto one of the couches and leaned the crutches against the arm. "Erin or I would walk into her office to find her staring at nothing. Getting any work out of her was like pulling teeth. Then about an hour before you would be due, she'd be in a total panic, trying to get everything ready and perfect for you."

Mare sat down next to Paula. "You're kidding me, right?"

"Yeah, like I'd make this up. She was as antsy as a kid waiting to open her presents on Christmas day. And let me tell you something, if it were you in there and her out here, she'd be ten times worse."

"I guess we're lucky it's her then, huh? I can just see her tearing up and down the hallways in that wheelchair of hers. God, it would be bedlam."

"You said it. Michael would be lucky if his unit was still standing by the end of it." That image set both of them off laughing.

"Oh, Lord," Mare said as the laughter subsided. "Thanks, Paula. I think I needed that."

"You're welcome. I needed it, too."

"Are you and Erin holding up okay?"

Paula ducked her head, and her hands fiddled with a thread on her jeans. "I'd be lying if I said we were great. This has hit us both pretty hard. We thought we'd gotten through the worst of helping TJ recover from the mugging, but now that this has happened, it seems as though we're back at square one."

Tears glistened in Paula's dark eyes, and Mare quickly pulled her into a hug. "Hey, hey," she whispered, rocking her friend, while slowly rubbing her hand up and down Paula's back. "Everything's going to be all right. TJ's going to make it through this, and so are we."

"I'm sorry," Paula said, wiping at her face. "I didn't mean to get all weepy. I was supposed to be keeping your mind off the operation."

"Hey, you did a good job. Besides, we're friends, aren't we? And that's what friends are for."

Paula wiped her fingers on her shirttail. "Yeah, you're right. You want to go get that coffee, or go back?"

"I'd like to get back. I'm sure Dad's secretary, Sheila, would get us coffee, if we really want it."

"Come on, then." Paula grabbed her crutches and Mare stood and gave her a hand up. The pair walked back the way they had come.

Paula pushed open the door with an elbow and walked in. She saw Erin leaning forward, arms resting on her legs, her face a picture of concentration. "How's it going?"

Erin looked up, her expression grim. "They've had to stop. TJ's blood pressure fell again."

"Shit!" Mare said as she walked in. "They have any idea why that keeps happening?"

"Your dad and the anesthetist think she's having a reaction to the anesthetic."

"What are they going to do?" Mare dropped into the seat next to Erin.

"From what I heard, lighten the anesthetic and see if that makes a difference."

"Has Dad said anything about the time?" Michael had told them to expect the operation to last about four hours. But with all the problems, minor though they were, that time estimate was proving too short.

"Another couple of hours maybe. He was just about to go in for the bigger fragments. He said something about just getting the one that was compressing the cord the most and getting out, if they couldn't stabilize her pressure." All eyes turned to the monitor as Michael's voice came over the speakers, and the operation resumed.

Time ticked by slowly. TJ's pressure dropped on two more occasions, and Michael decided to call it quits after he removed the larger fragment. Due to the critical nature of the operation site near the spinal cord, it took almost as much time closing up as it had opening. Each layer of muscle had to be perfectly replaced and sutured to prevent over-buildup of scar tissue. Michael had wanted to insert metal rods to stabilize the damaged vertebrae once he had removed the fragments. That procedure had to be postponed, however, until TJ could be put under without the unpredictable and mysterious drop in her blood pressure. For now, the hardest part had been completed.

ONCE THE CAMERAS were turned off, the women scrambled to their feet, left the office, and headed for the waiting room outside the recovery area. Mare knew her father would stay with TJ until he was satisfied that she would be okay. Then he'd come out and tell them what was happening. With any luck, she'd be able to go right in to see TJ.

She hurried through the hallways, leaving Erin and Paula to get to the waiting room at their own pace. She rushed into the tan-colored room, avoiding the potted rubber plants by inches. Brown leather couches were placed around the room, and there was even an entertainment system installed. Mare ignored all of it and paced before the green door with the portal window that led into the recovery area.

As Paula hobbled into the room, Erin walked slowly by her side and guided her to the couch nearest where Mare was pacing. The dark smudges beneath Paula's eyes were more pronounced, and she looked paler than she had that morning.

"You must be tired," Erin said to her.

"I'd bet we all are."

Erin inclined her head toward Mare. "Look at her, off in her own world. She's so worried about TJ, I don't think she even knows we're here."

"Probably not. She ought to save some of that concern for herself. She isn't going to be well enough to help TJ if she's not careful."

"We need to be careful, too." Erin dropped onto the couch. "How about we stay in town tonight?"

Paula had rested her head on the couch back and closed her eyes. "Sounds good to me."

Chapter
Two

MICHAEL PULLED OFF the green surgeon's cap and removed the blue facemask he'd worn in the operating theater. He was disappointed, and his face showed it. The surgery should have been pretty straightforward, despite the potential risks involved. He was at a loss to explain why TJ's blood pressure had persisted in falling. They had done everything that the protocols demanded: given fluids, administered vasoconstrictors, even reduced the depth of the anesthesia. And still, her pressure remained unstable. Nothing in the notes from her previous operations had suggested that there would be a problem. In fact, they had gone without incident.

The laceration in TJ's side and her dislocated shoulder shouldn't have had any bearing on her blood pressure. Michael was beginning to wonder whether he'd missed some other injury from the accident, but nothing had showed up on the blood tests, EKGs, or the scans they had performed. It was quite possible that TJ's body was just letting them know that it had had enough. His eyes wandered over the room to where green-clothed nurses were administering to his patient. He'd ordered more blood tests and another EKG, just to be on the safe side, and he had directed that TJ be measured for a turtle shell brace to be used later.

Now, he had to explain to Mare what went wrong. Taking a deep breath, he looked through the portal window in the green door and could see her pacing. He swiped at the moisture on his forehead and pushed through the door, letting it swing closed behind him.

Mare heard the door open and redirected her pacing to take her straight into Michael's embrace. She clasped him tightly, and his arms wrapped around her in a comforting hug. Then she slowly released her hold and looked him straight in the face.

"'TJ's fine," he said. "It will be a while before she comes around, but all things considered, she's done well." He put as much conviction as possible into his words, wanting to ease the worry he saw in Mare's face.

The tension that had taken over Mare's body relaxed its hold somewhat. "Her blood pressure?" she asked.

"Let's sit down, and I can tell all of you what's going on." He took Mare's elbow and guided her to a seat near Erin and Paula. Michael smiled at the two women. He still found it hard to accept the type of relationship that Erin and Paula had, found it even harder to accept Mare's relationship with TJ. But he had spent enough time in their presence to see the love between the two couples and the joy each woman stirred in her partner. Certainly, he couldn't begrudge either couple the love he still sought.

"Okay then, first things first. TJ is stable. Her blood pressure is still a little low but nowhere near as low as it was during the operation. The operation itself was pretty successful. We managed to remove several smaller bullet fragments, one of the larger ones that had us concerned, and some bone debris. There are still several fragments at the injury site, but they're unlikely to cause any trouble even if they do shift slightly. Because of the problems with TJ's blood pressure, I wasn't able to insert the metal rods along her spine to help stabilize it. So, she's being measured for a turtle shell brace for when she's able to sit up and start her physical therapy."

"A what?" Mare said.

"It's a plastic brace that will be fitted around her torso, from pelvis to sternum." Michael took hold of Mare's hand. "She'll wear it during the day to support her spine until she has healed sufficiently and built up enough strength to do without it."

Mare took a deep breath and released it. "How long will that be?"

"That's hard to judge, sweetheart. Her records show she was in one after the initial injury and recovered very well. But it may be up to three months, or even more if there are complications."

He looked over to Paula and Erin, who were listening intently. "We'll start physical therapy in the next few days. I want to make sure that her legs are kept flexible. We'll also concentrate on building up the shoulder she dislocated and helping her regain her upper body strength. Then we hope to get her standing and possibly walking with braces and crutches."

His eyes came back to Mare and softened sympathetically. "But this isn't going to happen in the next few weeks, Mare. We're talking months of rehab."

Mare's lips pressed together in a tight line before relaxing. "Okay, Dad. I understand that." She obviously was struggling to get her emotions under control. "What about the rods you wanted to insert?"

"If her spine hasn't stabilized by the time the brace comes off, we'll consider another operation to insert them. That's if she has recovered enough to undergo further surgery." He let his gaze linger on Mare, making sure she understood before letting his eyes drift to TJ's anxious friends.

"What was the problem with her blood pressure?" Erin asked when Michael's gaze reached her.

"I'm not too sure. This didn't happen in any of TJ's previous operations, and there's no clinical reason I can find for it to have happened today." Michael slowly shook his head. "'I know she's been through a lot of emotional upheaval in the past several months, and the last few days since she woke up have been pretty hard on her. The most reasonable assumption is that she's worn out, and this is her body's way of telling us to leave her alone, at least for now."

He squeezed Mare's hand and stood up. "Now, I have a few other patients I need to see. Nancy, TJ's nurse, is in recovery with her, and she'll let you in to see her. Just go through the door. I'll be back in a few hours, but Nancy will call me if I'm needed, okay?"

Mare caught hold of his hand again, stood up, and pulled him into a hug. "Thanks, Dad."

"That's okay, honey. You know I was glad to do it. Now go see TJ. But," he said, looking intently at Mare, then at Erin and Paula, "as soon as she's moved back to her room, I want all three of you to go to my place at Dorburton Lakes and get some rest. Stay as many days as you wish. I'll be here in Springerly for some time yet, so the house at Dorburton is just sitting there empty.

"Mare, you've been camped in this hospital living out of a suitcase long enough. You really need to get out of here for a while." He put a finger on Mare's lips. "No arguing. You wouldn't accept my offer to stay in Dorburton before the operation, but I won't take 'no' this time. TJ will be asleep for most of the day. The pain medication we're going to put her on is pretty strong."

"Don't worry, Doc, we'll make sure she gets some rest," Paula said. "And thank you. We really appreciate everything you're doing."

"Only the best for my family, young lady. And that reminds me." Michael pulled a pad and pen from his pocket and quickly jotted a note. "I'm going to notify my chauffeur—he and his wife live at Dorburton—that he's to be available to drive wherever you need to go. That will allow you a little more freedom of movement, especially since you two are hindered with casts." He pocketed the pad. "Now go in and see TJ, then go home. I'll see you all later." He left the room, waving off their further attempts at thanking him.

Mare went straight through the recovery room door. Nancy was already waiting for her, green gown in hand. She handed it over and grabbed a cap to cover Mare's blonde, shoulder-length hair.

"Thanks, Nancy, I appreciate your help." Mare quickly pulled on the gown and slipped the cap over her hair. The recovery room was large and airy with curtains between patient bays. Each of the bays had the same set-up of monitors and suction and oxygen equipment. TJ was currently the only occupant.

It always amazed Mare that no matter how big people might be, hospital beds always made them seem half their size. The bed TJ lay in swamped her. Her black hair flared out across the top of the bed, and her head was wedged between two blocks of thick foam. Heavy straps held her head securely in place. Earlier, Mare had provided some soft padding that Erin had picked up for her, and she was pleased to see that Nancy had remembered to put it under the straps to prevent chafing.

Mare leaned over the bed and kissed TJ softly on the forehead, her hand gently caressing the side of TJ's head. A pressure behind her knees let her know that Nancy had brought a chair over, and she sat down, her other hand automatically taking hold of TJ's hand. She was happy to note that TJ's arms were no longer secured to her sides as they had been since the accident. She glanced over at Nancy. "No arm straps?"

"Dr. Gillis didn't see any reason to restrict arm movement anymore, but you'll still have to watch that she doesn't try to twist too much. Of course, that tender shoulder will slow her down a little."

"Cool, I get to have a hug when she wakes up." It had been one thing that had bothered her beyond belief. With TJ strapped into her spinal bed, movement totally restricted, it had been virtually impossible to have any type of physical contact. Mare had been able to crawl next to her and try to hug her, but TJ hadn't been able to respond in any way. It had upset them both, but Mare more so than she had imagined it would.

"I'm sure you won't be the only one who thinks it's cool. She's been chafing at the bit to get her arms undone since she woke up after the accident. Maybe now she'll give us a moment's peace."

"Ha! No such luck until she gets out of here," Mare said.

"You want to try talking to her for me?" Nancy turned back to the monitors. "She should be coming around soon. When she wakes up, ask her what her name is and where she is — things like that — just so we can tell how oriented she is. Okay?"

"Yep, no problem." Mare returned her attention to TJ, the

fingers of her hand constantly rubbing TJ's slightly cooler ones. "Come on, honey," she whispered into TJ's ear. "I want to see those baby blues of yours, and I want my hug. Can't have either until you wake up, now can I?"

The first three days after the accident, when TJ had been unconscious, Mare had talked nonsense to her just so TJ had the constant reassurance of her voice. Now she launched into telling TJ what was going on in the world. "I think we need to send Erin and Paula on vacation. This last week has taken a lot out of them. Paula's leg is still giving her a lot of pain, and though Erin is putting a brave face on it, I can tell she's worried about her. They decided not to go back to the ranch tonight, and Dad has given us the run of his place at Dorburton Lakes. I think they made the right choice—the shorter the drive the better." Mare continued to talk to her slumbering partner for nearly thirty minutes before TJ started to come around.

"She's just beginning to stir," Nancy said, looking at the monitors. "Remember, she might be a little disoriented and will probably have a lot of discomfort. Until she's conscious and responsive, we won't be able to figure out the correct level of pain relief she'll need. If she indicates to you that she's in pain, let me know, and I can increase her medication."

Mare looked up to the heart monitor as the beeping increased. When she looked back down at TJ's face, she could see her eyelids fluttering. "Come on, sweetie, open those eyes for me." TJ blinked several more times before her eyes finally stayed open. Mare stood up and bent over so that TJ would be able to see her without straining. "Hi there, precious," she said before she noticed TJ's grimace of pain. TJ took a deep, gasping breath, and a shudder passed through her. "Nancy, I think she needs that pain medication."

Nancy picked up a nearby syringe and waved over to another nurse whom Mare hadn't noticed. The two of them checked the prescription chart Dr. Gillis had left. Then Nancy moved around to TJ's side and administered the medication through an IV line.

Within seconds, the tension and pain that had clouded TJ's features lessened and eventually disappeared. Mare leaned closer again and smiled as TJ's eyes finally focused on her. "Hi there." Her smile broadened as TJ's face lit. "I'm going to ask you a really dumb question, but you have to answer. Okay?"

"Sure. Go 'head." TJ's voice was quiet and slightly slurred.

"Good. What's your name?"

"Taylor Jade Meridian," TJ said so quietly that Mare could hardly hear it.

"I'm sorry, Nancy couldn't quite hear that. What did you say?"

Mare bent closer, her lips tantalizingly near TJ's.

"Taylor Jade Meridian. Okay? Do I get my kiss now?" TJ said, scowling.

"Sure do, but I want my hug as well." Mare leaned down and gently placed her lips upon TJ's, and an unhampered arm wrapped around her shoulders. "Now that's what I call a 'hello.' How are you feeling?"

"Tired and sore." TJ kept her arm around Mare, holding her as close as she could without disturbing the healing shoulder.

Mare barely heard the mumbled response. "Dad said he put you on a pretty strong pain reliever and the anesthetic would make you a little drowsy. They're going to keep an eye on you in here for a while, then move you back to your room. All three of us are going to head off to Dad's when they have you settled. We'll come back tomorrow, okay?" Mare could already feel the loosening of TJ's arm as her eyes began to close once more.

"Hmm, sure. Say 'hi' to the girls for me."

"They're here. Stay awake for a minute and you can tell them yourself." With a wave, Mare beckoned Erin and Paula who stood silently over by the door, gowns already on. She carefully pried TJ's arm from around her and moved out of the way, as Paula and Erin went to either side of TJ's bed.

Paula leaned against the bed taking the weight off her leg. She grasped TJ's hand and squeezed. "Hey, boss, how are you doing?" Her voice was barely above a whisper, emotion taking the strength from it.

"Much better now that I've seen you two. You'd better take it easy for a while, too. Let the corporate office deal with everything, okay?"

TJ was owner and CEO of Meridian Corporation, a multi-national company. The Meridian ranch, overseen by Erin, and the Meridianville packing plant, overseen by Paula, were among its holdings.

"Don't worry about the company," said Erin, brushing a lock of hair from TJ's face. "We've got a handle on that. I want you to concentrate on getting yourself out of here."

"Yeah, that goes for me, too," whispered Paula as she leaned down and lightly kissed TJ on the cheek. "Get some rest, and we'll see you later."

Mare kissed TJ again and caressed her face as the intense blue eyes lost focus and closed. The women waited another hour until TJ was moved to her own room. Then, with little prospect of their friend awakening soon, they decided to leave. Mare gathered her few belongings, joined Erin and Paula in the Land Rover, and drove toward her father's home.

Chapter
Three

MICHAEL'S HOUSE WAS set on several acres and surrounded by trees and hedges that screened it from the road. Mare navigated the long driveway and parked in a paved area near the front entrance.

Mr. and Mrs. Claude Escher, employed as butler/chauffeur and housekeeper/cook, ran Michael's household at Dorburton Lakes, but Mare had assured her father that she and the other women were used to doing for themselves and wouldn't be expecting any special treatment. Michael had let the Eschers know his daughter and her friends would be staying, but that the women preferred to fend for themselves. His chauffeured car, however, was to be readily on hand.

Mare grabbed the bags and then unlocked the door while Erin helped Paula from the vehicle and up the few steps to the doorway. Once inside, the three exhausted women went into the living room and collapsed on the couch and easy chairs.

"At least we've got the worst of it out of the way." Mare sighed and relaxed back into the plush chair.

Erin and Paula looked at each other sadly. They'd discussed this earlier. Even if it was upsetting, Mare needed to be prepared properly for what was to come. Paula nodded at Erin and gave her a wan smile. Erin stood up and headed for the kitchen. "I'll see if I can find something to eat."

As Erin walked out of the room, Paula ran her hand through her dark brown hair and sat forward as far as she could with her leg elevated. "Mare, we need to talk. I know you're probably fed up with Erin and me saying this to you, but we have a long, long road to travel here. TJ's always been an active person, and she doesn't take well to being restrained. Four weeks confined to that bed is going to be hell for her. Believe me when I tell you that she'll make it hell for everybody else as well."

Mare's eyes widened abruptly. "But—"

"No." Paula held up her hand. "I'm not being nasty. She

doesn't do it on purpose. Last time, she got depressed enough to try to kill herself. That's not likely to happen again, but you have to be prepared for the likelihood that things are going to get a lot worse before they get better."

"Is it really going to get that bad?"

"Yes, and it's probably going to get worse than that. We'll bring her laptop in and make sure she has work to keep her occupied. But that room, no matter how big it is, is going to seem like a prison to her. She's going to resent that you can leave it whenever you like, and she can't. One day she'll be fine, and the next, you'll walk in with a smile on your face and she'll rip you to shreds for being happy while she's held prisoner. The next, she probably won't even acknowledge your existence. For some time, it's going to be like living with a spoiled child."

"Don't worry. I'm not leaving her, no matter how bad it gets." Mare reached out a hand and patted Paula on the leg.

"I'm glad to hear that. I really am. TJ has a lot better chance of getting through this with you by her side. But you're going to get caught up in the situation and have your own reactions as well."

Erin entered the room with a tray that she placed on the coffee table. "I found hot coffee in a coffeemaker and sandwich fixings in the fridge. I'm sure we have Mrs. Escher to thank."

She sat on the couch. "I heard Paula's last remark, and I'd like to add something. You're going to resent TJ's attitude, and you'll get frustrated and depressed at the lack of progress. You'll take it out on everyone around you the same as she will."

"I doubt that," Mare said.

"I'm not kidding. Paula and I nearly split up the last time we had to go through this. It's going to be worse for you. You just need to remember, even when she's hurting you, she does love you. Paula and I will be here to support you, but we'll all have some times when we need to let off steam."

Erin's warm smile broke the tension that had begun to build. "Now that we've told you the gloomy side of things to come, let's eat and then get some rest. You never know. Maybe we'll get lucky, and it won't happen."

TJ KNEW EVERY blotch, every mark on the ceiling. At least she could see the entire ceiling and the upper regions of three walls. She'd been asleep for pretty much the whole day and had missed most of Mare's second visit, though she vaguely remembered getting a kiss and a hug at some point. She didn't recall seeing Erin and Paula at all. Michael had been in several times during the day to check on her, but she only had a clear memory of the last visit.

After arguing for what seemed like hours, she had persuaded first Nancy, and then Michael, to release her head from the strapping that had kept it immobile since the accident. Her arms were free, too, but hooked up to a myriad of new IVs that Michael had thoroughly explained: a prednisolone drip was connected to her right arm, and a morphine pump was connected to her left. Michael said he had also considered putting up a dopamine drip to bring her blood pressure back up if the fluids didn't do it. But that hadn't been necessary, and she was connected just to Ringer's and a million beeping machines that were slowly driving her crazy — as was the pain that was clutching at her back. However, every time she hit the button that provided pain medication, that same medication put her to sleep. Sleep wasn't a bad thing. She just didn't want to spend all of her time doing it. And this was only the start. She had months of this ahead of her.

It wasn't yet ten o'clock. The lights had been dimmed, and one of the nurses was sitting just outside the door at the nurse's station. TJ could have had the television turned on, a video or music playing, but that wasn't what she needed.

Temptation trailed a teasing finger through her lonesomeness. She reached for the phone, but her hand stopped in mid air. No. Mare needed a break from this hospital as much as TJ wished she could leave it. She would lie here staring at the ceiling, wishing she were tucked up next to Mare. TJ let out a long sigh and felt tears prickling in her eyes. *She'll be here in a few more hours. I'm just going to have to wait.*

THE NEXT MORNING was dismal. A cold front had drifted in overnight and brought rain with it. Mare wasn't able to park close to the entrance of the hospital. As soon as she stepped from the Land Rover, she started to run. Inside, she brushed the worst of the rain off her coat. She waved hello to the receptionist on duty and made her way up to TJ's floor. Erin and Paula would be along later, after they had contacted the ranch and packing plant to make sure everything was okay.

Last night, the three women had talked over the necessity of returning to Meridianville. Mare had to be there while Barry Cassel, her new assistant, moved into her veterinary practice. Erin and Paula felt they could alternate, with one visiting TJ while the other stayed at the ranch seeing to business affairs. Guessing that TJ would be on her better behavior for the first few days, Paula persuaded Erin to stay at the hospital for now while she went back home with Mare.

Mare really didn't want to leave. She knew it was going to upset TJ because she had been in Springerly by TJ's side since the transfer. Nine days wasn't that long, but she had neglected her practice as long as she dared, and TJ was on the road to recovery. Now she had to get back.

She approached the nurse's station. "'Morning, Nancy. How's my favorite patient doing?"

Nancy shifted her attention from the paperwork she was shuffling around on the counter. "She'll be a lot happier when she sees you, I'm sure."

"Why? What's she been up to?" Mare put her bag on the counter and pulled off her wet coat.

"Janice's working the night shift this week, and she said TJ had been awake most of the night. Seemed to be in some pain but refused to use the patient-controlled analgesia. So in the end, Janice had to give her a needle to relieve it and put her to sleep. She's a little grouchy this morning."

"Did TJ say why she wouldn't use the PCA?"

"Here, I'll take that." Nancy reached over the counter and took the coat. "No, she hasn't said why, but she hasn't been that talkative. Wouldn't eat her breakfast this morning, either. But, as I said, now that you're here, she's bound to cheer up."

"Yeah, until I tell her I have to go back home for a few days."

"You'll be fine."

"I guess I'll just have to promise to make it up to her."

The door to TJ's room was ajar, and Mare poked her head around it. She saw TJ staring up at the ceiling and looking miserable.

"'Morning, love." Mare pushed the door open and bustled in. She walked straight up to the bed, leaned over, and kissed TJ on the lips, barely getting a response. "I can see you're in a good mood this morning. Didn't sleep well?"

"Would you be in a good mood if you were stuck in this bed? Sounds like Nancy's been telling on me."

"She mentioned you'd had a bad night." Mare pulled up a chair and sat. "She said you were in pain but wouldn't use the PCA pump they'd set up for you, and that you wouldn't eat breakfast this morning. Care to tell me why?"

"Not really, but if I don't, you'll just sit here and grill me about it." TJ's tone softened, and she lifted her hand and brushed it across her forehead. "The medication puts me to sleep. Then, when I wake up, my head hurts and I feel sick. Plus, you weren't here whenever I woke up, like you had been. And I just didn't want breakfast."

"I'll tell Nancy about the side effects of the medication. They might be able to do something about that. But you could have used it last night, honey. At least you would have gotten some sleep."

"I didn't want to sleep."

"Why not?" Mare asked, although she had a pretty good idea what the answer was going to be.

"I missed you."

"Well, I'm here now." Mare rose and clambered onto the bed. "So you close those baby blues and go to sleep. I'll wake you for lunch." She settled down next to TJ and soothed her tense brow with gentle caresses.

TJ snuggled as much as she was able, and after a while, her breathing slowed and became deeper.

THE DAY WAS almost over, and TJ had slept through most of it. She had been wakened by Mare for lunch and a short visit from Paula and Erin but hadn't roused for the constant checks from the nurses or Michael on his rounds. Now she and Mare were just snuggling, taking comfort from being together.

Mare knew she couldn't put it off any longer. Resting on the bed, wrapped in long arms, she had her head tucked just beneath TJ's chin. The end-of-visiting-hours warning sounded gently but firmly from the room's speaker. She raised her head to kiss TJ's cheek, then pushed herself up and sat on the bed, gazing down into the blue depths of her eyes.

"Sweetheart, Paula and I are going back to the ranch tonight. Erin's going to stay here with you during the next few days. Then we'll rotate."

"What? Why?" TJ's eyes flooded with disappointment, momentarily pushing away the clutching pain that seemed to have found a permanent perch there. "Do you have to go?"

Even restrained to a half-whisper, TJ's resonant voice fanned the embers of desire that Mare, so far, had kept carefully banked. She pulled in a quick breath, and her hand brushed TJ's bangs. "Yeah, we do. Barry's moving his family into my house Sunday, so that gives me only one day to have it ready for him. Paula's arranged for the movers to bring my furnishings from the house to the ranch tomorrow, but I have to be there to let them in and make sure everything goes all right."

"I guess. Is everything ready at the ranch?"

"The painting was all finished a couple of days ago. Paula ordered the furniture I wanted for the office and got your foreman, Bill, to send someone to oversee its arrival yesterday. So that's all done." The hand moved to caress TJ's cheek. "She arranged for the regular cleaning service to spend some extra time going over my office and the rooms you insisted I pick out for myself. She's bound and determined not to let anything slow this move down."

"What do you mean slow the move down? You're not having second thoughts, are you?"

"No, of course not—"

"I mean," TJ said, "I wouldn't blame you after all that's happened. You didn't need to be stuck with a cripple in the first place."

"Hey, hey." Mare put a finger on TJ's lips, halting her flow of words. "Shh, sweetheart, calm down. All I meant was that Paula wanted to make sure everything was perfect for me when I moved in. You know how she is about details. And you were injured before I met you. This is just going to make things a little more complicated. But we'll get through it together. Honest."

TJ sorted through Mare's words for a few seconds, then said, "Yes, that's our Paula." One corner of her lips lifted into a hint of her lopsided grin. "You haven't told me which rooms you picked."

"I chose the suite on the first floor, next to the back stairway, just beyond the music room. The one you suggested in the first place. It's so big: two bedrooms, bath, living room, and kitchenette." Mare's eyes gleamed. "I don't think I have enough belongings to fill those huge rooms."

"First floor, huh? That's good. At least I won't have to struggle upstairs to chase after you."

The smile and arched eyebrow reached out and grabbed Mare's heart. She leaned over, bracing her arms on the bed on either side of TJ, and her voice thickened with sudden emotion. "You won't ever have to chase me, my love. Just crook your finger, and I'll come running." She lowered to meet TJ's lips and let her body sink gently against the firm one beneath her, barely touching. TJ's arm encircled her as heat seeped through clothing and sheet, sizzling between them while the kiss deepened.

Reluctantly, Mare ended the kiss. She lightly pressed her lips to TJ's cheek and throat before raising herself and leaving the warmth of the embrace. The silent women gazed intently at each other, their eyes glistening with unshed tears. Mare slipped off the bed, took TJ's nearer hand, and raised it to her lips. Turning it over, she kissed the palm and watched TJ curl the hand and place it against her heart.

"Good night," Mare whispered and walked to the door. She looked back, and her soul ached at seeing TJ's forlorn expression. They exchanged small waves, and Mare left.

Come back! Don't leave me. A heavy pall dropped over TJ's

spirit. Her mind told her it was an unreasonable reaction. Mare would be back as soon as possible. But her emotions weren't up to the fight, and she lay there staring at the ceiling, not even attempting to stem the tide of tears running down the sides of her face onto the pillow. At last, exhausted, she fell asleep.

AFTER SLOWLY BRUSHING the sky with velvet black, dusk slipped away. The Rover's headlights brightened the line down the middle of the road into a yellow ribbon that constantly unraveled into a dark hole—an illusion that portrayed Mare's feelings perfectly.

With Paula seated awkwardly in the front passenger seat, Mare drove toward the ranch outside Meridianville. That last look on TJ's face kept darkening her thoughts, and she couldn't block out the terrible expression of abandonment that had crossed those beloved features. She was still wondering what had prompted TJ's sudden outburst. All those insecurities. Had she picked up on some of Mare's fears?

Last night, while talking to Paula and Erin, she had realized some things were going to be more difficult than before. Juggling the responsibilities of her practice and her new associate, as well as traveling back and forth to the hospital, would force some tough adjustments. And they hadn't been kidding about TJ's mercurial moods either, as evidenced this morning.

Blinking rapidly to clear her vision, Mare swiped at the moisture on her cheeks. Ah hell, why fight it? She felt lousy. TJ was in constant pain, tied to a bed in a hospital, while Mare was going back to an empty house instead of being with her. *You've got every reason in the world to cry, so go ahead—wallow in it.* Surprisingly, giving herself permission to cry gradually halted her need to do so. She snickered softly at the irony.

Paula had been uncharacteristically morose, lost in her own thoughts. The snicker startled her, and her head jerked toward Mare. "What the hell's so funny?"

Mare glanced quickly at Paula, who sat with her arms hugged tightly against her lean body. Mare had almost forgotten that Paula was with her. The abrupt question was a dash of cold water, waking Mare from her self-absorption.

"Sorry. I gave myself permission to cry all I wanted, but all of a sudden, I didn't want to. Just struck me funny." Mare reached a hand to Paula's forearm and shook it. "Hey, you okay?"

"I'm fine." Paula unfolded her arms and patted Mare's hand before it returned to the steering wheel. "We all will be if we can just stick together."

"You're worried about Erin."

"Uh-huh. Erin has always felt responsible for TJ's well-being. The fact that she was at the wheel of the van when the accident happened is really bothering her, and I'm not sure how to handle that." Paula shrugged. "Besides that worry, TJ's going to be a bear now that you've gone, and Erin will catch the brunt of it. TJ will try to behave, but the physical pain and the emotional pain of missing you spell double trouble."

"I saw a little of that when I was with her this morning. I think I got an up-close preview of things to come. It's going to be every bit as hard as you said."

"This will be a bad time for all of us, and especially TJ. I hope like hell that she takes it easy on Erin. Erin's got a really soft heart, you know?"

"And you haven't? You're the tough one, right? Remember when I first met you in TJ's office? She wanted to throw me out, and you grabbed my arm, prepared to do just that. I thought she was a spoiled brat and you were an arrogant bitch."

Paula slid an amused glance at Mare. "I know you've changed your mind about TJ."

Mare laughed out loud. "Paula, I've seen how you try to keep things on an even keel at the ranch. TJ's definitely the boss, and Erin works hard to please her, but you're the Mistress of Ceremonies, pointing everyone in the right direction. How do you keep so calm?"

"Calm? Me? I churn inside all the time. Erin's the bellwether in the calm department. I can be boiling inside, and one look or one word from her can cool me right down. Most of the time," she said. "Erin now, she reacts differently when she's upset. She just endures TJ's yelling and hardly ever yells back. She tries her best to keep TJ happy. When that doesn't work, she doesn't blame TJ. She blames herself. She may look as if it doesn't affect her, but she buries it all inside."

"How do you cope with TJ's temper tantrums? I feel like our minds lock together, and there's a battle that she lets me win sometimes, but not before I feel a bit battered."

"Yeah, it's funny, isn't it? Even when she loses, she's still in control."

Mare turned this idea over in her mind and decided that Paula was right. The statement gave a new perspective to TJ's acquiescence to anything. "You're a pretty strong-minded person. How do you keep your balance?"

Paula sucked in her lips against her teeth, then loosened them with a soft swishing sound. "With studied ignorance."

"Studied ignorance?"

"Yeah. When TJ gets wild with her hands or her mouth, I make an effort to ignore all the hurtful parts. I know that's not the real TJ, just her frustration—and partly the result of her childhood. After all those years of growing up with her father bullying her and his employees, it's not surprising that she tries it occasionally." Paula paused for a moment, obviously touched by the physical and emotional horror TJ had survived.

"Over the last couple of years, the three of us have become closer, and she's gotten a lot better. So I try not to let her nastiness affect me. But, like I said, Erin takes it to heart. Oh, she puts on a great face for TJ, but I can tell when it hurts, and that's my Achilles heel. When TJ gets mad at Erin, I get ticked at TJ. Usually, I can step between them and deflect TJ's anger in my direction. That's when TJ and I have our all-out yelling matches that Erin usually breaks up. But I can't always manage to be at the right place to do that."

Paula shifted in her seat, leaned over to grasp her cast leg, and moved it to a more comfortable position. She sat back up and looked toward Mare with a mischievous grin. "Fortunately, I'm usually the one TJ gets mad at."

"Erin's going to be on her own tomorrow."

"I've asked her to call me a couple of times, tell us how TJ's holding up."

"Will she tell you if there's a problem?"

"She won't have to. I can tell by her voice. Remember, we've been through this before. Just talking to each other will help us both."

Mare nodded in understanding. *They have the same connection TJ and I have.*

They rode the rest of the way home in companionable silence.

Chapter
Four

THE NEXT MORNING at breakfast, Mare and Paula agreed to meet in the afternoon to put Mare's office and suite in order when the movers brought her belongings. Then they separated, with Paula going to TJ's office to catch up on some business and Mare jumping in her truck and driving to her home in Meridianville.

Mare saw the green and yellow moving van from Bodley and Sons coming behind her, so she parked in front of her house, allowing the van to pull into her driveway. She sat in the truck for a moment, unexpectedly rocked by a wave of nostalgia. She and her mother had lived in this home for a lot of years. She would really miss it. The enormity of giving up her home and moving into someone else's—taking on an entirely different lifestyle—hit her for the first time. Was this really what she wanted? Was she ready for it? Mare pushed the thought away, vowing to examine it more thoroughly at a later time.

She climbed out of the truck and inhaled the fragrance of the red roses her mother had planted, years ago, along the edge of the front yard. In the small flower garden nearer the house, splashes of chrysanthemums brightened the early autumn morning, poking their yellow and russet heads up behind the late-blooming petunias and impatiens. Why are good-byes always so hard? Even when it's not a person? Again, Mare tucked her thoughts away.

"Hi, Lee," Mare greeted the young black man who tipped the corner of his hat and flashed her a bright smile. "How's your dad?" Lee's father owned the moving business and had put his two sons, Lee and Linc, in charge of it when he hurt his hip in a bad fall. Both young men were tall and strong-looking, their rippling muscles a legacy of growing up in the business.

"He's coming along pretty well, Doc. He's already graduated from crutches to a cane, but I don't think he'll be moving any heavy stuff ever again. That hip took a real beating, and Doc Hunt told him to consider retiring."

Lee lifted his hat off and laid it on his van seat as Mare turned the house key in the lock. "How are your friends doing?" he asked. "Miss Meridian was hurt pretty bad, wasn't she?"

Mare tried to suppress the quick grimace of anguish this question brought to her face. "Yeah, her back was just operated on. We'll have to wait and see what happens there. The other two are doing well. One has a broken leg and the other a broken wrist."

"I saw Miss Meridian at that Town Meeting when she first got here. She was something else." Lee turned his palm up and curled his fingers in a grabbing pose. "She sure had those people by the...uh...I mean..."

Mare grinned at his obvious embarrassment. "Let's just say she was in full control, huh?"

Lee rubbed his wayward hand across the back of his neck and showed a rueful smile. "Yeah, that, too."

They walked into the house together as Linc and another man pulled up in a smaller truck to help with the move. Lee said, "And you know what else, Doc? Me and my brother live upriver, and our kids were getting sick, and no one could figure out why until Miss Meridian discovered the pollution and fixed it. Our houses were the first to get those filtration units connected to our water supply. She saved the lives of our kids. Tell her thanks for me when you see her, will you?"

"I'll be happy to, and I know Miss Meridian will appreciate hearing it." Mare looked around the room. "Now, how about we figure out what goes and what stays?"

Mare had agreed to leave her piano for Barry's family rather than put it in storage. But he and Berta had insisted that it was just a loan. If she ever wanted it back, it was hers. With that understanding, Mare left a few other pieces of furniture and the whole kitchen: tables, chairs, plates, utensils, pots and pans. The only things she took from that room were her mother's set of recipe books and two of her favorite mixing bowls. Shortly before noon, the house was emptied of what was going, and the men headed to the diner to eat lunch. Mare went back to the Meridian ranch.

PAULA WAS READY to sit down to soup and a sandwich. She was pleased that she could now manage in the kitchen with only minimal aid from her crutches, which were close by. When she saw Mare pull in, she returned to the counter and began to put lunch together for her.

Mare came barreling through the door and took a quick glance at the situation. "Hey, woman," she said, "you sit down and let me fix my own lunch. I'm not a guest anymore." She sidled up to Paula and playfully nudged her with her hip.

Paula dropped the sandwich makings and grabbed the counter, teetering off balance. "No-no-no!"

Mare threw an arm around her waist to steady her. "Sorry, I forgot you're unbalanced," she said with a twinkle. "You okay now?"

"Yeah," Paula said, "but next time, warn me first. So, you're all packed up?"

"Yep. Lock, stock, and barrel, as the saying goes."

"Great. And as far as your being a guest, Erin and I do take turns with the meals, but we all wait on each other. Figure it doesn't matter who does what, as long as it gets done. Grab yourself a cup of coffee, and let me finish the food."

"Right." Mare fixed herself a mug and sat down. She took a few sips and consciously tried to relax. The last few weeks had been a real roller coaster ride. First, there was the decision to move to the ranch, then the accident, then TJ's operation. And she still had the actual move to contend with, and a new assistant to get oriented, and running back and forth to the hospital, and the constant worry about TJ.

"Have you heard from Erin?" She curled her hand around the back of her neck and rubbed it.

"She called right before I came out to fix lunch. TJ's not a happy camper, of course, but Erin said she's at least making some effort not to be too miserable—yet." Paula passed the plate holding the finished sandwich to Mare and poured the remaining chicken noodle soup from the pot into a bowl. She handed over the bowl and a box of crackers and joined Mare at the island.

"That's good news. I know how rotten I felt having to leave. I can imagine how TJ must feel."

"Yeah," Paula said.

The two ate quietly.

"You want to talk about it?" Paula asked when they were finished. When Mare's eyebrows lifted in inquiry, Paula elaborated. "About whatever's bothering you. Is it TJ?"

Mare pushed her dishes away, put her elbow on the table, and rested her head in her hand. She splayed her fingers into her hair and turned her eyes toward her friend. "Yes and no. It was weird packing up the house—realizing that it wasn't going to be my home anymore."

"Are you okay with that?"

"I think so. I mean, it's time to move on with my life." Mare looked down at the table. "But do you think moving in with TJ is the way I should go?"

Paula rubbed her head and grimaced. "Isn't it a little late to be asking that?"

"I suppose it is. With TJ and me, though, once our relationship started, it was like the proverbial rolling stone. Nothing was going to slow it down. But the accident put the brakes on to some extent. Now that I have this bit of time to step back and look at it, I find myself questioning whether moving in together is a good idea. You know TJ better than just about anyone. Are we doing the right thing?"

Paula gave the question a few moments of consideration. "In TJ's case, I'd have to say yes. Your relationship has made an obvious positive difference and given her a reason to pick herself up, a reason to keep going. But you're the only one who can decide whether it's right for you."

"Yeah, I know. When TJ was here, it seemed the most natural thing in the world for me to come here to live with her. But she's not here now, and I think I'm having a touch of cold feet about moving in. I'm just a small town vet, and here I am pulling up all my roots and moving into the home of the owner of a multi-national corporation. It's an enormous step, and now that it's actually happening..."

Paula sat back in her chair, and a shadow slipped down over her eyes. "You change your mind about TJ?" she asked in a quiet, flat voice.

"No." Mare grasped Paula's hand and gave it a quick squeeze. "Never. This is not a Mare-TJ issue at all. It's..." Mare sat up and fluttered her hands back and forth to include the expanse of space around her. "I feel sort of uncomfortable moving in *here*. My body's making the move, but my emotions aren't going along so quietly. I'm not really sure what it is. Maybe I feel like I'm giving up my independence. Or submerging my identity."

The shadow lifted from Paula's eyes, and she gave a little laugh. "Anyone who's around TJ for five minutes is in danger of submerging her identity. TJ's presence is almost overwhelming, and we all feel that." Her arm made an all-encompassing move through the air. "This is a huge house, and no matter who else is in it, it seems empty without TJ. But when she's here, it doesn't seem empty at all."

"Yes," Mare said, "and that's probably causing part of my uncertainty. I'm not really sure whether I'm moving here because I want to or because TJ wants me to. Once she put the idea in my head, I accepted it without giving it a whole lot of thought. Now I have a chance to think about it, and I'm not convinced that it's the best thing for me to do." She shook her head in confusion. "I'm giving up my home, hiring an assistant, splitting up my practice, just so I can be here with TJ. I don't know if I can handle being responsible for her happiness twenty-four hours a day. What happens if I fail her?"

Mare got up, cleaned the remnants of lunch from the island, and stacked the few dishes in the dishwasher. "Then again, everything seems to be touched with a brighter light when TJ's around. I'll probably be okay when she's back here with us."

"Nobody," Paula said, "can be responsible for TJ's happiness except her. I know it feels like you have to be. You probably even want to be. But TJ has to learn to be emotionally responsible for herself. You know, nothing you're doing here is burning any bridges. If you decide there are things you can't handle, you can always ask your new assistant to find another house to rent and move back into yours. But we all hope you stay. TJ's not the only one who would like to have you here. Why don't you give her a call and talk to her? It might make you feel better."

"I tried first thing this morning, but she was still sleeping. I'll try again after I've got this moving sorted out." Mare wiped the island, rinsed the dishrag, and hung it next to the sink. "Thanks, Paula, you and Erin have made me feel very welcome."

"You *are* welcome. Besides," Paula said, "nothing like having a vet handy on a ranch. Oh, that reminds me. We have a small problem —"

"Can it wait until later? Here come the movers." Mare put a restraining hand on Paula's shoulder. "Don't get up. We can take care of this."

"Okay, I'll tell you all about it when you're finished. I have some more office work, anyway."

Mare went out to meet Lee and Linc and left a thoughtful Paula making her way to TJ's office.

MARE STOOD IN the center of the suite's living room, surveying her surroundings. The transfer of furniture was complete, and the movers had gone. At least she had a small piece of her identity here. And a piano available in the next room. What more could she want? The question made her heart thud. *TJ. I want TJ.* Her eyes misted, and she swung around and half-ran from the room.

She ventured down the hallway, past her office and made the right-angle turn toward TJ's office. At the open door, she tapped on it and walked in. The sight of Paula's dark head at the desk conjured up a split-second memory of enticing blue eyes and a glorious smile. It was so vivid, Mare's breath caught for a magical moment. Then reality returned, and the magic dissolved.

Paula looked up from the papers she was perusing. She checked her watch. "All done?"

"Yep. I am now a bona fide resident of Meridian ranch, cold feet and all." Mare clasped her arms across her body for just a moment as a quick shiver went through her.

"You'll be okay when TJ gets back." Paula's eyes gleamed. "She'll warm those cold feet for you in more ways than one. You try phoning her again?"

"Keep it up. You may convince me." Mare gave Paula's shoulder a playful slap. "And no, I haven't phoned her again. I'll do it later when I can sit down and relax and devote all my attention to her."

Paula picked up the papers she was reading and waved them at Mare. "One of the ranch hands brought the mail, and we got the investigative report on Mrs. Gloria Raphaele and her son, Thomas Joseph Meridian Raphaele."

"Great! What does it say?" Mare was suddenly fully alert.

"It looks like they lead a pretty uneventful life. Wealthier than most people. Of course, being Thomas Meridian's mistress and son could account for that. The mother does volunteer work with a couple of charities. They live in an exclusive section of their city, and the son just graduated from a private prep school. Other than that, there's nothing particularly unusual. You want to read the report?"

"I'll put it in my office and take a look at it later." Mare took the large envelope Paula handed her. "What was that little problem you spoke of earlier?"

"Come out to the barn." Paula stood and reached for her crutches. "I want you to take a look at Flag."

"Be right with you." Mare hurried to her office and placed the file in the top drawer of her desk, safe from any wandering eyes of clients. Then she returned to the kitchen.

Paula swung through the kitchen and out the door, with a curious Mare following. Though the air was still warm in the bright sunshine, a tinge of coolness and a woody scent warned that autumn was here to stay.

Inside the barn, Mare enjoyed the warmth and even the pungent smells: horses, hay, oiled leather, earth, manure. A vet spent many hours in barns, and whenever she entered one, a finger of familiarity touched and welcomed her. She walked quickly to Flag's stall.

"I can't figure out what's wrong with her," Paula said. "She's not eating right and is acting really skittish. Bill's been sending some of the hands over each day to take care of the horses, and he said they noticed it first. They wondered if maybe she was getting sick with something."

While Paula explained, Flag nickered and came to the front of the stall, as though looking for someone. Not finding the person for whom she was looking, she dropped her head and moved back.

Mare could see that the palomino had lost some weight and indeed looked skittish. "Hey, girl," she called and reached out, but Flag just backed away some more, then tossed her head and pawed the ground nervously.

"What do you think is wrong?" Paula asked.

"I'll get my bag and check her out, but I'd guess she's pining for TJ. It's been a while since she's seen her, and Flag's used to TJ riding her every morning." Mare gave a wry grin. "Just what we need, a lovesick horse."

"How come the other horses aren't affected? Erin and I haven't been around them that much either."

"Probably because Flag's been with TJ for so long. And you said yourself, there seems to be a special bond between them."

"That's true. What can we do? Is it dangerous?"

"She's lost some weight, so she's probably not eating properly. If she stops eating altogether, that can be dangerous. At the moment, it will just affect her overall health." Mare considered her options. "Look, I'll go in the house and get a blanket that TJ has handled, then bring it back here and put it in the stall. Just TJ's scent may help calm her down."

"Great idea." Relief flooded Paula's face, then her expression turned uncertain. "Do you think it's okay to say anything to TJ about this? You know how particular she is about Flag."

"I also seem to remember that the last time you and Erin tried to keep Flag's condition a secret, she found out anyway and told you guys off about it. So far, this isn't as worrisome as the heatstroke was. I'll explain it to TJ when I phone her." Mare frowned in thought. "Only other thing I know to do for Flag at the moment is keep a close eye on her. Ask the men to give her a lot of attention, maybe take her mind off TJ for a while."

"Will that work?"

"Darned if I know, but at least it will let us think we're doing something to help."

Chapter
Five

ERIN QUICKLY ANSWERED the ringing phone, hoping that she could prevent it from waking TJ, who hadn't had the best of days. But the slight jerk of the blankets showed that her hope had been in vain.

"Hello?" Erin said softly, then smiled as she heard Mare's voice on the line. "Hold on one second. I'll pass you over to her. She just woke up, so she might sound a little groggy." Erin stood up and handed the phone to TJ. "It's Mare. I'll give you two a little privacy. Be back in a while. You need anything before I go?"

TJ gave a slight shake of her head. "No, thanks." She spoke into the phone, not even noticing when Erin left the room. "Hey..."

An hour later, the phone still fixed to her ear, Mare was curled up on the couch, staring at the flames that flickered merrily in the fireplace. It wasn't really cold enough for a fire, but she enjoyed the cozy, homey atmosphere it produced. In the course of the conversation, Mare had told TJ about Flag's condition. Her reaction had been what Mare expected: short, sharp, and to the point. After answering a few probing questions, she had convinced TJ that the palomino was not in danger, but she could tell TJ was still upset about it.

"Okay, I'll sleep with an extra blanket you can put in her stall. Wish I could bring it to you myself," TJ said.

Mare could hear the frustration and tension coming through the phone. "I know you do, sweetheart. Good night. I love you. Now, if Erin is back, I want you to put her on the line. You get some sleep, and I'll call you in the morning, okay?" She listened as TJ passed the phone and quietly spoke to Erin.

Erin's voice came through, accompanied by some background commotion. "Mare? Let me call you right back from a hall phone. TJ's nurses have just come in to turn her."

Mare could hear TJ complaining loudly. Then the phone clicked, cutting the connection. Mare sighed, knowing that TJ wasn't going to be the easiest of patients over the next few months. The phone rang and Mare quickly picked it up.

"Hi, I'm back," Erin said.

"Hi. How's she doing?"

"Oh, Lord. I'd forgotten how hard this was. I think at the moment she's just testing the waters, but she's been a little trying today. That nurse Nancy isn't taking any nonsense from her though. Your dad thinks they'll be ready to start physical therapy on Monday. That is, if TJ hasn't escaped from her bed by then."

Mare chuckled. "Has she really been that bad?"

"Actually, no, she hasn't. She's still in a lot of pain, and the medication tends to knock her out. So, it's just when she wakes up that she's a bit of a handful. The simplest thing sets off her anger and frustration, so don't be surprised if she takes some of that out on you when you see her next. One of the nurses made some comment on how nice a day it was outside, and TJ nearly took her head off."

"You okay?"

"I'm fine. Been catching up on some reading for the ranch, and I've got a few reports to go over. You moved in okay?"

"Yep. Paula had everything moving smoothly. Thanks for looking after TJ. We should be back there in a few days."

"No problem. I'm just going to say good night to the 'terror,' then I'm off to your dad's. I think Mr. Escher's waiting outside. Tell Paula I'll ring her from there."

"Okay. Good night. Talk to you later."

ON MONDAY MORNING, Mare woke up in TJ's large bed with a death grip on one of the pillows. She lay there with her eyes closed, pretending she was holding TJ's body up against hers, imagining the feel of her warmth and firmness. A pleasant glow spread through her as she conjured up TJ's unique scent, her salty taste, the slick feel of... *Get up, you dope, you're just torturing yourself.*

Mare rolled out of bed, took a badly needed cold shower, and dressed. She sat on the bed and placed a call to TJ on the off chance that she might be up but was informed by the nurse that she was still sleeping. She left a message, then set the phone in its cradle and headed to the kitchen.

"Good morning," Paula said. She had managed to set two places at the island and was getting out the cereal, milk, sugar, and bananas. "All ready to start your new assistant on his duties?"

"Hey, I still have another hour. Let's not rush things," Mare groused good-naturedly and helped herself to the coffee. "First, right after breakfast, I'm going to check on Flag again. I want to see if the blanket from TJ's room has had any effect on her feeding. If it hasn't, I'll tell TJ when I phone that Flag is still pining for her, and we'll need her current sleeping blanket. A fresh scent will be stronger and might help her baby out. What are you up to today?"

"You remember Fred Morales, the packing plant manager? He's coming out for a meeting with me." Paula counted off on her fingers: "I have to check on the packing plant's production, go over the figures, see how the hiring is working out, find out if they have any problems, that kind of stuff. Then organize the information and report it all to TJ."

"Sounds like fun." Mare grimaced, wolfed her food, and started for the door.

"Let me know how Flag is, will you?" Paula said.

Mare lifted a hand to acknowledge the request and dashed outside. Another beautiful day. How she wished TJ could be there to enjoy the run of gorgeous weather they were having.

She strode into the barn and heard the palomino nicker but not move in her stall. Flag stood in the same corner as yesterday where Mare had hung the blanket from TJ's bed. "Well, that's something, girl," she said. Mare was frustrated, however, to see that a large portion of Flag's feed again was untouched. "But you have to pick up on your feeding. We sure don't want TJ coming home to a sick horse." At least, now that Flag had responded to the blanket, she wasn't acting as agitated.

The stable hands were just coming in to turn out the horses. Mare greeted them and bestowed a parting pat on Flag's rump. Then she scooted back to the house, gave Paula an encouraging report, and headed to Meridianville.

When she pulled up in front of her old home, Mare had to smile. With the curtains changed and a stroller sitting outside the door, it already looked different. Barry Cassel and his family had moved in on Sunday, and this would be Barry's first day on the job.

Mare had left her original vet office just as it was. It would continue to be the main surgery and animal treatment center. The office at Meridian ranch would serve as headquarters for the practice and was being set up with new furniture and supplies. Mare felt a little tug of uncertainty about leaving all the familiar furnishings behind.

She couldn't figure out what was wrong with her. She knew that starting something new often carried some trepidation with it. But without TJ, the prospect of living at the ranch was looking downright uncomfortable. Was she getting too dependent on TJ? *Is that what I'm leery of? Is that what love does to you?* Mare shook her head and got out of the truck.

As she was walking up the path, the front door opened and a

six-foot-tall, well-muscled man appeared. "Hi, Mare." Barry beckoned to her. "Come on in and meet my wife." Barry had a round, boyish face, short brown hair, and hazel eyes. His cheerful expression, enhanced by dimpled cheeks, lifted her spirits.

"Hi, Barry, I'd love to."

He held the door as she entered, then turned to introduce her. "Mare, this is my wife, Berta."

"Hi, Mare. I'm really happy to meet you. And I love your house." Small and sturdy, with medium-length, light-brown hair, Berta smiled attractively and held out her hand.

Mare shook it and smiled back into gray-blue eyes. "Thanks, Berta. Please think of it as your house. Your family will be a great addition to Meridianville. Speaking of family, where's your little boy?"

"I think the move must have worn him out. He's still sleeping." Berta pushed soft curls off of her forehead. "Not that I'm complaining, mind you. I'm pretty worn out, too."

"Yeah, moving can be tough on everyone."

Berta's laugh sounded soft and mellow. "But if we never moved, we would all still live in caves."

"Hmmm. I never really thought of it that way. Good point." Very good point. She should stop being a stick-in-the-mud about moving to the ranch. She and TJ had a wonderful future ahead of them. What kind of future did she have in sight before they met and fell in love?

"Maybe we better get moving." Barry gave Berta a kiss, picked up his bag, and started for the door. "Shall we take your truck or mine?"

"A man of action, I see," Mare said. She took Berta's hand. "Glad to have you here, Berta. We'll probably see a lot of each other."

"I hope so. So long, you two."

Mare moved to the door Barry was holding open. "Let's take your truck, Barry. Might as well get everyone familiar with it." With a sudden thought, she turned back toward Berta. "By the way, don't expect Barry back for lunch today. We'll be at the Meridian ranch at midday and eat there." To Barry, she said, "The ranch has become our biggest client."

"Isn't that where your new office is?" Barry asked as they moved toward his truck. The capped Dodge, almost a twin to Mare's, was the same truck he had used for calls at his last job. It was fully equipped with veterinary needs.

"Yes, it is. In fact, I live at the ranch now. But there will be times that an extra vet might be needed there, and I want you to be familiar with the layout."

"Okay, you're the boss." Barry's enthusiasm to start his new job cast a bright spell on the whole day.

WHEN TJ AWOKE, the room was as quiet as any hospital room could be. It was still relatively early, and Erin hadn't arrived yet. A quick glance at the clock on the wall told her that she would have the company of the nurses in a few minutes, and her daily routine would begin. The staff personnel were extremely good at their jobs, Nancy especially.

However, in TJ's opinion, they were all too cheerful. It didn't matter what type of day she was having, they always had smiles on their faces and kind words of encouragement. When she was tired and in pain, those words felt condescending and hurtful, because no matter how much they empathized with her and their other patients, none of these nurses were in the same position or the same pain, either physical or mental. Sometimes what she needed most was the peace and quiet of her room while she gathered herself for the upcoming trials she knew she had to face.

The door opened and Nancy bustled in with an unknown colleague and an orderly. "Good morning, TJ," Nancy said as she opened the curtains and let the sunlight in.

TJ grunted in reply and closed her eyes against the bright light.

The orderly and the second nurse prepared for TJ's morning bath. Nancy crossed from the window to check the medication pump, taking note of the levels before touching TJ to take vital signs. "Not in a talkative mood? How's the pain this morning?"

"Still there."

"Any change from yesterday?"

"Nope." The door opened, and Erin walked in. "About time you showed up," TJ said, then she turned back to Nancy. "It's the same. Any other stupid questions?"

Nancy ignored the remark. "Good morning, Erin. We were just going to get TJ up." She forgot the slip of paper she had been given by the departing night staff.

MARE HAD COLLECTED her new calls and callbacks from the vet in Sharlesburg, and she and Barry proceeded to make the rounds. At each place, Mare introduced him as her new assistant and stood back, lending a hand only when necessary, while he handled the animals' problems. After they finished the urgent calls and washed up at their last one, they stopped at Meridian ranch.

Mare unlocked the outside door to her office and led Barry in. At one time, this had been the office of Thomas Joseph Meridian, TJ's father. The father whose beatings and constant derision had left TJ with both physical and emotional scars. TJ hated him so much that she hadn't entered the office since Erin and Paula had rescued her from his final beating of her, when the women were at Harvard together. TJ had reluctantly allowed Mare to use the room for her vet office, on condition that every vestige of her father be removed. TJ swore she would never enter the office again.

When Mare, Paula, and Erin cleaned out the office, they discovered hidden papers that showed Thomas Meridian had a second, secret family and TJ had a half-brother. They decided not to tell TJ until Erin had the facts investigated. Then the van had crashed, and telling TJ had been put on hold.

The renovated room bore no resemblance to the heavily curtained, dark and foreboding one it had been. Light peach walls and a nut-brown rug set off the walnut desk, file cabinets, bookcases, and credenzas that were placed in one end of the large room. Two dark-green couches and several straight-backed chairs, randomly gathered near a fireplace, graced the other end. Yellow, green, and peach throw pillows supplemented the casual, welcoming ambience. Twin glass doors, newly covered with decorative ironwork, filled part of a wall and opened onto a closed-in porch. Two eight-foot-tall windows, complete with muted-yellow, cushioned window seats, gave a wide view of open range.

As Mare came through the door, she caught a reflection in a mirror of the intensely bright room. TJ wouldn't recognize this room. Someday, Mare would get her to come in and see the change. Maybe it would help chase TJ's nightmares away. The thought of nightmares sobered Mare. No one was with TJ at night to hold her while she suffered through her painful memories. Maybe she didn't have the nightmares in the hospital. Mare suddenly realized her thoughts had taken her miles away, and she pulled herself back to the present. "Sorry, Barry. What did you say?"

Barry was walking around, closely examining the various articles in the room. "I said this is a great office. I've heard the Meridian ranch is the largest in this area, and Miss Meridian is bringing it to full capacity. Is it there yet?"

"Not quite, but soon. I'll have plenty to do here when it is, but it won't take up my full time. I'll still be helping with the other calls. Depending on the load, we can work out a routine where I work here maybe three days and help you on the other days.

Except for emergencies, of course."

Mare opened the hall door. "Paula? You here?" No one answered her hail. "Come on into the kitchen, and we can find something to eat."

After lunch, Mare took Barry to callbacks at some of the larger farms and ranches that would produce most of his work and introduced him to the owners. A few moments of shop talk at each stop apparently satisfied them that the new vet knew his business.

About two o'clock, Mare directed that they return to town, since she was planning to make an early start for the hospital. "I'll make sure that you get around to the rest of the farms and ranches soon. I'd like all the owners to meet you and feel confident about calling you when they need a vet."

"I like that idea. It will help me feel more confident, too."

He drove home and parked in the driveway. Mare said, "I'll work with you for the next couple of days, then you'll be on your own. I'm going to have to ask you to take over as much of the work as possible for a while." A look of concern crossed her face. "TJ Meridian is still in the hospital in Springerly, which is a two-hour drive from here, and I'm spending as much time there as I can. When she gets home, I'll be more involved in the practice. Will you have any problem with that?"

"Not a bit. You give Miss Meridian the attention she needs. I figure the more work I do, the sooner I'll know everyone, and they'll know me. I want my family to become a part of this town, and I think working with people is one of the best ways to do that."

"I think so, too." Mare shook his hand. "You did nice work today. I'll see you tomorrow."

"Thanks. See you."

Mare drove back to Meridian ranch with a happier heart. Barry had made a good start. He was competent, sociable, and had a good head on his shoulders. Her responsibilities would be a lot lighter with him around. She and TJ just might have time to make a life together. If she ever got back home. The dull ache that seemed to take over her heart when she wasn't near TJ thrummed into an actual pain, and she unconsciously rubbed her chest.

She parked in the driveway, jumped out of the truck, and loped to the house. Pushing open the door, she hurried through and almost ran smack-dab into Paula.

Paula grabbed her shoulder and brought her to a halt. "Whoa, Mare. What's your hurry?" She gave a short puff of laughter. "Hey, you don't know how long I've waited to say that."

"Yeah, I'll bet. That's not the worst of what I caught as a kid." She made a face at the momentary recollection. "But I'm dying for a cup of coffee."

Paula let go of her. "You've come to the right place. I just made some fresh. Have you spoken to TJ at all today? I tried to get through to Erin but only got the nurse's station. They were running some tests on TJ, and both of them were away from the ward." Paula poured two cups of coffee, set them on the table with the cream and sugar, then sat down.

"Nope. I rang early this morning, but TJ was still asleep, so I left a message with the nurse." Mare sank gratefully into a chair and fixed her coffee. "Sorry I almost ran you down. I just seem to be jumpier than usual." The hot coffee nearly burned her lips, and she quickly wet them with the tip of her tongue. "Hey, I brought Barry out here for lunch, but you weren't here."

"Yeah? Sorry I missed him. I took a little walk to get some fresh air. Wasn't so easy with the crutches, but I get antsy sometimes, too. I was tempted to try riding Runny, but I took one look at that hoist and soon got over that idea. How does TJ do it? And ride? I don't think I could ride a horse that I couldn't snug my legs against."

The front doorbell rang, and Mare and Paula exchanged inquisitive looks. Mare raised a hand to keep Paula seated, swallowed a quick gulp of her coffee, then got up to answer the door.

She paused briefly at the front window and saw a tall, slim shape, wearing jeans and a blue T-shirt, facing away from her. When she opened the door, a young man turned toward her and dipped his head for a moment, then lifted it and looked right at her.

"Hello, ma'am. Mr. Jacobs sent me. Are you Miss Scott? Or Miss Tanner?"

He wasn't a man at all, just a boy. A tall, dark and handsome boy with a face she recognized from a photo. And blue eyes that astonished her. *My God, it's TJ's brother!*

"I...uh...hello. No...I..." Mare stopped and swallowed. "Sorry, my mind was out of gear for a minute. I'm Dr. Gillespie. Come on in and have a seat. I'll get Miss Tanner for you, Mr....?" She held the door wider and he entered.

"Russell. Tom Russell."

Mare noticed his broad shoulders and smooth walk, as he moved to a chair in the living room and sat down. She hurried into the kitchen and found Paula still seated, now talking on the phone she had moved from the counter to the table. Making a "T" with agitated hands, she demanded Paula's attention. "Paula, time out!"

Paula looked up, surprised at the urgency in Mare's tone. "Hold just a minute, please." She pushed the hold button and her eyebrows rose. "What is it?"

"He's here."

"Who's here, for Pete's sake?"

"TJ's brother. He just came to the door and asked for you. Said his name is Tom Russell." Paula's eyes widened as she and Mare just stared at each other for a minute.

Paula jabbed the phone button. "Sorry, I'll have to get back to you later. Good-bye." She cradled the phone. "What the hell is going on?"

"Maybe he thinks TJ is here, and he wants to see her — find out who she is. He's probably just as curious about her as we are about him, maybe more so. After all, they are related."

"Why not just say, 'I'm TJ's brother'?"

"Come on, Paula. We were concerned what finding out she had a brother might do to TJ. Maybe he's got sense enough to worry about that, too. He doesn't know anything about her or how she would react." Mare grimaced. "We know her pretty well, but even we don't know the answer to that one." She walked over and put her hand on Paula's shoulder. "He's in the living room, waiting for you. Why don't you go see what he wants?"

Paula leaned onto her own hand for a moment and rubbed her forehead. She stood up, took a deep breath, and blew it out audibly through pushed-out lips. "Right. You coming with me?"

"You bet. Wild horses couldn't keep me away."

Paula reached for her crutches, then threw an arm around Mare's shoulders. Giving her a quick hug, she grinned. "I'm glad you're here. With TJ hurting and my not getting much chance to be with Erin, I need all the support I can get."

Mare slipped an arm around Paula's waist and hugged her back. "Well, you've got my support, absolutely."

Alone in the living room, Tom felt like his heart was beating a mile a minute. His mind went back over his last day at home. He had told his mother that he didn't want to start college right away. He wanted to experience a bit of life for a while. But that had been only a small part of the reason. His mother didn't know that he had had his computer set up to gather any reference to the name "Meridian" found on the wire services and that it had fed him information about his father's other family. Tom recalled his exact thoughts when his mother asked him why he was so set on not starting college right away.

"I want to know how other people live," he had said, but his thoughts had streamed unchecked. He had a sister who was in a terrible accident two years ago. She was almost killed then, and she could have been killed in the accident she just had. He wanted to meet her, to see what she was like, to get to know her — before anything else happened

and he lost her for good. Like he lost his brother, a brother he never met. But he couldn't tell his mother that. He knew she had signed some papers when his father was alive, agreeing not to interfere with his other family or the Meridian Corporation, and his father gave her Raphaele Consultants in return. But he wasn't his mother. He hadn't signed anything. He wanted to meet his sister! He had cherished the dream for years.

Now, in this room, that dream was nearer to becoming a reality. This was where TJ lived. He was sitting in her living room. Tom looked around and examined his surroundings more closely. A shelf against one wall of the living room held several photos. He moved closer and was delighted to find that one was a portrait of his sister. From magazine images, he already knew that her eyes were similar to his, but this photo made him catch his breath. Their eyes were practically identical. Getting some wraparound sunglasses looked like a good idea. He heard women's voices coming nearer, and he hurried back to his seat on the couch.

Mare and Paula entered the living room from the hall, and Tom stood up. Pleasantly surprised at his good manners, Mare did the introductions. As Paula shook his hand, he said, "Please, call me Tom."

The women sat, and Paula indicated that Tom should, too. "What can I do for you?" she said.

Tom's weight hadn't yet caught up to his height, but it was already apparent that he would be a powerful man. Although reminiscent of TJ's, his features were slightly different: narrower jaw, longer nose, and thinner lips. But if you covered the lower part of his face, there was no denying the relationship. The raven brows and black hair were identical to hers, and though his eyes weren't as compelling as TJ's, they were the same unique shade of blue and had an intensity of their own. He wasn't yet mature enough to realize his eyes could be potent weapons.

"I hitched a ride up to the end of the drive. I'd heard you were looking for hands. One of the men directed me to Bill Jacobs's office, and Mr. Jacobs told me I would have to speak to you."

"Why did he tell you that?" Paula said. "He hires the ranch hands."

"He said you had to give the okay for anyone under eighteen, and I'm just sixteen."

"Why aren't you in school?" Mare asked.

"I graduated this year. I skipped a grade, so I graduated earlier than most kids." He couldn't hide a faint blush.

"Where's your family?" Paula said.

"My father's dead, and my mother and I just don't seem to get along anymore. I've been going to boarding schools all my life, and now she wants me to board at college." He drew in and released an audible breath. "I want to work a year or two, first. I need a change, and I wanted to learn ranch work, so I came here. I'm not afraid of hard work."

Mare reached over, took hold of Tom's hand, and turned it over, exposing its smooth surface. She touched the palm gently. "Lots of calluses, huh?"

A lopsided grin and a brow that arched above amused eyes won Mare over instantly. "I didn't say I had done hard work, Dr. Gillespie, only that I'm not afraid of it. I'm ready to start building calluses if Miss Tanner will give me a chance."

"You're going to have to get permission from your mother to work. You're still a minor," Paula said.

"I can't get in touch with her just yet. She's on vacation," Tom said. "I can write her a letter, and the post office will forward it to her. But I need work now. Couldn't you bend the rules just a little bit? I'll get the permission as soon as I can get in touch with her." Tom turned his eyes full on Paula and pleaded, "Please."

Paula pursed her lips and hesitated. Then she pulled her notebook out of her pocket and unclipped the pen. "You any good with horses?" She started writing.

"Haven't done much except ride them for my whole life, but I'd sure like to learn to take care of them."

"Okay, I'll have Bill start you on some stable work. If I get good reports from him, we'll talk some more. In the meantime, make sure you call or write your mother."

"Where are you staying?" Mare asked.

"I was hoping there would be an extra bunk here I could use."

Paula wrote some more on the note then tore out the page and put the notebook away. "Usually, those bunks are for the cowhands, but I'm sure Bill can find something for you. Give him this note." She stood up, slid the crutches into place, and handed Tom the note.

Tom stood, too, and they shook hands. "Welcome to Meridian ranch, Tom. I hope your stay here is a happy and productive one."

"Thanks, Miss Tanner, Dr. Gillespie. You'll see. I'll work hard. You won't be disappointed."

Tom left and the women returned to the kitchen. Watching through the window, Mare and Paula saw him leave the parking area and start to jog across the fields that led to Bill Jacobs's office, about a half-mile away.

"What do you think, Mare?"

"I think you've done as much as you can for right now. But at some point, I suppose we'll have to make sure he has contacted his mother. She may not know where he is." Mare walked over to the island and clicked her fingernails on its surface, thinking. She glanced at Paula with a roguish grin. "Of course, there's no reason why we have to know who he is, is there? At least, not until he has a chance to meet TJ."

"Well, I'll be darned. You surprise me. I'd never suspect you of being so devious."

Mare tapped the side of her forehead. "I have hidden talents, my dear." Then her brows climbed. "Do you think TJ will recognize him? Does he look much like Lance?"

Paula perched on one of the chairs, and Mare settled on another. "Recognize him? Remember, she doesn't know she has a brother, so she would probably think the resemblance to her was coincidental, if she noticed it at all. And, no, except for his eyes, he doesn't look like Lance." Paula's hands accompanied her voice descriptions. "Lance was a little shorter than TJ and built squarer. This kid is built like a male version of TJ: tall, broad shoulders, slim waist, moves like a cat."

She gave an admiring nod. "And Tom seems to have TJ's assertiveness. Lance always deferred to TJ's judgment. Always. I get the feeling that, even at sixteen, Tom has a mind very much his own. I think it will be quite interesting to see him and TJ together."

The roguish grin hadn't left Mare's face. "So you think maybe we should let fate take its own course? Not interfere at all?"

Paula looked Mare in the eye, and her grin grew until the two matched. "And we won't tell anyone but Erin." They clasped hands. "Deal?" Paula said.

"Deal. Now, let's go see our sweeties."

Chapter
Six

THE CO-CONSPIRATORS HAD a two-hour drive in which to cover all the ups and downs, ins and outs, and pros and cons of the situation and their decision not to reveal Tom's identity. They arrived at the hospital with their resolve intact.

They got off the elevator at the sixth floor and hurried toward TJ's room. Near a section of mirrored wall, Paula jabbed a crutch in front of Mare and brought her to an abrupt stop.

"What's wrong?"

Paula nodded toward the mirrored wall. "Take a look at your face. One of your hidden talents better be the ability to wipe that grin off. One glance at you, and TJ will know you're up to something."

Mare looked. "Ummm. You're right. Sometimes an expressive face isn't an asset. If she notices, I'll say I'm excited because Barry has turned out so well."

"Good thinking. That should work."

Mare and Paula stepped into TJ's hospital room with smiles plastered across their faces. Paula gave TJ a quick kiss and greeting, while Mare waved at Erin, seated on the far side of the room. As Mare moved toward TJ, Paula swung around the end of the bed. Rising, Erin tried to speak but was prevented from doing so as Paula pulled her into an embrace and kiss.

Paula finished the kiss and gave Erin a tug toward the door. "Come on, let's give the kids some space."

"Hi, sweetheart." Mare placed her hands on both sides of TJ's face, leaning down for a kiss, and was shocked when TJ turned away. "What's wrong?" Mare frowned as TJ ignored her presence. She turned to ask Erin what had happened, but the door was just swinging shut behind the pair. No help down that avenue. "TJ, if you don't talk to me and tell me what's upset you, then I can't help. Now what's going on?"

ERIN WATCHED AS the door closed and then looked at Paula. "I think maybe that was a bad idea."

"What? Leaving them alone? Why?"

"Did Mare say that she'd called at all today?"

Paula thought for a second. "Yeah, she mentioned that she'd spoken to the nurses this morning. Why?"

"Because, my darling Paula, TJ's under the impression that she hadn't. In fact, I was worried myself, since I hadn't heard from you either."

"Damn it. I phoned but you were out. TJ was having tests or something. I asked the person who answered to let you know I'd called. Actually, now that I think about it, Mare said she had left an earlier message with one of the nurses. Thing is, something radical happened at the ranch this afternoon that took our focus off the hospital for a couple of hours."

"What was that?"

Paula looked over her shoulder as she heard TJ's raised voice coming from the room. "I'll tell you in a minute. You think maybe we ought to go back in there and help Mare?"

"No, let Mare take care of it. She needs to see TJ like this, and she might be able to handle it better if TJ doesn't have to keep up the tough front just because we're there."

MARE LOOKED DOWN at TJ with increasing frustration. "You know, TJ, this is wearing a little thin, especially with someone your age. If you don't want me to be here, then just say so, and I'll go." TJ's eyes turned to her, and for the first time, Mare got a reaction. "Well, that's better. Now what has you all tied up in knots?"

The eyes narrowed. "Last night, you promised you'd phone me this morning. I've been waiting all day, and you didn't call."

"Honey, I did. I phoned this morning, but you were still asleep. I left a message for you with the nurse. Didn't you get it?" TJ eyed Mare suspiciously. "Obviously not," Mare said. "What's the matter? Don't you believe me?"

"I find it a little convenient to pass the blame to someone else."

TJ's petulance angered Mare. Did TJ honestly believe she would lie about phoning? Didn't she trust her? "In that case, let's call Nancy in and see if she knows anything about it. Just press that call button. Go on."

TJ studied Mare for several seconds before making the deliberate move to press the call button.

Nancy opened the door and walked in, looking a little ragged.

"Everything okay here, ladies?" She looked at TJ, then Mare.

"Go on, TJ, ask her." Mare crossed her arms and scowled.

TJ stared at the ceiling, considering for the first time that maybe her anger was unjustified. Did she really think Mare would lie to her? The damn pain was playing tricks with her mind. She turned her gaze to Nancy. "I've been expecting a call from Mare all day and never received it. She says she phoned first thing this morning and left a message with a nurse. Know anything about it?"

Nancy pulled a crumpled piece of paper out of her pocket. "Actually, yes, I do." She held it out to TJ. "I was given it when I came in this morning, but things got a little hectic, and I forgot about it. Sorry."

Silence descended over the room, and Mare was first to react, taking the paper from Nancy's hand. "Don't worry about it. No harm done. Was there, TJ?" Mare stared hard at TJ, daring her to pass judgment or comment to Nancy.

"No, no harm done. Thanks, Nancy," TJ said quietly.

"Okay then, if there's nothing else, I'll see you both later." She walked out.

"Well?" Mare said. They stared at each other a while longer before TJ replied.

"Okay. I'm sorry. I should have known better, and I reacted like an ass."

"Yep, you sure did. You should have had more faith in me." Mare uncrossed her arms and went to sit by TJ's bedside. "Look, I know things are hard for you." She stroked TJ's forearm. "You're frustrated and bored, but you can't let that get to you. We both have to work hard at understanding each other while you're in here, otherwise this could tear us apart. Now, I'm trying my best, and I need you to try, too. Okay?"

TJ realized she was being let off very lightly for her earlier display of childish behavior. "Yes, I will."

"Good." Mare leaned forward until their lips met. Each time they kissed, Mare warned herself to refrain from what TJ called a "wake-up-TJ" kiss, figuring that it would only make their situation more difficult for them both. But today, as she started to move away, TJ twined her fingers in Mare's golden hair and pulled her back.

"Will you give me a real, gods-be-damned kiss?" Mare didn't need a second invitation. She melted against the heat of TJ's body and lost herself. One strong hand supported her head during an erotic battle of tongues, while the other hand, hampered by a healing shoulder, pressed firmly against her back, trying to pull her even closer. At last, they parted, panting.

"Now that," TJ said, "is a kiss."

"Wow," Mare said. "I've never had kiss guidance before. At least, not mouth-to-mouth." A rumble of laughter started in TJ's chest, and Mare soon joined in. "It's great to hear you laugh, you know?" Mare drew a finger across TJ's bottom lip.

TJ still bubbled with the echoes of her laughter. "Sorry, I didn't mean to give you a hard time. It's just that sometimes my brain goes into overdrive, and I start thinking the worst. I guess it doesn't help that I gave myself some extra 'happy juice' a little while ago."

"The pain was so bad you had to take more medicine than usual?"

"Yeah. Starting therapy this morning kind of set it off. It's been pretty nasty all day." A plaintive note replaced the laughter. "You know I hate to take much of the medicine, especially if you're going to be here. I want to be awake for you. But I just had to. Now, I'll probably fall asleep in a few minutes and miss your whole damn visit." TJ's face clouded, her frustration showing again, then her expression lightened a little. "Did the blanket help Flag at all? I have the extra one that I slept with the last couple of nights, like you asked. It's there at the foot of the bed."

"Good, I'm glad you remembered. We might have better luck with a fresher scent. The other blanket soothed her a little, but she still isn't eating right. I don't think there's anything to worry about though. She just wants you home, same as I do." Mare ran her fingers down TJ's jaw line. "We're lonesome."

They kissed again, then Mare, being careful not to jostle TJ, crawled up into the bed and lay as close as she could. She knew the nurses might not like her climbing on the bed, but if it helped soothe TJ, she didn't give a damn. It soothed her, too. TJ's arms wound loosely around her. Mare curled one arm across the top of the black hair and teased the far ear with her fingertips, while she nuzzled the ear nearest to her and slowly rubbed her other hand against firm stomach muscles.

"You keep that up, sweetheart, and I may not fall asleep," murmured TJ in a lazy, throaty voice that vibrated through Mare's being.

"I just want to make sure you have sweet dreams."

TJ was starting to drift. "Mmm. Where were you last night? Could've used...sweet..."

"You had a nightmare? TJ?" Mare pulled her head away and looked down. TJ had already fallen asleep. Tears pricked Mare's eyes. She knew how terrible TJ's nightmares were. No wonder she was in such pain today. She probably didn't sleep at all last night and was too tense during the therapy.

Even in sleep, TJ's face was not as relaxed as usual. Mare could see that her jaw was tight, tension pulling at her muscles. She stroked TJ's cheek and placed random kisses on it before climbing down from the bed. Very gently, she smoothed TJ's sheet and covered her with the top sheet.

She picked up the blanket, hugged it to her, and buried her face in it, inhaling TJ's scent. Lucky Flag. She could use one of these herself. She walked out into the hall, carrying the blanket over her arm.

Erin was seated on a couch at the end of the hallway. Stretched out comfortably, Paula had her head in Erin's lap and her cast leg propped against the top of the couch's back.

Mare strolled up to them, leaned down, and kissed Erin's forehead. "You look nice and comfy."

Paula said, "Didn't sound like it was too comfy in there with TJ."

Mare gave a small shrug. "It could have been worse. TJ was a little upset about not hearing from me. There was some mix-up with the message I left. She also said that she had to use her medication more today."

"Yeah, sorry," Erin said. "I was hoping to warn you about her mood." She tilted her head toward Paula. "Seems I got distracted. TJ's therapy started this morning but had to be cut short. She was a witch, but it was mostly because she had a bad night and was tired. I try to ignore the acid remarks when she's like that."

"Good girl." Mare squeezed Erin's shoulder, then dropped into a chair. "Did Paula tell you our news?"

"She sure did. Unbelievable, isn't it? Maybe I can meet him tomorrow."

Paula had insisted that she and Erin alternate times at home. In her mind, whoever stayed with TJ earned the right to a day or two away, when it could be managed.

"Maybe so. I know we both were sure surprised. If all you could see were his eyes and hair, you would swear he was TJ." Mare grinned at the recollection, then remembered her other news. "Did Paula tell you about Flag?"

"Yeah, she did. Have you told TJ?"

"I told her over the phone Saturday night. She was a little upset but not too bad. I asked her to sleep with an extra blanket to put in Flag's stall." Mare indicated the blanket folded over her arm. "I'm taking it with me. You coming back to the ranch with me tonight?"

"Yeah, it's Paula's turn to get dissed." She threw her hand up as Paula smacked at her. "Ouch!"

"Whoops. Sorry, honey, I'll kiss it and make it better." Paula stretched up and kissed Erin's lips.

"Yum, nice. But it was my hand you hit."

"Yeah, but I was aiming at your mouth."

"Then I'm glad your lips have better aim than your hand did."

"They've had more practice. So far." Paula ducked the pinch aimed at her cheek.

"You guys might as well get on your way," she said. "TJ probably won't wake up again this evening. Mare, you have to be getting tired. Why don't you go home and get some extra rest?"

"I think I have to agree with you, but I wish TJ had been awake a little longer so we could visit more. I really miss her." Mare stood up and gave Paula a kiss on the cheek. "What do you say, Erin? Just about ready to go? I'll wait for you downstairs."

Mare left and Erin turned her attention back to Paula. "Michael's driver brought me in today. All you have to do is phone the house, and he'll come and pick you up. Remember, he's at your beck and call while you're here, so you won't need to worry about getting to and from the hospital. Okay?"

"Sure, honey. Thanks. Now you'd better get going. I hate to shoo you away, but Mare could sure use some sleep." They leaned together for a kiss, then Erin helped Paula to her feet and walked with her back to TJ's room.

Erin joined Mare a few minutes later, a look of mild frustration on her face. "I'll sure be glad when we don't have to leave anybody behind."

"Yeah, me too," Mare said. "Let's change the subject. What are you doing tomorrow?"

"Bill Jacobs is meeting with me at the office, and we're going over the books: payroll, upkeep, how stocking the ranch is progressing, that sort of thing. Two more shipments of cattle and we should be up to capacity." Erin pulled a packet of mints from her pocket and offered them to Mare, then popped one into her own mouth. "You know, Bill really knows the cattle business. I've learned to trust his judgment, so all I really have to do, unless something goes wrong, is keep an eye on things. I'm learning a lot from him."

Mare pulled from Springerly's main street onto the highway. "When I was helping him cull the herd, I saw that he knew what he was doing. He's been a great find."

"Now that we have that out of the way, tell me your impressions of young Tom." The rest of the drive home was lively with speculation.

MARE DID PLAN on going to bed early. After putting the blanket in Flag's stall, she showered and donned one of TJ's T-shirts. Once again, she discarded any thought of using her new suite and climbed into TJ's bed. It was a large bed, specially built, but tonight it seemed too large and too lonely. Mare tossed and turned and finally gave up the notion of sleep.

She got up, slipped her feet into her sneakers, and padded to the music room. She sat at the piano and began playing quietly. She became totally immersed in the music, investing it with her spirit and letting it soften the ache in her heart. She played for more than an hour. Calmed and soothed, she rose to leave and was surprised to see Erin lying on one of the couches.

Erin sat up and said, "You can really talk with your music. Thanks a lot. I feel better, now."

"Glad I could help. I tried to go to bed early, but I couldn't sleep. I thought at first it would be good to use TJ's bedroom. Maybe it would keep me closer to her. But I'm finding that it just makes it harder to be separated from her. I think I'll use the bedroom in my suite," Mare said with a sigh.

Erin stood up and patted Mare's arm, taking some of the sting from her words. "Cheer up. The worst is yet to come."

"You really think so?"

"I can see the frustration building in TJ. She's trying to contain it, which is admirable, but it will probably be bad in the long run. She's been sniping at me and will be at Paula, too, but she hasn't yet dragged out the heavy ammunition. When she does let loose, I figure we might all get blasted away. TJ never does things halfway. But we have lots of time to worry about that. Let's get to bed." Erin started to walk away then turned back. "By the way, the blanket you brought from the hospital for Flag? Did it help?"

"Yeah, I took it out to Flag's stall and replaced the other one. TJ had used this one for several nights, and her scent was stronger. Flag snuffled at it right away and stayed right next to it. I'll check in the morning to see if this one improves her appetite. I'm not sure what else to try."

"Right. Maybe we'll get lucky." Erin stifled a yawn. "Good night."

"Good night. Sweet dreams."

Erin grinned wryly and wiggled her fingers in acknowledgment.

In the suite bedroom, Mare wasn't constantly assailed with reminders of TJ. She did manage to get some sorely needed rest.

THE NEXT MORNING, after sharing breakfast time with Erin, Mare checked on Flag before heading to Meridianville. Sure enough, the palomino was standing next to the blanket she had hung on one side of the stall wall. The large head swung around to see who was there, then swung back, seemingly disappointed. Mare noted that at least the calming effect had lasted.

"Hey, Flag, how are you doing this morning?" Mare opened the stall gate and entered. She stroked a hand against the large body and noted that Flag's ribs were more prominent than they should be. She moved toward the horse's head, checked the feed bin, and saw that quite a bit still remained uneaten. "What are we going to do with you, girl?" She hugged the long neck and was rewarded with a nicker. "If you don't start eating soon, we're both going to be in trouble with your mommy."

A couple of truck doors slammed. Two ranch hands came through the door, and Mare turned to greet them. She recognized the first man as one of the two who'd helped her when she'd been thrown from Paula's horse, Runny, during a thunderstorm. "Hi, Mark. How are things going?"

"Hi, Doc. Not quite as exciting as last time I saw ya, but pretty good." He tipped his head toward the fellow beside him. "This here's one of our new hands, Tom Russell."

Mare came out of the stall and nodded to the youngster. "Tom and I met the other day."

"Hi, Dr. Gillespie."

"Just call me Doc, Tom. Everyone else does."

"You got it, Doc."

His eyes swept past to Flag. "Wow, what a beauty!" He checked the name on the post, then walked into the stall and laid a hand on Flag's flank. Mare and Mark watched as he patted the palomino's shoulder and murmured to her. Flag nickered and bumped him with her head. Laughing, he swung his long arms around her neck and squeezed. His head lay up against the strong neck, muffling the sound of his voice. "Is this Miss Meridian's horse, or is that a dumb question? I guess they're all Miss Meridian's horses, right?"

"Yes, no, and no," Mare said. "Flag is Miss Meridian's pride and joy. The other two horses belong to Miss Scott and Miss Tanner."

Tom lifted his head and began stroking Flag's face. "She's magnificent. Is there any chance I could ride her?"

Mark opened his mouth to speak, but Mare grabbed his arm, and he stopped.

She considered the idea for a moment, then wondered why not. Maybe it would be good for Flag. Might get rid of some of that nervous energy she had. Might even take her mind off TJ for a while. "You said you've ridden horses before, right?"

"Ever since I was two years old."

"I'll have to check with Miss Scott, but I think it might be all right. In fact, maybe you could exercise Flag every morning as part of your chores. I'll go ask her and let you know in a few minutes."

"Great!"

Mare went back to the house and looked for Erin. She found her checking the supplies file on the computer in TJ's office and explained Tom's request. "So, what do you think? Shall I tell him it's okay to ride Flag each morning? Or should you ask TJ first?"

Erin hesitated. "This is putting me in a tough spot. TJ isn't going to take too kindly to someone riding Flag, but if you—as Meridian's vet—are telling me that it might help Flag, then we should at least try it." She thought for a few more seconds. "No, I don't think I'll ask TJ. That will just bother her more, thinking that she can't ride Flag but some stranger can. Why don't you have him take her out now for a short ride? If Flag has a good response, then okay, we'll have justification for it. If not, we'll stop."

"Good idea. Thanks. If Paula calls, say 'hi' to TJ for me. Tell her I'll call her around lunchtime, if I can. On second thought, don't tell her that. I'm not sure where I might be." And if TJ expected her to phone and she couldn't, Paula would have to listen to TJ's bitching. Mare made a quick call to Barry to let him know she would be a little late and would meet him at his first stop. She hung up the phone and walked back to the barn.

"Tom, Miss Scott okayed giving it a try on my recommendation. But when Miss Meridian returns to the ranch, this particular job could end at a moment's notice."

Tom walked over next to Flag again, reached up, and caressed her neck. "Getting a chance to ride this beauty would be a real pleasure." He turned and grinned so engagingly at Mare that she just had to grin back.

"Good enough," Mare said. "Flag's been off her feed and a bit skittish—lonesome for Miss Meridian, I think. Take her for a short ride right now, and we'll see how it goes." Mare tilted her head toward the tack room door. "You'll find everything you need in there."

Mark turned the other two horses out while Tom saddled Flag. Mare leaned against the outside of the stall and watched his sure movements. When he had finished, he held the reins and turned to lead Flag out of the stall, but the stubborn animal shook her head and didn't want to come. He looked perplexed and kept a steady pressure on the reins, but Flag didn't budge, so he grabbed the halter to try to bring her head forward. "What's the matter, girl?" he asked.

"Wait a minute, Tom. That blanket hanging there has Miss Meridian's scent on it. I think Flag doesn't want to leave it."

"Heck, that's no problem." Tom unhooked the blanket, tied it over his shoulders, and tried again to lead Flag out. This time the palomino followed right after him.

Mare thought he made a cute picture as he swung into the saddle, blanket flying behind him. "Hey, Superhero, there's a trail over to the right that eventually goes into the foothills. Just take her about ten minutes out for right now."

Tom saluted and clucked to Flag. His body jerked as the horse broke into a trot before his feet touched her flanks. Mark had halted his work to watch, and he laughed out loud. "Guess we shoulda warned him that Flag reacts to sound signals."

"He sure knows now." Mare marveled at how Tom seemed to become one with the horse, just as TJ did. Must be in their genes.

While she waited for Tom to return, she cleaned out the back of her truck. About twenty minutes later, she saw him bringing Flag back at a walk and went into the barn to meet them.

Tom's cheeks were flushed and his eyes shining as he slid off the palomino, patted her shoulder, and unsaddled her. "What a terrific horse." He put everything away, then approached Flag to turn her out into the corral. "Hey, Doc, she's eating." Sure enough, Flag ate a good portion of the meal left from her first feeding.

Mare grasped Tom's shoulder and gave it a shake. "That is super. Looks like you just got yourself a job. Can you be here an hour earlier to take Flag out each morning?"

"Sure."

"Not that early in my truck," Mark said in protest. He was mucking out Ebonair's stall and had stopped to listen when he heard Mare mention a new job for Tom. "Maybe Bill will let you use one of the ranch horses."

"No problem," Tom said. "If nothing else, I'll run over here on foot."

"Wonderful." That was one less thing she had to worry about. "Make sure you put the extra time on your time card. Oh, and Tom, Flag means a lot to Miss Meridian. Be careful with her, and if you think there's any problem, no matter how small, let me or Miss Scott know." Mare waited until Tom acknowledged her warning, then got in her truck and headed out to meet Barry.

Chapter
Seven

THE REST OF the week played out fairly calmly. Mare and Erin made the two-hour drive back to the hospital to be with TJ and Paula on TJ's first day out of the bed and in the turtle brace. TJ was grouchy and in no mood to be poked and prodded, but the bonus of being able to sit in a chair for part of the day was enough to make her cooperate.

The days settled into a routine of hospital visits and ranch activity, punctuated by the four-hour-round-trip drives. This schedule became progressively complex for the three women to handle, as their presence at the ranch became gradually more necessary.

Another shipment of cattle had arrived, and Mare found that, even with Barry on the scene in town, she had her hands full at the ranch and was bone tired by evening. Driving two hours to and from the hospital almost daily was out of the question. The infrequent physical contact with TJ, however, made Mare's burden even heavier. Phone calls just weren't as satisfying.

On the days when Erin was at the hospital, she had tried to keep a handle on the ranch activities by phone but found that wasn't working well. She needed to see things with her own eyes in order to feel confident that her judgments were sound. Spending more time at the ranch was the only answer.

Paula's presence became urgently needed at the packing plant when General Manager Fred Morales came down with pneumonia, and she had to take his place. She finally gave in and commandeered a Meridian Corporation car and driver to ferry her between the ranch and the packing plant. At TJ's urging, she also had him take her back and forth to the hospital on the days when she was able to visit.

As a result of this increased activity, the hospital visits were cut back to the point that each of the three women visited TJ on alternating days, arriving around ten o'clock in the morning, then driving back early that same evening. Even though she readily understood the necessity, the change in visitations and the additional solitary time weighed heavily on TJ's moods. The visits made Erin and Paula apprehensive, and TJ's sniping at Mare had increased.

Paula returned from one of those uneasy sessions to find a dismal, darkened house. As she exited the chauffeured car and collected the crutches, she remembered that Mare was staying overnight in Sharlesburg. It was Mare's turn to take over Dr. DiNicola's practice the next day. She was surprised, though, that Erin wasn't home. It was way past dinner time.

She managed to hobble upstairs and shower and change into a pair of beige lounging pajamas. After partially towel-drying her dark-brown hair, she ran her fingers through its short locks to smooth it out, then carefully descended the stairs and maneuvered into the kitchen.

She brewed some fresh coffee, stuck a frozen Salisbury steak in the microwave, and sliced together a simple tomato, pepper, and onion salad for dinner. After eating, she put the leftover steak and salad in the fridge for Erin. Carefully, she then took her coffee in one hand and one crutch in the other, limped into the living room, and plopped on the couch to watch sitcoms. Her mind skittered about, wondering what was delaying Erin. She knew her partner had planned to ride the range with Bill, scanning for an area on which to graze the current cattle shipment.

When Paula finally heard the back door slam shut, she grabbed the crutch and scrambled to the kitchen, calling out, "Erin, where on earth have you been?"

Erin threw her hat down on a chair and yanked off her jacket. A fine film of dirt covered her from head to foot. "Where the hell do you think I've been? I've been busting my ass on a horse all day, trying to keep this ranch going. What have you been doing?"

"Hey, I do my share around here. Spending all day today putting up with TJ's load of baloney wasn't any fun. Neither was running around that packing plant all week on a broken leg."

Erin's lip curled as she hung her jacket on the back of a chair and started toward the bathroom. "You'd think you were the first person to ever have a broken leg." She looked at the empty range. "I guess it's too much to expect that there's any dinner saved for me."

"Don't leave your dirty hat and jacket there."

"Who the hell put you in charge?" Erin barreled out of the kitchen. As she passed Paula, she swung her shoulders to clear both the doorway and Paula. She stomped out, unaware that she had clipped Paula, who lost her balance and tripped over her crutch.

As Paula went down, she dropped the crutch and grabbed hold of a chair. The chair, the crutch, and Paula went over with a clatter, bringing Erin charging back into the kitchen.

"Paulie! Paulie, are you all right?" Erin dropped to her knees.

"Yeah, I'll be okay as soon as I can get out from under this damn chair," Paula growled. "Fat lot of good that stupid crutch was."

Erin helped Paula to stand, then grasped her shoulders and waited for downcast eyes to meet hers. "I'm really sorry, Paulie. You know I didn't mean to do that." She saw sadness and pain flicker across Paula's face. She pulled her close, put her arms around her, and started a soothing pat on her back. "Look, we promised ourselves that we wouldn't let the pressures hurt us this time, right?"

"Right," Paula murmured against the side of Erin's neck. Her arms moved up and closed around Erin's back.

Erin mentally kicked herself as she felt Paula trembling. She blinked rapidly against the dampness in her eyes. "Then let's keep that promise. I'm really sorry I took my bad temper out on you. I'll try not to let it happen again, okay?" Paula's head nodded against the side of Erin's face. "I love you, Paulie."

"I love you, too, sweetheart." They hugged for a moment more, relaxing in the welcome closeness. Then Paula pulled back and looked into Erin's moist, hazel eyes. "I did save you some dinner. Go get out of those dirty duds and take a hot bath, and I'll have it all ready for you."

Erin bit her bottom lip as a wave of gratitude swept through her. She gave Paula another hard squeeze then bent to retrieve the crutch. When she handed it over, their eyes met, and she patted Paula's flushed cheek with her fingertips. "You're always so thoughtful."

Paula leaned forward and placed a soft kiss against Erin's lips. "I learned it from you, kiddo."

Erin came downstairs wrapped in a double-thick terry cloth robe and ate dinner. Afterward, with an arm around Paula's waist, she helped her climb the stairs to their bedroom. They disrobed without fanfare, and Paula offered a massage.

She sat on the bed next to Erin's waist, with her cast barely resting on the floor. When the massage was almost complete, Paula had mentioned an idea that Erin was resisting.

"What do you mean, you can't do it? Of course, you can. It's simple. I go there instead of you." Paula finished the massage and gave Erin's backside a pat.

Erin's arms were crossed under her face, partially muffling her voice, but it still sounded weary. "It's my turn to go see TJ.

She's expecting a report from me about the ranch. You know she won't like it if I'm not there."

Paula moved her mending leg up onto the bed, turned over, then slowly lay down against Erin's back. Sliding her arms under Erin as she moved, she luxuriated in the feel of Erin's warm skin as it came into gradual contact with her descending body. She caught her breath as she felt and heard the low moan summoned by her moving palms. She almost didn't continue the conversation. There were a lot of other things she would rather be murmuring into Erin's perfectly shaped ear. She sighed. But first things first.

"You've had a long day on horseback, sweetheart, and I know you're in no shape for a two-hour drive first thing in the morning. And you know you gave that wrist too much of a workout today. You can phone in your report. I say you should stay here, and I'll go in your place." She nibbled Erin's neck. "Not to mention that TJ will probably welcome you with her usual acid comments. Are you really looking forward to that?"

"Not especially, but if you go in my place, you're liable to hear a lot worse from her." Another nibble, and Erin moaned again. "You know how TJ hates to have other people change her plans. She's expecting me to come tomorrow and report to her about the ranch. If you turn up instead, she'll just be more stressed. And you know the more we can keep her calm and free from stress, the better it is for her and everyone else."

"And what about you? Who do you think is in the best position to know what's less stressful for you?" Paula pressed her body harder against Erin's back. "We have to look after ourselves as well, remember?" Her hands squeezed softly against silky skin.

Erin shifted and squirmed delightedly against Paula's body and hands until she was on her back, face to face with Paula's gleaming eyes. She wrapped her arms around Paula's neck. "I'd have to say your position beats hers, hands down, or up, or anywhere you want them. You win."

"I win the argument?"

"Yes. And me." Erin tightened her arms, pulling Paula into a body-melding embrace.

PAULA'S GUARD WAS up as she swung into the hospital room on her crutches. TJ's eyes were closed, affording Paula the opportunity to walk closer and examine the face of her friend and employer. Paula's expression softened as she saw signs of fatigue that went unnoticed when TJ was awake, including dark smudges under those magnetic eyes.

"Today's Erin's day." The voice startled Paula, and she moved back a step as TJ's eyes popped open. "Why isn't she here?"

"And hello to you, too, TJ. I know you're not feeling all that great, but is it too tough to be civil?" The blue eyes widened a bit and focused a stare on Paula, who waited, not sure what reaction was coming. Damn, it was hard to look into those eyes and stay mad.

"Hello, Paula," TJ said in a flat voice. "Is something wrong with Erin?"

"She was riding all over the ranch yesterday from dawn to dark. She was tired and sore, so I offered to switch places with her."

"That's part of her job. I was expecting a report from her today, and she knew that."

"She can give it to you over the phone. I didn't see any need for her to push herself to show up here today. No sense in her getting sick over it. Nothing's that urgent."

TJ glowered. "As long as I run Meridian Corporation, I decide what's urgent and what isn't. You should have called me about it."

"Look, TJ—"

"No, you look." TJ's voice hardened. "When I tell Erin to be here, she damn well better be here. If you two don't understand that, then maybe you'd better—" TJ stopped abruptly and grimaced as another wave of pain hit her. She closed her eyes, then forced them back open.

Paula's anger turned into compassion.

TJ's eyes dulled, and her voice lowered wearily. "Don't go looking at me like that. I don't want your damn sympathy. I count on you to give as good as you get. Don't change horses on me now. Erin's an appeaser. Every time I yell at her, she backs off. I don't expect that from you." TJ gave a small snort. "Or Mare. She at least still puts her two-cents-worth in."

Paula set her crutches against the foot of the bed, skidded a chair closer, and sat down. "There's something I have to tell you, TJ. Sort of a warning."

TJ's head swung sideways to focus her gaze on dark-brown eyes glittering with concern. "A warning?" A spark of interest glowed in the depths of the pain. "About what?"

"I think you ought to be a little more careful about what you say to Mare and how you say it. You don't want to drive her away, do you?"

"What's that supposed to mean?" TJ scowled, then her eyes narrowed from another jolt of pain.

Paula hesitated, not sure of how much more to say or whether she should be saying anything. She knew TJ and Mare loved each other, but sometimes that made spats worse—the cuts went deeper and the acid remarks burned even more.

"Spit it out, Paula. Has Mare said something?"

Paula shifted uncomfortably in her chair and looked away from TJ's compelling glare. Finally, she made up her mind and looked TJ straight in the eye. "Mare seems to have some insecurities about a few things. After all, she's had a lot of emotional upheaval: falling for you, finding her dad, seeing all three of us hurt in the accident—"

"Yeah, yeah, I know all that," TJ said impatiently. "What are these insecurities about?" Another kind of pain came to the fore in TJ's eyes. Paula thought she saw a hint of fear there, too.

"Look, a lot has changed in a very short time for her. Hiring a new assistant was a big step for her, and so was opening a second office at the ranch. But I think that the move to the ranch—especially without you there—has been unsettling for her. I think that's been a bigger change for her than she expected, and it's really bothering her."

TJ's expression froze, and she seemed to suddenly shut down all her feelings. Paula grabbed her hand. "I'm only telling you this because I want you to go a little easier on her. We all recognize that you're pulling a heavy load, but Mare is, too. Give her a break, will you?"

"Sure. Sure. Thanks for letting me know." Another surge of pain made TJ pull away from Paula's hand and reach for the anesthesia pump. "I need to take some more painkiller and that always puts me to sleep. Why don't you go to the cafeteria and grab yourself some coffee or lunch or something?"

Paula reached for her crutches and stood up. "Okay, I'll do that. I'll come back and keep you company when I'm finished."

"Right." TJ watched Paula amble out the door with her distinctive crutch cadence. Then the doubts hit her full force, and tears welled in her eyes. Mare couldn't leave her. She couldn't. That would tear TJ's heart out. TJ's thinking began to falter as the anesthesia took hold. *I can't let her do that to me. I'll...leave her first...if I have to.* Nightmarish images stalked through TJ's sleep, dragging her down into oblivion.

Chapter
Eight

WHEN GLORIA RAPHAELE returned home from her volunteer work at the hospital in Ridgeton, Pennsylvania, she went upstairs to change her clothes, choosing brown slacks and a gold tunic. She had just finished dressing when the phone rang, and she picked it up.

The apologetic voice coming over the line was not saying what she wanted to hear. "We're still trying, Mrs. Raphaele. He has no car or credit cards, and that makes it very difficult to trace your son. We've checked buses, trains, planes and showed his picture all over town. No one has found anything yet. We'll call tomorrow with our regular update. Good-bye."

In her mid-forties, Gloria Raphaele presented a handsome picture. Short, thick, black hair combed straight back from her face set off her large, brown eyes and fine features. She was of medium height and build and projected the warmth of her personality with her quick smile and expressive hands. One of those hands was now rubbing knuckles against the creases forming between her eyebrows. Where could Tom have gone? What would have made him run away? She'd been asking herself the same questions for weeks.

The truth was that Tom had been growing farther away from her for a number of years—ever since his father's death. She considered part of that was her own fault. Indeed, she hadn't wanted Tom to grow up in a house with a lonely woman for company. For his own good, she had sent him to a private boarding school where he could get an excellent education and have some father figures to emulate. When her son had graduated at the head of his class, she easily convinced herself that she had done the right thing in sending him away. But the look on his face when she had told him of her plans for his college education still tore at her heart.

"Away? You want to send me away to school, again?" Those *marvelous blue eyes he had inherited from his father pinned her to*

her chair. *"I'm not going, Mother. At least, not yet."*

"Tom, don't argue with me. I know what's best for you. You'll get an education at Harvard that you can't get anywhere else in the world." She stood up and put her hand on his forearm. *"Right now, Raphaele Consultants is just a name on a piece of paper, but you could bring the business to life, make it a reality. Your father always wanted that."*

She saw Tom's jaw set and his eyes tighten. He stood taller and straightened his shoulders in a pose so reminiscent of his father that Gloria caught her breath. He already had his father's stubborn streak. He'd soon be a grown man and would need the education. She had to make him understand that she was only concerned for his future.

Tom's voice pitched lower. *"But Father's not here, now. It's time for me to start deciding some things for myself. I want to wait a year or two before starting college. I was the youngest in my class — two years younger than most of them. I won't lose a thing by waiting until I'm eighteen."*

"I suppose we could arrange for you to start in the January semester. But why do you want to wait? What do you want to do?" Tom's reluctance puzzled her. He had always consented to her suggestions in the past, even when he wasn't especially fond of them.

Tom walked over to one of the living room windows, pulled the drape, and gazed out. *"I feel like I've been too protected. I want to see what's going on out there in the world. I want to experience how other people live."*

"I'm sorry you feel that way. I can't agree with your thinking, and I'd like to make an appointment for you to speak to Harold Benns. I think, as a lawyer, he might be able to give you some good advice about it."

"Sure, make an appointment with Mr. Benns."

On the day of the arranged meeting, Tom didn't answer Gloria's call, and she went to his room to get him, thinking he must have music piping through earphones to not hear her. In place of her son, she found a letter on his bed.

Dear Mother,

    I know you feel that you have my best interests at heart, and I love you for it. But I've been shut away from the world for the last four years, and I need a chance to be a part of it, to find my way in it. Please don't be too upset. I'm not running away forever. I'll get in touch with you when I think the time is right.

Love,

Tom

Gloria had stood a few moments in shock. Then she had reached for the phone and had dialed a familiar number. "Harold, Tom has run away from home. Please get me a detective agency to find him. Yes, please come over. I'd like that. Good-bye." Then Gloria had dropped into a chair and cried until she couldn't cry anymore.

The recommended detective agency had been searching for weeks and didn't seem any nearer to finding Tom. She sat thinking. When nothing new came to mind, she rose and went into Tom's bedroom.

Her eyes roved around the room, and she imagined Tom seated at his desk, speaking to her. She went over to the flat-topped desk and sat down. Idly, her hands played with a letter opener and an empty CD holder. Then a picture frame caught her eye. The frame was stuck facedown into one of the pigeonholes lined up on the back edge of the desk. Gloria's lips curved. Probably a girl friend. She reached for the picture, turned it over, and saw that it was an image cut from a magazine.

She sat up in surprise. She was looking into the face of another dark-haired woman leaning over the neck of a palomino horse as it jumped a water barrier. Her breath caught. My God, look at those eyes...Thomas's eyes...her son's eyes. If she had any doubts about the person in the picture, the caption erased them: *Taylor Jade Meridian and Faithful Flag on their way to another win.*

With trembling hands, she reached for the desk phone and called the detective agency. "This is Gloria Raphaele. I think I may know where my son is. Find out for me where Taylor Jade Meridian is living. That's right, the head of Meridian Corporation. Just get me her current address. If he's anywhere near there, don't approach anyone, just let me know." If Tom was with Taylor Meridian, she'd take care of it herself.

Chapter
Nine

TJ SAT QUIETLY in the turtle shell brace, fingers impatiently drumming out a beat on the arms of her chair. She repeatedly examined the clock on the wall. Mare was late, only by a few minutes right now but enough to make TJ nervous. For the past couple of weeks, TJ had allowed herself to be poked, prodded, and measured everywhere possible, at Mare's insistence that she at least give the leg braces and therapy a go. Today was supposed to be the first time she would wear the braces and start some very intensive physical therapy. Mare had promised faithfully that she would be here for the session.

TJ had made it abundantly clear to everybody who cared to listen that the braces were going nowhere near her legs unless her hand was being held by Mare. She had already caught the looks of annoyance and pointed glares at the clock from the therapist and her assistant. And as far as TJ was concerned, the therapists could mumble and mutter all they wanted that her relationship with Mare, and therefore Mare's father, meant she was getting special treatment.

The fact was the therapists were the ones getting the special treatment. Compared to the first time she had been in this position in a hospital, TJ was being a positive angel. They wouldn't have a clue what hit them, if she decided she really wanted to be nasty about this. She took another quick look at the clock. Fifteen minutes late. Where the hell was she? Mare had been late before on several occasions but had always managed to phone ahead to let her know why. *She had better be okay. If she's crashed or hurt herself in any way, I'll, I'll...I don't know what I'll do.* TJ's heart lurched at the very thought of anything bad happening to Mare.

"Miss Meridian?" TJ looked up at the petite, ginger-haired therapist who had been giving her the evil eye for the last twenty minutes. "We really need to get started with this."

"Not until Mare gets here," TJ said.

The therapist tapped her foot. "Miss, we don't know when she'll get here, and we all have other patients besides you who need our attention. Now, please, stop being childish, and let us get on with this."

"Obviously," TJ said as she leaned forward and peered at the small woman's name badge, "Jackie, you don't hear too well. I said I'm waiting for my partner to get here. If you have other patients to see, please go ahead and see them. But those," she said and jabbed her finger toward the waiting braces, "don't come anywhere near me until she gets here. Was that clear enough? Or would you like me to write it down for you?"

Jackie blanched at TJ's tone and was about to reply when the door opened behind her, and a large, black woman, wearing therapist's whites, walked in.

"Can I help you?" Jackie asked sharply.

"I doubt it, but I might be able to help you." The newcomer leaned around Jackie and looked at TJ, who was concentrating on trying not to be noticed. "Morning, TJ."

TJ looked up from beneath lowered eyebrows. "Sacha."

Jackie looked back at TJ, then to the new arrival TJ had called "Sacha." Sacha stepped around the smaller therapist, knowing that she needed to get TJ busy with something before she killed Jackie and totally ruined the day. And judging by what she had heard from outside the door, that action wasn't far off. "So why aren't we doing our exercises?" She placed herself in front of TJ and blocked her view of the other therapist.

"I'm waiting for Mare to arrive," TJ said quietly.

"Does that stop you from working on your upper body strength?"

"No."

Sacha bent down so her eyes were level with TJ. "Then you just wheel yourself over there and get on with them. We'll give your Mare another twenty minutes or so and then decide what to do, okay?" TJ nodded, then turned her chair and wheeled over to the free weights. Sacha watched her go, a smile creasing her face.

She turned to face Jackie and her assistant, who were standing there stunned. "Didn't think that was possible, did you?" The two shook their heads. Sacha held out her hand. "Hi, I'm Sacha Courtney. Dr. Gillis just hired me. I have a lot of experience with paraplegics and with this one in particular," she said as she shook each woman's hand.

"Jackie Fletcher," said the therapist. "This is my assistant, Max Hess."

"Nice to meet you both. How long have you been working with TJ?"

"This is our first session. One of the other therapists had been working with her. But he went on compassionate leave a couple of days ago."

Sacha glanced at her watch. "Well, you lasted thirty minutes. That's pretty good with TJ. Most don't get past ten."

"Excuse me?" Jackie said.

"TJ is rather renowned for having people flee in terror. You were just about to be the recipient of the world-famous Meridian temper."

"She's a spoiled brat is what she is. All this special treatment because she's seeing the boss's daughter."

Sacha indicated that they should move to the desk at the back of the gym. "TJ's not spoiled — far from it, my dear. She just knows what she wants. You have to remember she's been through this before. She knows the script, and the last time she remained in the wheelchair. The more you try to force the issue, the more she'll buck your authority."

"She did what you told her to do."

"Yeah, but TJ knows me. She doesn't have a clue about your abilities, or who you are, except for the fact that you obviously don't like her. Your attitude stinks, quite frankly. TJ's an intelligent woman, and this isn't the first time she's been offered the hope of walking. Today is an important step in seeing whether she's ever going to get out of that chair. It's understandable that she wants her support system with her. We'll wait and let TJ make the decision. If her partner doesn't arrive, and TJ doesn't want to go ahead, then we'll reschedule for another day. On the other hand, TJ may decide to go ahead and try the braces out. But you can't force her into it. It has to be her decision."

Sacha's words proved to be prophetic. TJ wheeled over twenty minutes later.

"Come on. Let's get this over with."

TJ SAT IN her bed listening. She could hear Mare's voice outside in the hall. She was late by two hours. At first, TJ had been extremely worried and even tried to call Mare on her cell phone, but it had been switched off.

Now she was still waiting as Mare chatted and laughed with Nancy at the nurse's station. No doubt Nancy was telling Mare that she wouldn't eat breakfast and had upset the nurse last night. Then after they finished giggling over what they did last night, Mare would come in and tell her off. TJ picked at the blanket that covered her. She sat watching the minute hand of the clock progress nearly twice around its route, and the previous worry turned to anger. She looked up at the door as the laughter stopped and Mare walked in.

"Nancy tells me you upset the nurse last night and that you also didn't eat breakfast." Mare leaned over and kissed TJ on the head. "Want to tell me about it?"

"Did she also tell you how many times I sneezed?"

"I see we're in one of those moods, are we?" Mare sat down in the chair by the bed, catching hold of TJ's hand as she did. "So, what's up?"

TJ looked over at her incredulously. "What's up? You want to know what's up?"

Mare sighed, wondering what she was supposed to have done wrong this time. "Yes, that's what I want to know."

"You should have been here two hours ago," TJ said, pulling her hand away from Mare.

"I know, I know. I'm late and I'm sorry. I got caught up at work." Mare took TJ's hand again and squeezed.

"You're sorry? That's just great—you're sorry. I get shoved around, fitted with the leg braces you insisted I try, but you don't show up as promised, and you're sorry?"

"Omigosh. That was this morning? I thought that was tomorrow."

"Yeah, well, it was today, but please don't let it interfere with your social life."

"TJ, honey, come on, that's not fair. I was working."

"Not fair? I'll tell you what's not fair. Not fair is being stuck in here while other people are out there enjoying themselves. Not fair is sitting in a wheelchair for the rest of my life. Not fair is going through all this crap with the leg braces and finding out it isn't going to make the slightest bit of difference."

"I'm sorry about the braces. I know you're frustrated but—"

"How could you possibly know? You're not stuck here, are you?" TJ yelled.

"No, I'm not. Do you want me to be? Is that it? You expect me to be at your beck and call all the time? I have a life and a business to run outside of us, you know, and unlike you, I can't sit behind a desk to run it or have my lackeys do it for me." Mare stood up and started pacing the room.

"I'm not forcing you to be here. If you don't want to be, you don't have to be." TJ watched warily as Mare strode back and forth.

"What? I can't believe you said that. Is this relationship getting a little too hard for you, and you want to trash it and back out?" Mare stopped at the foot of the bed and stared daggers at TJ.

"No, but it seems you might want that."

"Oh, really? Do you have any idea what I've given up for this relationship? I stood up to a town that hated the Meridians and took all the crap that they threw. I moved out of my home and brought a partner into my practice so I could be with you. What have you done? What have you sacrificed?"

My heart? Mare's right. She has given up a lot to be with me. So why am I pushing this? Why am I pushing her away? TJ looked up at Mare and saw pain in her face. *Because you know, if she stays, that look will be on her face all the time.* Mare had already told Paula that she thought she'd got in over her head, that she couldn't handle this. Letting her out of it now would be less painful for them both.

"Nothing, apparently. And I think that's how it should stay. We should bring this sham of a relationship to an end."

Mare was stunned, and she took a shuddering breath. "Sham? You think what we have is a sham?" She could feel her heart pounding, and the ache brought tears to her eyes. Her hand flattened against her chest, trying to push the pain away.

"I think it's pretty obvious that neither of us is happy. It's only going to get worse if we keep pretending that we are."

"Fine." But nothing was fine. Was TJ giving up on them? Mare was battered into numbness. She couldn't believe what was happening. "If that's the way you feel, I'll start looking for somewhere else to live. I'll be out of the ranch before you get home." She walked around the chair and picked up her bag.

"Don't worry about it. You can stay there. I'm going to ask your dad to have me transferred to Atlanta. I'll be going back there to my townhouse when I'm released."

"You're going to close the ranch? And the plant? Again?"

TJ barked a sarcastic laugh. "I'm not my father. I'll appoint a general manager, or Erin and Paula can run them if they want. They do it already, so it wouldn't be that much of a change."

Mare hesitated, unsure of what to do now. "In that case, I'll stay at the ranch until I can find something in town. I guess I won't be seeing you around. Take care of yourself." She turned and hurried from the room, not wanting TJ to see the tears pouring down her face.

TJ let her head fall back onto the pillows, and tears rolled slowly from her eyes.

Just outside, Mare rested her back against the door and closed her eyes as silent sobs racked her body. She couldn't believe it was over. She thought they were stronger than that. She felt an arm wrap around her shoulder and opened her eyes to see Nancy standing by her.

"You okay, honey?"

Mare cried harder at the sympathetic tone, and Nancy pulled her into a hug. "Hey, hey, come on, it will be okay." She guided Mare to a nearby seat. "Now, tell me what's wrong. You two had a fight, huh?"

Mare brushed the tears from her face as she sat down. "Yeah."

"A bad one, huh? Don't take it to heart, Mare. You both have been under a lot of pressure. You both had to let it loose sometime." She dug a clean tissue from her pocket and handed it to Mare.

"I think this one went a little too far, Nancy. We broke up." Mare blew her nose and sniffed, getting her breathing back under control.

"Nonsense. TJ's had a rotten day, and from the look of it, so have you. Let everything calm down. Come back tomorrow and straighten it out."

"What do you mean TJ's had a rotten day? You didn't say anything when I came in."

"I know, but I didn't think you'd be having an argument as soon as you walked in the door either. TJ was really upset that you weren't here this morning. I tried calling your cell phone, but couldn't get you. And the fitting didn't go exactly as planned. Without you there, she wasn't in a cooperative mood."

Nancy's face softened, and she looked Mare in the eye. "I think TJ finally realized that, even with the braces, there isn't any chance of her walking. I know your dad has spoken to you about this, and that at first the surgeons had high hopes of some return of function. But, as you know from the tests, there's been very little change. She's a fighter, Mare. You know that. But with the added frustration, she needed to lash out at somebody, and you were the one available." Nancy patted Mare's knee. "Now go home and come back tomorrow, and you can sort this out when you're both thinking more clearly."

Nancy got Mare's coat for her.

"Thanks, Nancy. I'll see you tomorrow."

"Drive carefully."

"I will." Mare gave her a hug and walked down the corridor to the elevator.

Nancy waited until Mare had disappeared before she entered TJ's room. She picked up TJ's chart, ignoring the silent crying. She walked around the bed and checked the readouts on the one monitor still attached to TJ and the PCA pump that administered the patient-controlled analgesia.

"Feel better now?" she asked as she put TJ's chart down. TJ continued to stare up at the ceiling. "No? Well, neither does Mare. I sent her home after I got her to stop crying. What am I going to do with you, huh?" She still got no reply. "Look, TJ, I've seen this a hundred times. I can't say I understand what you're going through, because I've never been in your situation. I do know that we all say things in the heat of the moment that we regret. Mare will be back in the morning, and I expect you both to work this out." Nancy squeezed TJ's hand before leaving her bedside.

Chapter
Ten

PAULA WAS SPRAWLED in T-shirt and shorts on the couch, cast outstretched, while she idly flicked through the TV channels with the remote. With all the channels available via cable and satellite, she still couldn't find anything that would capture her attention for more than a few minutes.

With Fred Morales recuperated from pneumonia and back on the job, the factory was running smoothly. There was no longer a need to struggle around the plant floor on her cast. In truth, she was grateful to be off her feet. But waiting on several reports to come through from the head office didn't occupy her enough today. And she couldn't even pester Erin, who was out giving Runny and Ebonair some extra exercise. It almost seemed like their horses were getting jealous of all the attention Flag was getting from Tom.

Flag had calmed down remarkably with both the constant supply of scented blankets that Mare brought back from the hospital and the care that Tom was giving her. Paula knew they would have to be careful when TJ returned home. TJ had already been told it would be months before she would be able to ride again. She'd be even more annoyed when she found out that Tom had been taking Flag out. Never mind what she'd think when she found out that he was her brother. Oh yeah, Paula could see a happy family reunion around the corner. Now, why couldn't she actually believe it was going to be happy? Maybe because nothing was ever that easy around TJ? Still, she might surprise everyone.

Paula sighed and switched off the TV. Tossing that remote to one side, she picked up another and turned the stereo on, hoping that she'd be able to find some music that would satisfy her. She found a sultry rendition of an old country tune and decided to stay on that station. Since she'd moved to Texas, she'd acquired a liking for the country music scene.

Flopping back onto the couch, she relaxed into a light doze. She didn't know how long she had napped when she was startled awake, hearing the engine rumble of a car swing by the front of the house. She wondered who it could be. They weren't expecting any visitors. Mare was with TJ, and Erin was riding. Bill and the ranch hands always used the back road. Guess that meant she had a guest. Groaning, she pushed herself upright and grabbed her crutches, hesitating as she heard the back door open. Okay, that wasn't a guest.

The door slammed shut as she moved toward the kitchen. She entered the room and saw Mare leaning against the island. "Hi! You're back early, aren't you?"

Mare looked over at her and shrugged. Paula recognized the red puffiness around her eyes and the slump of her shoulders.

Quickly, she hobbled to Mare's side, rested one of her crutches against the island, and put her hand on Mare's shoulder. "You okay?" Mare shook her head. Paula slipped an arm around her shoulder and pulled her into a hug. Mare hugged her back, and the tears that had dried on the journey home started anew.

Mare was sobbing inconsolably, and the only reason Paula could think of for that happening was that something was terribly wrong with TJ. "Mare, I need you to calm down and tell me what's happened." Mare took some deep heaves to ease her breathing. "Is it TJ?" Mare nodded. Paula shuffled back, holding Mare at arm's length so she could see her face properly. "Listen to me carefully. Is TJ okay?" Her heart was pounding as she waited for the answer. Mare nodded again, and Paula sighed in relief. "So tell me, what's wrong?"

Mare looked at Paula with wounded eyes. "We—we had an argument."

Paula felt her heart stop for one painful beat, then restart double time. This was crazy. Mare was a wreck over a stupid argument?

"You had an argument? You want to tell me what it was about, and maybe we can sort it out?"

Wearily, Mare sat on one of the stools cluttered around the side of the island as Paula maneuvered herself onto another. Mare swiped at the tears that still fell down her face and spoke haltingly. "TJ was in a really bad mood this morning. Nancy told me that she'd upset Janice on the night shift again. Why she has to antagonize her I'll never know. Anyway, I walked into her room and said something about it, and she blew up on me, big time."

"Was that the only reason for her outburst?"

Mare grimaced. "No, I'm afraid not. I was late getting to the hospital this morning. I got tied up in surgery. I missed her brace fitting and physical therapy."

"Ouch. How late were you?"

"I totally forgot about the fitting. I got called out near dawn for a collie that had been hit by a car. I didn't even think to phone and say I wouldn't get there until mid-morning." Mare glanced at Paula's questioning expression. "Two hours. I was two hours late."

"Ah, hell. What did she say?"

"Basically, she said—" She stopped and turned as the kitchen door opened.

"Hi guys, what a great day," Erin said in a bubbly voice that trailed off as she saw Mare's face. "Or not, as the case may be. What's up?"

"TJ and Mare had an argument. Mare was just telling me about it," Paula said as Erin came over and kissed her on the cheek.

"Guess I'll get us all a drink, then." Erin went over to the fridge and got out the perpetually full jug of iced tea. She grabbed some glasses and returned to take a seat at the island. She handed Mare a glass of the tea. "So what happened?"

"TJ," Paula said, "was in her usual rotten mood this morning. More so, though, because Mare got tied up with some surgery and missed her brace fitting and therapy. That's as far as we've got. Go on, Mare, tell us what happened next."

"Basically, she said if I didn't care enough to be there, then I shouldn't have pushed her into trying the braces. I told her she was being unfair, and she lit into me, shouting that unfair was being stuck in the hospital and being in a wheelchair for the rest of her life." Mare absently pushed the glass around the island top. "Yeah, I know. I should have phoned her. I should have known she would be worried that maybe something had happened to me. It was my fault. On top of that, the braces didn't do her any good." Mare rubbed a hand over her forehead.

"We were both being nasty, but, for some reason, today her attitude got to me. So, I pointed out to her that I had a life and responsibilities outside our relationship." Her glance went back to Erin and Paula, wondering whether she'd just lost them, too.

"Is that all that was said?" Erin asked.

"No, we said a lot more than that. Now that I'm sitting here telling you guys, it all seems so petty. Yes, I do have outside responsibilities, and so does TJ. Before the accident, she accepted that without question. But something has happened to make her doubt what we have together." She brushed her hands against her damp cheeks. "I should have called her and let her know what was going on, and I should have kept my temper. Instead, I made it a lot worse when I told her I'd given up a lot for her—my home, part of my practice—and that essentially she'd given up nothing. That seemed to really set her off." She glanced over to Erin and

Paula again. Paula had gone pale, and her eyes had taken on a stricken look. "Hey, are you okay?" Mare leaned forward and took hold of her arm.

"Yeah, yeah, I'm fine, but I think I might have caused a part of this problem," she said.

"How?" Erin asked.

"Well, when I went to see TJ a few days ago, she was in a horrendous mood. And I sort of told her that her attitude might drive Mare away because Mare was already having second thoughts about moving in. And that if she wasn't careful, Mare might leave."

"You said what?" Mare jumped to her feet.

Paula flinched. "I didn't mean to cause a problem. Honest. I thought it would just make TJ think a little before she spoke, that's all."

Erin reached over, took hold of Paula's hand and squeezed. "It's okay. You only did what you thought was right."

"Okay? Okay?" Mare shouted as she paced across the kitchen floor. "It wasn't okay, and it didn't help. TJ has decided to transfer back to the hospital in Atlanta and live in the townhouse."

Paula dropped her gaze. "I'm sorry, really I am."

Erin patted the hand she held, while her eyes shot daggers at the still pacing Mare. "That's okay, sweetheart, you didn't do anything." Mare snorted in derision at the comment, not noticing the change in Erin's expression. With one more reassuring pat, Erin stood up and faced Mare. "Mare, please sit down, and we'll figure a way to sort this out."

Mare's eyes were defiant, and she opened her mouth to speak. But both she and Paula jumped when Erin's palm smacked down on the island's surface.

"Dammit! I said sit down. You want to get this straightened out, or not?" Mare's harangue halted under Erin's intense glare, and she sat back down.

"That's better." Erin sat down, too, took a moment to calm herself, and spoke firmly. "Over the past few weeks, I've been with TJ more than either of you, and I can tell you, Mare, that once she has business matters out of the way, all she talks about is you. How wonderful you are, how your presence brightens her day, how much you've changed her life, and how much she loves you." Mare hung her head and shifted uncomfortably in her seat. "And I've been around you, too. I know this has been hard for you and you've had some worries. But frankly, you gush about TJ in the same way. So, it seems to me, you have a solid foundation to work on to put this relationship back together."

She looked at both of the women. "We all know that TJ has

been depressed the last few weeks. We expected it and we tried to prepare ourselves for it. And we all know that we've been under a lot of pressure, too. We knew it was going to be hard. So let's quit moaning about it and fix it." Erin took a breath. "Mare, what exactly did TJ say about moving back to the city?"

"She said that our relationship wasn't working, and we should call it quits." Mare stopped for a moment, wrestling for control of her voice. "I told her to give me a week to find a place to stay, and I'd move my stuff. She said not to bother because she wasn't coming back here. She said she would be transferring to the hospital that treated her originally, then moving to the townhouse."

"Well, that isn't as bad as it could have been, I suppose."

"What do you mean?" Mare said.

"She didn't throw you out, for one thing. It shows that she still cares for you. Our problem will be convincing our stubborn, pig-headed friend to cooperate with us. I'm assuming here that you want to work this out, Mare."

"Of course I do."

"In that case, we have to convince TJ that you're not about to walk out on her and that she can trust you. And you're going to have to be stronger than ever."

"And how do we do that?" Paula asked.

"Pretend that today never happened."

"What?" Mare and Paula said in unison. "How?"

"Easy. Mare walks in there tomorrow, acts normal, and ignores any remarks TJ makes about today. We'll deal with this mess when things aren't as heated."

"I'm not sure that will work, love. You know how stubborn she can be," Paula said.

"It wouldn't be as bad if she were here at the ranch," Mare said, "where she can't hide from us."

"She's right, Erin. You know as well as I do that if she goes back to Atlanta, she'll lock herself away in that fortress of hers. Even we can't get in there if she doesn't want us to."

"In that case," Erin said, "we need to find out how soon we can get her home."

"I'll phone Dad and see what he says." Mare finally felt a little more optimistic.

Chapter
Eleven

MARE PROJECTED AN air of determination as she walked briskly down the beige-carpeted hallway. She had spent three hours on the phone with her father last night, figuring out a way to get TJ out of the hospital. The end result had been that TJ would be leaving the hospital today.

Paula and Erin were in the physical therapy department, arranging for the delivery of a great deal of equipment that would be needed at the ranch. Mare was eternally grateful that Sacha had agreed to live at the ranch with them until TJ no longer needed a full-time physical therapist.

Michael had made several strict conditions for TJ's early release from the spinal unit. Most of yesterday afternoon and evening and all of this morning had been spent sorting out the details. TJ was to have as strict a regimen at home as she would have had at the hospital. Michael would conduct regular checkups, and if TJ's condition deteriorated in any way, she would be readmitted immediately. This morning, Mare had arranged for a special mattress for TJ's bed. Then she had asked Erin to contact a contractor about expediting the plans for a pool so that construction could begin next week.

The tough part, Mare admitted to herself, would be getting TJ to cooperate. The other major condition her father had insisted on was that TJ be happy with the arrangement. Mare was hoping that the shock of what she was about to do would keep TJ quiet at least until she was deposited into the private ambulance waiting downstairs. Mare strode around the corner and walked straight up to Nancy at the desk.

"Hello, Mare. You're looking much better today."

"Thanks, Nancy, I feel much better, too. How's TJ today?"

"About the same. Didn't have such a good day yesterday—as you might expect."

"She didn't give you any trouble, did she?"

"Nope, she hardly said a word to anyone. Didn't even give

Janice a problem last night either."

"She was checked on at regular intervals, right? And you've been to see her this morning?"

"Yes, we've checked on her hourly. We know her history of depression, so we kept a close eye on her."

A wave of relief passed through Mare. "Thanks. I take it that Dad has spoken to you and told you what's going on?"

"He did indeed. Spoke to me this morning, in fact. Told me all about the rules he'd made. TJ was a little anxious this morning, so I gave her a sedative to calm her down. She'll be a little dopey when you see her." Nancy winked. "I hope it all works out for you."

"So do I, Nancy, so do I," Mare said. "Well, once more 'unto the breach...'" Mare turned toward TJ's door and took a deep breath.

THE ROOM WAS chilly, and it wasn't from the air conditioning. TJ didn't even look over as Mare entered.

"Good morning," Mare said in the most cheerful voice she could muster. Stony silence was her reply. She hadn't really expected anything different. It was a wonder TJ hadn't thrown anything at her. Better get started before the sedative Nancy gave her wore off.

"Not in a talkative mood today? Well, don't worry. You already know I can talk enough for both of us." Mare took off her coat and draped it over the chair by TJ's bed. TJ wasn't even looking toward her. This was going to be harder than she had thought. How was she going to get TJ to agree to get taken out of here if she was going to pull the infamous Meridian silent treatment? Mare wished she'd thought of a Plan B.

"Look, I know you're not entirely happy at the moment, but Erin, Paula, and I hashed out a plan with Dad last night to get you home today." TJ shifted on the bed, and though she was still ignoring her, Mare was pretty sure she was listening. "We have to meet certain conditions at the ranch, of course, but we've already started on them. The only thing standing in the way is you." Mare saw the eyebrow lift and knew she had TJ's full attention.

"Dad has insisted that you agree to all his conditions and follow his rules to the letter. That means physical therapy at the ranch, and Sacha has agreed to stay with us until you don't need her full-time. When that happens, you'll come to the hospital on a part-time basis. You'll have to resume your counseling sessions with Peter Tauper, and Dad, or one of his associates, will make spot checks at the ranch to make sure we're following the protocols he's set down." Mare took a seat in the chair and waited. What happened now was up to TJ.

TJ stared at the same spot on the ceiling that she had been staring at since the day she had awakened in this room. She had spent many hours trying to figure out how a perfect, circular hole could have found its way to being precisely above her bed, though it was a little fuzzy today after the pills Nancy had given her. She heard every word that Mare had said and had even felt a thrill of excitement go through her at the prospect of going home. It was perfect—except for one small matter. Mare wanted her space. She'd already told Paula that. They had moved too fast, and after the accident, Mare knew she had gotten in over her head. TJ wouldn't let her sacrifice her happiness out of pity and a sense of duty.

"I said I was going back to the townhouse, and that's where I'm going," TJ mumbled around the effects of the drugs.

"Not for a few months, you're not. Paula and Erin gave Dad a plan of the setup you have there, and it's a no go. There are too many stairs and not enough space to set up for therapy." She paused, knowing this was going to hurt TJ. "And no one to look after you. Paula and Erin will be staying at the ranch to run it and the packing plant."

"So I'll buy somewhere else, hire a nurse or something."

"You think it will be easy to find someone you can get along with or, more importantly, someone who can put up with you?" Mare looked away, not wanting to see the pain she knew that remark would cause. "Besides, that option would still take time to set up."

"I suppose you'd get your dad to veto anything I wanted anyway," TJ said. She finally looked toward Mare, her expression bitter.

"I could try, but I doubt it would make much of a difference. You're his patient. Your needs come first in his book, before anything or anybody else's. All it really comes down to is whether you want out of here or not. It's your choice—stay or go back to the ranch? Dad will be in to see you on his ward rounds. Think it over, and let him know what you want to do. There's an ambulance waiting downstairs, if you decide to go." Mare stood up and collected her coat from the back of the chair. With one last glance at TJ, she walked out.

TJ squeezed her eyes shut, trying in vain to prevent the escape of tears. She knew she said things that hurt other people, but most times she couldn't help herself. When the physical pain was acute, it seemed as though she stood back watching someone else say all those hurtful things and could do nothing to stop her.

Now, there was pain set deep in her chest that didn't come from the injuries she had sustained or from the surgery. She understood she had lost the woman she loved most. If she went back to the ranch, she would only prolong the inevitable. But if she pursued returning to the townhouse, she would also lose the friendship of Erin and Paula. What was she to do?

MARE WAS SITTING in the small waiting area outside TJ's room when Erin and Paula approached with her father. "Look who we found prowling the corridors," Erin said as she helped Paula sit down.

"Hello, sweetheart." Michael bent to kiss Mare's cheek. "These two have been causing havoc in my physical therapy department. What is it about your friends that has that department always in an uproar?"

"Hi, Dad. I have no idea," Mare said with a wry grin. "Maybe your people thought TJ was following behind them."

"No, Sacha has her well under control. And speaking of TJ, have you talked with her?"

"Yeah, I have, but I don't know what she's going to do. Or what I can do either."

"I'm on my way in to see her. Then we four will talk."

"TAKE A SEAT." Michael walked behind his desk and sat down. He waited quietly while the three women settled themselves. "I have no idea what's been going on, what has or hasn't been said. But I'll tell you this. It hasn't helped TJ at all."

Mare cringed at her father's angry tone. "She said no?"

"She didn't know what she wanted to do. So, let me be very clear. This accident and the operation have depleted TJ's physical and mental resources. I can't stress to you strongly enough that she cannot, and I mean cannot, take any more. If I allow you to take her back to the ranch — and I'm seriously rethinking my position on that — there can't be a repeat of yesterday. And I'll also want her counseling sessions to begin again right away."

"You mean you're letting her go back to the ranch?" Erin leaned forward.

"Yes, I'm going to let you take her home, for a trial period at least. I've come to the opinion that her staying in the hospital any longer is probably going to do more harm than good."

"Thank you, Michael," Paula said. "We appreciate your help." She and Erin stood and prepared to leave the office.

"You coming, Mare?" Erin asked as she pulled the door open.

"I just need a few minutes with Dad. Why don't you let Nancy know that TJ's coming with us, and she can notify the ambulance crew?"

"Okay, we'll meet you at TJ's room when you've finished."

"Sure." Paula and Erin left, and Mare turned back to her dad. "So, are you angry with me?"

"Not in the least, honey." Michael stood and walked around his desk. "In a situation like this, I have to put TJ's well-being first. But I do understand that this isn't easy for you either. You didn't actually expect to have to go through this type of thing when you signed on with TJ, did you?"

Mare sat back in her chair, eyes downcast. "No, but if I love her, it shouldn't make a difference, should it?"

"I'm not questioning your love for her. I'm just saying that this puts a strain on you, too, and unlike Erin and Paula, you haven't been through this before or seen TJ like this. It was bound to stress you somewhat. However, I have to protect TJ, and I really need you to hold back from putting any more pressure on her. That doesn't mean you let her get away with blue murder. It just means you have to be careful what you discuss with her. Okay?"

"Okay. I understand."

"Good. Remember, you can always pick up the phone and yell at me, instead of TJ, if you need to. I suspect, though, that when she starts her counseling sessions again, most of the anger she feels will be worked out. Come on, I'll walk you back to her room."

Chapter
Twelve

IT DIDN'T TAKE long to prepare TJ to leave the hospital. The ambulance service Mare had hired was quick and efficient, and thanks to Nancy, TJ was too sleepy to notice much of what was going on. Mare double-checked that nothing was left behind in the room and then followed the ambulance crew with the stretcher. She stopped at the nurse's station and waited as Nancy approached.

"I guess you'll be pleased to see the back of us, huh?" Mare said.

"Not really. You and TJ livened up the place, that's for sure. Still, it will be nice to return to the normal peace and quiet." Nancy tilted her head to look more closely at Mare. "You two are a good match, you know. But that doesn't mean things won't be hard for both of you. You take care of TJ—and yourself—and if you ever need a shoulder to cry on, feel free to come by. Or just come by to say hello."

The welling of emotion brought tears to Mare's eyes, and she clasped Nancy in a fierce hug. "You've done a lot for us. Thank you. I really mean that. We wouldn't have gotten this far without your help."

Nancy squeezed back and then released Mare. "I'll see you around."

"Be sure of it," Mare said.

She caught up with TJ and the ambulance crew at the elevator. Paula and Erin were already on their way back to the ranch, and Mare would be riding in the ambulance. The two-man crew was young, but from the conversation that Mare had had with them before they arrived in TJ's room, she knew they were experienced. TJ had been placed on the stretcher with the utmost care, and the men had been thoughtful enough to explain what they were doing and why. TJ was securely strapped to the stretcher and appeared to be dozing.

TJ kept her eyes closed during the whole ride to the ranch,

although Mare could tell by the breathing that she had come wide-awake partway home. Mare sat beside her, her hand resting just above TJ's head but not touching her. Even when they pulled into the ranch and TJ was finally settled into her own room, she didn't utter a word. Mare decided to just wait her out, no matter how long it took.

According to the plan, TJ's schedule at the ranch would closely follow her hospital routine. Erin or Paula would wake TJ in the mornings and assist her with cleaning up and getting dressed. Both of them had been shown how to put TJ in the turtle brace. Once that was complete, everyone would eat breakfast, and then Sacha would take over with TJ's physical therapy program. The aim behind the sessions was to strengthen the muscles in TJ's back to such an extent that the brace could eventually be removed. TJ would have up to three PT sessions a day depending on Sacha's evaluation of her condition.

On the first morning back at the ranch, breakfast was a strained affair. Mare had briefly made an appearance but had had to rush off to an emergency at one of the nearby ranches. She and TJ had not exchanged a word, and that put a damper on the conversation. Nevertheless, TJ's turbulent gaze flicked toward the window as Mare's truck left the parking area.

After her first grueling session of therapy, TJ bullied Paula and Erin into taking her out to the barn to see Flag. As soon as TJ's chair came through the barn doors, the palomino whinnied and pawed the ground until TJ reached her stall. Flag lowered her head to TJ, who raised her arm and encircled the horse's neck in an eager hug. She whispered her affection through a throat tight with emotion. When she had calmed herself, she recognized the blanket hanging along the side of Flag's stall. She had to admit Mare had been taking good care of Flag, even if their relationship was over.

Satisfied with Flag's condition but brooding over her own, TJ allowed Erin and Paula to take her back into the ranch house. She wheeled into her office, curtly told them she didn't want to be disturbed, and slammed the office door. They looked at each other and shrugged, then went about their business.

Later that morning, Mare returned to the ranch and then left almost immediately with Bill and Erin to have a look at the herd grazing on the northern pasture. Those cattle were the next scheduled for slaughter, and the herd needed an inspection to assure a clean bill of health.

Two more therapy sessions that day did little to improve TJ's outlook or behavior. Bitching and yelling at Sacha came from the gym on more than one occasion. That evening, TJ had dinner in her office while dealing with a minor crisis at the main office in Atlanta. Mare claimed she wasn't that hungry, grabbed a sandwich, and went back to her office. This left Paula, Erin, and Sacha around the table.

"Nice to see those two getting along so well, isn't it?" Erin put down plates of steak and salad in front of Sacha before turning to get hers and Paula's.

"They'll be fine." Sacha reached for the Italian dressing. "It's the first day back, and they weren't on the best of terms before we left the hospital. Give them a couple of days and they'll be okay."

"I think you might be expecting too much," Paula said.

"You'll see." Sacha looked unperturbed. "Maybe things have to come to a head before the air starts to clear, but it will happen. Those two are too good for each other to think they won't stay together."

"I hope you're right," Erin muttered.

THE NEXT SEVERAL days unfolded in the same way. One morning, however, the sun hadn't yet risen and TJ lay in her bed, listening intently. Each morning since arriving home, she had heard a horse come to the barn area at a very early hour. After a short period of time, a different horse rode away from the barn and then returned about an hour later. After another short interval, the first horse rode away again. Initially, TJ's emotions had been in such turmoil that she didn't take notice of the unusual activity. But today she noticed it and questioned it. She could swear the second horse was Flag. If it was, then someone was riding her without her permission. How could anyone dare let that happen?

TJ reached out and pulled her chair against the bed. She locked the brakes, pushed the nearer arm up, and grabbed for the handle above the bed. Grimacing at the pain that assailed her when she raised her arms, she wiped her hand across the bead of sweat forming on her upper lip. She waited for the pain to recede, then pushed the button to adjust her special mattress to a raised, almost-sitting position. With numerous tiny scoots, she maneuvered herself into the chair's seat. She grabbed the assist belt that was secured to the back of the chair and quickly wrapped it around her torso to keep herself upright. After manually dragging her legs off the bed, she sat for a moment, breathing heavily but smiling at this little victory.

She wheeled her chair over to her bedroom window and looked out. Apparently, the rider took off in the opposite direction, because no one came past her side of the house. Damn.

After all that trouble. She wheeled from the window, eyed the bed, and huffed out a sigh. At least getting out of the chair should be a lot easier than climbing into it. And with patient persistence, it was.

Chapter
Thirteen

ERIN HELPED TJ get up, then accompanied her to the kitchen for breakfast. Mare and Sacha were already seated, and Paula had just added places for Erin and TJ. The women ate quickly and quietly. Then TJ pushed her dishes away and leaned forward, placing both arms on the table.

She spoke very softly. "Who's been riding Flag in the morning?"

Erin swallowed hard before answering. "He's a new fellow named Tom."

TJ said even more softly, "And just why is one of the hands riding Flag?"

"Because I encouraged him to," Mare said with a tilt of her chin. TJ's eyes bored into hers, but she struggled on. "Flag wasn't eating properly even with the blankets near her. She had improved a little bit but not enough, and she was still skittish. Tom asked if he could ride her to try to get rid of some of that extra energy. We all thought it would be a good idea, and I told Tom to give it a try. Flag took a shine to him right away. She started to calm down and began eating right after the first time he rode her. And she's been eating well since."

"And who gave you the right to make that decision?"

Erin spoke up. "I made that decision." Paula's body jerked, and Erin rested a hand on her arm. Sacha seemed less concerned, but she watched with interest.

TJ looked sharply toward Erin and opened her mouth to speak, but Mare jumped in. "Flag was sick. I convinced Erin that Tom's attention might help. As vet for this ranch, I take full responsibility for that decision."

"As vet for this ranch?" TJ said. "Well, that could be subject to change."

Mare stood up so fast, her chair toppled over. The bang as it hit the floor made everyone jump. "We all know you're the one in charge here. You don't have to shove it down our throats by doing something so damned childish." So Dad didn't want TJ upset, huh? That was an impossible task. Mare stalked to the door and flung it open, then looked back at TJ. "But if that's your choice, just leave it in writing — as the contract states — in my office." Mare went through the door and slammed it behind her.

Erin nervously cleared her throat. "Do you want me to draw up a letter canceling Mare's contract?"

TJ slumped back in her chair. "No." Pain swept across her face as she recalled that Mare might decide to leave her, but the cold look was back in place when she addressed Erin. "I want to meet this man."

"He's not a man," Erin said, "so please don't be too tough on him. He's just a boy."

"What? You let a boy ride my Flag? She's irreplaceable — "

"Take it easy," Paula said. "The kid's a great rider. You can tell in two seconds that he was born to the saddle."

"I'll see if he was born to the saddle, and I'll say whether he can ride Flag. Have him come by the house so I can check him out."

Sacha stood up, looked at her watch, and calmly announced, "You can settle this later, TJ. It's time for your therapy." TJ was so disturbed by the news about Flag's rider that she didn't even protest when Sacha walked behind the chair, grabbed the handles, and pushed her toward the door. "I can't believe they let some kid ride Flag," TJ said, almost to herself.

Erin looked at Paula and they both blew a breath of relief. "What do you think?" Erin said. She and Paula rose and cleared the table as they talked.

"I think we might be okay. Tom and Mark were in town to pick up ranch supplies yesterday, and I ran into them at the grocery store. I hardly recognized Tom. He's growing a beard — actually a pretty heavy one for a kid — and wearing reflective wraparound sunglasses. I guess it must have dawned on him that his eyes might give him away. I can't say how TJ's going to treat him, but she sure as heck shouldn't suspect he's a relative."

"Good. Tom will still be exercising Flag every morning unless TJ stops him, but I asked Bill to switch him away from stable duty for a while, just in case."

Paula put an arm around Erin's shoulders and squeezed. "That was good thinking, sweetheart. Remember, Peter's coming here for TJ's counseling session this afternoon, so why don't you ask Bill to send Tom over sometime tomorrow? Let TJ know when he'll be coming, and we can try to be available, too. The kid might need some moral support."

Erin slipped an arm around Paula's waist and leaned into her.

"Speaking of moral support, I definitely plan to be here for lunch. TJ's been entirely too quiet about Peter's visit."

"You're right. After this morning's upset, who knows how she'll act?"

"Let's just hope for the best. Now, I guess we better get to work."

"HEY, TOM!" BILL Jacobs hollered as he saw Tom walking toward the cookhouse, his assigned job for the day. Tom stopped and waited until the foreman caught up to him. "Miss Meridian wants to see you tomorrow right after lunch, around one o'clock."

Tom's heart began to pound so hard, he wondered if Bill could hear it. "Did she say what she wanted?"

"No, I just got a message for you to be there. Maybe she doesn't like your sunglasses."

"Right." Tom was the only hand who wore sunglasses, and the others teased him about Easterners being wimps. "I don't wear them when I'm riding Flag. It's still dark out."

"You just be sure to be there, okay?"

"No problem, Bill. I'll be there." Tom entered the cookhouse, but he had trouble keeping his mind on his chores. All he could think about was the upcoming meeting with his sister. He remembered Doc Gillespie's warning that the job could end at a moment's notice. But even that possibility didn't dampen his joy. At last he would meet his sister face to face. TJ didn't know who he was, so there wouldn't be any hard feelings messing them up. He'd get to meet the real TJ Meridian.

ERIN ENTERED THE kitchen through the side door and walked into the middle of a full-blown argument. TJ was at one side of the table with Paula and Sacha seated across from her. Erin noticed that the lunch preparations lay in front of them, temporarily abandoned.

TJ's hard-edged voice hurled words like shrapnel. "The last thing I need right now is a chummy chat with Peter." Although they were barely speaking, TJ had hoped to find a way to ask Mare to come to this afternoon's session, but this morning at breakfast, nothing had gone as planned. She had been arrogant and unfair to Mare, and that just made TJ angrier and more defensive.

Paula and Sacha were trying hard to persuade TJ that she shouldn't miss Peter's visit. Erin joined forces and added her plea. "Come on, TJ, you know Peter has been helping you."

TJ silenced the nagging women by screaming, "I am the boss

here! I will not be pushed around!" She turned the wheelchair with such vehemence that it teetered for a moment. She wheeled through the hall into her office and banged the door shut.

Moments later, Sacha opened the mistreated door without knocking and walked into the lion's den. At least that's what Erin and Paula had called it, warning her that TJ might throw something more substantial than words. Sure enough, Sacha had to duck the pencil caddy that hit the doorjamb and splattered pencils, pens, and paper clips on the floor. Without a word, she bent down and methodically picked up every item, keeping an eye on TJ's movements, just in case. But nothing more was forthcoming. Throwing the caddy seemed to relieve some of TJ's frustration, though her eyes remained turbulent.

Sacha approached the desk with the rescued caddy, and rather than set it back down, she offered it to TJ, patiently waiting to see if she would reach for it. TJ finally grabbed the caddy and slapped it onto the desktop. "Put the damn thing down," she said, already berating herself for having thrown it.

Sacha placed her hands on the desk. "If you want to have sensible control of your life, then you have to learn to handle your emotions — and sometimes, you have to make some difficult decisions." She leaned in a little more toward TJ. "There are many roads and choices in life. Do you want to struggle up the hard road that goes forward? Or do you want to coast down the easy one that goes backward?"

TJ covered her face with her hands. "You know which one I want."

"Don't you think your counseling session will help you go forward?"

"But I wanted Mare to be here for it with me." TJ pushed her head deeper into her hands and splayed her fingers through her hair.

Sacha moved behind TJ and began to massage the tightness in her neck and shoulders. "That's not going to happen today, but you're a big girl now, and you can handle it. Maybe Peter can help you resolve some of your anger and give you and Mare a better chance of sorting out your problems."

"Maybe." TJ's muscles started to relax as this idea sank in. Sacha ended her massage, and TJ straightened back up. "Thanks, Sacha, that feels a lot better." Sacha moved alongside the chair, and TJ looked up to meet her gaze. "Okay, okay. I'll see Peter this afternoon. You win."

"Right decision," Sacha said. "You're the one who wins." Then she patted TJ's cheek. "Come on, let's go eat."

ERIN LOOKED OUT the window and saw the psychologist, Peter Tauper, arriving for TJ's first counseling session since the accident. Until TJ's back healed enough to ride comfortably in a vehicle, Peter had agreed to come to the ranch to see his patient. Erin let Peter in and quickly filled him in on the morning's happenings, including TJ's reluctance to have the session. She then showed him to TJ's office where TJ sat at her desk. Her eyes looked stormy, and her restless fingers flipped a pencil. She nodded to Peter as Erin announced him.

"Hello, TJ." He walked over, reached across the desk, and shook her hand. Peter was of average size and had a beard and mustache slightly darker than his light-brown hair. Disconcerting eyes — one blue, one brown — looked through small, wire-frame glasses. "I thought you would be in bed. You just got home from the hospital, didn't you?" He sat in one of the chairs pulled up in front of the huge desk and laid his briefcase across his knees. He had half-expected Mare to be here.

"They put me in a brace that supports my back." TJ knocked her knuckles against the turtle shell brace she wore under her clothing. "As long as I can sit up, that's what I'd rather do."

"Independent as ever, I see." Peter snapped his briefcase open and withdrew a tape recorder, which he laid on the desk. He closed the briefcase, set it on the floor, and looked at her.

"Why don't you come around here and sit near me, TJ?"

"I'd rather stay here."

"Okay, that's no problem." Peter got up, lifted the chair that was nearest to TJ, and moved it behind the desk. He set it near TJ, then reached across, turned on the tape recorder, and sat down. "Would you like to talk about what's upsetting you right now?" Peter asked gently.

TJ fidgeted for a moment. She still found it difficult to talk about her emotions, and the first few minutes were the worst. "Mare and I were...I kind of pushed her away. I...didn't want to have a session without her here, but I wasn't willing to ask her to stay with me." TJ shrugged. "So, I wanted to cancel this appointment."

"Well, I'm glad you didn't cancel."

"You can thank Sacha for that. She talked me out of it."

"What happened that you pushed Mare away?"

TJ explained the scene she had with Mare at the hospital and told about practically being blackmailed into coming home.

"Do you want to discuss your feelings about that?"

"Not right now."

"All right. Maybe we can talk about what happened between you and Mare this morning?"

TJ rubbed her neck. "I...ah...I guess this sounds pretty unreasonable, but I got upset when I found out somebody else was riding my horse."

"Why do you suppose you got upset?"

"No one else has permission to ride Flag. She's my horse."

"Why is someone else riding her?"

"Because Mare said he could. He's just a kid, too. How do I know he'll take good care of her? And Paula and Erin thought it was okay, too." She tapped the pencil against the desktop.

"Do you know why Mare let him ride Flag?"

"She said it was because Flag missed me and wasn't eating right. Seems like when this kid rode her, she began to eat better." TJ twisted the pencil in her hands.

"Do you think that was good for Flag?"

TJ blew out a breath of frustration. "Of course it was. I'm mostly angry that they said he could ride her without asking me first. What do you want me to say?" She suddenly felt exhausted.

"It doesn't matter what I want you to say. I'm just trying to help you learn to cope with how you feel about different things in your life. Since you say you're angry about it, how do you think you can handle that?"

"It doesn't really matter, does it? I already yelled at everyone and threatened to fire Mare. I can't take back what I said." Suddenly she yawned, and an abrupt wash of discomfort made her realize that her back pain was returning with a vengeance. "I'll try to think this through, Peter, but right now, I'm too tired and sore to even care." She put the pencil back in the caddy.

Peter glanced at his watch. "All right. We'll address this again in our next session. I'll have Mrs. Haddon call you to set up an appointment."

TJ pushed a button on the desk console, and Erin came in to show Peter out. She quickly returned to the office. "Are you feeling okay, TJ? Do you need anything?"

"I'm going to take a nap. Come help me out of the chair, okay?" TJ wheeled toward the hall doorway.

"Sure." Erin walked next to the chair and put her hand on TJ's shoulder. "You know I'll help you anytime you want me to."

TJ patted Erin's hand. "You're too good to me, kiddo."

THE NEXT MORNING, Tom arose as usual and rode to the barn. After saddling Flag, he cantered her from the corral and turned to the right-hand trail. A sharp whistle sounded and Flag reared, whinnied, and tried to change direction. Tom fought for control until another whistle came, and Flag reared again. This time, he let the palomino have her head, and she raced across the back of the ranch house, trotting up to a lighted window. A form silhouetted against the open window came into view as Flag neared. The palomino stopped just beyond some shrubbery.

"Bring her closer," a woman's low voice commanded.

"There are shrubs here, ma'am," Tom said.

"The hell with the shrubs, I said bring her closer." Tom clucked and Flag's hooves flattened the shrubs, as she poked her head into the window and bumped her nose against TJ. TJ kissed the golden head while her fingers scratched Flag's forelock. "Good girl, Flag," she said.

Tom's heart was so full he thought it would burst. He wished he could get a clearer view of TJ, but the light behind her kept her face shadowed.

TJ couldn't see him clearly either. As Flag had approached, she could tell the rider was tall, but that was the extent of what she could see. She pulled her head back away from Flag, and her voice hardened. "What are you doing on my horse?"

Tom tugged the brim of his hat. "Miss Meridian, I'm Tom Russell. Your horse missed you, and she wasn't eating. I thought maybe if I could ride her for a while, it would help take her mind off of missing you, and she would start to eat again."

TJ snorted, but Tom continued. "You're right. It wasn't easy, ma'am. The only way I could get Flag to leave the barn was to bring one of your blankets with me." He showed her by lifting the edge of the blanket he had laid across the top of the saddle. "The combination of your blankets and my riding her has worked." He patted Flag's shoulder. "She's been eating real well lately and is in great shape."

"Who are you?"

Tom took a deep breath and answered firmly, "Miss Meridian, I'm just a guy who loves Flag, same as you do. And I sure wish you were the one riding her instead of me."

"Good answer. Have we met before? You seem familiar to me."

He paused, then responded in a lower voice, "No, ma'am, we've never met. I wouldn't have forgotten you."

Something in the timbre of Tom's voice intensified the feeling of familiarity, muddling TJ's thoughts. They must have met before. Was he lying? "Finish your ride." She shooed him away with her hand. "I'll see you this afternoon."

Tom touched the brim of his hat again. "Ma'am," he said, then pulled Flag away and rode off.

TJ watched Flag and Tom until she couldn't see them anymore. He did ride like he was born to it. A pang of jealousy struck her. But that didn't mean he should be riding her Flag. She'd get that straightened out this afternoon.

Chapter
Fourteen

SINCE RECLAIMING TJ from the hospital, Mare had spent the nights at the ranch alone in her own suite, and this morning, she didn't even show up for breakfast. Erin shared the information that Mare had made an early start on her appointments for the day and would be back late, possibly missing supper, too. TJ just grunted, suspecting that Mare was purposely making herself scarce for the moment.

Throughout the morning, thoughts of Tom and Flag alternated through TJ's mind with thoughts of Mare's part in the arrangement. She could accept that Mare had Flag's interests at heart. What she had trouble accepting was that Mare had made the decision without asking TJ. That seemed too much like trying to take over TJ's life, and she had enough of that with her father. They had to get this straightened out. Then TJ felt a tugging on her heart and she grimaced. If they ever talked again.

A movement outside caught her eye. She watched as Tom dismounted and tied his horse to a corral post. He pulled off his hat, dropped it over the saddle horn, and ran long fingers through his heavy hair. After settling his sunglasses firmly on his face, he straightened his shoulders and proceeded to the house.

TJ wheeled to the door and let him in, then led him to the kitchen table and invited him to sit. The table legs had been fitted with lifts so that TJ's chair slipped beneath the tabletop, and she jockeyed it into place across from Tom. A pad and pencil lay in front of her with a pitcher of iced tea, two tumblers, and some napkins nearby.

Neither spoke as TJ filled both tumblers and slid one across to Tom, who nodded his thanks and took a long drink. TJ sipped at hers while she trained her eyes on him. Tom seemed to examine her just as intently and finally a tiny smile whispered around the edges of his lips.

TJ studied the youngster across from her. Hard to think of him as a kid. With that beard, he looked pretty mature. And seemed to have plenty of poise, too. Or else he's not much of a talker. She picked up the pencil and twirled it through her fingers. "So, Tom. I looked you up in our personnel files, and there isn't much there. Says you come from Pennsylvania, you've graduated from high school, and you've been riding horses since you were two years old. There's not even a Social Security number for you. Care to explain?"

"I forgot my Social Security number and have to write to my mother to get it. I haven't gotten around to doing that yet."

"Your mother doesn't have a phone?"

Tom started to drum his fingers, then intertwined them and clasped his hands together. "Actually, she does." He cleared his throat. "She's on vacation right now, and I haven't been able to get in touch with her." TJ stuck the pencil's eraser between her teeth and nibbled it for a moment. "Does your mother know you're here?"

Tom's head lowered. "No."

"And you don't want her to know?"

"No." His head came back up. "I mean yes, I don't want her to know. She wants to send me away to college, and I'm not ready for that yet. I want to live a little first." Tom scooted his chair in tight against the table, and his voice deepened. "I've been in boarding schools all my life. I don't even know what the real world's like, and I want a chance to find out before I get cooped up again. I've never had a chance to decide anything for myself. I figure I need to learn to make little decisions before I have to make big ones that will affect my life. Mother didn't agree with that, so as soon as she left for her vacation, I left home...and wound up here...and fell in love with your horse." He took a deep breath and clasped his hands more tightly. "I'm hoping you'll let me stay." Tom tensed and his breathing became very shallow. He stared at TJ as she considered what he had told her.

She could relate to Tom's wanting to make decisions for himself. And his words this morning, *"I sure wish you were the one riding her instead of me,"* had let her know he wasn't making an emotional claim on Flag. And she needed to know that.

TJ pursed her lips and then said softly, "I want you to get in touch with your mother as soon as you can, but you can stay."

"Thanks, Miss Meridian. I'll work hard for you. And I'll take great care of Flag. If you'll let me, that is."

"Well, Flag does seem to be pretty used to you," TJ said. Now that the final decision was up to her, the idea of Tom riding Flag didn't bother her as much.

"That's probably because of the blankets," Tom said.

"Whatever it is, it seems to be working. I'll let you keep riding her until I'm able to."

"I know you have to be missing her just like she's been missing you, Miss Meridian. I know I would. I sure hope you can ride her soon."

TJ compressed her lips as the sincerity of the young man's words threatened to overwhelm her. "Yeah," she whispered, then swallowed and tried again. "Let's go outside and see her."

"Right." Tom jumped up and held the door open as TJ wheeled through.

TJ found his enthusiasm contagious.

MARE DROVE THROUGH the cemetery entrance and parked in her usual spot at the base of the slight rise on which her mother's grave rested. She reached across to the passenger seat, picked up her tote bag and a spray of wildflowers, and climbed out of the car. She took a deep breath and inhaled the light scent of flowers, mown grass, and turned earth. Cemeteries had a look and feel and even a smell all their own. The hump of the rise leveled out, and Mare crossed beneath the hovering limbs of the guardian tree. She knelt next to her mother's grave and placed the flowers on it in a colorful fan. From her tote bag, she took grass shears, a knife, and a whiskbroom and made the grave clean and neat.

When she was done, she sat quietly for a while. In life, Jane Gillespie had often shared her shrewd insights into human nature with her daughter, and Mare frequently used her visits to the gravesite to reflect on her mother's teachings. No matter what was troubling her, she found that opening her mind to those insights and teachings often helped potential solutions rise to the surface.

As she always did, Mare brushed her fingers in greeting across the chiseled letters of the polished, gray monument: Jane Arnold Gillespie. Then she spoke in a quiet voice.

"Hi, Mom. Sorry I missed some visits with you, but I'm sure you understand. I was in a rat race there for a while — moving to Meridian ranch, getting Barry started in the practice, taking care of my end of it, and traveling to Springerly to see TJ. If you could hear my thoughts during that time, you knew they were pretty jumbled.

"Barry's doing really well, which is a blessing. Everyone's crazy about him. I wish you could see his little boy. He's a roly-poly whirlwind, and Berta's the perfect mother for him. She never bats an eye, just keeps doing whatever needs doing.

"Jess is still away. He picked up some extra new business in the same area, so he decided to stay awhile and get that off the ground. I'll get the full report when he gets back.

"But here's the tough part, Mom. We've brought TJ home. She's having a really rough time with pain, and when she feels miserable, she seems to want everyone to feel miserable with her—the old misery loves company syndrome, I guess. It's tough to see TJ giving Erin and Paula such a hard time, but it's kind of sweet to watch them stick up for each other.

"TJ said she wanted to leave me, but Erin said it's not her talking, it's the pain. What can I do to help her deal with the pain and stop making everybody else miserable, too?"

Mare focused on her heart's connection with her mother and waited, as always, for thoughts to blossom gently in her consciousness. Talk to TJ. Mare sighed as she recognized that this was not a new idea. Talk to her? They all had talked to her, a hundred times, and it hadn't done much good.

Her Mom's adage that "listen" and "silent" share all the same letters tickled Mare's memory. She frowned in concentration, then her face cleared. Okay, she needed to listen to TJ and talk with her, not at her.

A fresh notion gently unfolded. Walk in her shoes for a while? Hmmm. That had a slightly different meaning in TJ's case, but finding a way to experience her frustrations firsthand might help.

"The good news, Mom, is that TJ's continuing with her counseling. She's making a strong effort to overcome her past, and I hope to help her. If love can do it, we'll get it done. TJ and I have gotten pretty angry with each other a few times, but our love has never quit. How I wish you two could have known each other. TJ's the best thing that ever happened to me."

Mare hugged her arms against her body, wishing that TJ were enclosed within the embrace.

Before yearning for TJ completely undid her, Mare stood and brushed pieces of grass from her jeans. She kissed her fingers and touched them to the stone. As she headed home, she felt both comforted and enlightened.

BRINGING TJ BACK to the ranch was supposed to make life easier, but it hadn't. First, the contractors had been brought back to reorganize the gym to Sacha's standards, disrupting the entire household until they were finished. Tired of the turmoil, TJ had insisted that building the pool be postponed until a later date. And though the insurance claim was processed easily, the purchase decisions for a new van to transport TJ were also put on hold.

And after just over two months away from home, TJ was

having problems adjusting to life back at the ranch. Although she was able to fend for herself to some extent, she needed help to get in and out of her chair and assistance with several other everyday activities that she previously had been able to do for herself. She was still in some pain, and although her therapy was progressing nicely, her recovery was going at a slower rate than she wanted. The depression that had settled on her in the hospital hadn't lifted, as expected, with her return. And of course, TJ was still hardly talking to Mare.

After a very lonely night spent in her own suite, Mare sat in her new office at Meridian ranch. She looked longingly out of the window at the bright sunshine, then back down at the mountains of paperwork that had been neglected over the last few days. She sighed and pulled the next stack toward her.

Thoughts of TJ were seriously interfering with her progress. She could understand TJ's reaction to Mare missing the therapy session at the hospital, especially after hearing what Paula had told her. Still, enough time had passed since then that TJ should realize that Mare wasn't about to up and leave her. How could Mare regain TJ's trust when they were hardly even talking? Or hardly seeing each other, for that matter.

Mealtimes were so uncomfortable for Mare that she wolfed her food and departed the table as quickly as possible. When she wasn't out working, most of her time at the ranch house was spent in her office.

A light tapping on the door roused Mare from her dismal pursuits. "Come in," she called as she pushed the paperwork away.

Sacha's head poked around the door. "You busy?"

"Yes, but, please, interrupt me."

"That bad, huh?" Sacha closed the door behind her and sat across from Mare.

"Worse. I hate paperwork, and that's all I'm doing at the moment. Is TJ okay?"

"Actually, that's what I wanted to talk to you about. I know you two aren't exactly hitting it off at the moment. But I want you to know that she still needs you, in spite of the problems you guys seem to be having."

"Really? I was beginning to wonder whether she even knew I still existed."

"Oh, she does, believe me. She's always looking for you when we're in session, and she's always disappointed when you don't show up."

"She told me she didn't want me there."

"I know she did, but that was pride and bravado speaking.

You know TJ well enough to know that when it comes to emotional issues she does the exact opposite of what she needs."

"You mean she's pushing me away on purpose?"

"Essentially, yes. Ask Erin and Paula. She's done it before. She needs to know you still love her and need her."

"But I've told her that, I don't know how many times."

"I know that, and so does she. But she's terribly insecure at the moment. Telling her and showing her are two different things. Both of you are depressed. Everybody is on tenterhooks, and the only way to clear the atmosphere around here is to get you two back together, or at least on speaking terms. So, TJ's therapy is at ten o'clock tomorrow morning. I expect you to be there to give me a hand. Okay?"

"Yeah, okay. But TJ might not like it."

"TJ will be ecstatic. She just won't let you know about it. Besides, I'm going to have the same little chat with her shortly," Sacha said as she stood up.

"Well, when I see your death throes, I'll know you've done your best."

"Ah, TJ's a pussycat. A large and potentially lethal one, true, but I have her wrapped around my little finger. See you later."

"Yeah, I'll see you later."

Chapter
Fifteen

THAT EVENING, SACHA, Erin, and Paula went into town for a change of routine. Of course, TJ and Mare had been invited. But both had declined, citing unfinished paperwork.

Sacha was secretly pleased by their absence. She hoped that their being left to their own devices would mean they'd have to communicate—especially TJ, who'd been a little more resistant than Mare to her plan of therapy interaction. And Paula and Erin could do with a break from all the tension that muddled the air at the ranch. They were the ones taking the brunt of the hostilities between Mare and TJ, both again missing from the dinner table.

Around eight o'clock, Mare finally finished going over the last invoice of the day. She shut up her office and wandered toward the kitchen. She saw the glow of light beneath the door of TJ's office and assumed she was burning the midnight oil, too. She entered the kitchen and immediately noticed the big colorful note on the island. It was from Paula, addressed to both TJ and Mare. It said that dinner for each of them was in a covered plate in the fridge and to microwave the plates for three minutes before eating.

Mare was touched by the thoughtfulness behind the gesture. No matter how many times she told them not to, Paula and Erin insisted on looking after her in much the same way they did TJ.

Mare switched on the coffee maker. The trio of caretakers had been gone for a while, and it was unlikely that TJ had had a hot drink since they left. For the past couple of nights there had been a chill in the air, and Mare would gladly settle for hot chocolate with cream and marshmallows. On the other hand, TJ, who had been shut up in her office all afternoon, would want the comforting fragrance and stimulating kick that coffee would provide.

A look in the fridge established that both plates of food were untouched. Another glance at her watch confirmed that it was way past the time that TJ normally ate, and it was pretty important for her to stick to her routine. A wry grin crossed Mare's face. She could see Sacha's devious workings in this little night out. When the coffee finished dripping, she carried a mug of the brew out of the kitchen and down the hall to TJ's office. Mare knocked on the door and entered at TJ's beckoning call.

"Hey," Mare said as she entered, "thought you might like some coffee." She put the mug down on the desk.

"Umm...Thank you."

"You're welcome. You about finished? Paula left us food to be nuked. I'll put it in to be warmed if you're ready for it."

"That sounds like a plan." TJ sat back with her coffee, taking a sip. "And this is good. Thanks again."

"You've got five minutes to wrap up. Would you like to eat in the living room or the kitchen?"

"Living room, if you don't mind. I've been in this chair all day. I'd like to get out of it for a while."

"No problem. Five minutes," Mare said, then left the office. A warm glow of joy heated her chest. That was the most civil talk they had had in days.

They ate their meal in silence. Mare had helped TJ onto the couch, and they switched on the television to the Discovery Channel. It was Shark Week. Mare thought she felt TJ's eyes on her, but whenever she glanced over, TJ was concentrating on the show.

When they finished their food, Mare took the plates into the kitchen and washed them out by hand. They sure weren't making much progress yet. Mare sighed, set the dishes in the drainer, and returned to sit on the couch.

TJ shifted several times. "You okay?" Mare said.

"I'm a little sore and can't get comfortable. Think I've been sitting for too long today."

"You want to go to bed?"

"Nah, it's a little early for that. I'd just lie awake for hours." *Thinking about you.*

"What about if you lay on the couch, would that help?"

"Maybe. I'd need something to support my back though."

"I'm sure that could be arranged." Mare swung her legs onto the couch. "Come on, you can use me as a back rest." She patted the space between her legs. The raw yearning suddenly visible in TJ's eyes destroyed any doubts Mare may have harbored. She opened her arms and beckoned. "Please."

"You sure?"

"I've never been more sure of anything in my life. Time away from you has been hell on earth for me."

TJ felt a chunk of ice melt from around her heart. She used her powerful arms to pull herself along the couch, and Mare helped lift her legs up to make her comfortable. TJ leaned back against Mare's body, and welcoming arms enclosed her. They sighed simultaneously.

Mare's eyes drank in the strong profile resting next to her. "I'm really sorry for the dumb things I've said and done that have hurt you. I want us to go back to where we were."

"Me, too." TJ looked deeply into Mare's eyes for several breathtaking moments. The tip of her tongue darted out and moistened her parting lips, and her gaze dropped to the mouth so temptingly near hers. Mare readily accepted the invitation, and they joined in a kiss, letting the warmth of their love seep through them.

SACHA AT FIRST thought the evening out would be a failure. In spite of welcoming a change from the stress at the ranch, Paula and Erin were having difficulty unwinding. The bar they picked to visit had a three-piece combo, providing good, but loud, music for the patrons' enjoyment.

Erin had started walking toward the band when Paula grabbed her arm. "Where are you going?" she lifted her voice above the music.

"I want to sit at that table over there." Erin tilted her head toward the table she had her eye on.

"Let's sit at the bar," Paula said. "I'm ready for some serious drinking." She tugged on Erin's arm with little success.

"I've been sitting in a saddle most of the day," Erin said, "and I need a chair with a back. You want to sit at the bar, go ahead."

Paula stopped dead in her tracks. Just as her mouth opened to argue, Sacha wrapped a hand around each woman's upper arm and steered them to a table halfway between the bar and the band. "Haven't you two had enough contention at the ranch? You need more?"

The women looked at her, at first angrily, then guiltily. "No," they answered in unison.

"Then sit." Sacha pulled out a chair and sat down. Erin and Paula fidgeted for a minute, then joined her.

After a waitress took their order for hot wings and a pitcher of beer, Sacha leaned forward with her elbows on the table and looked from one tight face to the other. "Okay, ladies." She raised her voice above the song. "Let's clear the air. You two aren't mad at each other. You're just letting our boss and her situation with Mare get under your skin. Am I right?"

Erin gave Paula's hand a quick squeeze. "She's right. I didn't mean to — "

"Forget it," Paula shouted, then blushed as she realized she had spoken into a lull in the music. The other two women laughed, and she joined them.

"At least you weren't cussing," Erin said.

"I sure feel like cussing at TJ sometimes," Paula said. "I know she's having a tough time, but she keeps taking her anger out on us, and that's not fair."

The beer and wings arrived, and Sacha picked up the pitcher and poured a mug full for each of them. "How about you, Erin? How do you feel?"

After taking a sip of beer, Erin put her finger on the wet ring on the table. She traced it then pushed it out of symmetry as her eyes followed the movement of her finger. "She does get testy with us, just like last time. I guess I would, too, if I had the pain she has."

"Could be," Sacha said. "She not only has the physical pain, but also the pain from being out of sorts with Mare." She picked a wing from the basket.

"Yeah," Paula said, "she wasn't as bad this time while she and Mare were getting along. Now..." She shrugged and grabbed a wing for herself.

"But that wasn't all TJ's fault," Erin hastened to say. "Mare did promise to be at that therapy session, and she did say the things that Paula tried to warn TJ about."

"But let's be fair to Mare, too," Paula said. "She has a veterinary practice to keep up or she would have been there. And I should have kept my mouth shut."

Sacha broke in. "Looks like there's plenty of blame to be shared, but finger-pointing doesn't solve anything, does it? Sounds like TJ and Mare have to make up. Maybe being together by themselves tonight will have some good results. What do you say we assume that it will, and we relax and enjoy ourselves?"

"Fine with me." Paula picked up her beer and gulped a long draught.

"Me, too." Erin looked at Paula with a soft smile. "Pass the wings, will you?"

The three women had a good evening, and Sacha ended up driving home a very relaxed and mellowed-out Erin and Paula. It wasn't that they had too much to drink. They'd had an exhausting couple of weeks that were now beginning to catch up to them. The few drinks they'd had only served to put them both to sleep on the trip back. Sacha was hoping that, when they got back to the ranch, TJ and Mare wouldn't undo all her hard work in getting these two to relax.

She nudged Erin awake as they pulled up to the house. "Come

on, rouse sleeping beauty by your side, and let's get in the house."

Erin stretched and yawned as she opened her eyes, then gave Paula a shake. "You mean, let's see if they've left each other alive."

"I didn't say that."

"No, but that's what you meant."

The three women tiredly got out of the truck and entered through the kitchen. The room was dark, as was most of the rest of the house, with just the light of the TV flickering from the living room.

"Well, if they did kill each other, they did it after they ate." Paula gestured toward the clean dishes in the drainer.

"They must have left the TV on," Erin said softly. "I'll switch it off. You go on up. I'll be there in a second."

Sacha and Paula had just reached the bottom of the stairs when Erin backed out of the living room, waving at them and pointing into the living room. Paula and Sacha hurried back across to Erin and peered in.

"Is that precious or what?" Erin said, as they all looked in to see TJ and Mare fast asleep on the couch. TJ had her head pillowed on Mare's abdomen, her arms wrapped securely around Mare's thighs. Mare had an arm across TJ's shoulders and the other hand buried in her hair.

"Yep," Sacha said. "That is too cute for words, but we'll have to wake them up. TJ can't sleep in that position, and she still has her brace on."

Paula eased around the couch on her crutches. "Damned shame, if you ask me," she muttered.

"You said it, honey." Erin joined Paula at the couch.

Waking the pair was easier said than done, and in Mare's case, it proved impossible. The first shake got no response from Mare, and TJ just tightened her grip. The second got a rambling response from Mare, and TJ opened her eyes.

"Hello there, sleepyhead." Erin gazed at TJ, who slowly lifted her head and yawned. "Don't you think we ought to put you in the correct bed?"

"Don't wanna," TJ mumbled, putting her head back down on the warm cushion of Mare's stomach. "I'm comfy here."

"Well, you might be now, but you won't be in the morning if you stay there. Come on." Erin patted her arm.

TJ sleepily complied as Erin and Sacha unwrapped her arms from Mare's body, got her back into her chair, and wheeled her to her own bed. Mare slept on, oblivious to TJ's absence. Paula grabbed one of the afghans from the back of the couch and draped it over Mare. She switched off the TV and made her way upstairs to bed.

TJ WAS RELAXED enough that she fell right back to sleep. The next morning, waking to a remembrance of their tentative reconciliation, she became excited at the prospect of seeing Mare. Erin came in and gave her a hand climbing out of bed and getting ready for the new day. TJ wheeled into the kitchen only to learn from Paula that Mare had made another early start. But Mare had promised to be back at ten o'clock, in time for TJ's physical therapy session with Sacha.

TJ was in the gym when ten o'clock came, then ten-fifteen, and still no Mare. "TJ, obviously something has delayed Mare, but we need to get started," Sacha said.

"Let's just skip this session. I'm not in the mood."

"Skipping a session is like taking two steps backward. Do you really want to do that?"

TJ made a sound between a sigh and a groan. "No, I don't." She looked at her watch for the umpteenth time. "Let's go." She wheeled over to the first apparatus for her daily regimen.

At that moment, Erin came though the door. "Mare just called. She's on her way and should be here in fifteen minutes."

TJ only nodded.

"Wonderful!" Sacha gushed. "Thanks for letting us know."

"Glad to be the bearer of good news." Erin knew the feeling of relief Sacha was experiencing. She gave a little salute, then left to attend to her own duties.

Mare arrived as promised and hurried into the gym. "Sorry I'm late, folks. Barry ran into some problems with an injured bull over at the Meredith farm, and he needed my help. I have to run back over there as soon as we finish here."

"Too bad my therapy session had to interrupt your important work." TJ didn't look at Mare.

Mare had approached TJ to greet her with a kiss, but TJ's attitude stopped her. She stood in front of TJ and put her hands on her hips. "My work is important to me. And so are you. This time the work seemed a bit more urgent since there was no other vet in the immediate area who could help Barry. He's my associate, remember? We help each other. That's the name of the game."

TJ's knuckles whitened on the bar she grasped, and Sacha threw Mare a warning look. Mare removed her hands from her hips, placed her palm on TJ's forearm, and rubbed it softly with her thumb. "I'm sorry I upset you, sweetheart. I thought you would understand. I would much rather have been here than there."

TJ saw a raw, red mark on the back of Mare's hand. "What happened to your hand?"

"It's just a rope burn. The bull didn't care that we wanted to help him. He only knew he was in pain. His instincts told him to fight us. Sort of like some people I know."

Sacha held her breath, but little by little, the corners of TJ's mouth curved.

"Haven't the slightest idea who you could mean."

"Me either," Mare said airily. "I was just generalizing." Her hand transferred to TJ's cheek as she leaned into a kiss. Cool lips quickly warmed, and TJ put a hand around the back of Mare's neck, holding her for an extended moment.

Sacha clapped her hands. "Okay, you two. Let's save the pleasure for later and start concentrating on business."

Mare and TJ ended the kiss, reluctantly. "We're ready," they said together, then grinned impishly at each other.

Chapter
Sixteen

ALL AFTERNOON, TJ had an ear cocked for Mare's return from the Meredith farm. Finally, Mare telephoned around suppertime and said they had managed to get the injured bull tranquilized and tended to, but she needed to stay for a while to keep checking his condition. She would eat with the Meredith family. That night, TJ lay in her bed in the dark, trying to relax. Yearning for the company of a certain green-eyed, golden-haired woman, however, prevented release of the tension that was tying her stomach in knots. *Of all times for Mare to be called away!* Although she knew it wasn't fair, TJ had a hard time keeping resentment at bay.

After disquieting thoughts had tumbled through her mind for about an hour, her sharp hearing alerted her to the arrival of Mare's truck. She pushed herself up onto her pillows, reached to the wall just past the headboard, and flipped the three-way switch that lit the lamp next to her bed. Would Mare come in, or wasn't she ready to yet? That question was more than TJ wanted to wrestle with at the moment, so she thrust it away.

A soft knock sounded on the door, and TJ's heart leaped. "Come in," she called.

The door opened and Mare stepped in, keeping her hand on the knob. She was exhausted and had planned to just say "hi," go back to her rooms, take a shower, and hit the bed. Her eyes met TJ's and a tired smile crossed her face. "Sorry, I didn't know you were already in bed. I'll see you in the morning. I just wanted to..." She stopped and quickly reconsidered as a shadow of disappointment crossed TJ's face. Mare walked up to the side of the huge bed. She trailed her fingertips down TJ's cheek and lightly touched her lips, teasing them into a tiny smile. "I just wanted to see you, beautiful."

"You're the beautiful one," TJ said as her tiny smile spread into a wider one. Strong fingers enclosed Mare's hand and tugged. "Come here."

Mare wrinkled her nose and resisted TJ's pull. "I washed my hands and face, but I still kind of smell like that bull. I desperately need to go take a shower."

TJ's smile vanished, but she didn't release Mare's hand.

Tired as she was, Mare's own desire to be near TJ began to build, energizing her. "Tell you what. If you'll let me have a spare T-shirt to wear, I'll shower here."

TJ didn't trust her voice. She sucked her bottom lip in between her teeth and nodded.

Mare turned to leave, and TJ squeezed her hand. Mare's laugh bubbled through her voice. "I'll be right back. I promise." TJ released her hand, and Mare hurried to the closet, selected a shirt and towel, and dashed into the bathroom. Ten minutes later, she came back, toweling her hair as she walked toward the bed.

"That shirt looks damn good on you, Mare."

Mare looked down at herself. The T-shirt was plastered to her body, leaving very little to the imagination. She reached for the bottom edge to pull the shirt loose.

"Don't you dare touch that." TJ lifted the covers next to her. "Come on, get in the bed before you catch cold, and I'll take care of the shirt."

TJ jumped when the wet T-shirt touched her warm body.

"What's wrong, sport?" Mare said. "Don't like wet T-shirts?"

"On the contrary," TJ's silky voice answered, "I love this particular wet T-shirt." Her fingertips slowly rubbed back and forth across the damp cloth, pausing here and there to bestow extra attention.

TJ turned Mare back toward her, then carefully maneuvered herself off the pillows and followed her fingertips with her tongue and teeth.

Moaning, Mare tangled one hand in TJ's hair while her other hand dug against TJ's muscular shoulders. Unconsciously, her nails bit into back tissue when her body began to jerk in response to the contact of a persistent TJ. Longing for fulfillment, Mare willingly surrendered.

TJ WOKE JUST after sunrise, immediately comforted by the blonde head resting just below her chin and the soft firmness of the body spread over hers. This just felt so right. No one who made love like that could be thinking of leaving...could she?

Mare stirred and TJ's arms tightened about her. Mare tilted her head back into the hollow of TJ's shoulder and grinned lazily up at her. "Good morning."

"That it is. Best morning I've had in months." She kissed the end of Mare's nose. "The kind of morning I'd like to have forever."

Mare blinked. "It's been a long time since you've said anything about forever, sweetheart."

TJ's eyes filled and she looked away. "I've never really changed my mind about it. I know I've said some nasty things to you when I was in pain. I probably will again. I don't mean to, but I get so frustrated, angry, depressed — you name it, I've got it." She drew a ragged breath. "I can't blame you if you want to leave."

"You left out 'afraid,' TJ. You really are afraid that I won't stick by you, aren't you? Even after last night and the night before, you really are afraid that I might leave you." TJ's jaw clenched but she didn't say a word. Mare could feel the heaving of the chest that she lay against. She lifted a hand along that strong jaw and brought TJ's face around to confront hers. "What do I have to do to convince you that I won't leave? Do you want me to leave?"

TJ forced a single word from her constricted throat. "Never."

"Then why is it so hard for you to understand that I feel the same way about you? I love you. I never knew what love really meant until I met you. I can barely believe my luck when you say you love me, too. But when you don't trust my love, and you tell me to leave, that hurts way more than anything else has ever hurt me."

"It's not you I don't trust, Mare, it's me. I don't trust myself to be the kind of person you can love forever. The kind who won't ever hurt you."

"TJ, we can work through anything either one of us does that hurts the other as long as we're together. Please don't push me away. I need you. I don't want to live without you."

"Mare...Mare...God, Mare, I don't want to live without you, either." TJ closed her eyes.

"I promise you'll never have to." Mare waited until TJ's eyes opened and looked into hers, then she sealed her promise with a deep, tender kiss.

Fear and pain ceased for that moment of commitment.

"COME ON, TJ, just one more rep," Sacha said.

"Do you always have to bully me?" TJ lay flat on her back on the weight bench, pausing from her rhythmic working of an overhead pulley. Withdrawing her gloved hands from the leather nooses attached to the ropes, she stubbornly laced her fingers together across her abdomen.

"Bully you?" Sacha said in feigned surprise. "When I bully someone, I put my heart and soul into it, woman. I haven't even broken into a sweat with you, yet." She tapped TJ's shoulder with the backs of her fingers. "But I just might—so stop whining and get moving. You know I won't let you cheat."

TJ pouted. "That's easy for you to say. You aren't the one who's doing all the work. I feel like I'm in prison, and you're the damn warden."

That statement roused Sacha's sensibilities, and she pondered it for a few moments. "Are you and Mare getting along all right?"

"Mare and I are fine. Am I being that difficult?" TJ hesitated. "Yeah, I guess I am." She grimaced and looked off into space. "I'm just getting sick and tired of being cooped up here. When can I get away for a little while? I'm getting stronger. Can't I have just a short reprieve? How about a little trip into Sharlesburg? That's only an hour away." Her mouth crooked up on one side. "This is as close to begging as I get."

"Sharlesburg sounds possible. You have a session coming up soon with Peter. How about getting one of your friends to take you to his office, instead of him coming here? You can christen that shiny new van."

"Talk about underhanded tricks. You tease me with a chance to get out for a while, then you ruin it by making it be a visit with Peter."

"You can stop that pout. It might work on Mare, but it's wasted on me. I'm suggesting the trip to Peter's, because that gives me an excuse for why I let you go. It borders on being too early for you to go out at all."

TJ's mood began to lift as she realized that she might actually get some time away. "I know that I'm not all the way recovered yet, but I've been doing pretty well. And whoever takes me will be super careful."

"I'm counting on that. These women watch over you like mother hens."

"Yeah, but we all know who's guarding the henhouse. I've got to beg to get the damn door opened."

That earned a harder tap against her shoulder. "Get back to work before I change my mind."

MARE STRUGGLED TO help push TJ up the steep ramp at the red brick building that housed Peter's office. She stopped for a rest at the top, puffing. "Next time you have to come to a counseling session, Erin brings you."

TJ was in a good mood because her usual pain was only a dull ache this morning. "That's what you say now, sweetie, but you insisted on bringing me. Maybe you need some aerobic exercises."

"If you mean the ones that make me breathe harder, I think I just got some of those."

"You talking about now...or last night?" TJ chuckled and ducked as Mare swiped at her head.

"Behave yourself." Mare held the door open for TJ, and they proceeded into Peter's office. Mare was happy to note that TJ didn't cringe from these sessions as much as she used to. Peter finally seemed to be helping her.

"Hi, Mrs. Haddon," Mare said to the white-haired secretary. "How are you today?" She noticed that TJ at least waved, which was a huge improvement. She used to wheel right to the large windows and stare morosely out at the town's park. This time she stopped her chair near Mrs. Haddon's desk and glanced around at the pleasant room with its walls decorated with bright scenes, noting the sailboat that Mare claimed was her favorite. Two people were leaving as they arrived, but no other patients were waiting.

"Hi, Dr. Gillespie, Miss Meridian." Mrs. Haddon turned to her console and announced them to Peter, who immediately came striding from his office to greet them.

He walked to TJ and shook her hand. "Hi, TJ. Come on in and we'll get started right away." Turning to Mare, he shook her hand, too, and invited her to accompany them. "Unless TJ would rather see me alone," he said.

"No," TJ said. "Where I go, Mare goes."

And vice versa, Mare thought, except for her office. She still hadn't been able to get TJ to go in there. She patted TJ's shoulder, and the three of them entered the room.

Peter picked a chair forward of TJ's, with Mare on her other side. They chatted for a few moments to put everyone at ease, then Peter brought them back to business.

"Would you like to continue with what we've touched on in your last few sessions?" Peter glanced at Mare, then returned a questioning gaze to TJ. They had spoken several times of TJ's fear that Mare would leave her.

TJ's happy demeanor sobered so radically that Peter wondered if he should have rephrased the question. She shifted in her chair and started to rock back and forth, then caught herself and spoke guardedly, "I guess my not having enough trust in our relationship has been behind most of the problems between Mare and me. But we're working on that."

Peter waited with an expectant air while TJ sat looking at her thumbs, which she rubbed back and forth against each other. "Anything else on your mind that you'd like to talk about?"

TJ brought her eyes up to Peter's, unclasped her hands, and rubbed her jaw. "Yeah...I...ah...Remember when I said I got upset that somebody else was riding my horse?"

"Yes, I remember."

"I kept thinking, 'Why should someone else be able to ride Flag when I can't? It's not fair.' Then I talked to the youngster who was riding her, and he made me realize I was just being jealous. After some soul searching, I also figured I wasn't being very realistic. As you suggested in another visit, Flag's much better off having someone exercising her. No reason for her to suffer just because I won't be able to take her out for a while yet."

Peter prompted again. "And something else about it bothered you?"

TJ shifted ever so slightly toward the counselor. Mare's eyebrows lifted and her heart dropped. Why was TJ turning away from her?

TJ mumbled until Peter asked her to speak up. "Yeah, something else happened then that bothered me—a lot—and I've been kicking it around in my mind ever since." She stopped and took a couple of deep breaths before continuing. "You know, Peter, being in a wheelchair isn't easy. It puts a lot of constraints on your life, in ways that most people don't even realize. I've had to give up control of a lot of things, and that's been very hard for me." She glanced up at Peter, who nodded at her to continue.

"A couple of times, my friends have taken it upon themselves to make decisions that are mine to make...and I'm finding that very hard to accept." TJ hesitated and hunched her shoulders. "I know they think they're doing what's best for me, and I don't hate them for it, but they don't seem to understand that they make me feel..." TJ's voice lowered again, and Peter had to strain to hear her say, "helpless and inadequate."

"Why do you think it makes you feel helpless and inadequate?"

TJ closed her eyes tightly for a brief moment, squeezing tears from their corners. Peter handed her a tissue that she used to catch the tears and then mangled it in her twisting hands. "Because my father did the same thing to me," TJ answered hoarsely. "He tried to dominate my life...never being pleased with anything I did...always undermining my decisions...forcing me to do things his way." In spite of her valiant effort not to cry, tears began to slip silently down TJ's cheeks.

At these agonized revelations, Mare sucked in her breath and fought to hold it, but failed. She finally had to breathe, and every spasmodic intake of air hammered painfully against her chest. Her guilt-stricken eyes met Peter's, and he inclined his head toward TJ.

Mare rose and placed a kiss on top of TJ's bowed head. She

then put a hand on TJ's face and kissed her wet cheek. TJ reached blindly for her armrest, moved it away, and opened her arms. Mare moved onto her lap and into her embrace. "I'm so sorry, TJ. Can you forgive me?" She pulled TJ's head against her breast as she kissed and stroked her hair, crooning soothing sounds.

TJ broke down completely, crying so hard it hurt to hear it. Battered by the strength of the heart-rending sobs, Mare's body shook, too. TJ clung to her, instinctively trying to absorb the love that would help calm her soul.

At last, TJ began to quiet down. An occasional gasp passed her lips, jerking her body. Peter handed Mare a box of tissues, and she dried TJ's face, laying soft kisses on it as she did. TJ continued to cling to Mare. When she could speak, she lifted her head and touched Mare's lips with her own before turning to Peter. "I'm going home now."

Peter rose and Mare did, too. "Fine, TJ. I'd like you to think about having a discussion of today's session when you come back for your next visit. Okay?"

"Sure," TJ said quietly. "Right now, I just want to go home." She looked back at Mare. "What do you say, Mare?"

"Anything you want, sweetheart." She followed TJ to the outer office, waited as arrangements were made for TJ's next visit, and walked beside her out into the sunshine.

"Hey, Mare, I just had a deep thought about this lousy ramp. Related to something Sacha said to me. You want to hear it?"

"Sure." Mare took hold of the chair's handles to keep it from rolling too quickly, and they started down the incline.

"This ramp is sort of like life. It's pretty easy to get down, but it's a darn hard struggle to get back up."

Before Mare could answer, she had to swallow the lump in her throat. "Right you are, sweetheart."

Chapter
Seventeen

BERTA PUT BOBBY into the child's car seat in the back, then admired her husband, Barry, as he packed the portable highchair in the trunk. "You look right handsome in that outfit, podner," she said, exaggerating her normal drawl.

Barry looked down at his khaki jeans, rust-colored cotton shirt with the sleeves partly rolled up, and tooled boots. "A lot better than those worn out jeans I work in, huh?" His eyes roved over Berta. "You look pretty charming yourself, ma'am. Is that a new pantsuit?"

"Sure is. I know Mare said to just wear casual clothes, but most of my casual clothes are pretty tired looking." She twirled around, showing off her burnt-orange pantsuit, emerald-green ribbed sweater, and high-heeled boots. "Think this is all right to wear?"

Barry encircled her waist and gave her a quick kiss. "You look super, honey. You'll be the best-looking woman out there."

"Just as long as you think so, that's all that matters to me." Berta patted his chest. "I'm kind of excited to be going to dinner at the Meridian ranch."

"I'm kind of excited to be driving somewhere in a car instead of the vet truck," Barry said. He got in the driver's side and started the engine while Berta hopped into the passenger seat.

"I've heard some people in town mention Miss Meridian with something close to awe in their voices," Berta said. "Apparently, she saved the town from some dangerous water pollution."

"Yeah, and people on the ranches and farms tell me that she brought this whole area back to life by opening the ranch and the packing plant and putting people back to work. They owe her a lot."

"She sounds like a real mover and shaker. Have you met her?" Berta glanced back to check on Bobby. Dressed in a bright blue Dallas Cowboys sweat suit, he had already begun to nod. Turning her gaze to the passing scenery and the huge sky, she rejoiced that they were out of the town. Homes in Meridianville weren't sitting on top of each other, but she loved the sense of freedom and boundless space that the open range provided.

"No, I haven't had a chance to meet her," Barry said. "I heard about how she rolled into the Town Meeting and just took over the pollution problem, though. She must be quite a force. One reason I haven't met her is because of her accident. Remember when we first moved here and Mare was running back and forth to the hospital? Miss Meridian had an operation on her back, and she just recently returned to the ranch."

"She and Mare must be pretty close friends if Mare pulled up stakes and moved out there to live," Berta said. She glanced back and saw that Bobby had fallen asleep. As she brought her eyes back to Barry, she sensed his discomfort. "Are you blushing?"

"Berta...uh...maybe I should have said something sooner, but some people say that Mare and Miss Meridian are...a lot more than just friends."

"More than just friends?" Berta's brow knit. "You mean they're lovers?"

Barry stared straight ahead at the road. "Yep."

"Well, that's a relief."

Barry's head swung around so rapidly, he ran one wheel of the car off the road. He averted disaster by slowing the car and carefully steering it back onto the paved surface. "What do you mean, a relief?" he asked when his heart had gone from his throat back into his chest. "That doesn't bother you?"

"Barry, I've known a few gay people. Some I've been pretty close to, but I figure how they lead their lives is their own business. I'm not so perfect that I can go around telling other people how to live or expecting that they should live according to my rules. Besides, I've been kind of worrying about you traipsing around the countryside with Mare. She's a darn good-looking woman. Now I don't have to worry about it," she said. "That's what I meant when I said it's a relief. I'm more concerned about women who might chase my man, than I am about women who love women."

Barry let that thought sink in for a few minutes as he pulled into the parking area of the Meridian ranch house. "Are you saying you don't trust me?"

Berta unbuckled her seat belt, leaned over, and kissed his questioning lips. "I'm still with you, aren't I? Come on, let's go meet the savior of Meridianville. Grab the highchair, and I'll bring Bobby and the kiddie bag."

Holding the folded chair flat against his side, Barry pushed the bell. Then he stepped aside to let Berta, with the still sleeping

Bobby, precede him through the opening door.

Mare gave them her biggest smile. "Hi," she said quietly, in deference to the sleeping tot. "Come on in." She was wearing charcoal slacks and a silver-gray tunic top that shimmered with olive highlights when she moved, sparking green embers from her eyes.

"What a gorgeous outfit," Berta said.

"Thanks. You look great, too."

Erin got up and relieved Barry of the highchair. She set it on the floor against her leg and shook hands with Barry and Berta as Mare introduced her. "This is Erin Scott, CEO of the ranch." She turned to indicate Paula and Sacha, "Paula Tanner, CEO of the packing plant, and Sacha Gibbs, TJ's physical therapist. Ladies, meet Barry and Berta Cassel and their sleeping son, Bobby."

As the others shook hands, Erin took the highchair to the dining room, then returned. Mare ushered the Cassels to seats on one of the couches, directly across from the couch occupied by Erin and Paula and next to Sacha's chair. While the other women and Barry engaged in subdued chitchat, Mare helped Berta set her bag on the floor, then lower Bobby onto the couch. Berta pulled a light cover from the bag and placed it over him. "Might as well let him sleep until dinner's ready," she whispered.

"Our foreman's wife, Martha, is preparing dinner for us tonight. She assures me it will be served in about twenty minutes," Mare said. "Can I get you a drink?"

"Already taken care of." Paula waved as she made her way to the kitchen, having learned the proper drinks from Barry.

"Mare, where's your office from here?" Barry said.

A soft buzzer sounded, and Mare and Erin both promptly pushed a button on their respective pagers. "I'll get it," Erin said. She stood up and strode from the room while Mare answered Barry's question. They continued to chat as Paula returned with Martha, who offered drinks from the tray she was bearing.

Erin found an aggravated TJ, sitting in slacks, bra, and turtle brace. In her hurry to dress, she had tossed her shirt onto the couch in her room, and it had slipped and fallen behind it. The pants puller wasn't long enough for TJ to reach it, and the couch was too unwieldy for her to move, hence the pager call. Erin moved the couch out and retrieved the shirt, then pretended to torment TJ by waving it in front of her and giving her a pseudo lecture on taking proper care of her clothes. TJ trapped Erin in a corner, grabbed the shirt from her, and tried to snap it against Erin's rear as she dashed out and returned to the living room.

"TJ will be right in," Erin said.

Several minutes later, Berta heard a faint creak from the

hallway and turned to see its cause. Her breath caught at the sight of TJ, clothed in pale-blue slacks, a navy-blue turtleneck, and matching cardigan. Pearls circled her long neck, and compelling blue eyes gazed from a gorgeous face.

Mare had just completed the introductions when Bobby awoke screaming. Berta picked him up and bounced him in her arms trying to calm him down, but she wasn't having much success. TJ rooted in the pocket hanging from her chair and pulled out a peppermint stick. She unwrapped it, wheeled over in line with Bobby's vision, and held it up to him. He reached for it, jammed it into his mouth, and stopped screaming. She then held an arm out to him and patted one wheel with the other hand. "Hey, Bobby, I have a big wagon here. You want to take a ride?"

Bobby looked at Berta, who nodded. He moved into TJ's reach, and she picked him up and put him on her lap. "I'll be right back." She wheeled out into the hallway and rumbled down toward Mare's office door. As she got near it, she unconsciously slowed. Her heart started pounding and perspiration glistened on her upper lip, leaving her taken aback for a moment. *Shit, TJ, which one of you is the baby? You don't have to go in the damn office!*

She twisted her chair around and hurried back to the top of the hallway. In defiance of her ridiculous reaction, she gave Bobby a ride up and down the hallway two more times, coming as close to the closed door as she dared.

When she returned to the living room with Bobby, he kept saying, "Go, go," but TJ laughed and said, "Maybe after you eat." She set him on the floor, and he ran back to Berta, who thanked TJ profusely. Bobby turned his attention to playing with the toys that Berta had taken out of the kiddie bag and placed on the carpet at her feet.

Soon, Martha announced that dinner was ready, and they moved to the dining room where TJ sat at the head of the table and Mare at the foot. The Cassels sat to TJ's right. Bobby made it known that he wanted to sit near TJ, so, at her suggestion, his highchair was set up between TJ and Berta, with Barry next to Berta.

Erin, Paula, and Sacha sat to TJ's left. The convivial group enjoyed roast tenderloin with all the trimmings. Lively conversation included everyone, and even Bobby enjoyed himself. For him, the highlight of the dinner seemed to be the dessert: cherry pie topped with vanilla ice cream that he poked and pushed with his spoon.

With dessert and coffee, the conversation turned to celebrations held in Texas towns in the past. TJ, Mare, Barry, and Berta mentioned horse racing, food-tasting contests, dunking for apples, and shooting at targets. Erin and Paula added tales of tug-of-war and archery contests from their childhood memories in their native states, and Sacha recalled competitions for throwing softballs, footballs, and even frisbees.

"I'd like to see something like that happen here, in Meridianville," TJ said. "Maybe you and Barry could mention it around, Berta, and see if folks would be interested."

"Sure, TJ. I like the idea. And Barry meets a lot of people he can ask."

"Right," Barry said. "If enough folks are interested, maybe we could get the Town Council to set up a committee and get something started on it. I'll be happy to check it out. I'll get back to you on that."

"Paula and I can chip in as soon as we get back from vacation," Erin said.

"Super," Mare added. "I'll spread the word, too, and we can— oh my God!" Mare pointed at TJ.

TJ had pushed her chair away from the table, clasped her arms to her body, and doubled over. Sacha and Erin jumped up and hurried to her side with Paula right behind them and Mare dashing along the other side of the table.

"TJ," Erin said, "are you okay? What's wrong? Are you crying?"

Just then, Mare reached TJ's other side. She grabbed TJ's shoulder and hauled up on it. "No," she said, giggling, "she's laughing." Mare helped her sit up straight.

TJ had shining eyes and a smile that threatened to split her cheeks. The laugh she was holding in burst forth. As the others got a look at her, they laughed, too. When she lowered her arms, there was a dish in them. The front of her shirt was covered with a cherry pie-vanilla ice cream mixture. Still giggling, Mare lifted the dish from TJ's arms and set it back on the table.

TJ pointed at Bobby, who was sitting in his highchair with an empty spoon in his hand, banging it on the tray. "Bobby threw his plate at me," TJ barely managed to say, "when I wasn't looking. By the time I got my arms up, it was too late." She looked down at the front of her. "Guess he didn't like dessert, or maybe he wants to add pie throwing to our list."

Mare grabbed a napkin from the table and wiped TJ's hands, then cleaned some of the solid gunk off of her shirt. "I think you're going to need some clean clothes."

"Mare," Barry said, "this reminds me of what that bull did to you, when he pulled you on your belly through that pile of—"

"Barry! Don't you dare squeal on me."

"Okay, but TJ sure looks better than you did." Mare threw the balled-up napkin at him. He caught it easily and brought to his nose. "Smells a lot better, too."

"Can't argue that point," Mare said.

"TJ," Erin said, "I'll help you get cleaned up, and Mare can stay here with our guests." They went off to TJ's bedroom with Erin's voice trailing behind them, explaining that she thought TJ was having some kind of attack.

"TJ was really a good sport about that," Barry said to Mare, as Berta got Bobby down from the highchair. Paula showed them to the bathroom so Berta could wash Bobby's face and hands.

"Yeah, she was, wasn't she? I saw it happen, and she was really startled. But obviously the humor of the situation won out."

TJ returned, looking fresh and gorgeous, and she and Erin joined everyone gathered in the living room. She suggested that they top off the evening with a songfest. Everyone moved to the music room and spent the next two hours singing or just listening, while Mare played both popular and classical pieces on the grand piano. Erin and Paula joined in the popular songs with their guitars. To everyone's surprise, Sacha grabbed a set of bongo drums and set a lively beat for a number of tunes. The group even cajoled TJ into singing a couple of ballads, and her low, vibrant voice warmed them all.

It grew late, and the Cassels had to leave. "We had a wonderful time," Barry said. Both Barry and Berta shook TJ's hand, then Mare gave them each a hug. When they turned back around, they saw Bobby standing on TJ's lap with his little arms wrapped around her neck, and her arms encircling him.

"You get Mommy and Daddy to bring you back, soon, you hear?" TJ said.

"Go, go," he said.

"Okay, cowboy, one more time. Hold on." TJ turned the chair and took him for one quick ride down the hallway and back. Just before Berta reached for him, Bobby hugged TJ's neck and kissed her cheek.

"Thanks, TJ." Berta hitched Bobby up on her hip. "You've been most gracious, especially considering the mess Bobby made with the pie and ice cream."

"We loved having you," TJ said. "And don't worry about the mess. Next time maybe we'll give Bobby a doughnut for dessert. They bounce off."

Martha had cleaned up, leaving everything in perfect order before going home, so the only remaining chore was closing up the house. While Paula and Erin checked and locked windows and doors, Sacha expressed her appreciation of the evening and headed for her room. With everything secure, Paula and Erin waved good night and climbed the stairs.

"That was a lot of fun," Mare said as she turned off the lights. She dimmed the hall light, but left it on as usual. "Thanks for letting me invite them."

"Hey, sweetheart, this is your home, too, remember? You can invite anyone you want."

Mare walked to the chair, lifted the armrest away, and sat on TJ's lap. She leaned in and wrapped her arms around TJ's neck. "Go, go," she said.

"You betcha. Hang on." TJ wheeled out into the hall, then quickly into the bedroom. Mare stuck out her hand and pushed the door closed.

Chapter
Eighteen

DR. MICHAEL GILLIS drove up in front of the Meridian ranch house, turned off the motor, and took a moment to stretch his back and neck muscles. An early morning rain had assaulted his car for most of the two-hour drive from Springerly, and he felt stiff from the extra attention he had been forced to pay to the driving conditions. Fortunately, the storm had finally let up.

Before he could lift his finger to the bell, the front door opened, and he stepped in. He set his bag on the floor, enveloped Mare in a big hug, and kissed her cheek. "Hi, sweetheart, how are you?" As he released her, she returned his kiss.

"I'm fine, thanks, Dad. Seems like ages since I've seen you."

"It's been awhile, that's for sure. You and Sacha have done a good job with the phone calls, keeping me pretty well informed on TJ's condition. I appreciated your personal news updates, too." He shrugged off his windbreaker and handed it to Mare.

"We're all here, as you requested." Mare waved her free arm toward the other women. Sacha, in her white pantsuit, nodded to Michael from a flowered armchair, and Paula and Erin, seated side-by-side on the matching couch, nodded also.

On the coffee table in front of the couch sat a carafe, cups and saucers, mugs, sugar, cream, spoons, and napkins. "Would you care for a cup of coffee, Michael?" Erin asked.

Michael rubbed his hands together briskly. "Nothing I'd like better right now, thanks. The weather was nasty on the drive over. A mug will be fine. Black, please." Erin handed him a steaming mug. He settled in one of the armchairs and sipped the hot brew.

Mare returned from hanging Michael's jacket in the hall closet. "You want to talk to us for a few minutes or examine TJ first?"

"TJ's in her bedroom?"

"She probably heard you come up the driveway and wonders why you aren't in there yet."

"I purposely came a little earlier than our appointment was

scheduled. Surely she won't mind waiting while we have a brief chat?" Michael chuckled when Mare rolled her eyes. "A little impatient, hmmm?"

"TJ doesn't do impatient in a little way," Paula said.

Mare said, "I did tell her that you wanted to talk to us for a few minutes, either before or after you examine her, but I don't think that made much of an impression. I'll just go tell her you're here and will be in to see her in a few minutes." Mare headed toward TJ's bedroom.

"As soon as Mare gets back, maybe we better get right to the purpose I had in mind when I asked to see all of you together for a moment." Michael took a long swallow from the mug and set it on the edge of the coffee table. Mare returned and took a seat, and Michael continued. "I'd like a very brief rundown on how my patient is adjusting, physically and emotionally, to life here at the ranch. Would you like to start, Erin?"

"I know TJ has a lot of pain...maybe even more than the first time she was injured. And I see her getting tired sooner than usual. She always had a tendency to push herself to the limit, and she still does that, so we all try to make things easier for her." Erin glanced toward the other women. "When she first came home, she seemed really confused and depressed. But as soon as she and Mare made up, she calmed down a bit. I think she's really trying hard to keep her temper in check, but she's not always successful."

"And that makes her mad at herself," Paula added. "Which sets up a vicious circle, cycle, whatever you want to call it. She gets mad at us, then mad at herself, which makes her madder at us. I know you said to keep her calm, but that's a tough order, especially for me. I've got kind of a quick temper, and sometimes she and I butt heads. But I'll keep trying." Paula looked toward Sacha, but Michael interrupted by standing up.

"Thanks for your input, ladies. You've given me some idea of TJ's state of mind. If she's having trouble with her temper, I better not keep her waiting any longer. Sacha, how about if you hold your thoughts until after I examine TJ? We'll need to go over the next phase of her physical therapy, and we can talk then."

"No problem, Dr. Gillis."

Michael drained his coffee mug and set it back onto the table, then looked at Mare. "Shall we?" He walked to the front entrance and retrieved his bag.

Mare jumped up and led him down the hallway to TJ's door. She tapped, pushed the door open, and they walked into the room. TJ sat in buttery-hued sheets, propped up by several pillows bedecked with yellow and cream stripes. She looked toward them, but didn't speak.

Michael set his bag on a chair and greeted TJ with zest. "How wonderful to see you," he said as he walked over to her. He picked up TJ's hand and lightly squeezed it, then leaned over and kissed her cheek. "Sorry to keep you waiting. I came a little early because I wanted a few minutes to chat with your support team to make sure everything's going well." Michael still held TJ's hand, patting it as he spoke. "I thought Mare had explained that to you." His gleaming eyes challenged TJ, and he determined that he would hold her hand until she acknowledged him.

TJ clenched her jaw and looked past him into the distance. Mare glanced from one to the other, then moved closer and wrapped their clasped hands in both of hers.

"I guess you know you're the two people I love most in the whole world, don't you?" she said softly. "Please?"

TJ's expression gradually calmed. "Hello, Michael."

Mare let go of their hands. Michael held TJ's hand just a little longer, then released it. "Thank you for coming back from wherever you went just now," he said. "I'd hate to think I drove all the way from Springerly just to see you, and you weren't going to be here."

"Now I see where your daughter gets her blarney from."

"That's my Dad," Mare said.

"Looks like I'm outnumbered."

"How about we get started on this examination?" Michael opened his bag, took out his stethoscope, and hung it around his neck. He took TJ's blood pressure and listened to her heart, then returned his equipment to the bag. "Everything looks good so far. Will you move onto your stomach, so I can take a look at your back?"

Mare helped to remove the pillows while TJ scrunched down and turned over. Mare smoothed the sheet that covered the lower part of TJ's body and raised the bed jacket so Michael could examine the incision. Gently but firmly, his fingers felt the area around the incision. He pushed and probed until he was satisfied that the surface healing was completed. He finished his examination and motioned to Mare to help prop TJ up again in a sitting position.

"You've been wearing the turtle shell brace when you sit?" he asked.

"Sacha's trying to wean me away from it in little spurts, but yes, I usually wear it. My back still gets tired sometimes."

"It will for a while yet. Some of those muscles have had a pretty bad shock. It takes time for them to get as strong as they used to be. The therapy will help with that. Meanwhile, keep using the brace."

"Thing's damned uncomfortable."

"Well, Sacha's reports have told me that you're doing a lot better than we had thought you would. We might be able to get you out of it for longer periods soon. How's the pain?"

TJ's jaw clenched again but not from stubbornness this time. She glanced down at her fingers, which had been constantly playing with one of the ribbon ties of her bed jacket.

Michael's eyes softened. "Pretty bad, huh?"

TJ nodded. Mare swallowed hard and put a hand on TJ's forearm, rubbing up and down it soothingly.

"I can't give you anything stronger," Michael said. "I wish I could. I hope, as your back heals, the pain will lessen. I can't even promise it will go away. We'll just have to wait to find out."

TJ's eyes lifted and he could see the pain in their depths. "We knew that going in, Michael. It's something I'm trying to learn to live with." She frowned. "Something we're all trying to learn to live with."

Michael patted her shoulder. "You're a strong woman, and you have some great people here pulling for you. I'm going to have a word with Sacha, now. We need to get you started on your bladder training—see if we can do away with the bags and tubes."

"Now there's a thought to warm my heart. Tell Sacha I'm ready to start right away—today."

Michael took TJ's hand. "I'll do that. I'm always happy to leave a patient with some good news. I'll stop back in a few weeks. You try to take it easy on your caregivers, okay?"

TJ shook his hand. "Someone been telling tales about me?"

Her eyes leveled on Mare, who stammered, "Uh...I...uh... plead the Fifth Amendment."

"And I," Michael hurried to say, "need to find Sacha. I'll be seeing you." He picked up his bag and fled.

TJ grabbed Mare's arm as she started to follow Michael. "I think you need to stay here while we have a little discussion. About self-incrimination."

IT TOOK MICHAEL several minutes to find Sacha. She was outside, sitting on the corral fence, watching one of the ranch hands with the horses.

"Hi." Michael leaned against the fence and squinted in the bright sunlight.

"Hi, Doc. Are you satisfied with your examination of TJ?"

"Yes, I am. She's doing better than I expected. The operation site is healing well, and you've managed to get most of her upper body strength back." Michael turned his back to the corral and leaned again on the fence. "Mare and the girls seem to be happy with her progress, and TJ didn't mention any serious problems. I'd have to say I'm pleased on the whole, but..."

"But now you'd like to hear the truth, because none of them would say anything that would mean TJ has to go back to the hospital?"

"You know us doctors too well. So, what's your opinion of the situation?"

Sacha climbed down from the fence. "Walk with me." She started down the driveway and headed for the shade of the trees that lined the road. Michael settled into a slow walk by her side. "Physically, TJ is making excellent progress. She can spend longer periods out of the brace than we had predicted she'd be able to. In a couple of weeks she won't need it at all."

She swiped lazily at an insect that was buzzing around her head. "On the pain front, well, we're still in the mire there. It's not as intense as it was in the hospital, or at least that's what she says. Maybe she's just gotten used to it. I still occasionally give her a shot of pethadine at night, especially after a hard day, and she's still taking dihydrocodeine on a regular basis. You might want to think about reviewing that at some point. It makes her dehydrated, and that causes a wracking headache. Which leads us to the main problem." They had reached the shade of the trees, and Sacha wandered over to the trunk of a large oak and sat down on a perfectly dry spot at its base.

"And which problem would that be?" Michael asked as he leaned a hand against the tree and stuck the other in his pants pocket.

"They're all having problems adjusting mentally to what's happened, TJ especially. The physical independence she had fought for before was dashed in a heartbeat in the crash. Starting at square one again physically almost did her in mentally. The help of her friends buoys her spirits, but it also draws attention to her dependence on them. As Paula pointed out, TJ reacts badly when she's in pain, lashes out without thinking, and then beats up on herself for it. For a while there, I seriously thought about bringing her back in to the hospital. But Peter seems to be doing his job, and she's talking to him." Sacha stopped for a moment and gazed at her surroundings. "Peaceful out here, isn't it?"

Michael looked around at the quiet scene and took a deep breath. Fresh air, cleansed by the rain, was lightly touched with the earthy smell of horses and barn. "Yes, it is. Too bad we can't order up a sunny day to rest under an oak tree whenever we feel like it." He glanced down at Sacha. "How about the others? How are they doing?"

"Well, they're having their own fair share of adjustment problems, too. They don't know whether they're coming or going with TJ. One minute she's fine, and the next she's withdrawn or screaming at them. Obviously, walking on eggshells all the time isn't good for anyone." She picked up a twig, and her strong fingers worked to peel off its bark. "They also have a problem sometimes remembering that TJ's an adult and can make her own decisions. They're a little overprotective of her. Having said all that, however, they're coping, and the situation is improving. TJ's getting better at recognizing when she's overreacting, and they're getting better at not letting her get to them."

"Do you think TJ will be okay here when you leave?"

"Yeah, I think they'll all be fine. They might need a reminder every now and then, but they'll be fine." Sacha waved the bared twig and discarded it. "Too bad we can't peel problems away from people as easily as I peeled that bark."

"Right." Michael offered Sacha a hand up. "I think TJ has enough return of muscle tone to attempt retraining her bladder. It would be good for her to get rid of all the tubes and bags."

"I agree." Sacha started the walk back. "A little more independence will do wonders for her self-esteem. And I think it's about time I got back to the city. TJ knows what she has to do, and she can make the trip in to see me now."

"If you think it's time for TJ to take over for herself, that's okay with me."

"Yes, I do, and although I've really enjoyed being here, I'm looking forward to getting back home."

"SO, HOW IS my favorite patient today?" Sacha asked as she bustled into the room.

TJ had just maneuvered herself from the bed into her wheelchair. "Sacha, I'm your only patient."

"In that case, it isn't too hard for you to be my favorite, is it? Hmm?"

"Guess not. What does my personal torturer have in store for me today? More weights?"

"Nope, today I thought we would start on your independence from tubes and bags. Dr. Gillis reckons you have recovered enough tone down there to be able to do without having to wear a catheter constantly, and I agree. Before the accident, you had trained yourself to go without the bag for a period of several hours. We just need to retrain you."

"Sounds good to me. Let's get started."

"Hey, slow down there, champ. You've been through some of

this before, remember? You didn't exactly have a lot of fun with it, did you?"

TJ's enthusiasm dimmed as she recalled what needed to be done. The catheter would be removed and left out for a few hours, then reinserted to drain the buildup of fluid. This was easy enough to do if you could feel when your bladder was full or you had any control over when you opened the bladder. It was a lot harder when those normal senses and reflexes were impaired.

In fact, TJ had been through several embarrassing episodes at the hospital before it was decided that she would most likely have to use a catheter bag on a permanent basis. She had been mortified when she hadn't been able to control herself and ended up wet. The indignity of having the nurses come in to change her and replace the diaper-like pads she had to wear had made her all the more determined, and it was not an experience she particularly wanted to repeat. "Yeah, I remember. Do you think we'll have more success now?"

"Sure do. For a start, you're not under the same pressure as you were at the hospital. You're in the comfort of your own home. And let's not forget that, although you haven't recovered as much sensation as the doc hoped for, the removal of the bullet fragments has allowed you a little bit of extra control. I know you have more of an awareness than an actual feeling, but that should be enough for us to work with."

"Okay then, let's get started. What do you want me to do first?"

"We have to limit your fluid intake today, so we don't overload you too quickly, and you need to let Mare, Paula, and Erin know what's going on. That way they'll know that when you ask for help, you need it right away and not in five minutes. And, it means they can be prepared for any accidents that happen."

Telling her friends, and especially Mare, that for the next couple of weeks they might have to clean her up didn't appeal to TJ at all. But her previous experience had taught her a valuable lesson. If losing that little bit of dignity for the next few weeks was the price she needed to pay to get rid of the tubes and bags, then she would.

"I'll do that," TJ said. "Let's get on with the training."

Chapter
Nineteen

SACHA SPENT MUCH of the next three days regulating TJ's fluid intake and measuring her catheter bag contents at hourly intervals. Today was finally going to be the day that the catheter came out, and TJ would need to be checked every two hours or so, if she maintained her current fluid intake schedule.

Sacha walked into the gym that had become her base of operations during her stay at the ranch and found Mare and TJ waiting for her. "A little early today, aren't we?"

"Yes," Mare said, "just a little, but a certain someone decided she couldn't wait a minute longer." Her hand gently rubbed the shoulder on which it was resting.

"Hey, no baiting the handicapped," TJ said. "This is my big day. One more step on the road to freedom."

"Well, I wouldn't go that far," Sacha said. "But I can understand the feeling. So let's get rid of the catheter, shall we?" TJ nodded and wheeled herself to the treatment table in the corner of the room. "You have your alarm on your watch set?"

"Yep, and so do Mare and Erin and Paula. Do you think maybe I ought to get the operator, or Teresa, over at Meridian headquarters, to call as well? I mean, we should let the whole world know when I need to hit the toilet, shouldn't we?"

"Hmm." Sacha pretended to consider the idea. "Might save a few more pairs of jeans that way, but I guess five people with their alarms going off every two hours should be enough. Let's take the bag off and the tube out, and then I want to do some strength tests. If you can manage fifteen reps today, I think by the end of the week you should be okay running your own regimen and visiting me every other week up at the clinic. We can probably start to wean you off the turtle brace now as well."

"Really? I thought you said I'd need it longer."

"I did, but you've worked hard. We're further along in your recovery plan than I expected at this point, and that's good news on the home front. My apartment misses me, and I doubt that any of my plants have survived my next-door neighbor's loving care."

PAULA SAT PATIENTLY in the waiting room, watching cartoons on the overhead television fixed to the wall. She found it quite amusing to be one of only three adults in the room sporting casts on injured limbs. Erin was one of the others, and a young man, who just hobbled in, was the third. Her amusement soon turned into a headache as the six or so youngsters, heedless of their casts on legs and arms, proceeded to chase each other among the waiting room chairs. Thankfully, the parents finally corralled their offspring. She was sure she was next, since Erin was in the cast room having her cast removed now.

At this thought, the green door opened, and Erin appeared, her cast replaced with a plastic splint. She waved to Paula, who clambered to her feet using the crutches.

"Not totally free, I see," Paula said.

"No, and you won't be either, so don't get smug. I have a long list of strengthening exercises I need to do for the next couple of weeks, then the splint comes off. Now, my dear, go get that thing cut off, and we can celebrate our near-freedom from the dreaded unreachable itch."

"That sounds like a plan. When we get back to the ranch, I'm headed for a nice hot bubble bath first thing."

"Oooh, want some company?" Erin whispered.

"I might be persuaded to share." Paula made her way to the cast room for her turn at plaster removal. Twenty minutes later she was back, sporting a brace that covered her leg from thigh to ankle. She would only need her crutches for the next few days until she got her balance. She'd be more than happy to toss them.

SACHA RUBBED THE warm lotion into her hands and kneaded her fingers into the knotted muscles in TJ's shoulders and back. A groan of pleasure emanated from her patient.

"Lord, I'm going to miss this on a daily basis." TJ winced as Sacha hit a particularly sore spot.

"I seriously doubt that. You'll talk Mare into a daily rubdown in no time. In fact, I think it will be downright easy to persuade her." Sacha moved her hands to the new scar on TJ's spine and inspected it for buildup of thick scar tissue, which the massage was designed to help prevent. TJ was healing extremely well—much faster than when she was initially paralyzed. Mainly because Mare's presence had perked up TJ's emotional and mental health.

A saucy grin appeared on TJ's face. "Yeah, it might be, at that. But it just won't be the same. You know all my hot spots and how much pressure I like."

"With as much practice as Mare's going to get, she'll know them soon as well." Sacha paused for a second to get more lotion. "If you have any problems, you can pick up the phone and call me. And remember, I want to see you once every other week."

"Yep, and my keepers know too. Don't worry. I won't do anything too stupid."

"That's good to know." Sacha lifted the fingers of one hand and tapped them against TJ's back. "And try to take it easy on your friends, okay? You're doing well, and you know that, but there still could be setbacks. You need to maintain your regimen and not get so caught up in work that you forget." Sacha left TJ's back and started to work on her legs.

"Yes, ma'am."

"If I catch you slacking off, you know I'll come down hard on you."

TJ pushed herself up on to her arms and looked over her shoulder. "I promise. Honest. You, Mare, Erin, and Paula have worked too hard to get me where I am. I'm not going to disappoint you."

"I know you won't, but I couldn't leave without telling you that. After all, if someone found out that I was going soft on you, what would happen to my reputation?"

TJ lay back down. "Believe me when I tell you your reputation is set in stone, and nobody would dare say you were going soft." TJ's shoulders moved, as a small laugh escaped her. "Least of all me." Her voice became more serious. "You know you're welcome here on the ranch whenever you want to visit, don't you? I mean, you're part of the family now. I want you to consider this a home away from home."

"I'd like that. I'll try to get down when I can, but you know how busy it gets. Come on. Let's get you showered and dressed. I want to get on the road early this afternoon, so I have time to get some groceries. My cupboards at home are bare."

"Are you sure Paula or Erin can't drive you back?"

"Bill has volunteered one of the ranch hands to drive me. Paula and Erin have enough work to do without worrying about getting me home."

"You really ought to get a car for yourself, you know." TJ grabbed hold of the arm that Sacha offered and rolled over onto her back, then pulled herself up as Sacha moved her legs over the side of the table.

"Oh, I will, one of these days."

"Yeah, right. Like you just prefer riding around in other people's cars—no maintenance costs, no state inspections, no tags..."

"Well, one of the worst problems is parking. It's bad enough at the hospital, but it's even worse at my apartment complex. I'd have to park a mile away. Now, come on." Sacha pulled the wheelchair closer to TJ. "Let's get that shower."

PAULA TAPPED ON TJ's door. She heard, "Come in," and stuck her head into the room. TJ was seated in her chair in front of the mirror, brushing her hair, with Sacha nowhere in sight. "Sacha finished in here?" Paula half-whispered as she entered.

"Yeah." TJ grinned at the conspiratorial look on Paula's face. "She's doing some last-minute packing."

"Well, your little surprise has arrived and is all ready and waiting." Paula sat down on the bed and watched TJ's steady brush strokes.

"Great. Sacha mentioned something about parking problems. Is there anything we can do about that?"

"We've taken care of it already. Her apartment complex has an underground parking lot, and we've managed to acquire a reserved spot right next to the elevators. Her local garage will bill us for all maintenance costs, and the dealer will replace the vehicle every three years."

"Oh, I'm going to have fun with this." TJ put the brush down and spun her chair around to look at Paula.

"I'll just bet you are. Come on. Let's get your surprise on the road." She pointed her index finger at TJ. "Pun intended."

Lunch was a boisterous affair. Everyone felt that Sacha truly had become a member of the family, and each one had made the effort to be there for her going-away meal. Tall tales were told and much laughter ensued. Eventually, it came to an end, and good-byes were said.

Mare looked over at TJ, who was slowly wheeling her way to the door with Sacha at her side. TJ had a solid friend in Sacha, and Mare felt that she did, too. When TJ had first mentioned the surprise she had in store for Sacha, Mare's immediate thought had been that TJ's generosity might put Sacha in an awkward position. But after listening to TJ's reasons, she had supported the idea. Now, she was crossing her fingers that it didn't backfire on them.

Paula got to the door and opened it wide to allow TJ to wheel outside with Sacha right behind her. They paused in front of the sports utility vehicle parked there. Sacha's bags had already been loaded into the vehicle by Paula.

"Well, I guess this is where I say 'see you in two weeks.'"

"I guess so," TJ said. "Do I get a hug?"

"Sure you do." Sacha leaned down and wrapped her arms

around TJ.

"Hey." Mare walked up to the pair. "If she gets one, I get one, too."

"And me," Paula said.

Sacha gave them a hug and looked around. "Where's Erin?"

"She had to answer the phone. She'll be here in a minute." Right on cue, Erin came out of the house.

"Bill called and said there's some trouble out on the range. I'll have to get out there, and Mare, I'm afraid we'll need you. I'm sorry to say that means we don't have a spare hand at the moment to drive Sacha home."

"What's the problem?" TJ said.

"Couple of cattle got caught in some barbed wire. Bill's not sure where it came from, but he wants all the hands out checking to see if there's any more lying around."

"I'll just see Sacha off, then I'll get my bag and go out," Mare said.

"There's just one problem I see here." TJ looked at the group. "Bill hasn't got a spare hand, Erin and Mare have to leave, and Paula isn't cleared to drive yet. So, how are we going to get Sacha home?"

There was silence as everybody looked to each other for the solution.

"I'll just hang around until you can spare someone," Sacha said. "It's no big deal."

"No, no. I said we'd get you home today, and we will. You do have a valid driver's license, don't you?"

"Yes, but I've never driven one of these beauties. Besides, how would I get it back to you?"

"I'm sure we can figure that out. Erin, don't you have some papers Sacha will need?"

Erin pulled an envelope out of her back pocket. "Yeah, here they are." She handed the envelope to Sacha, who seemed puzzled as she opened it.

The envelope contained the title, insurance papers, and registration, made out in Sacha's name, for the SUV parked behind her. She read the papers, then looked, dumbfounded, at the SUV.

"Anybody have the keys?" TJ asked, thoroughly enjoying herself.

"Yeah, I've got them." Paula pulled a key ring out of her jeans and handed it to their stunned friend.

Sacha finally came back to her senses. "Oh, TJ, I can't accept this." She held the papers and keys out. "It's too much."

"Nonsense. What if your presence is urgently needed here at a barbecue, or God forbid, we need to have you come back and knock some sense into us? Don't you think it would be easier to jump in your own vehicle and get here?"

"Well, yes, but I don't have any place to park it, or — "

"Oh, we have that taken care of," Mare said. "Just drive into the parking garage at your complex, and you'll be directed to your reserved spot. You have one reserved at the hospital, too."

"But..."

"Sacha," TJ said, "please don't argue with me. This is the one skirmish I refuse to let you win. I owe you more than I can repay, and this is just a little something I can do that will go towards that."

"You're totally infuriating. You know that, don't you?" Tears welled in Sacha's eyes.

"Of course I do, and you wouldn't have it any other way. Now, you better get on your way, or you won't have time to go shopping when you get home."

"I don't know what to say except thank you." Sacha leaned down and gave TJ a heartfelt hug. "I've really enjoyed being here with you." She turned to Mare, Erin, and Paula to give them each another squeeze. "You'd better get to your animals," she said to Mare before noticing the slightly guilty looks on their faces. "Oh, I see. That was just a ploy, huh?"

"It worked, didn't it?" Mare said.

A surge of emotion choked off any reply. Sacha wiped a few tears from her face and climbed into her "surprise." A few seconds later, she was steering carefully down the driveway as her friends waved good-bye.

IT WAS SATURDAY, a day when plant and ranch responsibilities were left to Fred Morales and Bill Jacobs respectively, giving the women some time off. Paula sat in the lounge chair in the living room, reading. She and Erin had planned on riding their horses today, and she was waiting for Erin to join her. Since Sacha had departed, Mare had been assisting TJ with her exercises on the weekends, while Paula and Erin divided weekdays up between them.

Today was Mare's assistance day, but she had been called away in the early morning on an emergency. Erin was taking her place, and Paula had offered to help, too. TJ could be moody when her routine was interrupted. Her temper tantrums hadn't disappeared altogether, but they weren't nearly as volatile as they had been in the past. Erin insisted, however, that it was her turn to fill in for Mare, so Paula didn't bother arguing.

At last, Erin entered the living room and plopped down in a

corner of the couch. Paula glanced up at her with a smile that was soon stifled by the flushed look on Erin's face. Paula flapped the dust cover into the page she had been reading, closed the book, and laid it on the end table.

"Erin? What's wrong?"

"Nothing."

"If nothing's wrong, then you sure are wasting a nasty look. Did something happen between you and TJ?" Erin pursed her mouth but didn't answer. "Come on, honey, tell me about it."

"Don't 'honey' me. I'm not feeling very sweet right now."

Silence hung between them like a heavy curtain that resisted easy parting. Paula longed to walk over and push away the loosened curls that straggled onto Erin's face, but she held back. She knew TJ must have had a hand in this and, damn, that pissed her off.

"Why the hell don't you stand up to her, Erin? She only pushes you around because you let her. I know we're trying to keep her emotions on an even keel, but letting her walk all over you isn't part of the deal. TJ yells 'roll over' and you lay down like a damn puppy dog."

Erin's flush deepened, and she responded in annoyance, "That's easy for you to say. You don't owe her like I do."

"'Owe her'? For what? We carry our own weight here." Paula's surprise turned to a scowl. "Surely you can't still believe you owe her for saving you from those creeps in college? That was years ago. You've paid her back a hundred times by now."

"I'm not talking about any of that. I mean because of the accident."

"The accident?" Paula got up and moved onto the couch next to Erin, her voice softening. "You think you owe TJ because of the accident? None of that was your fault, honey." She reached up to put her arm around the tense shoulders, but Erin jerked away.

"Leave me alone. I'm in no mood for your sympathy. Besides, it *was* my fault. I was driving. I should have been able to outsmart those drunks. Instead, I let us get run off the road. You get a broken leg, and TJ gets close to two years of progress wiped out in a couple of seconds." Erin placed her elbows on her knees and bent her curly head into her hands. "She's going through this god-awful, unbearable, never-ending pain because of me." Tears dampened her cheeks, and she barely whispered as she repeated, "Because of me."

Again, Paula tried to put an arm around her, but it was shrugged off. Paula jumped up, jammed her hands in her jeans pockets, and paced agitatedly back and forth in front of the couch. "It was *not* your fault! The only ones at fault were the stupid jerks who attacked us. Nobody could have handled it any better than you did. You tried your damnedest to keep us on that road, and it just didn't work. It was an accident, pure and simple. Can't you see that?"

Erin kept shaking her head as Paula talked. Paula stopped pacing, stood in front of Erin, and put her hands on her hips. "Look, it was only bad luck for you that you were driving. It might have been me. Do you think I could have done anything that you didn't try?"

"How would you know what I tried? You were drunk."

The words scorched Paula like a flame-thrower, rocking her back on her heels. So, she got to claim a little part of this guilt, too, huh? The thought added fuel to her anger. "Where is TJ?"

"In her office. But stay away from her. Don't rile her up any worse than she already is. She's in a lot of pain right now."

"Right." Paula turned away and headed toward TJ's office.

TJ was sitting at a right angle to her desk, working at the computer. She had to have heard Paula come stomping in, but she didn't bother to turn around, which further antagonized Paula. She came up behind TJ's wheelchair, grabbed one of the push handles and yanked it, thinking to spin the chair around so she could confront TJ face to face. She hadn't considered that TJ had locked the wheels, as it wasn't her usual habit in her office. Instead of spinning around, the chair tipped precariously. Acting purely on reflex, TJ threw an arm toward the desk next to her and stopped the chair's descent just long enough for Paula to grab hold and right it.

TJ gasped as pain blasted up her arm, burst through her newly bruised shoulder, and forcibly merged with the nexus of agony in her back. "What the goddamn, frigging hell are you and Erin trying to do? Put me back in the hospital? First she tries to brain me with a damned weight, then you try to knock me over. I know you guys aren't exactly thrilled with having to take care of me, but for Christ's sake, if you want me back in the hospital, just tell me. You almost dumped me onto the floor, you stupid idiot."

"Oh, please, don't talk such trash. I wouldn't have let you go over, and you know it. Just because you happen to be having a bad day, don't take it out on Erin and me." Paula paused, hands on her hips. "Erin and I have been with you a long time, and we've put up with some real garbage from you. But I swear, if you don't stop hounding and yelling at Erin, I'm taking her, and we're getting out of here. You hear me?"

The two glared at each other for a long moment. Pain rebounded up TJ's back and surged across her shoulder blades. It spiked up her neck and exploded into her head. She gritted her teeth and closed her eyes. As Paula's words invaded her consciousness, her eyes flew back open and she continued to yell. "And just what the hell did I do to Erin to get you in here all riled up?"

"You tell me. You're the one who just had her so upset she was crying," Paula said. "I'm sick and tired of you using her for a verbal punching bag and expecting her to take it. Do you think that just because she works for you, you have the right to stomp all over her?" Paula's hands curled into fists, and she restrained them rigidly at her sides.

The pain had settled down a bit, but TJ still felt as though a tiger had dug its huge claws into her back. But she had never seen Paula so enraged, and it gave her pause. She fought for a moment to harness her own anger, then tried to speak calmly. "You know that anything I say or do has nothing to do with you and Erin working for me. You're my friends, not my employees."

"Well, maybe you need to be reminded of that 'friend' part again. I've told you before that I can take any shit you want to hand out, but Erin can't. You said something to her this morning that got her really upset, and it's not going to happen again, understand?"

Still fighting her pain, TJ managed to focus on just how distraught Paula was about some supposed confrontation with Erin. Hell, they knew she always yelled when she was in pain. What was so different about today? She stirred her memory as to what had happened earlier.

The exercise session was almost over, and Erin had been nagging TJ through the various moves. TJ was moping that Mare had been called away, and she didn't hesitate to complain about it. "You know, Mare doesn't pester me the way you do," TJ said.

"I see. Well, maybe you behave better for Mare than you've been doing for me today," Erin said with uncharacteristic tartness.

It was obvious that Erin was losing her patience. She had said that she and Paula had planned on riding together this morning. Mare's absence and TJ's exercise session had put those plans on hold. So, TJ thought, let someone else be frustrated for a change.

She lay on the weight bench, nearly finished with her last reps of presses. Her aggravation must have increased her adrenaline because the weights felt like feathers. "You didn't make these heavy enough," she said. "Take those five-pound weights off and put another ten on each side."

"I told you Paula's waiting for me to ride with her. At this rate, it will be noon before we get out of here."

"I want to push myself today. I need to work off some of this

feeling that I'm going to burst right out of my skin." TJ settled the bar in its rests.

Erin yanked off the lighter weights, set them on the floor at her feet, and dashed off to the next room to get the ten-pounders. She came hurrying back, carrying one in each hand with two fingers stuck through each hole for support. In her haste, she tripped over the weights left on the floor and yelped in helplessness. Still grasping the ten-pound weights, she threw her hands forward to stop her fall, but the reflexive action sent the weights on a precise arc toward TJ's body on the bench.

TJ grabbed the overhead bar and tried to move but could avoid only one weight. The other one came down on her shoulder with a thump, not hard enough to seriously injure her but hard enough to seriously hurt. The pain was momentarily unbearable. A scream burst from her throat that she transformed into a torrent of words aimed at Erin's clumsiness. "Son of a bitch, what the hell are you doing? Can't you do one simple thing without tripping over your own damn feet?"

Erin had scrambled to recover her balance. Alarm remained on her face as she laid down the weights and reached to administer to TJ's shoulder. "I tripped over the weights on the floor."

TJ grabbed Erin's wrist. "Oh, for God's sake, don't bother. You've done enough damage."

Erin winced as TJ's powerful hand closed around her wrist. "I'm sorry. It was an accident — "

"An accident?" TJ flung Erin's arm away from her. "You put the goddamned weights on the floor, which was pretty stupid in the first place."

"So, I'm not perfect." Erin's voice rose. "But at least I stayed here to help you. I could have just gone ahead and ridden out with Paula. I know you're ticked that Mare isn't here, but that's not my fault."

"See if you can push my chair over here without hurting anything. Then you can get the hell out of here. You're obviously not interested in helping anymore, and right now you're just a hindrance."

Erin shoved the chair close to TJ and tried again to touch the injured shoulder. TJ pushed her away and climbed into her chair by herself. She toweled off, adding a few more choice words about Erin's clumsiness. This appeared to infuriate Erin, and she stormed out. TJ wheeled herself to her office, wincing as she put pressure on the bruised shoulder.

"I did yell at her," TJ finally said, "but I had a good reason." If she would stop letting the goddamn pain control her anger, they

would all be better off. But just how could she manage that? Even
now, waves of pain thrummed through her, setting her teeth on
edge. It was a battle to speak civilly to Paula. "She tripped and hit
my shoulder with one of the ten-pound weights. It didn't really
injure me, but it hurt like hell, and I screamed at her. I don't
remember my exact words, but I do remember saying she was
more of a hindrance than a help."

"That's just great," Paula said. "Erin's been feeling guilty for
months about being responsible for our accident, and you make
her feel even worse by telling her she's practically useless. Why
didn't you just hit her with a club? That would have been less
damaging."

"Wait a minute. I'm the one who got damaged." TJ rubbed her
obviously bruised shoulder. Then the full import of Paula's words
penetrated. "You're not serious. She feels responsible for our
accident? That's ridiculous."

"Yeah? Well, try telling her that. I'm not having any success
convincing her. She's letting you walk all over her because she
feels guilty about all the pain she believes she's caused you."

"I had no idea." But she should have had. She was an expert
on guilt trips. If she hadn't talked her brother Lance into going
with her the night they were mugged, he would still be alive. That
guilt had never gone away.

Paula rubbed both hands down her face, massaging the tense
muscles. Her rage had burned intensely but swiftly. Now it had
burned itself out, and she was feeling the letdown. "Neither did I.
At least, I didn't know just how much it was bothering her. We're
both at fault here, I guess. Do you think you could talk to her? She
needs to hear you say that she's not to blame."

"Sure. Ask her to come on in — if she will. I was pretty nasty to
her."

"Thanks. I'll talk her into it. And I apologize for jumping on
you like I did. When Erin gets upset, I get upset, too, and I don't
have the greatest tact in the world, you know."

"Tact isn't even in my dictionary," TJ said. "But as long as we
can stay friends, I hope we can get over most of the hurdles." She
reached out, and when Paula grasped her hand, she pulled her
down into a hug and kissed her cheek.

Paula swiped at her eyes and sniffed as she straightened up.
"I'll send Erin right in." She hurried back into the living room
where Erin still sat looking angry. "TJ wants to see you."

"Like I give a damn."

"Come on. She wants to talk to you about our accident." Paula
sat next to Erin again but didn't attempt to put an arm around her.
Two rebuffs in one day were about all she could handle.

"What did you do, go in there and suck up to her about poor Erin blaming herself for the accident?"

"Get real. Did you ever see me suck up to anyone?" Paula said. These personal attacks from Erin were wearing her patience thin, and she could feel her defensive anger building again. She decided retreat was her best course of action and jumped up, heading for the stairs. "I'll be upstairs. You should go in and listen to what TJ has to say." Managing the steps as quickly as she could, Paula hurried away.

"It'll be a cold day in hell when I go running after her!" Erin shouted in the direction of the stairs.

A creak sounded from the doorway followed by a vibrant voice. "How about if she comes running after you?" TJ wheeled into the room and came to a stop several feet from Erin, who was momentarily dumbstruck. Her wary gaze rested uneasily on TJ, touching her heart. "Come on over here. Please?"

Erin's wariness turned to amazement. "Are my ears working all right? Did I hear you say please?"

"Yeah," TJ said softly, "please." She lifted up an arm of the wheelchair and patted her lap. "Come on over and sit here."

"Uh, TJ, I can't sit on your lap. That's Mare's place."

A small gust of laughter burst from TJ. "I'm not going to kiss you. I just want to have a heart-to-heart talk with you, like a mother and a daughter." TJ pointed a thumb at her own chest. "With me being the mother."

Erin hesitated, her anger at TJ not entirely gone. But TJ knew that when she really wanted something, Erin found it hard to resist giving in to her wishes. This generous nature won out, and she sat down on TJ's lap. A long arm wrapped around her waist, holding her firmly in place.

TJ saw the hardness of Erin's expression dissolve and the natural warmth of her personality return. "Paula tells me you're trying to take all the credit for our accident."

"Credit? You mean blame, don't you?"

"Well, all of us have some claim to the blame, and you seem to insist that it's all yours. I figure you must think it's something valuable, so it must be credit you're looking for."

"You're being ridiculous."

"Am I the one being ridiculous? Actually, it was Paula's turn to drive, but I told her it was her party, and she could choose not to drive. That choice moved you into the designated driver's spot. So, Paula could take credit for the whole thing."

"It wasn't Paula's responsibility. It was mine."

"Then again, Mare should get some of the credit. She's the one those idiots were chasing after when they showed up at our table.

If she hadn't *lured* them over, nothing would have happened, right?"

"But I was the one driving. I was the one who lost control of the van."

"Then, of course, there's me. Not only was I the hated Meridian bitch, who really set them off, but also I was the one who grabbed the guy's thumb and took him to his knees in front of the whole bar. I probably should be allowed to claim the greatest portion of the credit. Lord knows I worked hard enough for it."

"Look, TJ, no matter how hard you try to whitewash it, the van crashed because of my stupidity. Paula and I got hurt, and I can handle that. What I can't handle is what happened to you. You were making really good progress, and in a split second, you got knocked right back to the beginning—right where you were the first time. You have to go through all that pain again...because of me."

"I don't blame you for that, and I hope you can stop blaming yourself. You're no more to blame for what happened to me than I am for what happened to Lance. Let's both try to forgive ourselves, okay?" TJ felt a huge weight begin to lift from her soul. That made so much sense. Maybe, after all these years, she could start down the road of forgiving herself. Maybe.

Erin laid her head on TJ's shoulder and cried. TJ moved her arm up across Erin's back and clasped her upper arm, pulling her closer. The other hand smoothed the curly locks, over and over. "Go ahead and cry, kiddo," she murmured. "You'll feel better." She continued making soothing noises and gave Erin time to release some of her burden of self-accusation.

At last the tears stopped. "I've been such a fool," Erin said. "I couldn't see far enough past my own guilt to realize that none of us was to blame. Paula tried to tell me, but I wouldn't listen." She stayed there, resting in the security of TJ's arms. After a while, she raised her head and gazed into TJ's eyes. "She also told me to stop letting you push me around."

TJ chuckled. "You should listen to that partner of yours. She's one smart cookie."

"I have to warn you though, from now on when you yell at me, I'm liable to be screaming right back at you."

"I'll look forward to it. You know how I like a lively discussion."

Erin threw her arms around TJ's neck, moved close in, and hugged her. "God, TJ, even when I hate you, I love you."

TJ kissed Erin's cheek. "I love you, too. And I always will, no matter what happens."

WHEN MARE FINISHED the emergency call, she stopped at the post office to pick up some veterinary supplies that had just arrived. Riffling through the mail, she pulled out a postcard marked with her old address, and a warm feeling suffused her when she saw its sender.

Hi Mare, gonna be here longer than expected, more business contacts! I'll keep in touch. Love ya, Jess.

Mare was happy to hear from her long-time friend. Thank goodness he talked more than he wrote or phoned. She guessed she would have to wait until he got home to hear all his news. And for him to hear hers. And meet TJ. She slipped the card into her back pocket and walked out to her truck.

She drove to the ranch and entered her office through the back door. She loved her office except for the nagging disappointment that TJ had never entered it and probably never would. Mare had hoped TJ would change her mind, now that the room no longer held the slightest resemblance to its former appearance. In her determination to erase any memory of the space where TJ's father had beat his daughter so violently, Mare had not left one square inch unchanged.

All the other rooms on the first floor carried some imprint of TJ's presence: equestrian magazines, a horse-head mug, business charts, candy dishes containing her favorite fudge, and pencils everywhere. A feeling of completeness had returned to the rest of the house when TJ came back from the hospital. None of that feeling was evident here, and Mare missed it terribly. But she hadn't been able to entice TJ into the office, no matter what she said. The last time Mare had made a subtle suggestion, TJ had gotten agitated, forcefully reminding Mare of the agreement not to pester her about that subject.

"I'm not trying to pester you. It's just that the office is so much a part of me, a big part of my life, and I want to share that with you. I want to share everything with you. I guess I kind of hoped you felt that way, too."

"You knew how I felt when you moved in there. Don't be trying to lay some guilt trip on me. I won't go down that road." TJ's eyes narrowed, and Mare saw a storm brewing in their depths, so she quickly changed the subject.

The reminiscence brought forth a sigh. Ah, well, one could always hope. Mare placed the new supplies in the closet and sauntered toward the living room where she heard voices, keying on the velvety one that always thrilled her.

She reached the doorway just in time to see a tableau that startled her for a minute. Then she heard Erin say, "God, TJ, even when I hate you, I love you." Mare had to grin. There was some of that feeling in all of us, wasn't there? She heard TJ answer, "I love you, too. And I always will, no matter what happens."

"So." Mare walked into the room. "Just what did happen, if I may ask?"

Erin jumped about a foot in the air and scrambled to get off TJ's lap. "Nothing," she quickly said. "This isn't what it looks like." She waved her hands in agitation.

Mare glanced at TJ, who grinned mischievously behind Erin's back and winked. Oh, so it was tease-Erin time, huh? "Looks to me like you and TJ were hugging and kissing. Am I wrong?"

A blush rushed quickly up Erin's cheeks, turning them bright red. "Yeah. I mean — no. I mean, nothing was going on between us. I...uh...TJ, help me out here, will you?" She turned toward TJ, who raised her hands, shrugged, and looked apologetic.

"Well, we *were* hugging and kissing..."

Erin's mouth dropped as she stared at TJ. She swung her head quickly just as Mare was trying to wipe a smile off her face. Erin's eyes narrowed. "You guys are teasing me."

"I'm sorry. You looked so guilty, I couldn't resist," Mare said. "You and TJ have been friends for ages. If anything were going to go on between you, it would have happened long before now. Besides, Paula would have decked you both."

A begrudging grin crept onto Erin's mouth. "You're right, there." Then her expression changed as she said, "Yikes! Paula might still be mad at me. I better go see." She hurried to TJ and kissed her cheek. "Thanks, Mom," she whispered and dashed out of the room.

Mare dropped onto the vacated lap, put her arms around TJ's neck, and pulled her into a lingering kiss. As their lips parted, she murmured, "Good morning," then proceeded to nibble an irresistible ear.

"A very good morning, now." TJ squeezed her tightly.

"So, tell me about it. I want to hear every word," Mare said, then jumped as a warm hand met the skin beneath her shirt.

TJ bent her head for another kiss. "First things first, I always say."

ERIN WENT BUSTING up the stairs and into their bedroom where she came to a quick halt. There were clothes all over the room — on the bed, on the chairs, and even on the small table in front of the sliding glass doors that opened onto a balcony. "Paula? What's going on?"

Paula marched out of the walk-in closet with an armload of clothes that she added to those on the bed. "What does it look like? I'm rearranging my clothes." Paula's face was tight and her whole body tense.

"I thought we were going riding." Erin laid her hand on Paula's arm, but Paula yanked it away.

"My partner never showed up, so I decided to sort my clothes."

"Well, I'm here now. We can still go riding."

Paula started to put some of the clothes on the bed in different piles. "I'm busy now."

"This can wait, love. Come on. Let's go riding while it's still nice out. I'll help you with this when we get back," Erin said, but Paula wasn't giving in. She hadn't even looked at Erin yet.

Paula picked up two piles of clothes and walked back into the closet. As she came out, Erin startled her by grabbing her shoulders and shoving her against the closet door, pinning her there. "Paulie, I'm sorry we had the spat. I'm sorry I hurt your feelings, and I'm sorry I acted so nasty. Now, I'm not letting you away from this door until you agree to forgive me and go riding with me."

"You know, don't you, that I could knock you on your ass with one arm tied behind my back?"

"But you won't, will you?"

The two gazes mingled and spoke to each other. Paula's cheek twitched. "You know I won't," she whispered.

Erin leaned into Paula's body, lifted one hand from its hold on her arm, and laid it against her jaw. Tenderly, she drew her thumb back and forth across the unyielding lips until they began to soften. "I am really, really sorry I hurt your feelings. TJ and I had a long talk, and she convinced me that you were right. I shouldn't blame myself for the accident. But I do blame myself for being so mean to you. Please forgive me?"

Paula's arms lifted slowly to embrace Erin, and she leaned her head down on Erin's shoulder. Gently moving Paula away from the door, Erin wrapped her arms around Paula's tense back. She smoothed her hands over familiar muscles, feeling them gradually relax.

The two stood in silence for several minutes. Finally, Erin murmured, "What do you say we forget about what happened this morning? Let's go riding and have the great day we had planned, okay?" She felt Paula's head nod in agreement, then lift from her shoulder. She put both hands up to enfold Paula's face and touched her lips with a kiss. "Hi there, beautiful."

A slow, endearing smile and a squeeze answered her. "Hi there." Paula tilted her head and looked deeply into Erin's eyes. "Think you might like to go for a ride?"

"I'd love to."

Chapter
Twenty

MARE RUBBED AT her tired eyes as she put down the last of her papers. For the past two hours, she had been working over her financial books. Although she had an accountant, she liked to keep abreast of how her practice was doing. In the last few months, even with the addition of her associate, Barry, the practice was making enough money that it was paying its own bills with quite a bit left over. That knowledge filled her with a pleasant warmth.

Meridianville was on the upswing. The return of the packing plant and the ranch had indeed brought money into the economy, but more important, it had given the town back its self-esteem. Due to several federal grants, applied for with the help of TJ's business advisors, the Town Council now had the money to start renovating the town. Also due to the advisors, the Council had established an Enterprise Committee to encourage new industry to move into the area.

Mare leaned back and relaxed into her chair. Yep, TJ had really turned this town around, and people hadn't kicked and screamed about it either. Presented with the opportunity to better the community, they jumped at the chance. TJ had said that she would provide the resource people to help the town but she wouldn't force anything. As it turned out, the various advisors were rushed off their feet.

An odd thump drew Mare's attention to the wall her office shared with TJ's, and a chuckle erupted as she heard the muffled curses that followed. She stood up and wandered out of her office and down the hall to TJ's door. When TJ was annoyed, Mare had learned that discretion really was the better part of valor, so she knocked on the door and waited for a reply. "Hey, TJ? You okay in there?" She heard TJ moving around.

"Oh, I'm just fine, thanks."

"You sure?"

"Umm, well, actually, maybe I could use a hand."

Mare pushed open the door and stuck her head around it. "And how may I assist you, m'lady?" she asked, then frowned, not seeing TJ at her desk. She could, though, see the handles of her chair. "TJ?"

"Yes?" Her voice came from under the desk.

"What are you doing?" Mare walked up to the desk and looked over.

"I dropped my favorite pen, and I couldn't pick it up with my grabber." Mare glanced over at the long-handled stick that had a trigger action at one end and a three-pronged grasper at the other. Paula had presented it to TJ because she had gotten fed up with having to pick up the various objects TJ threw when she got angry. The grabber lay on the floor near the wall, and Mare guessed that it was what had been thrown this time.

"Come on, wheel yourself out of there, and I'll get it for you."

"Thanks." TJ tried to wheel herself out from under the desk but misjudged the distance and bashed her head on the edge. "Ow!" Her hand came up and rubbed the sore spot.

"Here, let me." Mare pulled the wheelchair the rest of the way from the desk, then she leaned down and kissed where TJ was rubbing. "Better?"

"Oh yeah," TJ said with an impudent grin.

Mare rolled her eyes at the implication in TJ's voice. "Brat! Now move out of the way, and I'll get your pen."

"Yes, ma'am." TJ rolled a few feet back but didn't move from behind the desk, watching with appreciation as Mare got on her hands and knees and crawled beneath the desk to retrieve the elusive pen.

"Got it." Mare held the pen out behind her so that TJ could see the evidence of her accomplishment, then she crawled back out and clambered to her feet. She turned to the grinning TJ. "Enjoy the view?"

"I always enjoy that view."

Mare sauntered over to her and handed her the pen. As she did, she noticed the dark, growing stain on TJ's jeans. "Honey, I think we need to go get you changed."

TJ looked down. "Ah, shi—" A finger touched her lips.

"Don't say it."

"I thought I'd got past this stage."

"You've done really well so far. You haven't had an accident for a few days. So no beating up on yourself or cursing to high heaven, okay? We'll just get you cleaned up and go on from there. Got me?"

"Yeah, okay," TJ said rather forlornly.

"I said no beating up on yourself."

"God, you know I love it when you get authoritative."

"Well then, I'll have to practice it with you more often."

"How about a little extra practice right now? Soon as I get cleaned up?"

Mare quickly followed TJ as she wheeled out of the office.

"YOU ARE SUCH a brat!" TJ lay back on the bed and smiled as Mare's voice echoed out of the bathroom. "And don't you dare lay there with that smug grin on your face either." Mare's voice grew louder as she poked her head around the door. TJ forced a startled look onto her face and pointed to herself. "Yes, you," Mare said.

"But what did I do?"

"The bathroom looks as though it went through the great flood, and I look like a drowned rat."

"Yeah, but you're a beautiful drowned rat. Besides, you started it. So don't blame me that you couldn't finish it."

Mare had to concede that point to TJ.

They had slowly wheeled down the hall to the bathroom with Mare trying to keep the atmosphere as light as she could, knowing that TJ hated the fact that she had soiled herself. But as Sacha told them, it was to be expected, and at least it had happened while Mare was there to support her.

She got TJ into her bathroom and helped her out of her clothes. Rather than go for a quick wash, they decided that TJ might as well take her bath. With the aid of the overhead hoist, Mare helped her into the warm water she had prepared.

TJ had been quietly washing herself when Mare decided that the situation needed to be livened up just a little. Swiping her hand down into the water, she arched a large splatter smack into the center of TJ's chest. TJ returned the favor with relish. An all-out water fight followed, and the bathroom sank without a trace.

In her zeal to make the biggest splash, Mare got too close to TJ and cringed as a large hand grabbed her shirt. Unable to escape, the squealing captive got her just desserts.

TJ showed no mercy. She pulled Mare forward and dunked her face in the tub, then pushed her back up. Sopping wet and out of breath from yells mixed with laughter, Mare finally begged for a truce. TJ tugged against the shirt, threatening another immersion. But after a moment of nose-to-the-water teasing, she took pity on Mare and let her go.

Mare dragged TJ out of the bathroom, helped her onto the bed, and tossed her a clean towel from the closet. Then she returned to clean up the flood. If nothing else, the zany deluge had brought back

TJ's incredible smile. The mess Mare now had to clean up was more than worth the trouble.

Finally Mare had soaked and blotted up the worst of the water. She leaned against the doorjamb and wiped her hands on the only towel that retained a trace of dryness. *God, TJ is gorgeous.* She gaped at the still glowing body sprawled on the bed. "Hey," she called, then hesitated, trying to regain the breath that deserted her suddenly as TJ looked her way. "Want some company?"

TJ looked into Mare's eyes. They promised more than she could imagine and evoked an immediate reaction. "Sure." Her voice was husky and barely above a whisper. Mare slowly walked over, her gaze drawn to the hand that TJ reached out to her.

As their hands met, Mare's eyes connected with TJ's, and she felt smoldering heat surge down her spine. Her heart rate increased, and a fine sheen of moisture coated her face as she felt the stirrings of desire. Her fingers lovingly traced the contours of TJ's strong hand, each ripple deeply ingrained into her mind. Even as her eyes never left the depths of TJ's, Mare was gently tugged and brought to her knees by the side of the bed.

"Hi," TJ whispered. She rolled onto her side to get closer to Mare and raised her other hand to caress the soft face before her.

"Hi, back," Mare said as she leaned in and tasted the sweetness of TJ's lips.

Savoring the moment, TJ slowly moved her hand through Mare's hair to the delicate softness at the nape of her neck. The gentle massage brought a purr to Mare's lips, and she settled closer. TJ ended the kiss reluctantly, but her body demanded that she breathe.

"I think you're overdressed for the occasion." She pulled at the still damp T-shirt until Mare took the hint and removed the offending article. TJ's hand then dropped inside Mare's bra to the inviting mound of her breast. She loved the fullness and weight in her palm and thrilled in the gasp her touch brought from Mare. As her lips began to nibble their way down Mare's neck, TJ fumbled left-handed with the bra catch. Mare reached behind her back and hastened to help. Her flesh was already tingling with the anticipation awakened by TJ's occupied hand.

The catch gave way beneath their combined efforts, and TJ unceremoniously threw the bra across the room. Totally freed, Mare's breasts summoned a low growl from TJ as her descending mouth latched onto an aroused nipple. Capturing it anew, her tongue played around and against its hardness. Mare moved to pull TJ closer, but the positioning was too awkward. She pushed up from her knees, rolled TJ onto her back, and followed her over until she was sprawled on top of her, TJ still firmly attached to her chest.

"Oh sweet—" Mare gasped as TJ continued the roll until Mare was pinned on her back. TJ moved her lips from the left breast to the valley between and over to the right, while one hand moved to the top of Mare's shorts. With a quick twist of her fingers, she had the button undone, closely followed by the zipper.

Mare's excitement grew at the proximity of TJ's hand, but she knew that TJ couldn't lift herself from the spot. With a nudge, Mare pushed TJ over onto her back and then supported herself while TJ removed the shorts and panties at an infuriatingly slow pace. She then pulled herself away from TJ's suckling to slide downwards and greet her face to face.

The feel of breast upon breast sent a hiss of desire through TJ. It still thrilled and amazed her how Mare's touch, her smell, her taste could elicit such response from her upper body and encourage the fantasy of sensation in lower areas. Their lips and tongues met with longing as Mare sank into the kiss. TJ groaned as the feathery strokes of Mare's smaller but incredibly arousing hands became more aggressive against her hungering breasts. Her eyes closed at the sensation, and her hands ran down Mare's back until they reached her shapely buttocks and pulled her closer.

"Oh, sweetheart," Mare whispered in desperation, "please..."

"Ask me, Mare," TJ's husky voice answered. "I'll give you whatever you want."

And she did.

THE MORNING SUN drew golden patches on the kitchen floor as Mare picked up her bag and prepared to leave. TJ wheeled into one of the patches, her eyes glowing even brighter from the reflected rays. Mare smiled inwardly at the lovely picture, even as her brow furrowed with concern. "You sure you're going to be all right?" she asked again.

"I'll be fine. Will you get out of here?" TJ said. Paula and Erin had gone to the packing plant for the day, and Mare had been called to fill in for Dr. DiNicola in Sharlesburg. This would be the first day they had left TJ completely alone, and Mare had misgivings about it.

Mare recognized the impatience edging into TJ's voice. She supposed she *was* being overprotective. "Okay, okay." She leaned down until she felt TJ's lips against her own, then lightly brushed the tip of her tongue between them, kissed her quickly, and pulled away.

"Wait." TJ grabbed the tail of the departing shirt. "Come back."

"Nuh-uh. That's just a little something to remind you of me while I'm gone." She yanked on her shirt and pulled the tail from TJ's grasp.

"Spoil sport." TJ made a face.

Mare took one step out, then turned back. "Remember, Martha will come over from the cookhouse and fix you some lunch. Erin or Paula should be back in time to fix supper, and I'll be back from Sharlesburg as soon as I can."

TJ raised her hands, turned the backs of them toward Mare and made shooing motions, sweeping her out. Mare put her fingers to her lips, blew a kiss, and left.

AFTER LUNCH, TJ returned to her office while Martha cleaned up the kitchen. When the front door bell chimed, Martha hollered that she would answer it. A few minutes later, she came to the office.

"Miss Meridian," she said, "there's a Mrs. Raphaele at the door. She says she needs to talk to you about something that concerns your father."

Her father? Just the reference to her abusive parent chilled TJ to the bone. *Suck it up, TJ. You're the head of Meridian Corporation. Now act like it.* Then her thoughts turned to the visitor. Who was she? What could she want? "Just a minute, Martha."

TJ called up the name "Raphaele" on the computer's Meridian database. The only reference was to Raphaele Consultants with a notation that they had been hired for some consulting work quite a few years ago. There was no specific information available. Why hadn't the woman gone to the Meridian office? Why had she come to her? "You can show her in now."

Martha left and returned. "Miss Meridian, this is Mrs. Gloria Raphaele." Martha left the office as Gloria walked to the desk and extended her hand.

TJ leaned over the desk and shook her hand. She noticed the firm, yet controlled, grip. There was no flash of recognition on TJ's face, only a touch of curiosity. "Please sit down, Mrs. Raphaele."

"Does the name 'Raphaele' mean anything to you, Miss Meridian?"

"We have a Raphaele Consultants listed in Meridian Corporation's records, back before I took over the company. Are you that Raphaele?" TJ shifted in her chair. The pain she usually managed to push out of her consciousness suddenly seemed concentrated into a new, burning spot in her back, and she was having trouble suppressing it. Oh God, she hoped this woman would get out of here in a hurry. She needed to lie down.

"Yes, I am. But I'm not here on business. Well, not exactly. I'm looking for my teenaged son. He ran away from home, and I thought he might be here."

TJ picked a pencil out of the caddy and started twirling it between her fingers. "And he'd be here because..."

"I found your picture in his desk," Gloria said as she put her bag on the floor next to the chair.

"Mrs. Raphaele, teenagers don't usually go running off to meet someone just because they have a picture of that person." TJ started tapping the pencil against the desktop. "I thought you said this concerned...umm...my father." The pain sent fingers of flame out from the central fire, torching her shoulders.

"It does." Gloria sat up straighter and lifted her chin. "Your father and I lived together for fourteen years. Up until his death."

"Excuse me?" TJ glared at Gloria, daring her to speak those words again.

But Gloria sat silent, as TJ's jaw clenched and her lip curled.

TJ trembled with the double struggle to control her temper and her pain. Anger tore the words from lips pulled tight against locked teeth. "Are you telling me you were his mistress? You and which ten other women?"

"That's not true. Your father was a powerful man with strong appetites, but he wasn't promiscuous. He needed love and companionship, and he found them with me."

Sarcasm dripped from TJ's voice. "I'll bet my mother would have found that comforting. Is this where you tell me that the bastard really loved you?"

Gloria blinked and her face paled. She reached into her pocketbook and brought out an envelope full of photos. She pulled several out and spread them across the desk. Each was a picture of TJ's father in a pose with Gloria, taken at various times through the years. In a couple of scenes, they were hugging or kissing, and others showed them beaming and obviously happy together.

"Very pretty." TJ shoved the photos back across the desk.

Undaunted, Gloria laid out several more pictures with three people in them: Thomas, Gloria, and a youngster. "This is my son, Tommy, your half brother." Then she put down one that showed father and son with their arms across each other's shoulders. The look of pride and love on the father's face was unmistakable.

The pain in TJ's back had worked up to her neck and into her head, but now she was overcome with a different pain. Lost opportunities, shattered love, and yearning fused into a white-hot agony that clutched her heart. She reached out her arm and violently swept the pictures off of the desk. *You pig! Why him and not me?*

Gloria's hands shook, but she had too much mettle to back off. She took out one last item—her son's graduation picture. Next to it, Gloria laid his birth certificate.

TJ's chest was heaving, but almost against her will, her eyes fell on the picture and halted there, mesmerized. It showed a handsome youth, full face, smiling, his gleaming blue eyes full of hope and promise. Her breathing gradually eased. She would have investigators check out every bit of Mrs. Raphaele's story, but after seeing the picture, there was no question in her mind about this young man. He was her brother, without a doubt.

She couldn't bring herself to hate the boy, though she did resent his presence in her father's life. For years, she had craved one tiny gesture of love from her father, a gesture that never came. That still hurt, even though she hated him. And here was this boy receiving the love she had been so viciously denied. That hurt, too. She laid her fingers at the base of the picture and leaned forward, looking into his eyes. "I'll bet he never laid a violent hand on you," she said quietly.

Gloria's eyes widened as TJ's meaning sank in. "Did your father beat you?" she whispered.

TJ's haunted gaze lifted from the photo and an ugly twist marred her lips. *Let's let her see what a wonderful man dear old Dad was.* TJ laid her arm down in front of Gloria and pulled up her sleeve, revealing the scars.

Gloria gasped and touched them with her fingers, making TJ's arm jump. Gloria kept her fingers where they were, outlining one of the crescent-shaped scars. "Thomas did this? What did he hit you with?"

"His belt buckle. He left seven of these marks down my back. Your perfect gentleman and partner was anything but that, to his family here."

Gloria shook her head in puzzlement. "But why?" Her eyes fell further down TJ's arm to her wrist. Her fingers stroked across the attempted suicide scar, and she looked up. They gazed at each other silently for a long moment.

"But why?" TJ finally said. "Because I wasn't the son he had always wanted."

"But, he *had* a son. In fact, he had two—Lance and Tom."

"Yes, but I was the first child, and even you must understand how important it was for my father to be first." TJ pushed herself back from the desk, taking the photo with her. She wheeled around, avoided the fallen prints, and handed the picture back to Gloria. "Your son's not here."

TJ fled the office without another word, not even considering that she'd left an almost total stranger sitting there. The inner torment precipitated by Gloria's revelations blanked out her physical pain. All she wanted was to escape. Wheeling through the house to the kitchen, she picked up the phone and tapped in the ranch manager's number. "Bill, send one of the hands to the barn to saddle Flag." She listened to the foreman for a few seconds before interrupting him. "I don't care what you think is wise, just get Flag saddled." She slammed the phone down on the kitchen counter and pushed her way though the outside door.

Gloria was a little stunned to see TJ leave so abruptly. Surely she was coming back. She retrieved the photos that had been brushed to the floor. Seeing TJ in a wheelchair was quite a shock, too. She'd heard about the mugging, the death of Lance, and TJ's injury, but she hadn't fully appreciated what that meant for the beautiful young woman who had been sitting before her.

She was at a loss now. She had suspected that coming to see TJ wasn't the most sensible thing to do, and that telling this powerful woman that her father had a mistress and son for fourteen-plus years wasn't exactly going to be welcome news. She hadn't reckoned on finding out that Thomas Meridian, the man she had loved, thought nothing of beating his daughter with his belt buckle. That horrible news tumbled through her thoughts as she waited for TJ's return.

TJ wheeled herself into the barn just as Mark, the ranch hand Bill had sent, guided Flag out of her stall.

"Afternoon, Miss Meridian. Flag's looking good today. I thought Tom had taken her out earlier," he said as he lifted the saddle onto the palomino's back.

"He did. Now I'm taking her out."

Mark paused, his hands stilling as he tightened the cinch. "Uh...do you think that's a good idea? Didn't the doc say you weren't going to be able to ride for a few more months yet?"

"I don't care what anybody else has said. I'm taking Flag out for a ride."

"But—"

"Mark, please don't question me. That isn't what I pay you for. Just finish saddling Flag and give me a hand up."

Mark hung his head. "Okay, Miss Meridian."

Gloria sat for quite a while, expecting TJ to come back. Finally, she decided that her waiting was in vain. She sighed, picked up her bag, and put the photos inside. She rose, took a quick look around the office, and walked out.

Chapter
Twenty-one

MARE SWUNG HER truck into the long driveway of the Meridian ranch. She had been hard at work all morning in Sharlesburg when the elderly Dr. DiNicola returned to the clinic much earlier than expected. Mare had offered to stay and work the rest of the day, but he had shooed her away, telling her to get back to TJ. Mare had given him a big hug and bolted from the office just before eleven o'clock. Unfortunately, traffic had been horrendous, and it took her more than the usual hour to get back. Still, if she could sweet-talk TJ out of her office, they would have the better part of the afternoon to goof off.

She frowned at the unfamiliar car coming down the drive toward her. Funny, TJ hadn't mentioned that she was expecting anybody today. As the car approached, Mare slowed the truck to a stop and leaned out of the window. The car pulled up alongside and stopped. "Hi," Mare said cheerily as she looked down into the car. "Can I help..." she began to say, then stopped as she registered who was in the car. "Mrs. Raphaele?"

"Yes, I'm Mrs. Raphaele."

"You haven't been up to the house, have you?"

"As a matter of fact, I have. I've just been to see Miss Meridian."

Mare's eyes closed, and her head fell forward onto the steering wheel. "I don't suppose..." She took a deep breath then lifted her head toward Gloria. "You didn't tell her who you are, did you?"

"May I ask who *you* are? And what this information has to do with you?"

"Sorry. I'm Doctor Mare Gillespie, a friend of Miss Meridian's. I'm the veterinarian for the ranch, and I also live here." Mare thought for a few seconds. "Look, I know this is kind of a weird request, but I need to talk to you. Would you mind coming back up to the house with me?"

"Dr. Gillespie, I came here looking for my son. Miss Meridian has already told me he isn't here. Now unless you can tell me differently, I don't think Miss Meridian wants me here."

"Please, I know this is hard for you. But I can help you find your son. Please come talk with me."

"All right."

"Thank you."

Once Gloria had turned around, Mare continued her drive toward the house. With her right hand, she rummaged in her bag and pulled out her phone. Hitting one of the quick-dial buttons, she waited until Paula's voice came on. "Paula, it's Mare. We have a problem. Think of your worst possible nightmare coming true, and this will beat it. Guess who turned up at the ranch and saw TJ?"

Paula put down the file she was holding and sat heavily in the desk chair behind her, as she listened intently to Mare. Her eyes closed and her spare hand lifted to rub her forehead. "Yes, I understand. Yes, not in the room with me, but I'll get her, and we'll head back right now." She looked up as a noise caught her attention.

Erin stood at the door with two mugs in her hands.

Paula put the phone down and waved her in. "We have a big problem. Mrs. Raphaele turned up at the ranch looking for Tom."

The mugs slipped from Erin's hands and crashed to the floor. "Shit."

MARE OPENED THE kitchen door and let Gloria pass by her. She thumped her bag into a corner near the door and walked into the living room with Gloria close behind her.

"TJ? TJ? Where are you?" Mare strode through the house opening and closing doors with Gloria following.

"I think she left," Gloria said. "She gave me back the pictures I'd shown her of Tom and said he wasn't here. She left me just sitting in her office."

Mare felt panic rising in her stomach. News like this wasn't something that TJ would react well to. And when TJ didn't react well, she tended to do something stupid. "Hell, where would she have gone?" She tried to get her brain thinking the way TJ's would and forgot for the moment that Gloria was still with her. "The barn. She will have gone to the barn." Mare turned around and nearly walked into Gloria.

"Sorry," Mare said. "I'm a little worried about TJ. She's had a pretty rough time over the last couple of months." Mare returned to the kitchen, with Gloria still following.

"I appreciate your concern for your friend, Doctor, but could you please tell me what this has to do with my son?"

"Please, take a seat. I'll explain what's going on as soon as Erin and Paula get here. They are TJ's associates, and they run the ranch and the packing plant that the Meridian Corporation owns here. I phoned them from the truck on the way up the drive. It will take them about twenty minutes to get here from the plant. In the meantime, I really need to find TJ."

"All right, I'll wait," Gloria said. "I've come a long way for information about Tommy. A few more minutes won't hurt." She took a seat by the island.

"Thank you. I do appreciate your patience." Mare crossed to the phone. She tapped out the number for Bill's office and waited for a reply. "Hi, Bill, this is Doc Gillespie. I just got back to the ranch, and Miss Meridian isn't around. Have you or any of the hands seen her today?" She was quiet as she listened to Bill on the other end of the phone. "Has Mark come back yet? No, no, that's okay. I'll call the barn. Thanks, Bill."

She hit the number for the barn. She was waiting none too patiently for an answer when she was relieved to see the Land Rover pull up outside. Paula and Erin came rushing through the door, and Mare's eyebrow lifted. "That was a quick twenty minutes."

"So I broke a few speed limits," Erin said. "That Rover can move." Paula stood next to Erin, looking at Gloria.

Mare followed Paula's gaze. "Paula, Erin, this is Gloria Raphaele, Tom's mother. Mrs. Raphaele, Paula and Erin. TJ's friends." Her attention turned as the phone was answered. "Mark? It's Doc Gillespie up at the house. Have you seen Miss Meridian today?"

Paula took a further step into the kitchen and shook hands with Gloria. "Mrs. Raphaele, good to meet you. Sorry we have to meet under such circumstances."

Erin walked up to Paula, her attention still on Mare and her phone conversation. "Hi," she said absently to Gloria.

Gloria said, "Can you tell me about my son?"

"We do have some information—" Paula stopped as she heard Mare shout.

"She did what?" Mare's face looked thunderous.

Erin left Paula's side and rested her hand on Mare's arm. She winced as Mare slammed the phone down.

Mare looked at Erin, then Paula. "You will never guess what that pig-headed, stubborn woman has gone and done." She didn't give anybody time to reply. "She has taken Flag out for a ride. That woman is going to drive me crazy. Doesn't she listen to anybody? The way she's going, she'll end up back in the hospital.

I'm going to take the pickup truck and go find her." Mare picked up the cell phone and strode toward the door, reaching for the truck keys on the hook by the door.

"I'll come with you," Erin said. "Someone will have to ride Flag back." Mare waved a hand, and Erin followed her out.

The kitchen was quiet for several seconds after the searchers left. Paula said to Gloria, "Let's sit at the table. It's more comfortable. Can I get you something to drink? Then I'll fill you in on what's been happening here."

MARE SLAMMED THE truck door and jammed the keys into the ignition. She ground the gears until she found first, released the emergency brake, and started to move off, barely giving Erin a chance to jump into the passenger seat.

"Pig-headed idiot. I swear I'm going to..." Mare pressed the accelerator down and sped out of the ranch parking lot, heading along a track toward the open plains. "I don't know what I'm going to do, but I'm sure I'll think of something."

Erin watched Mare drive up the track and shove the stick shift into second gear. She reached over and placed her hand on Mare's, which rested on the gearshift. "We need to be careful what we say to TJ. She's had a big shock today."

Mare glanced over at Erin, taking her eyes off the bouncing track for a few seconds. "I know. Why do you think I'm ranting now? I'm hoping that by time we find her, I'll have worked out the urge to yell at her and be able to help her."

"I'm sure that just your presence will help." Erin squeezed her hand tightly. "I have a question though."

"What's that?" Mare thrust the gearshift into a higher gear.

"Are you going to tell her that we knew she had a brother? That we knew her father had been cheating on her mother for all those years?"

"I'm not sure. I'll see how bad she is first, but we'll have to tell her at some point. And she isn't going to be happy that we kept it from her."

Erin looked out of the window as they passed clumps of trees and the last of the ranch outbuildings. Before them stretched the wide-open grass plains that made up the majority of the ranch holdings. "No, she isn't going to be happy with us at all, is she? Oh, God. Why isn't anything simple anymore? Every time we get ourselves onto an even keel, something comes along to rock us."

"Yep, we sure haven't had an easy time of it this year, have we? But we still have many roads to travel along. We'll just have to keep hoping things get better than this." Mare's eyes swept the horizon. "Now where would TJ have gone? The lake is a little too far. I doubt she'd make it there."

"I wouldn't put it past her to get anywhere, but I think you're right. I don't think she'd have gone there," Erin said. "Try going up to the small ridge line, the one over toward the main road. There are a few trees up there where she could get out of the sun, and it's a pretty good view. She rode up there occasionally when we first moved back to the ranch."

"Okay." Mare swung the truck off the track and headed cross-country toward the main road.

PAULA FELT AWKWARD as she placed the glass of iced tea in front of Tom's mother. Considering the upheaval going on around her, this woman had been entirely too accommodating and accepting. Paula had the uncomfortable feeling that the messy part of this situation was about to land in her lap. "So, what made you think Tom was here at the ranch?"

Gloria grasped the chilled drink and looked at Paula. "Because I found TJ's picture in his room, and he'd been asking about her a lot. He is here, isn't he?"

Paula sat on the stool opposite. "Yes, he's here. He turned up at the door about two months ago, looking for a job. Mare recognized him right away. Since then, he's been working around the ranch, but TJ doesn't know who he is. I'm not sure if you're aware of it, but we were all involved in an accident almost three months ago. TJ has only been out of the hospital for a short time. We decided not to tell her about Tom yet."

"I'm so relieved he's safe. I need to see him."

"Not a problem. I think he's out with a couple of the ranch hands seeing to the cattle up by the lake. They're due back this evening. You're welcome to wait here until he gets back."

"How did Dr. Gillespie know who Tom was when he turned up?"

Paula sat for a few moments considering her answer. "We were clearing out TJ's father's desk, and Mare found a hidden drawer. Inside were photos of you and Tom, a copy of his birth certificate, and papers dealing with transfers of money and shares to you. We had you investigated. In fact, we received the report from the investigators just before Tom arrived."

"That still doesn't tell me why you allowed a boy who is still a minor to stay here, without telling someone of his whereabouts. I was worried sick about him."

That rocked Paula slightly. They hadn't fully considered the legal implications of allowing Tom to remain here or the fact that his mother would be frantic about him. Rather selfishly, all they really thought about was the impact his presence would have on TJ. Paula remained silent as Gloria continued.

"I could report all of you to the authorities. I'm sure they'd frown upon such irresponsible behavior."

"Are you going to?"

Gloria put her hands flat on the island top. "No, I'm not. You seem like good people. And from what I've seen of the ranch so far, Tom will be having the time of his life. I don't know what he's told you, but like his father, he decides something and rarely considers the other people involved."

"Tom said you wanted him to go away to college, that he had been at boarding schools all his life, and he wanted to get out into the real world for once."

"Did he tell you I said it would be okay, if he would promise to start at Harvard in the spring semester?"

"No, he didn't mention that."

"I'm not surprised. He wouldn't have wanted to risk your sending him home. You have to remember that Tom's only sixteen. Although he occasionally acts like an adult, he's still a child, and a somewhat spoiled one at that. He's always wanted to meet his sister, and before Lance died, he wanted to meet him as well. He's always known that his father and I weren't married, and that meant he wouldn't be able to have a normal relationship with his siblings. But he's headstrong, and once he had decided he wanted to see TJ, there was nothing I, or anyone, could have done to stop him."

"He's a great young man. You can be proud of him. He has fit in very well at the ranch, and he's well-liked by all of the men. Although TJ doesn't know who he is, she likes him, too. She's even allowed him to ride her horse, Flag, while she hasn't been able to. And she's really particular about who rides Flag."

They sat in a comfortable silence, the ticking of the kitchen clock the only sound disturbing the peace. Gloria studied her surroundings. The kitchen was big and airy with an island set into the center of one end and the large, solid oak table and chairs at the other end, with the outside door between them. Its bright décor enhanced the spacious feeling. Personal touches were scattered around: character mugs hanging from the mug tree, magnets attached to the fridge, even the Post-its were of the cartoon variety.

Obviously the kitchen was a popular and well-loved area of the ranch house. The house itself wasn't the cold, loveless shell that Thomas Meridian had frequently described. It had a warm, caring feeling to it, and Gloria wondered how much of that was due to Paula and the other two women who were out searching for TJ.

THE SUN WAS warm, a delicate breeze ruffled her hair, and TJ was in heaven. She was out of her room, her office, and the house. For the first time since their accident, she was free and by herself. The anger that had begun to boil while facing her father's mistress drained away quickly once she left the barn.

She'd been as sensible as she knew how to be on Flag. She hadn't gone galloping hell bent for leather over the fields but had settled for a canter. Her back caused her some distress as she started out, but the joy of being out of the house outweighed it. She thought of going to the lake, where she and Mare had shared some wonderful moments, but that was too long a ride. She already would be in deep trouble with everybody, so she settled for a ride through the fields nearer the house. She had her phone with her. It wasn't turned on, but she could call for help if she needed it.

Her ride had done her good. Not only had it given her time to calm down and get rid of the stressful feelings, but also it had provided her time to think. So, her father had another family that he actually cared for and loved. Did that change her opinion of him? Not in the least, because if he had really cared for them, he would have divorced her mother and left. The only reason not to have left was the cost of a divorce settlement. That meant he was just as much of a bastard as she thought he was, if not more.

She had a brother she didn't know about. She couldn't even begin to describe how she felt about that. He probably wasn't anything like Lance, but it might be good to get to know him. And despite the fact that Gloria Raphaele loved TJ's father, she seemed to be a nice enough person. TJ knew she shouldn't have left like she did. Gloria probably wondered what kind of madwoman she was.

With a tug on the reins, TJ turned Flag up a small path to the top of a rise that would give her a better view of her holdings. She liked this area, and when she had first returned to the ranch, she had come riding out this way on most days. Before the accident, though, most of her longer rides had been with Mare up to the lake or out to see Mare when she was tending to the cattle.

The place wasn't as isolated as it felt. The main road into town was just a few minutes away, and there were several tracks that led into and out of this part. Still, it was beautiful. Even when her father had worked the ranch, this section hadn't been used extensively. Most of it was prairie, with streams and stands of trees scattered sparsely throughout.

She had been out for nearly an hour now and really ought to be getting back to the house. Paula and Erin would be home shortly, and Mare would be back not long after. TJ leaned forward and slapped Flag's neck, feeling the well-groomed hair beneath her fingers. With a flick of the reins, she moved Flag back toward the ranch house.

MARE GUNNED THE truck engine up the hill in front of her, and Erin held on tightly as they crested the top.

"There she is." Erin pointed across Mare and out her window.

Mare turned the truck toward TJ and Flag. Mare was determined not to yell. She was going to be calm about it. Yes, TJ hadn't shown the best judgment, but she'd had a major shock. And when TJ found out that Mare and Erin and Paula already knew about the Raphaeles, she was going to be more than a little upset. Mare slowed the truck as she drew nearer.

"Will you wait here, please, Erin? I think I might get further if I'm alone with her."

"No problem. Just give me a shout when you want me."

TJ pulled Flag up, as the truck appeared over the hill. She guessed it was finally time to face the music over this little excursion. She wondered who Bill found to come looking for her. At least Mare was in Sharlesburg. TJ don't know whether she could handle Mare being mad at her now that they were back on good terms.

She waited, unconsciously pulling herself taller and settling her face into a mask as the truck got nearer. She could make out two people sitting in the vehicle and slowly recognized the features of Mare and Erin. The confidence she had felt moments before fled rapidly, and her stomach curled into a tight knot. She closed her eyes. She didn't want to see the disappointment on Mare's face or the anger she knew would be there with it.

Mare stopped the truck, opened her door, and slammed it closed, noticing the visible flinch it elicited in TJ. Christ, she looked like a two-year-old kid waiting for the sky to come falling down on her. But Mare was going to be sensible about this. No yelling, no screaming, just lots and lots of support.

"Hi there. Good ride?" Mare asked without a hint of condescension or anger.

TJ sat stock still, then slowly opened her eyes at Mare's loving tones. "Aren't you mad at me?" She ignored Mare's question, totally puzzled at her reaction.

Mare relaxed at TJ's question. At least she wasn't going to get the silent treatment. "Am I mad at you? I could be, but that wouldn't be very understanding of your reasons for going against all the rules Dad told you about riding." She walked up to Flag and slung her arm under the golden neck so that she could pat the loyal steed. "Hi, girl. Did you enjoy having your mom take you out?" Flag nudged at her shoulder as though replying.

"That doesn't really answer my question," TJ said.

"I'm a little upset, but no, I'm not mad at you. I met Mrs. Raphaele as I drove up the lane to the house."

"Did she tell you who she was? Did she tell you I have a brother? That my father had another family? A family that by all accounts he loved?"

"She didn't have to," Mare said, quickly coming to a decision. "I already knew it."

"What?"

"Why don't you let Erin and me get you off Flag? Then we can drive back to the ranch, and I can explain everything to you on the way. Erin will ride Flag back for you."

TJ didn't want to wait for an explanation, but she knew she couldn't make an issue of it, since Mare was being so reasonable about her impulsive ride. "Sure, I can do that."

Mare took hold of Flag's bridle and led the horse over to the truck. Erin jumped out of the passenger side, lowered the tailgate, and climbed into the open back. While Mare tied Flag off and began to undo the straps that secured TJ's legs, Erin tackled the others that secured her to the saddle. Once all straps were loosened, Erin carefully pulled TJ's far leg over Flag's withers and helped TJ from the horse's back.

"Cat got your tongue?" TJ asked dryly.

Erin grimaced. "Can't lift you and talk, too." Erin held TJ steady as Mare quickly moved around to lend a hand. Mare clambered up next to her and helped her rest TJ on the floor of the truck. "Thanks, Mare," Erin said as she jumped back to the ground. "You ready?" she asked TJ.

"Yep." Erin scooped TJ into her arms and carried her around to the side door. TJ put her lips up to Erin's ear and whispered, "Are you Mare's right-hand girl now, Erin? In cahoots with my big, bad rescuer?"

"We're only trying to help you," Erin muttered with a little asperity. She placed TJ into the passenger seat, fastened the seat belt, and closed the door gently. She walked to the back of the truck where Mare had just finished untying the palomino. "Okay, Mare, I'll see to Flag and meet you guys back at the ranch."

"I told her I already knew about the Raphaeles," Mare said quietly. "I'm going to tell her the rest on the way back. If you cut cross-country, you can make it back before us. You had better warn Paula and Mrs. Raphaele before we get there. TJ might be in a bit of a mood."

Erin pulled Mare into a hug. "I think she's working on one, now. You sure you're going to be okay with her?"

"Yeah, I'll be fine. She might blow her temper, but she won't do anything I can't handle. We'll be home soon."

Erin released the hug and held Mare at arm's length. "You know, you really have made a change in TJ. Had this happened before you came, I'm not sure how she would have reacted, but it wouldn't have been pretty. Now, she knows she has you to lean on, and no matter how nasty she gets, or how loudly she shouts, you'll still be by her side. I think that's making a big difference."

"I hope so, because she's taking this way too calmly right now."

"I think she's just taking a leaf out of your book. She sees you all nice and calm and figures she had better act like a grown-up, too. At least, I hope that's the case. You had better get on your way. I'll meet you at the house."

Erin mounted Flag and headed out across the fields, while Mare jumped back into the truck next to TJ. She started the vehicle and pushed it into gear, slowly turning it and driving back toward the track.

"So." TJ's fingers nervously flicked at her cuticles. She wished she had her usual pencil to tap.

"So?"

"Yeah, as in, so are you going to tell me how you knew I had a brother? Or how you found out about the Raphaeles?"

"We found out about the Raphaeles when we started cleaning out your father's office."

"We? Paula and Erin knew about this and didn't tell me either?"

"Yeah. We were all together when the papers were found."

"And you were planning on telling me — when?"

"We would have given you the report as soon as it arrived, but we had the accident."

"What report would that be?"

"Look. I know you want all the information right away, but why not let me start at the beginning and tell you what happened?" Mare looked over, and TJ nodded. "Okay, then. As we were sorting through your father's desk that first day, Erin noticed that one of the drawers was too short for the space it occupied. When I checked, I discovered another drawer, a secret one, behind it. We found pictures, a birth certificate, and paperwork relating to funds and stock that your father had transferred to Raphaele Consultants. That's how we learned that the family existed. We knew you were already upset about me taking over your father's office, and we wanted to get all the facts before we told you what we found. So Erin got in contact with one of the agencies your corporation uses and asked them to do a background check on the Raphaeles for us."

TJ gazed out of the window at the passing trees and fields. She lifted her right hand and rubbed at her temple. "When did the report arrive?"

"A few days after your operation."

TJ raised her voice. "My operation was nearly three months ago. I could maybe understand your not telling me right away after the operation, but almost three months go by, and you still hadn't told me?"

"I know it looks bad, but we didn't want to give you another shock." Mare slowed the truck to a stop and looked at TJ's angry face.

"Then, maybe, but *now*? You think it was better for me to find out from my father's mistress that I have a brother? You think that was easy for me?"

"No, but—"

"Don't you think I might have appreciated finding out about him from my friends? Rather than have his mother accusing me of hiding him at the ranch? Hell, he can't be more than a teenager."

"He's sixteen."

"Fine, sixteen. If he was at the ranch, do you have any idea how much trouble I could be in for harboring a runaway minor? We already have one kid working for us, and Paula still hasn't had confirmation of permission from his parents." TJ looked over at Mare, catching a quickly hidden, guilty look. "What?" she said, barely below a yell, her temper getting to the boiling point.

"Promise me you won't do anything—"

"About what? For crying out loud, what the hell is going on?"

"We didn't know what to do when he turned up."

"Turned up?" TJ stared. "Oh no. Please don't say what I think you're going to say."

"We couldn't turn him away. He had obviously come looking for you." Mare sent a pleading look for understanding across the cab of the truck. "At least, if he was with us, we knew he wasn't in any danger."

"Didn't it occur to you that his mother might come looking for him? I could be looking at a lawsuit. Better yet, she might decide to report this to the police. Then I could be looking at charges of kidnapping," TJ yelled.

"TJ, please." Mare reached out a hand, but TJ flinched away

from her touch.

"Don't 'TJ, please' me!" TJ purposely slammed her arm into the side window.

Mare jumped at the impact of TJ's arm against the glass. She had seen TJ angry before but had never really been in this type of situation without Erin or Paula nearby. Talking to her didn't seem to be an option. She was way beyond being calmed down. Mare was reluctant to approach her physically, for fear that TJ would strike out in her anger. Deciding that silence was the best choice, Mare released the brake and started toward the ranch again.

Chapter
Twenty-two

ERIN HEADED OUT at a canter, then spurred Flag on to a gallop in her desire to get back to the ranch before Mare and TJ.

She breathed a sigh of relief when the ranch house came into view with no sign of the truck. She guided Flag into the barn, asked Mark to take care of the palomino, and sprinted to the house.

Paula and Mrs. Raphaele looked up from their places at the table as Erin rushed in, closed the door, and leaned against it. Paula frowned, concerned. "Is TJ all right?" Relieved by Erin's nod, she rose and got a glass from the cupboard. She poured more iced tea for all three of them and sank back into her seat.

"She seems to be fine," Erin said. "She was pretty calm. And, frankly, *that* has me a little worried."

Erin walked toward Gloria with her hand extended. "Mrs. Raphaele, I apologize for practically ignoring you earlier. My mind was more on TJ's well-being than on your search for your son." She shook Gloria's hand. "I assume Paula has explained Tom's situation here. I'll add what I can to the explanation, but first we have to get TJ settled."

"Please, call me Gloria. I understand you need to see to Miss Meridian's needs first. Besides, Paula told me that Tom won't be in from the range until later."

"And I invited Gloria to wait here with us," Paula said.

Erin chose a seat at the end of the table with Paula to her left and Gloria to her right, facing each other. She took a long drink of tea, then rubbed her palm across her face.

Paula patted her forearm. "You say you're worried about TJ's calmness. Did Mare confront her about disobeying Michael's orders?"

"We found TJ out on that low ridge where she likes to ride Flag. All the way out there in the truck, Mare ranted and raved. I'll tell you she has a temper when she lets it fly. But by the time we got there, she had reined it in, and she talked to TJ as sweet as you please. TJ didn't stand a chance. You know what effect Mare has on her."

Erin hesitated. "What I'm worried about is what will happen as they drive here and when they arrive. Who knows if they both will be able to keep their cool? TJ's like a coiled spring—the tighter she holds something in, the higher it bounces when she lets loose. Not that I could blame her. She's had a real shock, and a lot of that is our fault—all three of us."

"Yeah," Paula said. "We deserve to be yelled at."

Gloria pursed her lips and nodded. At Erin's surprised look, Paula said, "I've filled Gloria in on what has happened from square one, right from our discovery of the secret drawer up to the present, including the investigation." Paula squirmed in her seat. "I explained how we've been trying to protect TJ from any emotional upsets. But looking at this particular situation through another person's eyes, our actions seem pretty lame and unjustified." She clasped her glass of tea in overlapping hands, swirled it around and stared into it, as though a solution could be found in its eddying brown depths. For a prolonged moment, only the clink of ice broke the silence.

Erin lightly touched a fist against Paula's biceps. "Hey, we'll be okay."

"It's not us I'm worried about. It's TJ."

"We'll just have to count on Mare for damage control," Erin said.

"Please," Gloria said, "tell me more about TJ. I've read some things in the newspapers over the years, but I'd like to hear about the real person from her friends."

Paula looked at Erin. "You start, okay?"

Erin nodded. "I'll have to give you an abbreviated version. They should be here any minute. We all met in college..."

TJ GAZED MOODILY out the window as the truck bounced along the track. Her hands, lying in her lap, were in constant motion as her mind replayed the conversation she'd just had with Mare. They wondered why she lost her temper and hit out when they treated her like this. Didn't they understand that, in real terms, that was the only absolute control she had over her life? She looked over at Mare, who seemed as upset as she was.

"You know what I hate most about being in a wheelchair?" she said in a grating voice. "No matter how good a recovery I make, everybody still treats me as though I can't decide for myself on personal matters that count, never mind that I run a multinational corporation. When you came into my life, I was glad for the first time that the nurse found me when I tried to kill myself. I thought you understood how I needed to have some control over the direction my life should take. But in the end, you're just like everyone else. You have no idea what it's like to be me."

Mare struggled to focus as tears fell from her eyes. No, she didn't have any idea what it was like. And she'd give anything for TJ not to have to know, either.

PAULA AND ERIN looked up as they heard the truck pull into the parking area. "I'll get it," Paula said before Erin could stand to collect TJ's wheelchair and take it out to her. She looked to Gloria as she stood. "I won't be a minute, but please understand that TJ might not be in the best of moods."

"Don't worry," Gloria said as Paula went over to the wheelchair that Mark had brought from the stable. "I'm old enough to look after myself."

Mare slammed the door shut after parking the truck. Their short trip back hadn't settled into silence, even after brief tears. She had continued to talk to TJ, and surprisingly, TJ had responded, even if it was only in two-syllable words. Her comments about control, though, had sent Mare's thoughts straight back to Peter's counseling session when TJ had broken down so completely. It was true then, and it was true now. They were all guilty of not allowing TJ to make her own decisions on anything they thought might bring about emotional turmoil.

Paula pushed the wheelchair toward the truck, and Mare opened TJ's door. "Hi ya, boss. Enjoy your ride?" Paula said, as though nothing untoward had occurred.

TJ scowled at Paula as she swung herself from the truck into the chair. "Bring Tom to the house. I'll be in my office. Call me when he gets here." She wheeled toward the house.

Paula glanced at Mare. "Guess things aren't going so well, huh?"

"Better than I expected." Mare and Paula trailed behind TJ. "Let's ask Erin to get Tom. She knows the ranch better than we do."

TJ wheeled through the door into the kitchen, barely sparing a glance at Erin. "Mrs. Raphaele, I think we have some things to discuss. If you would excuse me for a few minutes, I'll have you shown into my office shortly." She turned toward the hall and looked back over her shoulder at no one in particular. "I'll buzz you when I'm ready."

Mare started to follow, but TJ waved her back. "I don't need any help," she said in a frigid tone.

"Would you like some tea or coffee brought in?" Erin said.

"Mrs. Raphaele?" TJ paused and turned partly around.

Gloria leaned across to Erin, who was on the receiving end of TJ's glare. "Not for me, thank you," she said and gave Erin's hand a pat.

As Mare sat down to a glass of tea, Paula asked Erin to retrieve Tom. When the promised buzzer sounded, Paula quickly escorted Gloria to the office, and then retreated to the kitchen.

TJ had already rolled herself behind her desk, and she waited for Gloria to settle into one of the chairs in front of it. "Mrs. Raphaele, I owe you an apology. It seems that I had very little idea about what was going on in my own home —"

"Please, TJ, call me Gloria."

TJ recognized her own tactic of disarming your opponent with the kindness of offering your first name, but she refused to be brought into the game. "I've sent someone for your son. He should be with us soon. All I can do, I'm afraid, is offer my apologies for what's happened. If you think this needs to go any further and you plan to bring legal charges, then I can supply you with the names of my lawyers, and we can go from there."

"I don't think legal action is absolutely necessary. Paula has explained to me what happened, and I'm satisfied that you weren't keeping Tom's presence at the ranch from me for any malicious reason."

"I wasn't keeping his presence from you at all. I didn't know he was here."

"Well, I'm not angry at anyone. I'm sure no harm has been done intentionally."

"It surprises me you feel that way, Mrs. Raphaele. I'd think all the worry you've been put through was harmful enough." TJ turned her head toward the window and gazed out implacably, her fingers beginning to torture a rawhide decoration on the vest she was wearing.

Gloria sat silently, contented that the conversation, or lack of it, be directed by the woman opposite her. For many years, portrait painting had been an avocation of Gloria's, and she welcomed the diversion of scrutinizing TJ's profile. What a fascinating face she had, even under such trying circumstances. Or maybe, even more fascinating because of such trying circumstances.

She believed that a person's character manifested itself through words and movements, but mostly through facial expressions, if one made the effort to read past superficialities. She studied the strong chin, wide cheekbones, full lips, and straight nose. The clenched jaw, flared nostrils, and tense body language spoke of restrained anger. But the eyes, those magnificent Meridian eyes, conveyed a different message. Even the lowering of the perfectly arched, raven brows couldn't hide the hint of vulnerability they displayed. TJ was angry, yes. But she was also hurt, and something else — was it betrayal she felt? Of course. She felt betrayed by her friends, no matter how well meaning they were. And Gloria had walked in and dumped her father's betrayal on her, too.

Gloria's face grew somber, and her heart ached for the young woman seated across from her. She struggled to think of something positive to say, something to lighten the heavy atmosphere in the room. "I think you and Tom will like each other."

TJ's head came slowly around and rewarded Gloria with a fleeting twitch of the lips. "We already do. But liking someone doesn't seem to preclude..." She hesitated.

"Hurting them?" Gloria said. TJ gave a brief nod and returned to her desultory gaze.

With no further conversation forthcoming, Gloria assumed that nothing more would be heard from TJ until Tom arrived. She sat back in her chair and centered her thoughts on her imminent reunion with her son. She couldn't wait to see him and know for sure that he was all right.

ERIN LOST NO time in going after Tom. She jumped into the truck, her ear already against the cell phone. "Bill, TJ wants Tom right away, so I'm going after him in the truck. Can you tell me the shortest route to get to him?" She headed in the direction he specified. She also asked Bill to call to the site and have Tom ready to leave. She drove as quickly as conditions would allow, gathering from the expression on Mare's face that TJ would brook no delays. As soon as the truck pulled into the work site, Tom hopped in.

"Hi, Miss Scott. What's happening?" he asked breezily.

Erin backed the truck to turn around, and before she changed gears to start forward, she hesitated. A half-smile stole onto her face as she looked over at Tom's jaunty grin glowing through his beard. Then the impending confrontation with TJ wiped it off of her lips. "Your mom happened."

Tom froze for a moment, then turned his body toward Erin and leaned back against the door, his left arm reaching up to lie along the seat back. "My mom? Did she call back about my Social Security number?"

"Tom, lay off the acting, okay? Your mom showed up at the

ranch today with the whole story." She shifted gears and floored the gas pedal. "And she told it all to TJ."

"All of it?"

"All of it."

"How mad is my mom?"

"Probably not as mad as she has a right to be. She's upset that you ran away but grateful to have found you. The better question would be how mad is TJ?" This time Erin's gaze caught a questioning frown on Tom's face. "You can take off your wraparound sunglasses now, too. TJ knows you're her brother."

"Hey, that's okay. I was going to tell everyone sooner or later, anyhow." He smiled widely, removed the glasses, and stuck them in his shirt pocket.

"Aren't you even the least bit sorry?"

"I...uh..." He seemed genuinely puzzled. "Sorry for what?"

"Sorry for worrying your mother half to death. Sorry for lying to all of us. Sorry for putting TJ in such a precarious position—"

"What precarious position?"

"You're a minor. Your mother could sue TJ to hell and gone for letting you work here under false pretenses."

"But TJ didn't know who I was."

"No, but the rest of us did."

"You knew I was her brother?" Tom's voice rose to a higher register. "Why didn't you tell her?"

"I wish now that we had. Right before you got here, TJ had a serious operation and she was in severe pain. Even now, her nerves are still stretched thin. We didn't want to slam her with any unpleasant news, so we kept putting it off."

"You think finding out she has a brother is unpleasant news? I was thrilled about TJ being my sister. Why would she feel differently?"

"Only TJ can answer that. What isn't pleasant, I would guess, is finding out her father had another family."

Tom hung his head. "I never thought of that."

"Seems like there are a lot of things you never thought of," Erin said. But he wasn't any worse than they were. They had all hurt TJ, the one person none of them wanted to see suffer.

"But I can explain—"

"We're here. Save your explanations for TJ."

They entered through the front door and went down the hallway to TJ's office. Erin led Tom in and watched as mother and son embraced. Then she turned to TJ, who was also watching them. "You want me for anything?"

TJ dragged her gaze from them to Erin, and Erin flinched as she saw her expression change from wistful to hard. "Not yet," TJ said in a flat tone.

Erin sucked in her lips and left the room, her heart aching for the totally unforeseen pain TJ was experiencing. They all loved her so much that it was easy to forget that her parents hadn't loved her. Erin recalled her own childhood: her intellectual dad nevertheless teaching her to ride a bike and coming to all her games, no matter what sport it was. And her practical mom allowing her to learn to do household carpentry, electrical work, and plumbing, as well as cooking and sewing. Her parents constantly hugged their children and each other, showering everyone with plenty of love. Meanwhile, TJ studied, studied, studied and knew that no matter what she accomplished, she would never garner her parents' approval or affection. She only had Lance to love her, and she had lost him. No wonder she loved Flag so much. Faithful Flag.

Erin walked into the kitchen where Paula and Mare were seated at the table. Paula took one look at her face and had just barely stood up when Erin walked right into her body and grabbed her in a fierce hug.

"Hey, what's wrong, honey?" Paula asked softly as she closed her arms around Erin.

"Just hug me for a minute, okay?"

Finally, Erin loosened her hold a little and turned her head toward Mare. "First thing you do, the first chance you get, make sure you give TJ the biggest damn hug she's ever had."

Mare pulled a chair out and patted the seat. "Please, sit down and tell me about it."

Chapter
Twenty-three

IN THE MIDST of welcoming her son, Gloria, too, had glimpsed the wistful look on TJ's face and filed it in her memory. Gloria ended the embrace and took a good look at the tall young man she barely recognized. In the short time he'd been missing, Tom had begun to fill out, and his muscles were bulking up from the physical nature of ranching. His tan skin and bearded face would have fooled her, had it not been for his eyes. Gloria could see why TJ hadn't realized that the pictures she showed her were of this young man. He wasn't her little "Tommy" anymore.

"Mother, I'm sorry I upset you. I had to meet my sister, and I just couldn't see any other way." He nodded toward TJ, but she made no acknowledgment of him.

Gloria sat back down and motioned for Tom to sit in the chair beside hers. "You could have told me you wanted to meet Miss Meridian. We could have discussed it. Instead, you dash off with no notice, no explanation, and needlessly worry me."

"But you know you wouldn't have given me permission to come here. You and Dad had an arrangement about that."

"That arrangement bound *me*, Tom. It never was intended to bind you."

Tom looked startled. "You mean you would have let me come?" A grin lit his face. "So what's the big problem?"

TJ's low, throaty voice answered. "The problem is the way you went about it. You should have contacted me first and received my permission, as well as your mother's."

"I don't get it." Tom bristled defensively. "I was thrilled to know that somewhere in the world I had a sister. Aren't you happy to have a brother?"

TJ set her elbows on the table, put her palms together, and propped her chin on top of her fingertips. Her voice was strained. "You have pleasant memories of your father, and I wouldn't attempt to take them away from you. But the father who loved you didn't provide a loving home for me. He was a monster. So sharing your blood with his is no recommendation in my book. In fact, it could be just the opposite, and that remains to be seen."

"I'm no monster." A guarded arrogance stole over Tom's young face. "Ask the men I work with, if you don't believe me."

"The men your father worked with knew he was a shark, but they had no idea he was a monster. He saved that for the *sanctity* of his home."

Although Tom didn't know about the abusive history, he picked up on the emotional undercurrents, and his arrogance diminished. "Can I stay? I'll prove I'm not him."

"You're not fired, if that's what you're asking. Whether you can stay is up to your mother, not me."

Tom turned to his mother. "Can I stay? Please?"

"We can speak about that privately. We've taken up enough of Miss Meridian's time. But before we leave, you owe her an apology."

"Sure. I'll apologize." He paused and looked perplexed. "But what am I apologizing for?"

"You lied to her, Tom. You put her in a situation that could be emotionally damaging and for which she had no preparation. You could have hurt her financially and harmed her reputation by working for her as a minor without parental consent. I think those reasons will do for a start, don't you?"

A flush rose slowly over Tom's countenance, and he got up and walked to the desk. Unable to meet TJ's eyes, he stared at the desk's surface. "I've been pretty stupid. I didn't think about your side of this whole thing. I'm sorry." TJ didn't answer him. Finally, he lifted his gaze.

TJ's voice was empty and cold, her words dismissive. "If your mother lets you stay, give your Social Security number to Miss Scott before you start back to work."

She looked at Gloria. "You're welcome to stay here until you're ready to return home, if you wish. We have plenty of room."

"Thank you," Gloria said. "I'm grateful to accept your offer. I just arrived today and hadn't checked in anywhere."

TJ buzzed and Erin soon appeared. "Erin, show Mrs. Raphaele to one of the suites upstairs, and let Paula know we have a guest for dinner."

Tom stared toward TJ, until Gloria took his arm and led him from the office.

Soon, Mare entered. Her heart plummeted when she saw TJ's head bent down, resting on the heels of her hands, with her fingers threaded through her hair. She went to her and put an arm across her shoulders. TJ tried to shrug it off, but Mare wouldn't let go.

"No, don't push me away. Please. I need you." She hugged the tense shoulders. "I'm really sorry. I know it's easy to say that we never meant to hurt you. I wish I could go back and change how stupidly insensitive we were, but I can't." Mare moved her hand onto TJ's back, rubbing circles on it with her palm. "We talked it over, and we admit we had no right making your decisions for you. We're sorry you had to get hurt before we learned that lesson."

TJ dropped her hands to the desktop and pushed herself away as she brought her torso upright. Her eyes looked wounded, and her mouth twitched down.

Mare lifted the chair arm, slid onto TJ's lap, and took her in her arms, giving her the biggest hug she could, just as Erin had suggested. TJ held on with a death grip until Mare could feel the thudding of TJ's heart slow to an even beat. "You okay?" she murmured.

"Not really," TJ said in a raspy voice, her turmoil taking a toll, "but I'll survive. I even suspect I'm getting a little bit stronger at coping. Maybe all the crap that's being thrown at me is toughening me up."

They sat and held each other for a long time, until Mare realized that TJ was starting to nod off. She leaned back and lifted a hand to replace a fallen strand of black hair as TJ's eyes struggled to focus.

"You've had a rough day, sweetheart. How about if I help you into bed and bring you some dinner? We can have a nice, quiet meal together, and then you can rest." She patted a tan cheek. "I might even be persuaded to feed you."

That prompted a small, tired grin. "Sounds good to me."

Mare stood and replaced the armrest, then pushed TJ to the bedroom. After a stop in the bathroom, TJ transferred to the bed. Mare helped her out of her clothes, removed the turtle shell brace, and slipped a pajama T-shirt over her head.

"Mare, do you remember when I talked about the struggle to get up the ramps of life?"

"Yeah?"

"Today I think I ran into a couple of broken boards."

Mare lay down beside her and gave her another giant hug.

ERIN SHOWED GLORIA and Tom to one of the upstairs suites. "You have a bedroom, bath, and sitting room with a small kitchenette, and you'll find milk, soda, and bottled water in the fridge. Please make yourself at home. Dinner will be in the kitchen in about an hour. We're having ham and yams tonight, one of my favorites."

"This is lovely," Gloria remarked. The rooms were decorated in an Old West motif with brown-dyed burlap furniture coverings, natural burlap curtains, and woven, multicolored cotton throw rugs on hardwood floors. Even the bedspread was burlap, hand-embroidered with a western landscape in hues to match the throw rugs. Colorful oil paintings of cowboys, Indians, and western scenery hung on the beige walls. "Please thank Miss Meridian, again, for us," she said to Erin, who nodded and left.

Gloria sat on the couch, and Tom picked the easy chair next to it. "Tom," she said and sighed. "I hardly know where to start." She raised her hands and let them fall helplessly into her lap.

Tom tilted his chin up, a pose that hinted at arrogance, but Gloria knew he used it to hide his insecurity. "I don't understand what I did that was so awful. I know I shouldn't have run away from home. I realize now that I really worried you, and I'm sorry. But when I got here, I went to work. I didn't just show up and dump myself on TJ. I've been making my own way."

"That's not the point. TJ had no inkling of your existence. Nor of mine. Your father had no intention of his first family ever learning about us. I don't know all his reasons, but it made great sense to me. *We* are living proof of your father's infidelity to *them*. Surely you aren't too young to see that it would be extremely painful to discover that?"

Tom's lips tightened. His loose fist scuffed at his chin whiskers, then his eyes gleamed as though he were about to win a point. "Yeah, I guess it would. But she didn't find that out from me."

"Thomas Joseph Raphaele! Don't you *dare* try to pass the blame. I would never have come here if I weren't following you. And if you had given any thought to anyone besides yourself, you wouldn't have come here either."

Her indignation finally got through to Tom. "You're right." He flopped back against the chair cushions and slouched despondently. "I could tell from the look on TJ's face that she doesn't care much about me. I thought she would be happy to find out she has a brother, but she didn't sound happy. She treated me better when she didn't know who I was." Fighting back tears, he blurted, "I liked her, and I thought she liked me."

"Has it occurred to you that TJ probably does like you and that makes your deception even more painful to her?"

Gloria's heart went out to Tom when she saw the tears welling in his eyes. Maybe, though, feeling some pain would help him understand how he had hurt TJ.

Tom swiped away the lone tear rolling down into his beard. "I didn't mean to hurt her. I only wanted to love her."

Gloria rose from the couch and settled on the edge of Tom's chair. She put her arms around his shoulders and pulled him to her, soothing him as he broke down and cried.

After Tom's tears had eased his pain, he dried his eyes and sat up. "Maybe I shouldn't stay here. I'd always be reminding TJ of Dad's betrayal."

"On the contrary. She could have fired you, you know, but she didn't." Gloria relinquished her embrace. "I'd like to see you stay here at least until spring semester begins. I think TJ wants you here and is willing to give you a chance to redeem yourself."

"I'd do anything to redeem myself. She only has to name what she wants."

"I don't think it's going to be that easy. Right now, TJ's probably leery of you, not sure of whether it's safe to let herself care about you. I suggest that you just go about your work and try to regain her respect. Then she might let you get closer to her."

"I'll sure give it one heck of a try." He slipped an arm around Gloria's waist, pulled her close, and kissed her cheek. "Thanks, Mother. First, for not yanking me home by my ear, like I deserve, and second, for helping me see where I went wrong and how I hurt TJ. I might lose my teenager badge for admitting all that, but I'm grateful."

"You keep on working to understand the results of your actions, and I'll be even more proud of you than I am right this minute. And that's saying something."

Tom blushed, took a deep breath, and looked at his watch. "I guess I better get on down to the cookhouse if I want any grub." They stood up, and he gave his mother a hug. "I'll be by really early in the morning to exercise Flag, just about dawn. Will you be up then?"

"I'll make it a point to be," Gloria said and watched with a sweet smile as Tom left. Grub? He was even talking like a ranch hand.

The phone on the end table rang, and Gloria looked at it curiously, then picked it up. "Hello?"

"Mrs. Raphaele, this is Erin. Dinner will be ready in fifteen minutes. Will you be available?"

"That's fine, thank you. I'll be right down," Gloria said and cradled the phone.

PAULA FIXED TWO dinners, complete with dessert, for Mare to take to TJ's room. She set them on a tray with silverware and napkins while Mare fixed two mugs of coffee. Gloria came in as they finished, and Erin indicated that she should sit across from her.

Gloria nodded to Erin and sat. She saw that Mare was just about to pick up the tray. "You aren't joining us?"

"No. TJ is pretty wrung out. I'm going to eat with her in her room and spend a quiet evening there. If you need anything, just ask. Paula and Erin will see to it."

"Don't worry about me. I always bring a book or two when I travel. I'll just go back to that beautiful suite of rooms and relax with a juicy murder mystery. Please tell TJ I said good night."

"I'll do that," Mare said. "Good night." She picked up the tray and tapped Paula's side with an elbow as she passed her. "Thanks for the help."

"You're welcome." Paula took her seat next to Erin and initiated the passing of the food.

"It has been a tiring day," Gloria said. "I'm not surprised that TJ wants to rest. She went through a lot of emotional upheaval." With that, she got to work on the pineapple-covered ham, which was tender enough to cut with a fork.

"Yeah." Paula's wry expression spoke volumes. "Her doctor told us to keep her calm. We didn't do much toward keeping her calm today." She pushed her yams around on her plate several times, shrugged, and began eating.

"I apologize for my part in this," Gloria said, "and Tom's. I didn't know that TJ was recuperating from an operation, or I would have used more discretion. Until you filled me in on the results of her earlier injury, I didn't even know why she had to use a wheelchair. When I first met her and she moved from behind her desk, I was startled to see that she was in one. And now I learn she recently had a second injury and operation. My news must have been a terrible emotional blow to her."

"Don't blame yourself too much," Erin said. "If we had told her about you and Tom when we first found out about you, this might not have slammed her quite so hard. So we made mistakes, too."

Paula cleaned off her plate, then got up to get the dessert. "Well, that's all water over the dam," she said. "We need to make sure we don't hide anything from her anymore because of what we consider her best interests. We'll let her be the judge of that."

"And keep ourselves out of trouble," Erin said. She nodded for emphasis and polished off the remnants of her food. She rose and cleared off the table, while Paula finished serving the cake with whipped topping. Gloria stepped around them and poured more coffee for everyone, then they resettled themselves at the table.

"TJ told Tom he could stay with my permission," Gloria said, "so I'm going to let him. I'd like to see the two of them get to know each other better. At the moment, and I can understand why, TJ seems a little ambivalent about her feelings toward him. I'm afraid it might take awhile before she thinks of him as family."

"TJ was crazy about her brother Lance," Erin said. "Truly, except for him, she didn't have much use for her family. Would be nice to see her get a second chance at one."

Gloria's expression turned sad. "She told me about how Thomas abused her. I still find that hard to understand. He had a terrible temper, but he never struck either of us. How horrible that must have been for her."

Paula's voice sounded rough. "She never knew love from her father or her mother. Erin and I were at her home and saw that for a fact. TJ has a heart as big as Texas, but she sure didn't inherit it from either one of them."

"She seems to be surrounded by love now." Gloria ventured a small smile. "You women obviously care about her and look out for her."

"Yes, we do," Erin said, "and she does the same for us. We have a mutual admiration society." She flicked a glance at Paula.

Gloria looked from one to the other. "I can't help but see that you two are very close to each other and — "

"We're partners," Paula said, her weariness stirring a touch of belligerence. "Lovers. Lesbians."

"And TJ and Mare?"

"Yep, they are, too. Does that matter to you?"

Erin cocked her head at Paula, wondering at her irritability. Gloria hadn't seemed aggressive in her questioning.

Gloria's eyes narrowed as she sat forward and pointed at Paula with her dessert fork. Erin held her breath. Just what they needed to end this rotten day. Another confrontation. She was too damned tired for this. She laid a soothing hand on Paula's arm.

Punctuating each strongly enunciated word with a movement of her fork, Gloria attacked.

"Does...it...matter...to...*you*...that...I...am...straight?" Gloria's glare rapidly disappeared, and she sat back with a grin. "I sure hope not, because I can't change any more than you can, though I do think you're pretty cute."

Erin clapped her hand over her mouth as she saw Paula's comical expression. She had seemed ready to counterstrike against an expected dig. Instead, she looked completely surprised.

Quickly recovering, she rubbed her jaw. "Hell, no. It doesn't matter to me." Then she retaliated with a grin. "Some of my best friends are straight."

Gloria chuckled and set the fork down. "I'm sorry. I know a lot of discrimination still exists, but not in my family. I would guess that some of your mood tonight comes from being tired, but you looked like you were just itching for a fight, and I couldn't resist egging you on a little." A puff of laughter blew past her lips. "I must be tired, too." Without warning, the laughter turned into an infectious giggle that she couldn't stop.

Erin joined her, and finally, Paula was engulfed, too. Paula kept trying to ask another question, but each time she started to speak, another wave of giggles hit them. Eventually, they were all giggled out.

"What were you trying to ask me, Paula?" Gloria said, her face red and eyes still wet from laughing.

Paula scratched her head. "Damned if I remember." Too worn out to giggle any more, they all laughed softly.

"I think I'll head on upstairs," Gloria said, wiping her eyes. "Tom's coming by early to ride Flag, and I want to be up to see him."

Paula's mind kicked into gear. "You know how to ride, don't you?"

"Yes, I've been riding since I was a child."

"Well, heck, why don't you ride out with Tom? You can use my horse, Runny. Tom can saddle her for you."

"Or my Ebonair, if you want a quieter one. Like her owner, Runny is a little spirited," Erin said, casting a lighthearted look at Paula. "And tell Tom he can have the rest of the morning off. It will give you some time to spend together. I'll let the foreman know. You can come back here for breakfast if you want. There's always something in the fridge."

"That sounds like a great idea," Gloria said. "Thank you for giving us the extra time together. I'll see you ladies tomorrow."

"Okay. We're going to watch TV for a while in the living room, so you might hear us coming upstairs later," Paula said. "Good night."

Gloria walked around the table and impulsively hugged Paula, then Erin. "And thank you for making me feel so welcome," she said and headed upstairs.

After Erin made the cail to Bill Jacobs, she and Paula talked about their upcoming vacation while they finished straightening up the kitchen.

"Gloria seems pretty nice," Erin said as they moved into the living room. She handed the remote to Paula, who found the channel they wanted and sat back to wait for their show.

"Yes, she does." Paula reached around Erin's shoulders and pulled her in close. "But no matter how cute she thinks I am, she doesn't stand a chance. My heart belongs to another nice woman."

"Oh yeah? And who would that be? Do I have to fight for you?"

"Why it's you, darlin'. Nobody but you."

Erin wrinkled her nose at Paula and patted her cheek. "Right answer." With a satisfied sigh, she leaned into Paula's kiss and settled down against her.

They talked a few minutes more, put the finishing touches on their vacation plans, and then relaxed and enjoyed the TV.

Chapter
Twenty-four

PAULA CAME DOWNSTAIRS the next day just a little ahead of Erin. Last night, when their show was over, the wrestling matches came on, and the two women started their own playful wrestling, ending in...well, it hadn't really ended, just moved upstairs.

This morning, Paula discovered her keys were missing and guessed they'd been dropped somewhere in the living room. When she entered the room in search of them, she found Mare sitting in TJ's motorized chair. Not TJ, just Mare, studying the controls.

"What the heck are you doing?" Paula asked.

"Hi. You know, TJ has mentioned several times that I have no idea what it's like being tied to a wheelchair, and she's right. So, I figured I would spend a day in a chair, just as she does, and get a feel for how hard it is. What do you think?"

Erin entered the room and came to Paula's side, a questioning look on her face. Paula's arm went around her waist. "Mare's going to spend the day in the wheelchair, to find out what it's like."

"Cool," Erin said. "We never thought of doing that, but it seems like a great idea. What are you going to do about your work?"

"I talked to Barry about it, and we rearranged our calls so he can handle them for today. Unless an emergency arises, I'm good to go."

"Does TJ know about it?" Erin said.

"Does TJ know about what?" TJ pushed her chair into the room. She steered around Erin and Paula and came to a dead stop.

Mare had absolutely no clue to TJ's thoughts, but being true to her nature, she jumped into the silence. "I'm going to spend today in this chair, shadowing your movements, so I can get a better feel for what you have to put up with." She cocked her head at TJ, whose face had become totally unresponsive, which made

Mare nervous. "Is that all right with you? I promise not to get in your way."

"And just what are you trying to prove?" TJ's tone was one Mare was beginning to think of as velvet ice — it sounded so quiet and smooth but could freeze the skin right off of its target. "Are you trying to prove how easy it is to sit in a chair all day without letting it bother you?" She snorted. "For one day?"

For a moment, Mare was dumbstruck. "No, you don't understand — "

TJ's eyes went out of focus and her voice continued, distantly, as though Mare hadn't spoken. "It's not one day that gets to you. I could do one day with my hands tied. It's the 'forever' part that really..." TJ's voice thickened and stopped.

Mare bolted from the chair and knelt next to TJ. She stroked TJ's arm until her eyes recovered their focus and met Mare's. "I didn't mean to upset you, sweetheart. I thought it would help me be more understanding of the frustrations you deal with everyday. I'm not trying to make you look bad."

Erin cleared her throat. "Hey, guys, how about we get some breakfast before it's therapy time? Paula and I will get it started, okay?" Mare nodded and they hurried away. Paula could look for her keys later.

Mare moved the chair arm and settled unopposed on TJ's lap. She took TJ's face between her hands, lightly kissed her cool lips, and drew back. "I swear I had no idea this would upset you. I thought you'd be enthusiastic about it. At last, one of us would have some firsthand experience of what you go through every day." She brushed TJ's lips again, and again pulled back. Her hands dropped to TJ's shoulders, and she waited, not knowing what to expect.

Long arms lifted and wrapped loosely around Mare's waist, then TJ laid her head against Mare's. "I had no idea it would upset me, either," she said. "I appreciate that your intentions were good. It was...well, just seeing you in that chair threw me for a loop. I wouldn't wish this on my worst enemy, and seeing you there..." TJ paused. "Maybe it's a good thing I'm the one in the chair." Her next words were a throaty whisper. "I couldn't bear the thought of you in one."

Mare slipped her arms around TJ's neck and hugged her close. "You'd love me just the same, you know. Our love's too strong to let anything stop it." Mare loosened her arms just enough to allow her to kiss TJ's forehead, eyes, cheeks, and finally her lips. This time, the full lips warmed under hers. They tightened their arms and pressed their bodies together, holding on until the contact had soothed them both. When their lips parted, Mare sat back and slowly ran a hand over TJ's head, smoothing her hair with a caress. "How about if we go get some breakfast?"

TJ's intense gaze softened as it moved from Mare's face, traveled admiringly down her body, and returned, stirring with a hint of desire. "Do we have to?"

Mare intercepted the hand that was sliding up her hip, aimed at slipping beneath her shirt. "Yes, we do," she said with a pretended pout. "You have exercises to do yet, remember?"

"Yeah," TJ said with a sigh. "Now *there's* something you could do in my place."

"Come on, let's have breakfast and then I'll help you with them. After that, I'm free for the day. We can do anything you want."

"Mmm, what an enticement. Let's go." TJ swiveled the chair and ran it through the doorway with Mare still on her lap. "How fast can you eat?"

"ERIN SAID RUNNY is spirited," Gloria said to Tom. "She may be a little too much for me." She saw how the horse danced around as Tom led her outside the stall, then put her back.

"Yeah, she always tugs against the lead, like she wants to be the boss." Tom patted Runny's rump as he left the stall. "I think you'll like Ebonair. She's more of a lady." Gloria watched Tom's smooth movements as he fetched the tack and began to saddle Flag and Ebonair.

"She's a beauty," she said, "and Flag is simply gorgeous. I can imagine TJ flying over jumps on Flag. What a picture that must have been."

"I try not to think about it," Tom said. "I feel too bad for her."

"I understand, but I don't think TJ would want you to feel bad for her. She seems to handle her disability pretty well. Look around this ranch, for instance. I know a lot of other people are doing the hands-on, physical parts of running it, but that would probably be the case no matter who the owner was. TJ's in charge of all this, and apparently it's doing all right."

Tom slowly nodded. "I've been so involved with Flag that I kind of took everything else for granted, but that's true. Bill gets most of his instructions from Miss Scott, but everyone knows TJ is the boss. The men talk about her with a lot of respect, too. When she started the ranch back up and offered them jobs, she gave them a chance to feel proud about themselves again."

"Paula gave me a quick explanation of all that. Don't forget, too, that TJ runs a major corporation. People use the expression 'big wheel' rather loosely sometimes, but even in the short time

I've been here, I can tell that TJ's the hub that everything else revolves around. Seeing the power of her personality, I'd guess that the corporation's no exception."

Tom shot a contrite glance at her. "I've been looking at what TJ can't do instead of what she can do. One more dumb idea I had."

"Not dumb. You've just been looking at TJ's situation with too narrow a focus." They walked the horses out into the soft light. The hidden sun nudged the top of its rim against the slowly yielding horizon, as if impatient to shine its face on a new day.

"Take a wider look," Gloria said. "That wheelchair might slow her down a little, but TJ will still be far ahead of most people. Don't feel sorry for her. She's well worth your admiration."

They mounted the horses and rode toward the emerging dawn.

"THIS PLACE IS gorgeous." Mare pulled the truck as close as she could to the trees that TJ indicated. A very slight breeze enhanced her awareness of the air's freshness and fragrance. Birds chirped their solos, while assorted insect sounds mingled with the chucking of squirrels to their playmates.

"Some small hideaways like this have springs and pools in them," TJ said, as her eyes drank in the beauty of the trees and late-blooming flowers, "but none of them are this close to the house."

They had decided to take advantage of Mare's being free for the day by spending some time outdoors, in a wooded area of the ranch. TJ had wanted to go to the lake, but bouncing that far across the range in a pickup truck didn't sound like a good idea. Besides, she might have to rely again on tubes and bags for that long a trip. That unwelcome thought helped Mare convince her that, after the prior day's adventures, a closer locale made more practical sense. The weather was too cool for swimming anyway, and the huge ranch offered many other delightful places that had yet to be visited.

Mare lifted the wheelchair from the back and helped TJ into it. She handed TJ a blanket, then followed her, laden with pillows and a six-pack of soda from the back of the cab. TJ wheeled through the scattered underbrush into a grassy dell, sprinkled with wildflowers.

Mare set the pillows and soda on the ground. She spread the blanket next to a tree and helped TJ out of the wheelchair. TJ laughed as she easily caught the pillows Mare tossed at her. Mare then picked up the six-pack and faked a toss with it but set it within reach, instead.

TJ pretended to flinch. "You throw those sodas at me, and you won't get any."

Mare flopped on the ground next to an outstretched TJ and leaned against her, happy that the turtle brace could be left at home and she could feel TJ's body with her own. She batted her sparkling eyes. "You keep threatening me, darlin', and you might not get any either."

"Woman, you are shameless." TJ's low chuckle rumbled through Mare's body, warming every single fiber of her being.

"Only where you're concerned," Mare murmured and lowered her lips to taste TJ's. She felt the buildup of heat in TJ's body and the acceleration of her breathing. Then she rolled away, and a startled TJ grabbed for her and missed.

"But first, a soda." Mare knelt up, out of reach, and freed two cans from the pack.

TJ rolled onto her side, propped her head on her arm, and narrowed her eyes. "You just love to tantalize me, Dr. Gillespie, don't you?"

"Yes, indeed, Miss Meridian. But as I keep telling you, it's just so much fun." Mare popped a top on a soda and made the tactical error of handing it to TJ.

A strong hand gripped Mare's wrist and pulled. The action dumped her right back onto the spot she had just vacated, lying prone next to her aroused lover. TJ grasped Mare's shirt with the arm she had propped against the ground and grabbed the soda with her free hand. "So, you want soda first, do you? Then soda you'll get."

"No, no." Mare protested in vain and wrapped her arms over her head and face. TJ poured the whole can of soda over Mare's squirming body, dousing every spot from her shoulders to her knees. When Mare realized the can was empty, she stopped squirming. "Now what, you nut?" she said, laughter bubbling out of her. "I'm soaking wet."

TJ rubbed a teasing hand over Mare, watching with a heavy-lidded smile as her body reacted. Then she reached for the top button of the clinging shirt and unfastened it. "I guess I better get you out of these wet clothes before you catch a cold."

"Oooh, yeah. Good idea." Mare helped by shrugging her shoulders out of the sodden garment. "But I'm still going to be awfully sticky when this stuff dries on me."

"Come here, you sticky-sweet thing." When Mare scooted closer, TJ dipped her head and licked at bare skin until Mare wriggled and gasped. Then, in a sultry voice, TJ said, "I think I can fix that."

And she proceeded to do just that, most thoroughly.

BACK AT THE house, Mare showered and changed while TJ took care of her own needs. Then Mare took a bucket of water outside and washed the truck seat. She returned to the kitchen and shook a finger at TJ. "Just remember paybacks."

"Yes, ma'am," TJ said, but her meek act was spoiled by a snort of laughter. "Okay, I'll be nice. I'll fix lunch."

"Oh yeah, like that's being nice. I'd be afraid to eat it." She grinned at the innocent, raised-eyebrows look that TJ fashioned. "I'll figure out something else you can do, later. I'll fix lunch. I saw Tom and Gloria coming across the fields. Maybe they'll join us." Mare busied herself making soup and sandwiches and setting a pitcher of iced tea on the island.

"Hi," Mare greeted Gloria as she knocked on the door and entered. "You're just in time for lunch. Is Tom staying?"

"Hi, and thanks for the invitation. I'd love some." Gloria walked to the sink and washed her hands. "Tom said he'd eat at the cookhouse. I'm flying home this afternoon, and we said our good-byes just now. He's not one for public displays of affection." She took a seat at one end of the island, diagonal to where Mare would sit.

"How was your ride?" Mare asked. "Did you get a good look at the ranch?" She set the food on the island and took her place next to TJ. The three women talked as they ate.

"Yes, I really enjoyed it. We rode for a couple of hours, then Tom took me back to the ranch office and introduced me to Bill Jacobs and his family. They invited us to join them for a delicious breakfast. After that, Tom showed me the bunkhouse, the barn, and outbuildings. This place is beautiful and quite impressive."

"Thank you." TJ inclined her head in acknowledgment of the compliment. "We have a lot of people working hard to keep it that way." She took a drink of her iced tea. "Would you rather have a soda to drink, Gloria?" she asked politely and swallowed a grin as Mare kicked her chair.

"No, thank you, tea's fine. I can see where teamwork would be vitally important in a ranch this size. Tom seems to be absorbing that knowledge from his work with the other men. I really appreciate that you're letting him continue here."

"A ranch is a great place to learn about life," TJ said. "Sometimes the lessons are hard, but they're all worth discovering. When you grow up and have to choose a road to take, there are hundreds of different ones available, and some you get pushed onto whether you choose them or not. A strong belief in yourself and your friends sure can make the journey a lot easier, even when the road's awfully hard."

Suddenly embarrassed by the realization that she had slipped into a revelation of her own personal experiences, TJ stopped talking. Her eyes slid to Mare, who gave her a small smile of encouragement and patted her on the arm. The three women finished their lunch in silence, and Mare then began to clean up, waving Gloria back into her seat.

Finally, Gloria spoke again. "TJ, I've told Tom he can stay here until spring semester starts at Harvard. I appreciate your telling him that I was the one who had to give him that permission, but you really are the one who has the last say. Is it all right for him to stay until then?"

"Yes, it is. And I want you to know I'll be keeping a close watch on him."

"Thank you. That eases my mind a lot. He's really happy here." Gloria hesitated. "He wants to get to know you better. Will you give him that chance? Please?"

"I'm not ready to make any promises," TJ said with a frown. "Beyond the offer to let him work here and keep an eye on him, I won't say."

"Very well." Gloria rose from the table. "I have to get packed. My plane leaves in a couple of hours." Mare and TJ nodded to her, and she headed upstairs.

Mare walked over to TJ and brushed her cheek with her fingertips. "You okay, sweetheart?"

TJ smiled up at her, a lovely, bittersweet smile. "Yeah, I'm fine. Some things only time can take care of."

"I'm glad you're feeling all right. Wouldn't want this morning's fun all undone."

TJ's expression turned happier. "No danger of that." She turned her head as Erin and Paula entered, carrying bags of food.

Paula set hers on the counter while Erin put her bag on the island. "I got finished at the plant earlier than expected," Paula said, "so I grabbed Erin and we went shopping." She glanced toward Erin, who was looking at Mare quizzically.

"Weren't you wearing something else this morning?" Erin said.

A flush started to creep up Mare's cheeks. "Ah, yeah. I...uh...got some soda spilled on—"

Paula had been looking from Mare's pink face to TJ's devilish smile, and she interrupted with a droll voice, "At least you got your shirt buttoned right this time."

TJ laughed out loud, Mare turned from pink to red, and everyone laughed.

MARE HAD CAST off her robe and picked up a T-shirt when she felt TJ's gaze on her. She glanced toward the bed with a gentle smile. "You always watch me. Don't you get tired of seeing me do the same old things over and over?"

TJ's silky drawl crawled right inside of Mare, warming her. "Every time you ask me, I'll tell you over and over. You are so beautiful, it pleasures me to watch you. Do you ever get tired of seeing a sunrise? A waterfall? A rainbow?"

These words evoked a small smile that widened as Mare lifted the T-shirt over her head and heard a softly in-drawn breath. "Careful, sweetheart, you're letting your sensitive side show." She slipped into the bed and entered TJ's embrace.

"Mmm." TJ hummed as her squeezing hand tested a few spots. "Seems like you're sensitive on all sides."

Mare giggled as TJ hit a ticklish area. She grabbed the wandering hand and pulled it up between them. "TJ?"

"Yeah?"

"Can we talk about Tom?" Mare felt TJ's body change abruptly from warm and yielding to cold and hard, as TJ withdrew into herself. Mare had never known anyone whose emotions could change as rapidly as TJ's sometimes did. Like throwing a switch. Mare pressed her lips against the bare skin above TJ's T-shirt collar then tilted her head back to look into TJ's detached gaze. "Are you angry about having a brother?"

"No!" TJ startled Mare as the detached gaze came frighteningly alive. "I'm..." TJ's face contorted with the effort to get her words out, but Mare waited, knowing how difficult it was for TJ to express her innermost feelings. "I'm..." TJ sucked in a breath and clenched her jaw. "I'm afraid."

Mare laid her palm against TJ's cheek, stroking tenderly with her thumb. "Why are you afraid?" she whispered.

"I'm afraid...to let myself love him."

"But why?"

TJ's breathing roughened, and Mare rhythmically patted her cheek in an attempt to soothe her. "What if he turns out to be a monster like our..." TJ gritted her teeth. "Like our father? He does have the same blood in him."

"Sweetheart, you have the same blood in you, and you aren't a monster. I don't think Tom is either. Surely there would have been signs of it by now. He seems to be a caring youngster who wanted to find and meet his sister. That doesn't sound like a monster." Mare kissed TJ's cheek. "You can keep an eye on how he acts here at the ranch. Check him out before you commit yourself," she said. "But something else is bothering you, isn't it?" Mare watched as TJ briefly closed her eyes.

The haunted blue eyes were moist when they reopened. "What if I let myself love him...and then I lose him?"

Mare slid up the bed, put her arms around TJ, and pulled that distraught face against her breasts, leaning down to kiss the top of TJ's head. She felt trembling arms encircle her waist. "Bad things don't always happen," she murmured against the raven hair. She strained to hear TJ's hoarse voice.

"When Lance died, a voice inside my head screamed for months and months. I don't think I could stand that again."

Mare could feel the dampness of TJ's tears soaking through her T-shirt, and she held her tightly, struggling to find the words to help her. "Would you rather not have loved Lance? Or me?"

There was a hesitation, then the embracing arms strengthened their hold on her. Mare could feel TJ's hard swallow and the shake of her head as she moaned, "Oh, God, no. You two are the best things that ever happened to me."

Mare dotted TJ's head with kisses. "The only safe way to protect your heart from being wounded is to build a wall around it and never let anyone in. But then, you're only half alive. Love's best when it's shared, and that means breaking down the wall and trusting that your family and friends will help protect you." Mare's hand caressed TJ's head for a long time, as they lay clasped together. She had just begun to drift off to sleep when TJ's velvet voice stirred her one more time.

"Mare?"

"Hmmm?"

"Thank you."

Mare fell asleep with a feeling of peace as her body welcomed TJ's good night kiss against her breast.

Chapter
Twenty-five

"ATLANTIC CITY? YOU could go anywhere in the world, and you want to go to Atlantic City, New Jersey? In the off season, no less?" TJ sat in her office and peered at Paula and Erin. They had just completed the weekly report on the ranch and packing plant and had switched to a discussion of their vacation plans. "I thought you were kidding when you said that last week. I still don't get it."

"Atlantic City is perfect for us," Paula said. "Besides, it's our vacation. We can go anywhere the hell we want."

Erin jumped in, forestalling any possible retort. "We've talked it over for a month now, and that's what we decided. We've been to a lot of plush resorts in a dozen cities, and they were fine, but this time we just want to relax and enjoy ourselves. I like beachcombing and museums, and Paula likes to gamble and hit the nightspots. So we figure Atlantic City makes a nice compromise. The ocean and the gambling are right there, and three big cities are within driving distance for almost anything else we would want to do."

"You don't even have to get in a car for some of the things I want to do," Paula said. She and TJ traded lecherous grins, complete with waggling eyebrows, and Erin annoyed herself by blushing.

"You don't have to go to Atlantic City for that," she said primly. "Might as well save some money and just stay home, if that's all you're interested in."

"Yeah," TJ said. "You could put one bucket of water and one of sand right next to the bed and just dip your hand in each one once in a while. And you could use a fan for the sea breeze. Close your eyes, and you'd think you were at the ocean. You wouldn't even have to get out of bed."

"Oh yeah." Paula nodded vigorously.

Erin made a face at them, then Paula leaned from her chair and took hold of a lock of Erin's curls. She pulled it to her nose and sniffed. "Ah, sweetheart, but I want to smell the ocean on your hair and trace the tan line around your swimsuit." She moved teasing fingers across Erin's breast and had her hand smacked by her red-faced partner.

TJ covered her mouth, trying to stifle a laugh, but her jiggling body gave her away.

"Mare!" Erin hollered. "Come here. I need help!"

Mare came running in so fast, she almost fell when she tried to stop. "What? What's wrong?"

"Oh hell, Mare, I didn't know you were actually here. Nothing's wrong. These two are just feeling oh-so-cutesy-sexy, and they're ganging up on me."

"I just got in. What have you two been doing?" Mare looked from TJ to Paula, and neither one would meet her eye. They cast totally innocent looks at each other and sucked in their lips to keep from laughing. "Okay," Mare said, "you can stay in here and torment each other. Erin and I are going to have some ice cream."

Erin jumped up and put her arm through Mare's. "Sounds good to me. Let's go."

"And these two inconsiderate oafs can't have any until they apologize," Mare said as she and Erin left the room. She then stuck her head back through the doorway. "Chocolate mint ice cream." She licked her lips and vanished.

"What do you think?" TJ said.

"That's my all-time favorite," Paula whined melodramatically and placed her hands over her heart.

"Mine, too." TJ whirled her chair around and headed for the door, but Paula got there first and blocked her way.

"Not so fast. You've got to promise something first. No more cutting us up about going to Atlantic City."

TJ pushed out her lips. "You just want to spoil all my fun." Then her face slowly creased into an ornery smile. "Okay, at least I'll promise not to be too nasty."

Paula unexpectedly leaned down and kissed her cheek. "It's great to see you in such a good mood, boss," she said softly.

"Thanks, Paula." TJ sobered for a moment. "Sometimes I actually feel pretty good." Then her eyes gleamed again. "But we have some apologizing to do and some ice cream to eat, so get out of my way." She went flying past Paula, who barely had time to jump away from the door.

THE DETERMINED COUPLE did have to take additional friendly teasing about going to Atlantic City. But sure enough, a week later, off they went for two weeks of fun and frolic. They had been concerned initially about dumping both the packing plant and the ranch responsibilities in the laps of the respective foremen for that long. However, both men had proven themselves capable and trusted, and TJ picked up the bare necessities of overall supervision.

Mare took over all obligations concerning TJ's personal needs, and TJ cooperated by sticking to her regimen and schedule. Sacha was alerted and agreed to be on call, if needed. When arrangements were finalized for the two bunkhouse cooks to fix dinner at the main house on alternating weeks, Paula and Erin felt really free to enjoy themselves without any misgivings.

And enjoy themselves they did. Overnight trips were made to New York, Philadelphia, and Baltimore to visit museums, catch some plays, and partake of the nightlife. Before going on vacation, they had planned a routine for the days they stayed in Atlantic City that worked well in practice. They spent each morning at a different casino, ate lunch there, and proceeded to walk the boardwalk or the beach in the afternoon. Later, they showered and changed and went out to dinner. After dinner, they stayed for a casino show or went back to their room and relaxed.

Today was their next to last one at the ocean resort. They would be leaving first thing in the morning. After breakfast, Erin and Paula returned to the casino where they had won the week before. Erin, not really a gambler at heart, plopped down in front of a slot machine and started feeding it coins. Paula, on the other hand, moved from one game to another, winning steadily.

Since blackjack was her favorite, Paula saved it for last. She focused her full attention on the game, kept winning more often than losing, and the pile of chips in front of her continued to grow. Finally, she looked at her watch and saw it was almost time to meet Erin at the dining room entrance. She cashed in her chips and was surprised that she had amassed more than two thousand dollars.

She stuffed the bills in her pocket and started toward the dining room. As she walked down the aisle past the roulette tables, she mused at the number of players who sat or stood around the green perimeter, mesmerized by the movement of a tiny ball. Suddenly, she was seized with an irresistible urge to try her luck with it. On the spur of the moment, she traded an even two thousand of her new winnings for one-hundred-dollar chips.

She stood at one end of a table, watched the action for a few minutes, and then stacked the chips in front of her and counted them into four piles of five hundred dollars each. What the hell was she doing? She should take her winnings and leave. The money would more than pay back what she had lost over the two weeks. She could go home a winner — not a bad deal, considering most people went home losers. Twice she picked the chips back up to leave, and twice she changed her mind. *Hell's bells, Paula, play the damn game or leave.*

She picked up one stack and looked at the various ways bets could be made. Debating whether to make several different plays on one wheel spin or to make a single play on several spins, she stood there tossing the chips from one hand to the other. She placed the chips on number 26, Erin's birthday. That way, if she lost, she could tell Erin it was her fault. Paula immediately felt remorseful. That wouldn't be fair to Erin. She'd been great the whole time. Paula should play some extra chips for her. She grabbed another stack of chips and set it on top of the first. What the hell, Erin had been perfect. A crazy urge grabbed Paula, and she plucked up the remaining two stacks and added them to the others. Might as well bet the whole farm. Her breath caught as the dealer spun the wheel.

As if in a dream, she watched the wheel turn. It slowed, and the ball kept spinning and bouncing around and around. Why had she done such a stupid thing? Her head went around and around with the wheel. She couldn't believe she had just thrown away two thousand dollars. Erin wouldn't hear about this little escapade. Paula would be in enough hot water as it was for being late for lunch.

Finally, her torture ended when the wheel stopped. The ball bounded and ricocheted erratically then bounced into the slot for number 12.

Paula swung swiftly away, chiding herself for her lack of control.

Snick.

She froze for a split second as she heard the ball move one more time. Get real. What were the odds against it being Erin's number? She took one more step.

"Hey, lady, you won." A pudgy young man grabbed her arm and stopped her forward progress. "You won. Your number hit."

Everything seemed to go into slow motion. Paula's feet weighed a hundred pounds each as the happy spectator slowly turned her around. Bewitched by her good fortune, she let him lead her back to the gaming table.

Suddenly, she was back in real time, and the dealer was shoving her winnings toward her. Number 26! Heart pounding, she let out a shout, threw a fist in the air, and pulled in her winnings. She handed five chips to the man who had grabbed her arm. "That's for hauling me back here."

"Hey, thanks," he said. "Hope some of your luck rubs off on me."

Paula cashed in her chips, and an attendant accompanied her to the office where she had to sign papers and have the income tax deducted from her winnings. When she was handed a check, she couldn't stop grinning. She finally stuck it securely in her pocket, knowing she could sneak it into the safe back at their hotel.

She could just picture how surprised Erin would be. She would tell her after lunch when they were on the beach. Keeping it a secret for a while made it seem even more delicious. She walked back and forth several times in one of the hallways to calm down, but she had a hard time stopping the grin that kept popping up on her face. Finally attaining some semblance of normalcy, she went to meet Erin.

"Sorry I'm late," Paula said, expecting the impatient look that had settled on Erin's face. "I got carried away with the gambling and forgot the time. Forgive me?"

"We'll see about that. I guess I'll have to keep you closer to me if I want you to be on time." She turned and started through the entrance to the dining room. Paula purposely walked so closely behind her that she kept bumping into her.

"Now cut that out!" Erin looked back with a frown. It disappeared when she saw Paula giving her one of her sweetest smiles. "You know I can't resist that smile, at least not while we're on vacation." She lightly punched Paula's muscular arm. "Come on, let's eat and go get changed. This is our last chance at beachcombing."

"Yes, ma'am." Paula pictured Erin on the beach, hearing her good news. A wisp of heat puffed through her body as she imagined the warmth of the hug she would get.

ERIN RUBBED HER arms and shivered. "It's kind of cool out here with this breeze. How come I'm wearing my swimsuit and you aren't wearing yours?" Her eyes roamed the nearly empty beach, seeking treasures to collect. Stooping, she freed a tiny, intricately shaped shell from its sandy prison. Carefully brushing it off, she stood and held it in the palm of her hand, admiring its exquisite contours.

Captivated by Erin's bemused expression, Paula put an arm around her and gave her a quick hug. "I'm wearing shorts and a tank top, so I don't have much more on than you do, but I'm not cold. Has Texas turned you into a wimp?"

"Better not let any Texans hear you say that. I'll be fine once we move around more. It just occurred to me that every day we've come here, you've asked me to wear a suit, but you haven't worn one yet." She placed the shell into a bag Paula wore belted at her side.

"There you go." Paula pointed to her action. "Someone has to carry the bag."

"Oh. Right."

"Okay, so I've been roaming the beach with you practically every afternoon, and I haven't complained once. The least you can do is let me enjoy a little eye candy."

Erin stepped away, cocked her head, and looked Paula up and down. Straight nose, high cheekbones, almost black eyes, and a wide mouth whose narrow lips were so perfectly formed that Erin loved just to look at them. The light breeze swirled tiny feathers of short, dark-brown hair around the edges of Paula's attractive face

Suddenly growing warmer, Erin quickly shifted her look to Paula's extremities, admiring the muscle tone of her well-shaped arms and legs. Two inches taller than Erin's five-foot-seven-inch height, Paula carried her wiry, but shapely, frame with casual ease. Until provoked. Erin smiled as the thought came to mind. Paula was such a softy most of the time, although she got embarrassed whenever Erin said that. And, oh God, how Erin loved her.

"Well?" Paula's mouth curved when she saw the heat growing in Erin's warm brown eyes.

"You aren't the only one who enjoys eye candy, you know." She stepped nearer Paula and murmured, "You want to cut this beachcombing short?"

"No, no, no." Paula took Erin's hand and pulled her along beside her as she started walking. "This is your last day, and I don't want to hear afterward that I seduced you out of it." Still moving, she pulled Erin in closer and kissed her cheek. "But keep that thought for later."

They continued on hand-in-hand until Erin found another shell that struck her fancy. She cleaned it and put it in the bag, and Paula said, "What are you going to do with all the shells you've collected?"

"You might have noticed that I've concentrated on small ones. I'm going to polish them, put them in a decorative jar, and put them in our bathroom. I think they'll look great in there, don't you?"

"Whatever you want is okay with me." Paula ruffled Erin's curls.

"Okay, how about if I fill the jar with maggots?"

"What?"

"Or maybe, cow flop."

"Horse shit!"

"Okay, I can work with that. Heaven knows we've got plenty of it."

"No way. Are you playing some kind of game?"

"Well," Erin said with her eyes twinkling, "you said anything I want is okay with you. I just was testing to see if there were limits on that statement."

Paula looked at her in mock disgust. "I think I'll go back to the casino and feed them some more of my money."

Erin grabbed her hand. "Did you lose much today? I know you were a little ahead, but did you play it all back?"

"No. I have something really great to tell you. I won." Paula spread her arms wide. "As a matter of fact, I won big."

"Wow! Where is it?" Erin searched in the nearer pocket of Paula's shorts but found nothing.

Paula turned so she could reach into the other pocket. "Try this one."

Erin did, but again she came up empty. She stomped her foot on the sand. "Why are you telling me to look in your pockets when there's nothing there?"

"Because that felt sooo good." Paula dodged as Erin poked at her with a finger.

"So you were just kidding about winning big?"

"No." Paula crossed her heart. "I really won big."

Erin grabbed her arm and shook it. "Stop teasing. How big?"

"I won seventy thousand dollars."

"How did you...?" Erin's voice failed her.

"Well, I kept winning all morning long, and when it was time for lunch, I cashed in my chips. On my way out, I walked past a roulette table, and I just got this urge to play your birthday number. I changed the money back into chips, put it all on number 26, and it won!"

Erin grabbed Paula's other arm and danced her around in a circle, ignoring the inquisitive looks of the few people on the beach. "That's wonderful! I'm so happy for you."

"You mean happy for us. This belongs to both of us." Paula's voice lowered. "It was your number I played. I always knew you were lucky for me. Now I have actual proof."

Erin's eyes filled, and she gave Paula a huge hug.

"THIS IS OUR last night." Erin snuggled closer to Paula in their bed. "I wish it didn't have to end. Spending these two weeks alone with you has been heavenly."

Paula pulled Erin's body over her own. They smiled at each other, and Erin nuzzled her lips into Paula's neck, savoring her taste and scent.

"You think we'll always stay with TJ?" Paula startled herself with her own question. Although it had passed through her mind at odd moments, she had never asked it of Erin. She knew that Erin had a special love for TJ, dating back to their first meeting. Paula also admitted that she would go along with whatever Erin decided to do. She loved and respected both women and would never purposely drive a wedge between them.

Erin's lips and tongue stilled, and she lay in silence for a few moments. "I don't know. I really haven't given it much thought. Do you have a problem with our living there?"

"Nothing major. But you said it yourself. These two weeks alone together have been great. Maybe it's time to think of getting out from under TJ's wing and having our own home."

Erin rolled off Paula, faced sideways, and propped her head on one arm. "You know I can't leave TJ as long as she needs us. I love her more than anyone in the whole world except you, Paulie. And you love her, too."

"Yeah, I love her," Paula said with a shake of her head. "But I don't always like her."

"That's because you're too much alike. Both of you are contrary, cantankerous mule-heads when you get crossed. You need to work on being able to disagree with each other without fireworks."

"Too true, my love. But I'm not talking about moving away or anything like that. I don't want to leave TJ while she needs us either. I was thinking more along the lines of buying a home of our own in the same area. That way, TJ and Mare would have their home, and you and I would have ours."

Erin chewed her bottom lip. "I'll give that some serious thought."

"You do that, sweetheart." Paula rose up and kissed Erin's tempting lips. "But let's forget about that for now. If you remember, before we came on this vacation, I talked about pursuing a tan line." She lightly pushed against Erin, pressing her back down on the bed.

"So that's why you insisted I wear my swimsuit while we combed the beach. You're a devious woman."

"Well, it's too cool to go swimming. I had to think of some way for you to get that tan line. For two weeks, I've been looking forward to tracing it. Like this one across your chest." Paula lowered her head and began playing her mouth along the demarcation above and below Erin's breasts. Erin breathed sighs of pleasure, which turned into little gasps when Paula detoured for a while into more sensitive areas. "And this one your bikini left across your stomach." Paula pushed her body further down the bed and started nibbling the next tan line while her fingers visited the areas that she had just traveled.

Erin clutched a handful of Paula's hair and ran her other hand in an ever-increasing tempo up and down Paula's back. Erin's legs drew up as mouth, tongue, and teeth crept tantalizingly along her stomach and Paula's free hand touched her inner thigh. When she reached Erin's hip, Paula paused and laid her head against Erin's abdomen, slowly working her cheek and chin back and forth against the smooth, heated skin.

"Paulie," Erin whispered thickly, "you missed a couple of...lower tan lines."

"Oh, no," Paula murmured, "I'm just building up my energy." With that, she resumed her pursuit with renewed vigor, urged on by the cries of her writhing lover.

Chapter
Twenty-six

TJ AND MARE were in the midst of eating breakfast when Paula straggled in, grabbed a mug of coffee, and sat catty-corner from TJ at the island.

"Tough to get up the morning after returning from vacation, huh?" Mare said.

"Yeah it is," Paula said. "Glad we allowed for an extra day at home before having to report to work." She glanced at TJ, who merely returned the look, her tight lips evidencing that she was in some discomfort.

"Yeah, thank goodness we don't have to worry about anything until tomorrow," Erin said as she entered and plopped next to Paula. She leaned into Paula's shoulder and blazed a dazzling smile at her. Paula pushed her untouched mug over to Erin and rose to get another. "Thanks, honey," Erin said. "My brain isn't back in gear yet."

This prompted a chuckle from Mare. Even TJ showed a small smile as she cut a piece of sausage and popped it into her mouth, chewing mechanically.

Mare looked from Paula to Erin. "Have you guys given any thought to how to spend your winnings?" Erin gazed toward Paula, who shifted in her chair. Paula glanced quickly at TJ, then at Mare, then at the island's surface, and back to Mare.

She hitched a shoulder in studied nonchalance. "We thought we might start looking for a home of our own. Our winnings will make a nice down payment."

TJ's forkful of pancake stopped short of her open mouth and hesitated for a long moment before it continued its journey. She laid the fork down next to her plate as though she had lost interest in eating, and her lips grew tighter even as she chewed. She picked up her coffee mug and washed the food down with a swallow.

Mare jumped into the moment of silence before it grew noticeably long. "Really? I didn't know you were thinking of moving out."

Erin seemed a bit flustered. "We don't know for sure that we are. Honest. It's just something that occurred to us when we won the money. We're just tossing the idea around."

TJ dabbed her mouth with a napkin, then folded it and placed it next to her plate, smoothing it down several times with her long fingers. She spoke in a low voice, without looking up. "I guess I should be glad you've stayed here as long as you have." Her gaze came up and locked on Erin's. "It can't be much fun having to take care of me every day."

Erin reached out a hand, "TJ—"

"Jesus H. Christ!" Paula jumped up and started pacing as everyone's attention switched to her. "We're not talking about running out on you. I couldn't even if I wanted to—Erin would never leave you." Paula stopped and rubbed the back of her neck, then lifted one shoulder. "Actually, I never would either. What kind of friends do you think we are? We both..." Paula's lips pursed as she struggled to get the words out. "Aw, shoot, TJ, we both love you." A red flush of embarrassment moved slowly up Paula's tanned cheeks, as TJ's eyes softened, then grew moist.

Paula hurriedly sat back down, put a hand on TJ's arm, and gazed pointedly at her. "We'll be honored to take care of you as long as you want us to, and that's a promise." She patted TJ's arm, then clasped her hands together. "We're talking about buying a home close by where we can still be available whenever you want us."

TJ worked her lips back and forth. "You're not happy here? You can have the whole second floor if it's privacy you're looking for."

Erin spoke up. "Of course, we're happy here. Who wouldn't be? It's not really a privacy issue. It's just that this is your house, and we'd like to have one of our own."

"'A man's home is his castle,'" Mare quoted.

"Exactly," Paula said. "I think we're ready to have our own castle. This one is yours and Mare's."

"You say you'll still be available?" TJ tugged an earlobe. That question lightened the heavy atmosphere considerably. A flicker of amusement crossed TJ's face when sighs of relief issued from three throats. "What? I'm not really the ogre you try to make me out to be."

Mare slipped an arm around her shoulders and kissed her cheek. "We know you aren't." Then she pulled away with a twinkle in her eye and said, "At least not today."

TJ narrowed her eyes and waggled a finger, pretending to threaten Mare. "You are going to get..." She hesitated, knowing the comeback that was waiting on Mare's lips. "Maybe I should say you are *not* going to get it." Mare made a cute crestfallen look.

"Of course we would always be available," Paula said through the laughter. "We sure wouldn't want to miss too many moments like this one. We figured we could eat breakfast at our house, then be here early in the morning of each weekday to help with your exercises. We can still help with lunch and supper if we're here, and go home in the evenings. And we'd have our weekends free unless you particularly needed us."

"Sounds like a plan. Keep me posted, okay?" TJ said. "Now, you gals might not have to work today, but I sure do. Will you be here for lunch?"

"Yeah, we will," Erin said. "We plan to just laze around today, maybe ride the horses, maybe not." She looked up at Mare, who had risen from her seat. "We'll take care of lunch today, Mare. You go ahead about your business."

"Great. Thanks."

TJ backed away from the island, turned around, and started for her office, with Mare following. Mare trailed her into the room and waited for TJ to place herself behind her desk. She walked over to her and kissed the top of her head.

TJ looked up, smiling. "What was that for?"

"For keeping your temper with Paula and Erin when I know you're in pain. I was afraid you might lose it, but you didn't, and I'm proud of you for that."

"Paula kind of blindsided me with that idea. I had a bit of a struggle there for a minute."

"I know, but you controlled it." Mare moved behind TJ, pushed aside her hair, and started a gentle neck massage.

"Ummm, that feels good." TJ leaned back into the warmth of Mare's hands and closed her eyes, relishing the tingle that Mare's touch transmitted through her body. "Then I figured that our having this place to ourselves in the evenings sounded pretty enticing, so why should I stand in their way?"

"You rascal, you." Mare lifted TJ's hair and kissed the back of her neck.

"Yes!" TJ's eyes flew open. "That's the kind of massage I want. All over my body."

"Oh, no, you don't," Mare said with mock sternness as she walked back to TJ's side. "I have to get to work soon and so do you."

TJ lifted a hand, and Mare slid hers into it. "What would you think of my giving Erin and Paula a piece of ground to build a house on? I want to do something nice for them. I owe them a lot."

Mare leaned against the edge of the desk and clasped TJ's

hand in both of hers. "Honey, I'm not sure that's such a great idea, not at the moment, anyway. I think it would be more satisfying for them to make their own way with this plan."

"But if they want to stay nearby, what could be better than to build here on the ranch? Besides, this place is so big, they won't be able to find any spot near enough that isn't part of Meridian ranch. Nearest other place would be the farm across the road, and nothing's for sale there."

Mare considered how she could help TJ understand the point she was trying to make. "Look, you have control of a huge corporation. You can pick up the phone and make a decision that could have an impact on the lives of hundreds of people. The rest of us don't have that kind of power. We only have power over some of the decisions that have an impact on our own lives. Can you see that?"

Mare waited for TJ's nod, then continued. "Building their own home is a decision that should belong just to Paula and Erin. You don't have to rescue them. The rest of us need to keep out of it unless they ask for our opinions or our help. If you offer the ground now, it will look like you're trying to take over management of their idea. Sort of turning it into a Meridian project, instead of letting it be a simple home building. They deserve a chance to do this for themselves."

"But I only want to give them a piece of ground. Why would they feel I was trying to manage it?"

Mare lifted a hand and combed her fingers through the raven bangs that always tempted her touch. "You just have no idea of your power of intimidation, have you?"

"Well, yeah, I do." TJ's lips hitched into her usual lopsided grin. "But I use that in the boardroom and sometimes at the hospital. I didn't intend to use it here at home. I don't try to intimidate my friends."

Mare tilted her head and elevated an eyebrow, skepticism painted on her face in bold strokes. "Oh, really?"

TJ gave a short laugh. "Okay, so I do sometimes. But not this time. I'm not planning on intimidating Paula and Erin into doing anything."

"Good. So, you'll let them call the shots. Just kind of hang back in reserve, and if they need reinforcement, let them ask for it. Okay?"

"Okay, I can do that. It's just that I want to help—"

Mare silenced her with a finger against her lips, then removed the finger and waggled it in time with her shaking head.

"Okay, okay, I surrender." TJ released Mare's hand and thrust her bent arms halfway into the air.

Mare chuckled and pushed her arms down. "No, don't surrender. You're the reserves, remember?"

"Right." TJ crossed her heart with her right index finger. "Silent, until called upon."

"Exactly." Mare looked at her watch. "Whoops, I have to get moving. I have a couple of calls this morning. I don't know if I'll be here at lunchtime or not, but at least with our travelers home, you can eat on time today."

"No problem, except I'll miss you." TJ tilted her head for Mare's kiss, and they hugged. "Hurry home."

"You know I will."

TOM SAT IN Bill Jacobs's empty office with his elbows propped on the desk and the phone pressed against his ear. He had been happy to hear from his mother, and they'd had a long and cheerful conversation. Now, Tom had a favor to ask. Picking up a discarded pencil, he began to tap it on the desktop.

"Mother, can I ask you something? I'm really happy working here on the ranch. The men have accepted me, and I'm beginning to feel more confident about my decisions. That's something I needed after making such a mess of things with you and TJ. I wondered if I could talk you into letting me stay awhile longer, maybe start college in the fall semester next year? I'd still be younger than most of my classmates."

He closed his eyes and grimaced as his mother reminded him of their earlier agreement. "Wait, wait, please," he said. "You know how important TJ is to me. I wanted to meet her and Lance for years, and I've missed out on Lance altogether. I don't want to miss out on TJ, too. I'm never going to have a better chance to get to know her, to get her to care about me. I want to work on that— having her accept me as her brother—and spend awhile just being around each other. It's been weeks since she learned that I'm her brother, and we've barely spoken. I need more time."

His expression smoothed and his eyes opened, as his mother didn't commit herself but agreed to think about it. "Thanks. Please, just remember how long I've waited for this chance to know TJ. It might never come again." Tom's knuckles whitened from his grip on the phone, but he spoke softly, "Harvard just doesn't seem quite as important to me right now as my sister does. Love you, too. Bye."

Tom hung up the phone and sat in deep thought, his fingers twisting the pencil around and around. He had to get a chance to talk to TJ. He couldn't make up with her if he never saw her. Maybe he could find a way to get her out to the barn when he brought the horses in later today. The snapping of the pencil woke him to his current surroundings. He looked at the broken pieces and realized his active fingers were the culprits. In his mind's eye, he recalled TJ at her desk, speaking with him, her fingers also tangling with a pencil. Maybe that was hereditary. He laughed at himself, knowing he was grasping at straws to show their connection, but his yearning couldn't be denied.

He looked at his watch and saw that it was time to round up Flag and the other two horses and put them back in the barn. With a heavy sigh he rose, tossed the pencil pieces in the wastebasket, and left to tend to that duty.

By the time he had led the horses into the barn and fed and watered them, he had invented a plausible reason for TJ to come to the barn. He went into the tack room and phoned the house, asking for Miss Meridian. He didn't feel comfortable calling her TJ without explicit permission. He waited while Erin got her on the phone. "Miss Meridian, this is Tom. I'm in the barn, and Flag has a bruise on her foreleg that I think you should look at. Could you — "

"I'll be right out," TJ said and hung up. Moments later, she wheeled into the barn and crossed the concrete hallway, coming right up to the packed earth of Flag's stall. The palomino had moved to the edge of the stall as soon as TJ entered the barn. She whinnied and bumped her head against TJ's chest, bringing a broad smile to the previously taciturn features. "Hey, girl, what have you done?" She circled Flag's neck with her arms. "Let's take a look at your leg."

"You don't have to...do...do that, Miss Meridian," Tom stammered. He rested his arms on the top of the stall's side and looked at her with trepidation. Even in his anxiety, he admired the picture before him of a beautiful woman greeting a beautiful horse. "There's, um, nothing wrong with her leg."

TJ dropped her arms and stroked Flag's nose as her lips pursed. "More lies?" she asked softly, not yet looking at him.

"I'm sorry." He exhaled a big sigh. "I wanted to talk to you, and I didn't know how else to get you out here." He ran a hand through his hair and licked his lips, and nervous tension suddenly dried his mouth. He had thought he was prepared for this, but she scared the heck out of him. One word from her, and he'd be gone off this ranch without even one chance in a million of ever getting to know her. He struggled not to flinch as TJ swung her powerful gaze onto him.

"You could have just asked to see me."

"I was afraid you'd say no, since you're kind of mad at me right now." Tom's nerves jangled so strongly, he felt like his insides were being flogged.

TJ stared at him for a moment, her face expressionless. "Well, I'm here. Talk." Just then, Flag bumped her again, and she turned back to the palomino with a small spurt of laughter. Looping one arm around Flag's neck in another hug, she rubbed her head against the golden cheek.

Tom was stung by the difference in demeanor TJ showed Flag as opposed to the way she was treating him, her own brother. "People are more important than horses, you know."

His strangled words stirred a resonance in TJ's heart. She turned her gaze back up to him, and pain arced between them. She laid her head against Flag's and continued her caress as she spoke in an emotionally vibrant voice, continuing to look at Tom. "Flag has never hit me, kicked me, or beat me with a belt. She has never belittled me as a person, disapproved my thoughts or actions, or condemned my lifestyle. And she has never, ever, lied to me."

The veiled accusation hurt all the more because of its truth. Tears oozed from Tom's eyes, and he swallowed with difficulty. "I want to make that up to you, if you'll let me. I know I've made some mistakes, but I promise to learn. I've kept track of everything I ever heard or read about you and Lance, ever since I was old enough to know I had a brother and sister. I've fantasized a thousand times about meeting you." He sniffed and wiped his sleeve across his face, but he immediately restored eye contact. "I'm not your father. I'm your brother. I missed out on knowing Lance, but I don't want to miss out on knowing you. I want us to be a family."

The turmoil twisting TJ's thoughts didn't show on her face, but Tom glimpsed a tiny breach in the pain in her eyes. The kernel of hope that he had stubbornly nurtured in his heart slowly began to grow. He walked to the end of the stall and knelt next to TJ, bringing his head nearly even with hers. "All I ask is a chance to let you get to know me. I don't ever want to hurt you. Please."

He felt like TJ was looking into his soul. A long moment passed before she spoke. "I'll give you a chance," she said softly, "but I won't promise anything more than that."

"That's all I'm asking. Thank you." Someone was approaching, and he stood up and dusted off his knees, as Mare came through the barn door.

"Hi." She gave Tom a wave and spoke to TJ. "Supper's ready. I tried to call you, but you must not have your phone turned on." She saw Tom's red-rimmed eyes and felt the emotional tension in the air. TJ seemed subdued, rather than rankled, so Mare turned to Tom. "Why don't you come and eat with us? You've probably missed supper at the cookhouse."

Tom looked at TJ, who said quietly, "Sure, come join us."

Mare and TJ started toward the house with Tom behind them. "Tom?" The velvet voice reached back to him.

"Yes?"

"You can call me TJ."

"Thank you...TJ." A small smile kept pulling at Tom's lips as he followed his sister into the house.

Chapter
Twenty-seven

"I DON'T KNOW," Erin said. "We've looked at everything on the list, but I honestly don't care for any of them." She brought her gaze back from the run-down property on view in front of their Land Rover and turned toward Paula. The real estate office had given them a list of the few houses for sale in the Meridianville area, and they had quickly worked their way through it. Neither one of them wanted something right in town, but with farms and ranches making up most of the outskirts, the number of small places for sale was limited.

Paula began to slowly thump the side of her fist against the Land Rover's steering wheel. Erin watched in silence as several expressions played their way across her tanned features. Paula blew air out through her lips, then turned to Erin with a bleak expression. "What do you think? Looks like we might have to stay at the ranch house."

Erin turned full face to Paula and laid a stroking hand on her thigh. "Not necessarily. We can keep checking. Maybe something will come on the market soon. I do have an idea, but you might not like it."

Paula glanced down at Erin's moving hand. "I like your idea so far," she said, getting an impish grin and a pinch in return. "Ow!" she yelped and smacked Erin's hand away. "I get pinched for saying something nice?"

"Do you want to hear my idea, or do you want to play around?"

"Do I have a choice? Ow!" Paula's leer changed to a look of mock pain as Erin pinched harder. "You're bruising me, woman."

"If you behave yourself, I might kiss it for you later."

"Okay, you've convinced me. What's your idea?"

"Suppose we check out empty lots for sale? If we find one we like, we can hire a builder. It would take some time, but we could have the house we really want."

Paula sank back against the Rover's door, propped an elbow

on the steering wheel, and put her fist against her chin. She sat there silent, gazing at Erin, her dark eyes narrowing and a small twitch pulling at her lips.

Not sure what the look meant, Erin fidgeted and finally broke the silence. "Well?"

Paula nodded as though in deep thought. "I'm reminded sometimes that you do have a brain under that curly mop."

Erin made a goofy grin and crossed her eyes. "I was smart enough to pick you, wasn't I?"

That earned her a snort of laughter. "Too bad you weren't smart enough to get a list of empty lots." Erin pulled a sheet of paper from her breast pocket, unfolded it, and waved it in front of Paula's shining eyes. "Good job, girl! Point the way. Who knows, maybe we'll get lucky." Paula sat up and moved back behind the steering wheel while Erin sidled over next to her.

Erin slid an arm around Paula's waist and kissed her cheek. "I'm already lucky."

"I'd say we're both pretty damn lucky." Paula started the Rover and pulled onto the road as Erin rested her head against Paula's shoulder.

TJ WHEELED THROUGH the hall and into her office. She slid the chair in behind her desk, activated the computer, and called up the daily reports for Meridian Corporation. Within minutes, she had settled down to her daily routine of running a multinational company. In truth, since the accident, TJ had been doing very little with the company: signing off on a few proposals, rubber-stamping certain real estate purchases, reading the interim reports, and just generally keeping herself up-to-date with what was happening. A quick tap to a button on her telephone got her straight through to her administrative assistant, Teresa.

"Good morning, Miss Meridian."

"Morning, Teresa. Please tell Sebastian I want a conference call with him and his department tomorrow. I want some research done on medical centers and resources."

"No problem, ma'am. What time would you like it scheduled?"

"Around eleven o'clock should be okay. Oh, and ask Richard to contact me sometime before that."

"Would you like me to get Richard for you now?"

"No, it isn't anything urgent. Just ask him to give me a call when he has a spare minute, between now and the conference call tomorrow morning. Thank you, Teresa." Another tap to the phone, and the connection was cut. TJ settled down to writing the proposal she had been considering since her return from the hospital.

Around lunchtime, she had no sooner gone into the kitchen than she heard Paula and Erin returning. It was a gorgeous day, and they had asked for the day off to go house hunting. TJ had willingly agreed, glad to have a chance to make up for some of the occasions when her needs had usurped their free time.

She looked out the window and saw Mare's truck come in right behind them. She headed to the counter, picked out four glasses, and was just removing the iced tea from the fridge when the three came pouring through the door, chatting. Erin and Paula greeted TJ, and then left for a moment to wash up before preparing lunch.

"Oh boy, just what I need," Mare said when she saw TJ filling the tumblers. "I would crawl across the floor for a glass of iced tea."

TJ held one up and crooked an eyebrow at her. Mare slinked across the room, making a show of swaying her hips, and kissed her. "Will that do?"

"One more walk like that, and you can have the whole pitcher." TJ handed Mare the glass of tea while a broad smile curved her full lips

Mare hesitated, captivated for a moment by that smile, and then gulped the tea and set the glass back on the counter for a refill. She rinsed her hands and splashed her face at the kitchen sink, grabbed a paper towel, and dried off just as Erin and Paula returned.

"Mare, you and TJ go sit at the island. Paula and I will take care of lunch," Erin said. Mare shook her head in vain protest when Erin nudged her toward the island, and she joined TJ.

"So, sweetheart, what have you been up to today?" Mare tugged on a lock of TJ's hair as she sat down.

TJ put her hand over Mare's and briefly rubbed the smaller one, just for the enjoyment of the touch. "I thought I'd get plans started for the hospital I promised to build in Meridianville. A couple of my resource people are going to call me tomorrow morning, and then I'll really get something moving on it."

"Great. Thanks to you this place is growing quickly, and they'll really need a hospital soon." Mare's whole face showed the pride she felt for TJ's generosity. In a moment, her face turned pensive. "Maybe you could talk to Dad about ideas for a spinal cord injury wing. He might be willing to oversee setting one up."

"That's a good thought. Maybe I will."

Erin and Paula finished putting lunch on the table and sat

down. TJ turned to Paula. "How did the house hunting go?"

"Didn't like them," Paula said with a growl and tore a bite out of her sandwich.

Erin said, "We checked everything on the market, and nothing suited us. They were mostly big, older homes, not really what we want."

"Not even a decent building lot," Paula mumbled around her mouthful of food.

TJ's brows went up, and Erin explained. "We thought we might be able to find a lot and build a house to our own plans, but nothing attractive was available there, either."

"Too many farms and ranches," Paula said. "Not much land left to build on."

TJ looked at Mare, touched her thumb against her chest, and lifted her brows even further until they almost disappeared into her bangs. Was it time for the reserve troops to come marching in? Mare nodded imperceptibly. TJ cleared her throat. "If you want, I could sell you a piece of ground."

Paula looked at Erin and saw her face light up as the idea struck a welcome chord. But Erin, with a nod, deferred to Paula, whose gaze then swung to TJ. "You're talking about a real, honest-to-goodness sale, right?" Paula's tone left no doubt that she wanted to pay her own way.

"Yep. You pick out any areas that interest you, and we'll have an appraiser come in and tell us what they're worth. When we're all satisfied on the one you want, I'll give you a ten percent discount, and that's what you'll pay. How's that sound?"

Paula looked again at Erin, who said, "I like the idea."

Paula reached across to TJ. "Sounds great then. Thanks," she said, and they shook hands. "I bet Erin will have me running all over the ranch picking a spot," she said in a teasing tone.

Erin made a face at her. "Thanks from me, too, TJ. And you forget, sweetheart, I've been running all over this ranch for months. I already can think of a couple of likely spots to show you as soon as we clear off the table."

"Guess I better get moving before you run off without me."

"You guys go ahead," Mare said. "I have a little time before my next call. I'll clean up." The words weren't completely out of her mouth before Erin was at the door.

"See what I mean?" Paula jumped up and followed her.

Mare cleared the table and stacked the dishes in the dishwasher. She turned around and saw a smile on TJ's lips. She walked over, bent down, and gave her a quick kiss. "Pretty pleased with yourself, huh?"

TJ took one of Mare's hands and brought it to her lips. "Pretty

pleased with you, as a matter of fact. You were right about
waiting to make them an offer. I think Paula, in particular, might
have resented it if I had mentioned it earlier. Like me, she
basically wants to be the boss."

"Really? I never would have guessed that about you." Mare
squeezed her lips together, trying to keep a straight face.

TJ pulled on the hand she held and brought Mare closer. She
reached up, slid her hand under Mare's hair to the back of her
neck, and spread her fingers up against her scalp. "That doesn't
mean I always get to *be* the boss. Sometimes a certain green-eyed
gal heads me off at the pass," TJ whispered huskily. She pulled
Mare's head down into a tender kiss of such sweetness that both
hearts were soon thudding.

"Lordy," Mare said when they parted. "You kiss me like that,
when I have to go on a call?" She glanced at her watch. "Like now."
She groaned. "Hold that thought, okay?" She gave a speechless TJ
another kiss. Only this one was a quick good-bye, and she hurried
out the door.

THAT EVENING AFTER supper, Erin pulled a map of the
ranch from the office files and stretched it across the kitchen table.
She and Paula searched for the three spots they had decided on as
possible home sites and pointed them out to TJ, who marked them
with a pencil.

"Three good choices," TJ said. "All of those spots have a few
trees to give you some privacy, but at the same time are within
reasonable walking distance of here." Her lips twitched as she
looked at Paula. "If walking is ever reasonable."

The teasing was well deserved. Paula had two opinions about
movement: why walk when you can ride, and why ride when you
can fly? "Well, that makes them within driving distance, too,"
Paula pointed out, bringing a chuckle from the rest.

TJ folded up the map and reached across to lay it on the
counter. "When I speak to Teresa tomorrow, I'll have her engage
an appraiser, and we can go from there. Okay?"

Erin got up and gave TJ a hug. "Thanks a million."

TJ took the hand that lay against her shoulder and brought it
down to clasp it in both of hers. "You and Paula are moving
toward a new home together, and Mare and I are moving toward a
new life together. We've come a long way from Harvard, haven't
we?"

"We sure have."

TJ's eyes softened as she looked up at her long-time friend.
"The damn road's been pretty rocky sometimes, but it looks like

we've finally reached smoother going." She squeezed Erin's hand. "And look at the great neighbors I'm going to have. Who would have thought it? Do you think maybe you neighbors could join us in the living room for some popcorn and beer? That is, of course, if you make the popcorn. I think I can handle the beer."

"I get the remote!" Paula's shout brought a disparaging glance from Erin and Mare, who then looked at each other.

"How come we never think to yell first?" Mare asked as she reached in the cupboard for the microwave popcorn.

"Maybe because we have better manners." Erin's teasing remark earned her a goofy face from Paula. She shooed Paula and TJ out of the kitchen. "You guys go fight over the remote. We'll bring the popcorn and beer."

TJ PAUSED IN her typing when the phone next to her rang. "Meridian," she answered as she lifted the receiver, wedged it against her ear, and continued typing.

"Hi, Miss Meridian. I have Richard on the line for you," Teresa said.

"Great. But before I talk to him, make a note that I'll need an appraiser here at the ranch. Try to find me someone who knows land values in this area well."

"I'll find someone today and have him call you."

"Thank you. Put Richard through now and remind Sebastian of the conference call with him and his department before lunch."

"Yes, ma'am. I'll get it arranged for you right now." Teresa's voice clicked off at the other end, and Richard came on.

"Hi, Richard, how's the family?"

Richard had been with TJ since the start. He was barely out of management training when they had first met. TJ recognized his potential and took him on as her assistant, showing him how she wanted things run and making sure that his vision for the company matched hers. Within a few months, they were working like a well-oiled machine, and she had given over the running of several sections of the company to him, making him Vice President of Operations. It had really ticked off a few of the older generation employees in the company, but TJ was sure the results that Richard could produce would soon have them eating out of his hand, and she hadn't been wrong. Richard now ran the company in her absence, only drawing her attention to the things in which he knew she'd be interested or those in which he wanted her input.

"TJ, great to hear your voice. Margaret and the kids are good, except that Cindy wants to know why she hasn't heard from her

Internet pen pal for a while."

"Tell her I'm sorry, Richard, and I'll write to her this evening. I've been sort of caught up in things here."

"Ah, don't worry. She knows you've had a lot of things on your plate recently. How's the therapy going?"

"Yuck. It's going, which is all I'm prepared to say on the matter. Which brings me nicely into why I wanted to speak to you. I want to start moving on the medical center I promised for Meridianville. I'm conferencing with Sebastian after this call. I'm going to give him the go-ahead to contact our usual medical consultants and work up a plan, incorporating some suggestions I faxed over to him. He'll provide you with copies of everything once we've settled the major issues."

"Well, our other projects are moving right along, and we definitely have the growth potential in that market. What do you have in mind?"

TJ relaxed back in her chair and stopped typing. "Everything."

Richard paused. "What exactly do you mean?"

"I want a complete wellness center, a hospital complex that will knock the stuffing out of that one we just finished building for Springfield General."

"That's one hell of an undertaking for such a small town."

"Maybe, but that's what I want."

"Okay, I'll work out the budgeting after you've spoken to Sebastian. You do realize we aren't going to see a return on this for quite some time, don't you? The shareholders might not be so pleased."

TJ picked a pencil from her nearby caddy and started tapping her new victim against the desk. "I'm not particularly worried about getting a substantial return at this point. I just don't want to have to make a two-hour drive or forty-minute flight to a hospital every time I need to see someone, and I'm not overly thrilled that anybody else who works for me has to either. And right this second, I don't really care what the shareholders think."

TJ freed the phone from between her ear and shoulder and eased her bent neck straight again as she explained her intentions to Richard. "Meridianville's in the early stages of a growth spurt and has new investments coming into the area. The Town Council has already decided to limit the environmental consequences by setting strict guidelines."

Richard said, "Preserving the cleanliness of the resources will be a big plus for companies looking for uncontaminated places to build."

"Right. Too many suburban enclaves are already overdeveloped and borderline polluted. A fresh, clean area like this is perfect for a large medical center. I want us to start as soon as possible, so that we're well on our way here before another company decides to jump in."

"Okay, I'll get right on it."

"Thanks. Give my love to Margaret and the girls, and tell Cindy to keep an eye out for that email."

"Will do. Take care. I'll get back to you as soon as we get something moving here."

TJ held onto the line as Teresa came back on and channeled her into the conference call she had set up with her Medical Division VP. "Sebastian, I have a little project for you and your wunderkinder..."

Finished with Meridian Corporation projects for the day, TJ pulled her To-Do list from the left-hand corner of the desk and perused it. She ran a pencil mark through the items she had just completed and sat there thinking for a few moments. Her restive fingers tapped the pencil against her pursed lips before jotting a few more notes onto the list.

Finally, she set the pencil down and stretched, reaching first high into the air, then dropping her fists to shoulder height and reaching out to either side, then back again. A growling stomach prompted her to check the mahogany clock on the wall. As her gaze lifted to it, she heard Mare's truck swing around the parking area.

TJ pushed away from the desk and hurried to the kitchen, but Mare didn't come in. After a moment of waiting, TJ wheeled to the window and looked out. There was no sign of Mare. She must have gone around to her office. Now why did she do that? Wonder if she had to go right back out? TJ decided to go ahead and start fixing lunch.

As she mixed a can of chicken-rice soup in a pot, she heard voices coming from the hallway. She set the pot on the range, turned it to low, and wheeled over to the hall. Mare was standing in her office doorway, holding the door wide open, and talking to someone behind her.

As TJ came into view, Mare looked up the corridor and spied her. "Hey, TJ, guess who's joining us for lunch?"

As soon as TJ realized Mare's office door was open, she glanced away, though Mare's body had prevented her from seeing into the room. She backed up quickly, returning at once to the kitchen, her emotions in turmoil. She couldn't work up any justifiable anger at Mare, but she was so disturbed that she had nearly been exposed to a sight of the hated room that her hands were shaking. She clasped them together in her lap, trying to hold them still.

Mare came running up the hall into the kitchen. Slowing to a walk, she moved toward her agitated partner. "I'm sorry."

"You promised to keep that door closed." TJ's eyes were glued to the hands in her lap.

"Yes, I did, and I always have. I didn't realize you would come out into the hall. Be fair about it, okay?" She put her hands over TJ's, pulled them apart, and held one in each hand. Their shaking stilled, and Mare lifted them to her lips for a kiss. "I've brought someone to share lunch with us." She gazed sweetly into TJ's now upraised eyes and tipped her head toward the doorway.

TJ turned slowly and forced a smile. "Hi, Barry, come on in."

Barry had hurried up the hallway behind Mare and stopped at the doorway when he saw Mare slow down. Now he was leaning against the doorjamb, with his muscular arms crossed.

"Hi, TJ. My fault, Mare was holding the door open for me. We wanted to surprise you, but I guess we should have been quieter." He straightened up and entered the room. "Sorry if we upset you."

Mare released TJ's hands, and TJ reached one out to Barry, who lightly clasped it. "Glad you could join us. You're more than welcome. Have a seat at the table. You'll be more comfortable there than at the island." Barry released TJ's hand and sat down. Mare took over the lunch preparations, and TJ wheeled her chair to the head of the table and slid it into place.

Barry turned his chair around to face both women and leaned an elbow on the table. "So," he said, "what's the big deal about the office door?"

TJ's head jerked back very slightly, and she just looked at him for a moment. Then a grudging smile played at her lip corners. "You certainly are direct."

Mare stopped putting the sandwiches together and glanced over at TJ.

Undaunted, Barry's grin turned into a full smile, crinkling his eyes. "Yep, I am. I learned a long time ago that most problems can be knocked down by some kind of direct action, even if it's only a promise to yourself to take care of them. You let them hang around without a fight, and they can take up permanent residence."

TJ looked down at her hands, clasped tightly together on the tabletop, and mulled Barry's rejoinder for a moment. She swept her powerful gaze up and smothered his smile as she pinned him with her eyes. "That room holds some extremely traumatic memories for me. I don't want to enter it, see it, or be reminded of it. Mare and I have an agreement about that."

She pulled her gaze away for a moment. She didn't have to explain herself, but for some reason she felt a need to. Slowly, she brought her eyes back to meet Barry's. "Surely, there are some things in your life that you'd rather not have to face. I've already had my share of them and had to face them down, but with this one, I can do something else. Mare wanted that office, and she got it, but I don't have to be a part of it. The choice is mine, and I choose to turn my back on it."

"Hey, whatever. It's your call." Barry gave a little shrug and said wistfully, "I just can't imagine having a house as beautiful as this without calling every single part of it my home."

Then Barry spoke again, with a nearly perfect diversion.

"You sure made a big impression on Bobby. We took him to the store to get a new red wagon, but he picked a black one with big, rubber-tired wheels, and named it 'TJ.' Every time he gets in it, I keep expecting him to yell, 'Go, go.'"

A laugh puffed from TJ's throat. "I had fun giving him a ride. I'm glad to hear he remembers it."

Mare set sandwiches and bowls of soup in front of each place, then added drinks, napkins, and utensils. She settled across from Barry, who followed her lead as she dug in. They ate in silence for a few minutes, then TJ and Barry got into a discussion about the town fair that had been mentioned at their dinner party.

Barry finished his last bite of sandwich and nodded his head when TJ asked about the Town Meeting. "I've been talking up the idea of an annual fair, and people sounded pretty interested," he said. "At the meeting, I brought it up on the floor, and it was discussed for about half an hour. The consensus was that people would like to have one, but the Town Council decided that the first one would need a lot of preparation and should be postponed until next fall."

Mare had gotten up to clear the table, and as she walked behind TJ's chair, she trailed her fingers across TJ's back. TJ gave her a quick smile before turning back to Barry. "I'm glad they're going forward with the fair but a bit disappointed that they want to wait so long."

"Me, too. I got everyone excited about it, and now they have almost a year to wait. Darn shame we couldn't do something ourselves instead of having to go through the Town Council."

"Why can't we?" TJ said.

"Do it ourselves? I don't think the Council would be too thrilled about us taking over the town without their say-so."

TJ started cracking her knuckles, then grinned when Mare handed her a pencil. She sat for a moment in deep thought, twirling the wooden cylinder around and around. She stopped and fastened her eyes on Barry. "Meridian ranch is a lot larger than the town, and we have loads more free space."

"Have a fair here? That's a great idea."

"Well, maybe not a fair," TJ said. "That's a pretty large undertaking, and the Council is right. It would need a lot of time to plan. But how about a barbecue that everyone's invited to? Meridian would provide the beef, and the people could bring covered dishes to share. That way everyone would be a part of it."

"Super," Barry said. "We could have games for the kids and the adults, too. Maybe even some of the local musicians would add their talents to it."

TJ looked toward Mare, who was leaning back against the counter, her arms folded, listening to the exchange "What do you think, Mare? You up for this?"

"Oh yeah, I love the idea," Mare said. "I'm sure everyone would like a chance to get a closer look at the ranch."

"Okay, then." TJ turned back to Barry. "How about you and Berta head up the planning committee for it? Maybe get some long-time residents on it, too, and get things moving?"

"Berta and I would love to help. Especially Berta — she's a born organizer."

"How soon do you think you could get it set up?"

"Mmm. Maybe six or eight weeks. That sound all right?"

"Perfect."

Mare pushed away from the counter. "I hate to be the party pooper, but we have to get back to work."

"Right," Barry said. He stood up and clasped TJ's shoulder before moving toward the door. "I'll get back to you about this."

"Fine." TJ looked up at Mare, who had walked over to kiss her good-bye. "Will you be here for supper?"

"As far as I know, I will." Mare leaned down for the kiss. "Bye-bye."

TJ went to the window and watched until they left. She wheeled out into the hall and turned toward her office. She hesitated as her eyes fell on the door at the end of the hall, and Barry's words jangled through her mind: *"I just can't imagine having a house as beautiful as this without calling every single part of it my home."* She shook her head but couldn't let the thought go. Why did she ever let Mare pick the one room in this whole place that she couldn't bring herself to enter? It was the heart of Mare's work life, and TJ couldn't share that with her.

With a heavy sigh, she continued into her office.

Chapter
Twenty-eight

"MERIDIAN," TJ SAID as she answered the phone that was preventing her from winning her game of solitaire. She was supposed to be working, but the proposals sent down from Meridian HQ hadn't held her interest for longer than an hour. Mare was out working, Paula was at the plant, and Erin was riding the range. TJ had been forced into playing mind-numbingly simple games to keep amused, especially since Mare had twisted her arm and made her promise not to ride Flag again until Michael had given the okay.

"Sorry, TJ. I didn't mean to disturb you," Gloria Raphaele said.

Immediately losing interest in the card game, TJ leaned back in her chair. "Mrs. Raphaele. What can I do for you?" She was still at a loss as to how to interact with this woman and felt more secure at a professional distance.

Less than a week ago, she had discussed this very thing with Peter at her last counseling session. No matter how she tried, she couldn't shake the feeling that if her father hadn't had another family, then maybe, just maybe, he would have been a more caring father with her and Lance.

She managed to hide that little bit of resentment from Tom and, more importantly, from Mare. She knew that if Mare found out about it, she'd be in for several long chats about how it wasn't Tom's fault or even Gloria's that Thomas Meridian had cheated his first family. She loved talking with Mare, but she knew this was something she had to come to terms with by herself, and Peter, strangely enough, agreed. He did point out, though, that when she had worked through the resentment and had come to terms with her feelings, Mare should be the first person to know, with Tom and possibly even Gloria next.

"You know, TJ," Gloria said, "I see no harm in your using my first name. You are looking after my son."

"Sorry, Gloria, I was involved in something." TJ softened slightly.

"That's perfectly all right. I was just phoning to see how Tom is."

"He's doing fine. I haven't had any complaints from the men, and Erin seems happy with his work."

"That's good to hear. Maybe he's found his niche there until school starts. And what about you? How's the physical therapy going?"

TJ almost dropped the phone she was so confounded by the question. Why on earth should Gloria care whether her therapy was going okay? It wasn't as if TJ was her concern. "Fine. I seem to be making some decent progress. My upper body strength's improving."

"I'm glad to hear that."

"Look, Gloria, while I have you on the phone, what do you think about my arranging an internship with the Meridian Corporation for Tom? I'd like him to see some of the business dealings of the corporation. It would give him a chance to see if he has an aptitude and desire for international business. Maybe he'd be interested in coming aboard when he graduates college."

There was a long silence, broken only by soft, slightly ragged breathing. Then Gloria's voice came through, quietly at first then gathering strength. "That's more than generous of you. Tom has a good head on his shoulders, and I think he'd be thrilled with the prospect of joining his sister's company."

TJ closed her eyes and swallowed hard, trying to overcome the lump that suddenly formed in her throat. What was she getting so emotional about? She was turning into a goddamned wimp. She took a deep breath to steady herself and said, "If you think he might be really serious about moving into this business, then he's going to need a varied work background, and I can give him that. Of course, I'd tie the internship in with his gaining sufficient grades at college. The company offers several placements to different colleges, and in order to qualify, he'd have to maintain the same grades that they require."

"Have you spoken about this to Tom?"

"No, I haven't. I figured it would be best to have your approval for it before I offered him something that you might not want." TJ heard a chuckle on the other end of the phone.

"I appreciate that, but believe me, right now I'd settle for him just going to college. Still, I'm sure with the incentive of the internship he'll be wishing the new semester were here already. Feel free to talk to him about it. If he wants it, then I'm all for it."

"In that case, I will. Was there anything else you needed?" TJ reached toward the stack of pencils in her desk caddy.

"Not really. I just wanted to check on Tom, and I didn't think he'd appreciate his mother phoning the bunkhouse to do it."

"No problem. Feel free to call me anytime. I'll make sure he picks up the phone and calls you this week. I'll present the offer to him before too long. He can call and talk to you about it then."

"Thank you, TJ. Give my best to Mare and to Paula and Erin, too."

MARE SHUT THE door to her truck and paused to take in the glorious sunset. She had had a long and tiring day and was looking forward to relaxing for the evening. After one last glance at the fading colors, she made her way into the kitchen. "Hi, guys," she said as she hung her hat on the stand.

Erin and Paula, who were seated at the island, looked up. "Hi, yourself," Paula said. "Busy day?"

"Yep, too busy. I thought that taking on an associate would lessen the load." Mare settled onto one of the stools.

"Ha! Didn't anybody teach you the first rule of business? More staff equals more work."

"Tell me about it. What about you two? Did you manage to keep out of trouble today?"

"Well, some of us did," Erin said. "Right, sweetheart?"

"Oh, now this sounds interesting," Mare said. "Care to tell me what happened?" She leaned forward, and Paula dropped her head and groaned.

"I'll get you a coffee, Mare." Erin stood up. "Want a refill, honey?"

"I'll give you 'honey,'" Paula mock threatened. "No, thanks, and really, Mare, there isn't that much to tell. I just got into a shouting match at the plant with one of our suppliers who tried to overcharge us. I told him Meridian Corporation didn't deal with cheaters and his company's conduct would be made known in corporate circles. They lost our business, and I got rid of a supplier who could have damaged our reputation. So all is now well."

"Sounds like you enjoyed that little argument way too much, just like another person I know. Speaking of whom, where is TJ?" Mare asked as she received her mug from Erin.

"Where do you think?" Erin said. "I tried to pull her out of her office at four o'clock, but she was having none of it. Teresa was on the phone, and it seemed to be getting a little heated in there, so I got out quick."

"Hell, wonder what's got her riled up now." Mare took a quick look at her watch and noticed it was just after seven. "Well, she's coming out now whether she likes it or not. Has she at least had something to eat?" Erin shook her head. "I'll kill her."

Erin laughed. "Haven't we heard that before? If you do decide to carry out those threats tonight, do it quietly, will you?" she yelled at Mare's retreating form.

Mare knocked on TJ's office door, pushed it open, and leaned against the jamb, staring in. TJ was lying back in her chair, looking out of the window. She had the phone wedged between her shoulder and ear. Her hands were fidgeting with her latest mistreated pencil, and she was totally oblivious to Mare's presence.

"No, Sebastian, I didn't ask for that. Well, change it. That's what I pay you for, isn't it?" The tapping of the pencil became harder. "Are you being obstinate for the sake of it, or are you trying to piss me off?"

Maybe I ought to go calm things down, Mare thought, entering the room. Then TJ burst into laughter.

"Aha, that's what I thought. You'd never get away with that if I were in Atlanta, sonny boy. Just remember I can still get you even from here. Now change that neon yellow back to my cool, calm pastels, and I'll be happy. Good, I'll talk to you later. Bye-bye."

"Sounds like you had a stressful day," Mare said from behind TJ, making her jump.

"Christ, woman, are you trying to kill me?" TJ looked over her shoulder.

"Hmm, well, I told Erin and Paula I was considering it, but no, I wasn't actually going to do it." She leaned forward and kissed TJ's cheek. "What're you up to?"

"Apart from contemplating firing Sebastian and his whole network of cronies, not a lot. You?" she asked, returning the kiss.

"Let me see. I was hoping that by this time I'd be snuggled up or eating a pizza or something. But it seems that my partner decided to work late, even though she promised me she wouldn't push it too hard." Mare walked around TJ's chair and looked at her accusingly.

"I wasn't pushing things too hard. Besides, I played hooky most of the afternoon." TJ tried to stare back but couldn't resist smirking. "Anyway, now that I have a good excuse to stop and play some more, I will."

"Oh, you think you're going to play tonight, do you?"

TJ wheeled forward until her chair was touching Mare's legs, and she took hold of Mare's hand. "You don't want to play with me anymore?" She put the most pathetic hangdog look on her face.

Mare gazed down at her soulful expression. "Ah, hell, what am I going to do with you?"

The hangdog look turned decidedly wicked. "Oh, I could suggest a few things."

Mare laughed and slapped her arm away. "Food, then we snuggle and watch some TV. And then, and only then, will I consider anything else." She turned and walked out of the office with an enticing swing of her hips.

TJ focused her gaze a little lower than Mare's face and felt a spurt of appreciative anticipation before following.

MARE HAD FINISHED her last call for the day at one of the farms on the other side of Meridianville. She headed home through town, stopped at the post office, and was pleased to see a card from Jess.

> *Mare, we finally have a break in the action here. May be home before you read this. Will arrive Monday, about noon. Love, Jess.*

Omigod, that was today. Mare loped outside, dropped the mail in the truck, and hurried over to the grocery store.

Maria Cidone, the young clerk, was behind the counter, and her face lit up when she saw Mare. "Hi, Doc. Did you hear that Jess is back?"

"Hi, Maria. I just got the news. Where is he?"

"He took his mom to Sharlesburg for dinner. He said she wasn't going to work on his first night home. He said if I saw you I was to tell you that he'll call when they get back."

Mare pulled out a business card and wrote the ranch house phone number on the back of it. "Leave this for him, will you, please? Tell him to use this number."

"I'd be happy to." Maria slipped the card under the counter mat.

"Thanks." Mare gave her a wave and left.

WHEN SHE GOT to the ranch, everyone was in the kitchen, nearly finished dinner. Mare gave TJ a quick kiss and set the mail on the counter. Erin jumped up to reheat the casserole while Mare went to wash up. She returned to the kitchen, loaded her plate with dinner, and gulped it down without a word.

"Hungry?" TJ said.

"Lord, I was starved. No matter what time I eat lunch, four hours later my stomach thinks it's dinnertime. Thanks, Erin," she said belatedly and gave her midsection a pat. "That hit the spot."

"No problem, Mare," Erin said. "Glad you liked it."

Mare looked around the table. "Guess what? Jess came home today."

"Jess?" TJ said. Erin and Paula, who had risen to clear the table, looked at Mare blankly.

"You remember. I told you about him. The guy I grew up with. Jess Longwood. My best friend."

"Your best friend?"

"My best *male* friend," Mare said. Oh hell, what if TJ was jealous of Jess? What if Jess was jealous of TJ? Mare had never given either possibility much thought. "I know I haven't told you a lot about him, but he's the one who's been out of town for months doing Web design for some big clients. His mom owns the grocery store."

"Oh yeah, now I remember." TJ cleared her throat. "Will I get to meet him?"

"Don't be silly, of course you will. I'm dying to have you two meet." At least she had thought she was. "I want him to meet all of you. You're my family."

TJ's frosty attitude seemed to thaw a little. "Why don't you invite him to dinner tomorrow night?" she said

"I'd love to. Maybe you could ask Tom, too, and I'll give Dad a call. We could make it a whole family gathering. What do you think?" She swept her gaze around the table. "Everybody okay with that?"

Erin looked at Paula, who nodded. TJ tapped her palm against the tabletop. "That's settled then, providing Jess can make it. I'll line up Martha to cook again."

"Nothing fancy, though, okay? Jess is a real down-to-earth guy. I'll tell him to come in jeans and a sport shirt."

"That's good. I doubt if Tom brought anything dressy to wear, anyway. Make sure you let Michael know, too."

Jess phoned later that evening, still out with his mother. He said he had called the store to pass on a message to Maria, and she had given him the number. Mare was thrilled to talk to him and ecstatic when he agreed to come to dinner the following evening. The chat was short. He had to get back with his mother, but he promised to fill Mare in on all his news when he saw her.

She hung up, her eyes aglow, and turned to see TJ watching her with an odd expression on her face. Mare walked over to her and picked up a hand, enclosing it with both of hers. "He's a very good friend. Nothing more, nothing less."

"Was he ever your lover?" TJ blurted out the words hoarsely.

Mare wasn't offended by the question. She understood it was TJ's insecurity speaking. "No. We love each other but never that way." She raised TJ's hand to her lips and kissed it. "I've been with other women, sweetheart, but I've never been in love with anyone else. Only you."

TJ still seemed uncomfortable, but Mare didn't know how to resolve that. Maybe she'd feel better when she met Jess. Maybe.

EVERYONE WHO HAD been invited to the dinner was coming. Dinnertime had been set at seven o'clock, a little later than usual, to give Michael time to journey from Springerly. And Mare had informed everyone that Jess was coming a bit early so he and she could visit before dinner.

TJ and Erin were in the kitchen, finalizing dinner plans with Martha, when they heard the sound of Jess's truck. TJ turned toward the window and looked out to see a new Dodge Ram come to a stop on the blacktop. A tall man with a blonde, curly mop of hair stepped out and opened his arms just in time to catch Mare as she ran from her office, flung herself at him, and wrapped her arms around his neck. He picked her up, swung her around twice, and set her back down, both of them laughing. They continued to hold each other for a minute, talking away.

TJ's voice sounded ragged. "Doesn't anyone in this county drive a car?"

Erin leaned down next to TJ to look out the window. TJ's hands had clenched around the armrests, her knuckles turning white. Erin reached toward her and rubbed her palm lightly against her tense back. "Hey, honey, relax. He's just a friend, remember?"

"Would you be so calm if that were Paula out there wrapped around him?"

"I see your point. But Paula doesn't go for guys, and Mare doesn't either, does she? Look at the bright side—at least she hasn't kissed him on the mouth." The words were no sooner spoken than Mare reached up, pulled Jess's head down, and gave him a quick kiss on his lips.

TJ's body gave a jerk, then she twirled the wheelchair away to the other side of the kitchen, her face a stone mask. A moment later, Mare entered, her arm in Jess's.

"Erin, this is Jess. We've known each other forever. Jess, this is Erin Scott. Besides being a great friend, she oversees the ranch."

Erin moved to shake his hand, looking up at a rectangular face with bluish-gray eyes, a high-bridged nose, and a narrow mouth stretched into a friendly smile. "Hi, Jess. Glad you finally made it home so we could meet you."

"Thanks, Erin, I'm glad to be back."

Mare turned him toward TJ. "Jess, I'd like you to meet TJ Meridian...my soul mate." That TJ's face was tightly closed wouldn't be obvious to someone who didn't know her.

Jess just stood there, staring. TJ held out a hand and said, "Hello," and Jess reached out slowly, almost as if in a daze. Then he seemed to become aware of his behavior, and he looked flustered as he shook TJ's hand.

"Mare told me you were beautiful, and I figured she was saying that because she's biased. But I was wrong. I mean, she was right, you're gorgeous. I mean..." An endearing blush appeared on his cheeks, and he quickly dropped TJ's hand. "Sorry, I'm not noted for my smooth talking."

His candor was disarming. A grin tweaked the corners of TJ's lips and grew into a smile. "You're doing fine, so far," she said in her rich contralto. "Welcome to Meridian ranch." She heard Mare release a breath and glanced her way.

"We're going to grab a couple of beers and go back to my office. I want Jess to see what I've done with it. Give me a buzz when Dad gets here, okay?"

"Sure, no problem," TJ said, doing a good job of hiding her disappointment.

Mare and Jess started to leave. She introduced him to Martha as the cook came into the kitchen from the dining room and busied herself at the counter.

TJ accepted that Mare wanted some private time with Jess. What was hard to accept was that he would be taken into the room that she wouldn't enter. She pulled her mind away from that thought as Erin put a hand over hers.

"He seems like a nice guy."

"Is that supposed to make me feel better?" TJ arched an eyebrow. "He *does* seem like a nice guy, and I know I'm having an attack of stupid jealousy. It's just..." For the first time in a long while, TJ's constant pain showed in her expression, and she expelled a big breath. "I can't walk arm in arm with Mare. I can't hold her hand and stroll next to her. I can't pick her up and twirl her around. Hell, I can't even stand up and kiss her."

Erin squatted down, leaned her arms on TJ's knees, and looked up into her eyes. "That's true. There are a lot of things you can't do, and we can't change any of that. But there's one huge thing you have to keep in mind that should help you cope with this little attack of jealousy."

"I'm listening."

"When Jess leaves here, Mare stays. And just about the time Jess goes to bed tonight, Mare will be crawling into your bed and snuggling up against you. I suspect you look at your relationship with Mare as her giving you the love you need and want, but that works both ways. You give her the love that she needs and wants, too. If she had found that with Jess, she'd be going home with him. But she's yours, just as sure as you're hers. You need to feel secure about that."

A lopsided grin worked its way onto TJ's face. "Why does everyone else see these things so much more clearly than I do?"

Erin grinned back at her. "Your brain's wired to run huge corporations. We people with ordinary run-of-the-mill brains are more in tune with the emotional stuff. But we'll keep working on you. Maybe someday you'll catch up."

"Yeah, like you guys have run-of-the-mill brains."

Erin stood up and gave her a hug. "Let's go find Paula. She was supposed to check on the supply of drinks."

MARE WAS PROUD of her office, and Jess showed genuine appreciation, giving it a thorough inspection and remarking on how it suited her. He stopped in front of a shelf that held four pictures and picked up one of them. "This is a great picture. What were we then — fourteen? This must be freshman year when I was on the Junior Varsity football team and you were on the high school newspaper. Look, you even have your interview notebook with you."

Mare walked over beside him. "That was the day you were picked to move up to the Varsity team — the first freshman in the history of Meridianville who had achieved varsity status. And I was interviewing you for the school newspaper. Mom took that picture."

"I'll have to get a copy of it." Jess put it back on the shelf and picked up another picture, a formal one of Mare's mother. He reached with his other hand and took the next picture, holding each side by side. "Your mom was a beautiful woman." Then his eyes moved to the picture in his other hand. "But this just has to be your dad. You look just like him. I don't remember ever seeing a picture of him. He died when you were little, right?"

"Boy, do you have a lot of news to catch up on. He's not dead. In fact, you'll meet him tonight at dinner. Let's go sit on the couch, and I'll explain everything."

"Wow. Sure," Jess said. He set the pictures back on the shelf and picked up the last one. It was a snapshot of Mare and TJ sitting on the living room floor, their legs stretched out in front of them and their backs against the couch. Their arms were wrapped around each other, and TJ's head was lifted in a hearty laugh that made her eyes sparkle while Mare looked up at her with a loving smile.

"You really love her, huh?"

Mare was watching Jess's face. She saw him purse his lips and give a small shrug. After seeing TJ's first reaction, she'd almost expected Jess's. "I do. And you'll see why when you get to know her. TJ's had a lot of problems, and she still has a lot of pain, so sometimes she gets pretty edgy. But she has a huge heart. And she's given it to me."

"If she makes you happy, that makes me happy. Even if I don't like sharing you."

"Thanks." Mare gave his arm a tug. "But don't worry, you'll always be my best male friend."

"Guess I'll have to settle for that," he said and sighed melodramatically. He took Mare's arm and moved toward the couch. "Now let's hear that explanation about your dad."

WHEN MICHAEL ARRIVED, he strode right to TJ and gave her a hug and a kiss, which she returned. Even in jeans and a flannel shirt, Michael projected an air of debonair sophistication. TJ took advantage of their few minutes alone to let him know that the project for a new hospital/wellness center for Meridianville had been put into motion. "I'd like to get your input for the spinal cord injury department we intend to incorporate into the plans. Would you consider sitting on our board of consultants?"

"I'd be honored to. Just have your people get in touch when they're ready for me."

"I'd also like you to consider being in charge of the department once the hospital's completed. You could have the latest technology and the best brains we could get together. Money is no object."

Michael rubbed his hands together in a familiar gesture. "Now, that's mighty tempting. I'll give it some thought and get back to you on it."

The mix of people at dinner turned out to be unexpectedly compatible. Jess held forth for a while about Web site designing and entertained them with some tales about the various unnamed companies for which he had worked. TJ, Michael, Paula, and even Tom asked astute questions about his business. He promised TJ to call for an appointment to show her his portfolio.

Michael added a few stories of his own from both the medical and musical worlds. Tom's private schooling had provided him with an education in classical music that enabled him to take part in an animated conversation led by Michael and Mare. Erin, Paula, and Jess were quick to champion current music trends, while TJ sipped her wine and moderated the friendly discussion with an occasional remark accompanied by an uplifted eyebrow.

The emphasis on music led to a natural migration to the music room. Erin and Paula plugged in their guitars, Jess pulled a beat-up harmonica from his pocket, and Michael and Mare took turns at the piano while everyone sang. After two songs, it was evident that Tom shared his sister's singing talent, and the two of them were persuaded to sing a few duets.

Finally, the evening ended. Each guest said good-bye, and the house quieted down for the night.

Mare had helped TJ prepare for bed and was just pulling on a T-shirt, finishing her own preparations. As she approached the bed, she saw a smile curl across TJ's lips, so she sat on the bed before turning out the light. "And what's that cat-that-swallowed-the-canary look for?"

"Just thinking about something Erin said to me earlier today. Did you enjoy yourself tonight?"

Realizing that the subject had been blatantly changed, Mare turned off the light and got under the sheet, snuggling against TJ's warm body. TJ's sigh of contentment melted right through Mare. "I had a super time. Jess seemed to fit in well with everybody, and that really pleased me. Dad obviously liked him, and even Tom was downright sociable."

"He was, wasn't he? I was impressed with Jess. And I had a good time, too."

"Glad you did. I was especially thankful that you and Jess didn't strike sparks off each other."

"Now why would we do that?" TJ grunted as a finger stuck her in the stomach.

"Because neither one of you sounded too friendly earlier today. Though I have to admit it's good for a girl's ego to have two people jealous over her."

This time it was Mare's turn to get a finger stuck in her stomach. "Well, I'm not jealous anymore. At least, not too jealous."

Mare's eyes had adjusted to the darkness, and when she tilted her head back, she could see the gleam of TJ's wide smile. "And what cured you so fast?"

"Something Erin told me."

"That's the second time you mentioned something Erin told you. What the heck was it?" She laid her head back against TJ's breast.

"She noticed that I wasn't being too sensible about Jess, and she gave me a reminder." A quiet laugh rumbled softly through TJ's chest. "She said Jess would leave tonight, but you would still be here in our home, snuggled up next to me." She gave Mare a squeeze and got one back. "And here you are."

"And here I'll always be," Mare said. They lay together quietly and were beginning to drift into sleep, when Mare murmured, "I love you."

Long arms tightened around her, TJ's head moved, and warm lips lightly brushed Mare's forehead. Then she felt the low rumble of the voice that caressed her soul.

"Mmm. Love you, too. Always."

Chapter
Twenty-nine

A COUPLE OF weeks had passed since Jess's return, and he and Mare had managed to have a few short visits in town when Mare's calls took her through Meridianville. Each time, she had made a full report to TJ, hoping to make her more comfortable about their friendship. It seemed to be working, as TJ gradually appeared to be accepting his presence in Mare's life.

This morning, Mare was standing in the barn, watching Tom come across the field. "Hi, Tom," she said as he entered the barn. "I asked Bill to send you over to help me give Flag a bath. You and this horse get along so well, I figured you both would enjoy it." Mare had a bucket of warm water with shampoo already mixed in. Next to it lay a couple of sponges for washing, and a scraper for drying. "I'd like her to look special for TJ."

"Sure, Doc, I'd be happy to help." Tom fetched a coil of rope hanging against the wall. "Better than being outside right now, anyway. Looks like a storm might be brewing. I saw a bunch of lightning bolts zigzagging off to the west." Tom's hand soared through the air, jumping jaggedly to imitate the bolts. "Then ka-boom!" He slapped his hand against the plywood side of an empty stall with a thunderous noise. Everybody jumped, including the horses. "Whoops, sorry," he said, not looking at all penitent.

Mare chuckled as she glanced outside through the back entrance of the barn. Tom was a little less stoic than his sister. "Yeah, I've been hearing it for a while, too. We get some weird weather here. One time you might just see lightning and no rain, and next time there's a downpour with it." She watched the irregular path of several bolts. "I'm not too fond of lightning," she said, recalling the episode when Runny shied and threw her in the mud. "Even the sky looks strange."

"Awesome, huh?" Tom followed her gaze. "We could use some rain." Flag fidgeted as he slipped a rope onto her halter. He led the palomino out of her stall to a post next to the hallway, and tied her to a ring. Paula's horse, Runny, started neighing and kicking the sides of her stall. "How's TJ today?"

"She was a little grouchy this morning, so I thought I'd better steer clear of her for a while," Mare said rather sheepishly. A little grouchy? TJ was a bear at breakfast, and none of them knew why. At least she didn't single out any one person to pick on.

Mare watched Runny's unusual behavior. Erin's placid black mount, Ebonair, also shifted restlessly in her stall but otherwise seemed to pay no attention to the ruckus outside.

Tom walked toward Mare, his expression eager. "Does TJ have a bad temper?"

"Bad?" Mare gave a snort. "Scary's more like it. Let's just say we all try to keep her nice and calm for a good reason." She stuck her hand in the bucket to test its temperature, then grabbed the handle to take the bucket nearer to Flag.

Suddenly, there was a bright lightning flash, accompanied by booming thunder, almost directly overhead. Mare cringed, then tried to make light of her nervous reaction. "Tom, will you stop hitting that plywood?"

Tom turned his twitch into a shrug and slapped the wood again in weak imitation of the real thing. "Wasn't me. I can't compete with that."

Another flash glared and a cracking thunderclap, even louder, made them both jump. The whole barn shook, and a strange rumble sounded in the loft overhead. "What the heck was that?" Tom looked up toward the loft. His jaw dropped.

Mare's gaze swerved up and her eyes widened. Sixty-pound bales of hay slid from a stack fifteen feet above the ground. They tumbled toward Mare and Tom. Momentarily frozen in disbelief, neither moved quickly enough to evade the avalanche. Two bales caught Tom full in his chest and legs. The impact slammed his head into a stall gate. He fell to the floor, unconscious.

A bale struck Mare's shoulder. She stumbled back, and a second bale took her down. Her head smashed into a post, and she plunged into oblivion. More of the dislodged bales piled on top of her. Their weight pinned her to the hallway's concrete floor.

The lightning had demolished the electrical box and charged through the barn's wiring. As it short-circuited wires throughout the structure, the overload knocked out the smoke alarm system. Wires began to smolder, then burn. Tentacles of fire extended toward anything flammable. Flames surged up a wall, hungrily devouring the loose hay in the loft. A tongue of fire licked at the remaining bales, then slithered relentlessly to the roof like a ravenous predator. Ignored—for the moment—were the helpless bodies sprawled below.

TJ SLUMPED UNEASILY in her chair, staring at the figures on the computer screen. The corporation was running relatively smoothly, the ranch was up to capacity, and the packing plant was chugging along at full steam — everything was moving along really well. She wondered when the bad news was coming. TJ grimaced at her own macabre attempt at humor. *Come on, stop looking for trouble. You've been antsy all morning.* With exaggerated care, she put down the pencil she had unconsciously picked up to twirl. Time for a coffee break.

As she wheeled across the hall, a great clap of thunder startled her. Wow! That had sounded right on top of the house. Funny that it wasn't raining. She entered the kitchen, and a bright flash of lightning surged outside the window. Thunder boomed simultaneously, seeming to fill the house, and making the windows rattle. TJ shivered, uneasy that the lightning was so close.

She ate a doughnut, then fixed herself a mug of coffee, stuck it in the armrest cup holder, and moved to the window. She wondered what Mare was up to in the barn. She'd been out there for a while. She probably was keeping out of sight because TJ had growled at everyone this morning. TJ felt a pang of guilt. She sipped her coffee and watched a tendril of smoke lazily emerge from the roof of the barn.

Smoke? she thought, then the word burst from her throat. "Smoke!" She pushed the button on the arm of her chair, and her heart sank as she remembered that Paula and Erin had gone into Meridianville. She wheeled to the island, slammed down her mug, and grabbed for the cell phone. Quickly pushing 911, she shouted to an inquiring voice, "Fire at Meridian ranch. In the barn!" Next she punched in the number for Bill's office. While waiting for him to answer, she tightened her seat strap and hurried over to the door. It took precious, frustrating moments for her to get the door open and maneuver outside. She smelled smoke as soon as she hit the outside air. "Bill!" she yelled as he picked up the phone. "Fire in the barn! Send some men."

"There's only me and Carlos, but we're on our way."

"Shit." TJ tossed the phone into the carrier pocket on the side of her chair and rushed toward the barn, noting with alarm that the smoke was growing heavier each moment. Flames did a devil dance along the roof peak. Wild neighing and kicking warned of horses in distress. Where the hell was Mare?

TJ hurried through the wide entrance and paused to reconnoiter the situation. Bales of hay, some smoldering, lay jumbled every which way in the open hallway, hampering free passage. Flames shot from the roof and loft, generating thick smoke, and in several places, the walls were rapidly becoming involved. Heat steadily built, already drawing sweat from TJ's body. It trickled down her face and chest, dampened her underarms, and made her palms slippery against the metal handrims of the wheels.

A few bales moved, and TJ's heart leaped. "Mare?" Before she could maneuver around other bales, they toppled out of the way, and Tom scrambled to his feet, coughing heavily. Tom was here? "Tom! Where's Mare?" TJ shouted at him, but he seemed dazed. "Tom! Wait! Where's Mare?" Still coughing, he stumbled through the bales to the entrance, just beyond TJ's reaching hand.

Flag pawed uneasily at the floor and neighed. Frightened by the billowing smoke, searing heat, and roaring fire, Runny and Ebonair screamed and thrashed about in their stalls. A blaze spread through the tack room, and exploding bottles and cans lent their sounds of destruction to the clamor. The fire burned off vapors as they formed, leaving acrid remnants to add their stench to the almost overpowering foulness of the smoke.

Fire raged up the walls, bouncing red reflections from every shiny surface in the building, including TJ's agonized eyes. "Mare! Mare! Where are you?" TJ yelled in vain, knowing that the noise level overpowered her voice. The discordant uproar clanged inside her head, heightening her soul-searing frustration. Heat surged against and through her as she searched the area frantically, her heart threatening to burst. Blood surged and pulsed through her brain, shrieking urgency. *For God's sake, Mare, where are you?*

She gasped when her frenzied gaze at last spied a black boot, barely visible beneath the fallen bales. Just as TJ started toward it, a burning chunk of loft flooring dropped onto several of the bales that partially covered Mare, setting them alight. TJ stopped and stared in helpless horror as the blazing debris tumbled farther, landing on the floor near Mare, its flames reaching for her face.

"Mare! Hang on. I'm coming." Her chest heaving for air and eyes running with tears, TJ quickly backed up to the entrance and grabbed a pitchfork from the wall behind her left shoulder. Stuffing it between her body and the chair, she headed toward the mound of bales imprisoning Mare. She rubbed sweat-slicked hands on her pants and retrieved the pitchfork, vaguely aware that her clothing felt super hot. But nothing else mattered. Mare needed her. Fear increased her strength to near superhuman proportions. Straining mightily, she forked up each of the burning bales and, fighting to keep her balance, pitched them away. But she couldn't push the flaming floorboard aside without endangering Mare even more. TJ's mind went into overdrive, racing for a solution.

Two agonizing seconds ticked past, seeming to take forever. Then TJ jerked into action, using the pitchfork's tines to snag the blanket still hanging from the side of Flag's stall. She tossed it over the piece of board and smothered the hungry flames. She swiped at her streaming eyes with her arm.

The raging blaze in the roof sucked at the oxygen in the barn. Hot air streamed across TJ's body and painted painful stripes on her exposed skin. Her sweat-soaked hair and clothing clung to her, providing temporary protection. Drafts drawn in through the open-ended hallway brought brief respite from the oppressive heat.

Frantic to reach Mare, TJ attacked the remaining bales with the fork. She fought like a maniac to move them, heedless of where they landed. Coughing hard, she had to stop often to catch her breath, frighteningly aware that a total collapse of the loft would drop flaming bales onto both of them. On grit alone, grunting with each painful exertion, TJ hoisted the bales, one by one, and furiously flung them out of the way. Finally, Mare was free.

TJ screamed in frustrated anger as another huge section of loft broke off and dropped behind her chair, blocking a clear way to the door. She had Mare free, now what? She looked at the maze of burning bales. No way could she take Mare through that. They'd burn trying to weave the chair through, and there wasn't enough time left to crawl out.

TJ's tearing eyes swiftly scoured the smoke-filled barn, searching for an answer. *Flag can do it!* She wheeled between two of the blazing bales to a singed coil of rope hanging from a stall post, and snatched it down. She dropped it into her lap and propelled her chair rapidly to Flag. "Come on, my faithful girl, you have to help me with this. Mare needs us." She spoke urgently but as soothingly as possible to the restless palomino, as coughing racked her body. The burgeoning heat beat against her and evaporated her sweat and tears. Time was running out. Quickly, she wrapped one end of the rope around her body and tied the other around Flag's neck, then unfastened her from the post ring.

Pieces of the barn roof crashed to the floor, igniting everything flammable that they touched. Runny and Ebonair pounded against their stalls, stung by hot embers. The animals' terrified screaming and crazed kicking, the fire's frightful roaring, and the ominous explosions of bottles and cans created a hellish, demented symphony.

TJ dashed furiously back through the bales to Mare, pulling a nervous Flag with her. She unbuckled her seat strap, thrust herself out of the chair, and dropped onto the concrete. Every pounding beat of her heart pumped hope that she could save Mare. She prayed that dragging her out of there wouldn't make any injury worse. That thought paralyzed her motion for a split second. *Suck it up, TJ. You've got to just keep moving, no matter what.* Hastily, she loosened the end of the rope from her body, looped it around Mare, and tied it tightly. She placed a second loop around herself, then her heart leaped with gratitude as Tom came charging back in. "Tom, get the horses!" TJ shouted and pointed toward the panicked animals.

Tom couldn't hear over the noise, but he saw TJ pointing from her sprawled position, and he trusted her judgment. Without breaking stride, he hurried to Runny. He struggled to put a lead rope on her and move her from the stall, and then he had a fight on his hands. The terrified horse tried to run deeper into the barn, away from the burning loft. Tom dug in his heels and used all of his strength to turn her. Feeling like his arms might pull from their sockets, he finally got Runny headed out the back door into the corral.

Bill Jacobs and Carlos came dashing into the barn. They made their way through the thick smoke toward TJ and Mare. Before the two men reached them, Flag moved.

"Okay, Flag, get us out of here, baby." TJ clucked a command, and Flag stepped quickly through the maze, dragging the two women toward the entrance. Mare and TJ swerved against the sides of some of the bales, but the flames shot upwards, never touching them. Bill and Carlos looked astounded. "Get the other horses!" TJ yelled, as she and Mare went past them.

The two men grappled with Ebonair to get a lead rope on her, then wrestled her toward the back door. Just as they exited, the main roof caved in with a loud whoosh, showering sparks high into the sky. Still hot, the glowing embers rained back to earth. Both horses were outside, and the falling sparks unsettled them even more. Tom tried at first to help out, but soon realized that Bill and Carlos could deal with the spooked horses. He raced around the fully engulfed building to check on TJ and Mare.

"Whoa, Flag," TJ called when they had been pulled across the driveway onto the grass, a safe distance from the inferno. Giving the palomino's leg a grateful pat, she untied herself and Mare. TJ's throat, eyes, and skin hurt, but she feverishly began to examine Mare for injury. "Mare, my God, Mare, speak to me. Please, speak to me," she begged over and over in a raspy voice.

Mare's eyelashes and eyebrows were singed, and her face and ears were slightly burned. TJ shuddered at how near Mare had come to having her beautiful face scarred by the fire. A bump protruded from the side of her head, but when TJ carefully lifted her eyelids, her eyes looked fine.

When the roof caved in and sparks fell from the sky, TJ pulled Mare close to protect her from the burning shower. Reaction to the heart-wrenching tension of fighting to save her set in, and TJ started to cry. "I love you, Mare. I love you. Please be all right. I'll do anything you want me to, if you'll just be all right. Anything." TJ caressed Mare's golden hair and brushed gentle kisses on her unresponsive lips and face. "I can't bear the thought of something bad happening to you." Tears streamed down TJ's cheeks.

The wailing sirens of the fire engines and ambulance caught her attention. She needed to call Erin and Paula, but she remembered that the cell phone was in the pocket of the doomed wheelchair. She dashed the tears from her eyes and lay there with her arms around Mare. Protectively hugging Mare's warm body close, TJ willed their nearness to convey a silent message of love.

The fire engines and ambulance pulled up at the barn and people piled out. The paramedics gently removed Mare from TJ's arms and laid her on a stretcher. TJ accepted a pillow to prop herself up but refused to be put in the ambulance. "No way. I'm fine. You take care of my partner first." TJ looked up at the paramedic. "And let me know how she is," she said in a scratchy voice.

Everyone in the area knew of TJ Meridian, the woman who had revitalized Meridianville. The paramedic looked at her with respect. TJ knew his practiced eye could see that she didn't appear to be seriously injured. He gave in to her demands and joined the other attendant at Mare's side.

Tom ran into the driveway area and saw TJ and Mare in the yard with the medics. Flag was standing quietly off to the side. The palomino, rope still hanging around her neck, nibbled the grass and totally disregarded the commotion of the firefighters.

Tom took a moment to speak to the fire chief to let him know there were no people or animals still in the barn. The chief was incredulous when Tom told him that TJ had entered the burning barn in her wheelchair and used her horse to save Mare by pulling them both out, roped together. Tom assured him it was true, and then hurried over to where TJ lay in the grass.

He squatted next to her. "Are you okay? How's Mare?"

"I'm fine. I'm waiting to find out about Mare." Tom reached out a hand, and TJ, attempting a tired smile, grasped it. "What happened to you two in there?"

"I'm not too clear on that," Tom said. "All I remember is hearing a loud crack that shook the barn, then I heard a rumble. I looked up toward the loft and saw a truckload of hay coming down on us. Then...boom! I was knocked for a loop. The next thing I remember was coming to, out here, and thinking that Mare must still be inside. That's when I went running in."

The medic left Mare's side and loped over. "Looks like the doc's lungs are clear, Miss Meridian. We're giving her oxygen, just in case. She's got a nasty bump on her head, maybe a concussion, and her face is a little singed. We'll know better what shape she's in after we get her to the hospital. But her vital signs are good, so she's probably not in any danger."

"Thanks." Relief flooded through TJ. "And thanks for helping out." The medic trotted back to Mare, and TJ's attention swerved to the approaching fire chief.

"It's going to take awhile to put the fire out, Miss Meridian. But your barn's a total loss. The lightning rod must not have been grounded. Looks like lightning struck the outside electric box. From there it would have traveled right along the wiring, spreading fire everywhere the wires went. That's why it burned so fast." He turned and looked at the men working the hoses, then swung back to TJ. "The roof had collapsed before we got here. There wasn't much that anyone could do. We'll just spray it down until there aren't any more hot spots." He took his helmet off and scratched at his damp head. "And your wheelchair got ruined, too. Sorry about that."

"Don't worry about it," TJ said softly. "We can replace a wheelchair. And you've kept the fire from spreading to the other buildings. Thank you, and thank your men, too." The fireman nodded and walked away. TJ's eyes returned to the ambulance that was just going down the driveway with Mare inside. Tears welled and TJ sniffled.

Tom squeezed the hand he still held. "She'll be okay. They'll take good care of her. Let me tie up Flag, and we'll get you back into the house." He released TJ's hand and stood. He took Flag's rope, patted her on the neck, and tied her to the corral fence. "I'll come back for you soon, girl."

"My other chair's in the garage. Would you get it for me?" TJ asked through a tight throat. "You can go through the house if the doors are locked."

Tom squatted down next to her again. He slipped an arm under TJ's shoulders and one under her knees.

"Whoa! Wait a minute, Tom. I'm as big as you are."

"No kidding? Guess I better be careful, then." He pulled TJ's body against his and stood straight up with little effort. With a great look of satisfaction on his face, he carried her to the house. TJ helped by opening the door, and Tom took her to the living room. He laid her gently on the couch and looked down at her with concern. "Your eyes are puffy and bloodshot, your face is as red as a beet, and your arms are red, too. You really should have gone to the hospital."

"Yes, Mom," TJ said dryly. "Will you bring me the phone, please?" TJ looked around the room. "There's one on the reading table. And don't worry. I'm going to the hospital as soon as I get Paula and Erin home."

Tom shook his head as he handed her the phone. TJ chuckled. "I just got out of the hospital. I'd have to be hurting a lot worse than this before I'd go back as a patient."

"You know, you saved the doc's life."

TJ looked up into Tom's hero-worshipping eyes. "Let's just be grateful that we didn't lose anything but the barn. It could have been worse. A lot worse." She grasped his hand and gave it a squeeze. "You were a big help, too. Thanks." Tom blushed and TJ said, "Well, look who's red now."

"You're family. I was glad to help," Tom said shyly. TJ's eyes filled, and she squeezed his hand again. Tom got even redder. "Guess I'll go get the chair now." He escaped to the garage.

TJ followed him with her gaze, and the affection that she had held back for so long came flooding into her heart. Her brother was a good man. Better than she'd been giving him credit for.

She picked up the phone and closed her eyes for a moment before calling. She wondered whether Erin or Paula would want to hear this pleasant news first. Neither, of course. She opened her eyes and sighed as she pushed in the number. "Paula? I want you guys to come home right away. You're on your way? Great. We've had a little excitement here while you were gone..."

TJ made several other calls: one to Barry, one to Michael, one to a business in Meridianville, and one to the contractors who would need to tear down the ruined barn before starting to rebuild.

ERIN AND PAULA bolted home. "TJ sounded like it was just another day," Paula said. "I can't believe she's really that cool about it."

"We'll find out when we get there, Paulie, so hang on tight." Erin was squeezing as much speed out of the Land Rover as she could and still stay on the road.

Paula noticed Erin's use of her nickname and grabbed onto the seat. Erin only called her Paulie when her emotions were in high gear. She better keep an eye on her, as well as TJ. "That ambulance that passed us must have been carrying Mare. Too bad we didn't know sooner. You could have dropped me at the hospital."

"Yeah," Erin said as they pulled in and parked, "but we'll hurry back."

They dashed into the house and found TJ at the kitchen table. Her head was buried in her arms, and her shoulders were shaking.

Erin rushed to her side, her face screwed up in distress. She put an arm around TJ's shoulders. "We're here, honey, we're here. Please don't cry. Come on, we'll take you to see Mare."

TJ raised a tear-streaked face. "I almost lost her. Just like Lance. I...I couldn't stand that, again."

Erin pulled out TJ's chair, leaned down to put her arms around her friend, and pulled her close. "Mare's not lost. You saved her."

TJ buried her face in Erin's shoulder. "But I couldn't save Lance," she said, sobbing.

Erin bit her lip and tears came to her eyes. She began to pat TJ's back. "Aw, TJ, we were going to forgive ourselves, remember? No one could have saved Lance, sweetheart. It was his time. But you haven't lost Mare." The hand moved to caress TJ's hair. "Come on, let's get you ready to go see her, okay? Maybe you can be there when she wakes up. You'd like that, wouldn't you?"

Gradually, TJ's tears stopped, and she nodded against Erin's shoulder. She raised her head, and Paula handed her some tissues, evoking a tear-stained smile. Erin took the tissues from TJ's hand and tenderly wiped her face and eyes for her. "Blow," she said, holding the tissues against TJ's nose. TJ did as she was commanded. "Better?"

"Better."

Erin patted her shoulder and said, "We'll have you to the hospital in about fifteen minutes." Paula had fetched a washcloth, which Erin used to freshen TJ's face. She kissed her cheek. "Ready to go?"

"I really have to bathe first," TJ said. "I was too shaky to do it when I was here alone." She indicated her body with a flip of her hand. "I'm a mess."

"Do you want me to help you? It might be faster," Erin said.

"If you would, please, at least with the undressing and dressing. That would speed things up a lot."

"Okay, let's do it. And your skin could use some ointment, too. You look like you have quite a sunburn." Erin followed TJ out of the kitchen as she engaged the chair's motor and headed for her rooms.

Paula quickly straightened the kitchen and went outside to look at the barn. Firemen were still hosing it down as a refilled pumper came up the driveway. She sadly surveyed the damage.

Damn! The barn really was totaled. She couldn't picture anyone having the guts to go into a burning building in a wheelchair.

She shook her head. She always had admired TJ's gumption, but that admiration just jumped up a couple of notches. What a remarkable friend. And Paula had threatened that she and Erin would leave her. Paula snorted. Not that Erin ever would, and Paula was finally starting to understand why. Loyalty like that couldn't be bought. TJ should've kicked her butt.

She walked over to speak to a couple of the firemen, and she got a better idea of just what had happened. She was even more awed with TJ's courage when she heard the amazed and respectful way the men spoke of her rescue of Mare.

A catering truck arrived and started handing out sandwiches and steaming coffee, bringing grateful looks to the faces of the tired men. "Compliments of Miss Meridian," one of the women with the truck announced.

The fireman next to Paula turned and gestured to her with his full hands. "Miss Meridian sure knows how to take care of people," he said.

"She sure does." *She sure does,* the words echoed in her heart, *and we'll take good care of her, too.* Paula jogged back to the house as the door opened, and TJ and Erin came out.

The firemen hollered their thanks to TJ, who waved back and thanked them in return. Then she flashed a brilliant smile that lifted everybody's spirits.

WHEN THEY ARRIVED at the hospital, Erin ran on ahead while Paula helped TJ into a borrowed chair and pushed her through the entrance.

In a few minutes, Erin came back. "Mare's still in emergency. They're waiting for x-rays. Let's see if we can get in."

"Oh, we'll get in, all right," TJ said. Her hands were white where they gripped the armrests. When the women reached the emergency room area, they were surprised to see Michael hurrying toward them.

"Just getting here? Me, too. I hopped a ride on a helicopter coming back here from Springerly Hospital. Perfect timing." Michael took TJ's hand and gave it a squeeze. "Give me a minute, and we'll go see Mare," he said. He left for a moment to speak to a clerk at the emergency entrance. He showed his credentials and waved to the women to join him. He walked beside TJ's chair and directed her to the proper cubicle.

A nurse turned and looked at them questioningly. "I'm Dr. Gillis," Michael said, "and the patient is my daughter. How is she?"

"She's still unconscious, Doctor. She has some contusions on her body and mild burns on her face and arms, but unless the x-rays show something, nothing else is evident." She stepped nearer Michael and lowered her voice. "However, we don't like that she's still unconscious. We're hoping she revives soon."

TJ had rolled right up to the bed. She lifted Mare's hand to her lips, then held it against her cheek, before lowering it to remain clasped between hers.

"Thank you," Michael said to the nurse. He walked to the other side of the bed, leaned down, and kissed Mare's forehead.

Erin and Paula touched Mare's shoulder, and everyone took a seat. TJ never left Mare's side, holding her hand and murmuring to her. Some time passed, and still the x-rays hadn't been returned.

"She's waking," TJ said as Mare's eyelids fluttered.

They came open, and Mare blinked. Finally her vision focused on TJ. "Hi there, beautiful. Is something wrong?"

"Not now." TJ pushed the words through quivering lips.

In spite of her obvious pain, Mare struggled up and reached for her as TJ's tears began to flow.

Chapter
Thirty

MARE HAD A slight concussion and a badly bruised body, but the x-rays showed no serious damage. Her position on the barn floor had saved her from the worst of the smoke. She was released from the hospital the next day but not before a steady stream of visitors had come to see her, including Jess, who rushed to her side as soon as he heard that Mare was hurt.

Of course, the most important person in her life had been there when her eyes first opened, but she was gratified to see that so many people cared what happened to her. Everyone was treating her like a hero because she got caught in the fire, but TJ was the real hero. She had risked her life to save Mare. Mare was somewhat awed by that, and the knowledge filled her heart until she thought it might burst.

TJ told her what had happened to her and Tom after the bales hit them. And she'd given Mare the bare-bones story of the fire and rescue. Mare subsequently learned that, after phoning Paula and Erin, TJ had called Barry to come check out the horses. Bill, Carlos, and Tom had taken them to the working barn near the bunkhouse where Barry had treated them for superficial burns. Next, she had called Michael to inform him of Mare's accident and rescue. Then she had called the caterer to feed the firemen, and lastly, TJ had called the contractor to start at once on building a new barn.

TJ's bloodshot eyes and reddened skin had told Mare more about the rescue effort than mere words could. That, and the fact that she had released Mare's clasped hand only when forced by necessity. Even today, she had held it until Mare needed to dress to go home. Once they were settled in the van, TJ immediately pulled her into an embrace and hadn't let go of her since.

As they motored up the driveway toward the house, Mare was saddened to see the blackened skeleton of the barn, pieces of its stucco shell spread across the ground. Men were already tearing it down. She shivered. She would have died in there, had it not been for TJ's courageous rescue. TJ could have died, too. But that didn't stop her.

TJ had Mare clasped tightly against her side, but she squeezed even tighter when she felt Mare shiver. "Scary, huh?" TJ murmured and kissed the top of her head.

Mare nodded. She sucked hard on her lips, trying to quell the tears threatening to spring forth, but the tears won. She turned toward TJ, and the arched eyebrow and lopsided grin unseated the last vestiges of her composure. She buried her head against TJ's neck and sobbed. Long arms wrapped completely around her shoulders as she slipped hers around TJ's waist. The warmth and security of being in TJ's arms worked its magic, and Mare's sobbing subsided. Their embrace was such a comfort to both of them that neither woman moved when the van stopped.

Paula got out to retrieve the new wheelchair from the back as Erin turned to Mare and TJ. "Hey, guys, we're home," she said.

TJ's arms tightened, and the slight hoarseness in her velvet voice tugged at Mare's heart. "I've been home ever since we picked up Mare."

"God, that is so beautiful," Mare managed to blurt out before the tears came again.

MARE CRAWLED GINGERLY into bed and sighed as she snuggled her aching body up against TJ's firm form. They lay quietly for a few moments, enjoying each other's warmth. "TJ?"

"Hmm?"

"Tell me what really happened in the barn."

"I did tell you. You were knocked over by some bales of hay. I went in and found you and brought you out—"

"Wait. Those are the parts I want to hear...in detail. The 'went in and found you and brought you out' parts. Paula told me some of the stories she heard from the firemen about the inside of the barn, and when Tom came by this afternoon, he told me about bales of hay thrown to hell and gone all over the hallway. He said they were spread away from me and farther apart than they could have fallen, and you must have moved them somehow. So, how did you do that and get me out of there? Please, tell me."

"All of it?" TJ asked and made a face.

"All of it," Mare said. "I'm disappointed that I was unconscious through the whole rescue. I know you did something pretty fantastic, and I want to hear about it. I think it's really exciting."

"Hmm." TJ pulled her head away and looked at Mare.

Exciting? More like heart-stopping. But she had promised to do anything Mare asked. She just hadn't expected to be called on it so soon. TJ's self-deprecating smile told Mare she would be rewarded. "Okay, I'll tell you."

TJ leaned her head against Mare's again and began her tale. Her descriptions were plain and unadulterated, but that made listening to the situation even more terrifying. Mare sucked in her breath several times during TJ's narration but didn't interrupt until she felt TJ's tension increase. She told of freeing Mare, then how the loft bits fell behind the wheelchair, and how the same bales she had flung away blocked her exit. "It was my own stupid fault we were trapped."

Mare patted her side. "You were frantic to get those things off me. It's amazing you could even move them. They'd be impossible to aim."

"I was trying so hard not to fail you...like I failed Lance."

Mare pushed away from TJ and sat up outside the covers, tucking her legs under her. TJ looked up, startled. "You did not fail Lance. All of us keep telling you that. When are you going to believe it?"

TJ looked away and bit her lip. Mare put her fingertips against TJ's jaw and turned her head back until TJ's eyes met hers. "Answer me this. What happened at the time you and Lance were attacked that you could have changed?"

"I should never have talked him into coming with me," TJ said thickly.

"That doesn't count. People are always talking each other into doing things. It wasn't the first time, was it?"

"No," TJ said slowly.

"But this time something bad happened. And you didn't foresee that. Who could have? Can you see into the future?"

"No."

Mare was distracted for a moment by the shape of TJ's lips when she drew out the word "no." She shook her head and blinked to resume her focus.

"Let me ask you again, did you have any real chance to save Lance? You've been telling me of your superhuman effort to save my life. I'm sure you would have made a superhuman effort to save Lance, too. Did you have that chance?"

TJ thought about it for several long moments. "No."

"Then you can't honestly keep blaming yourself. It isn't fair to you. Do you think you can ever admit that and forgive yourself?"

TJ's gaze moved away for a full minute and then came back. "I think maybe I can. Yes."

"Oh, TJ, that's wonderful."

TJ smiled at her glowing face. She'd save Mare a hundred times a day if she had to. And she knew, at last, the same was true of Lance. She would have saved him if she could. But she never had that chance. And it wasn't her fault. TJ's whole body relaxed as she took a deep breath and let it out slowly.

"Sweetheart, will you do me a favor?" Mare was using a wheedling voice, and a dark eyebrow arched up in question. "Would you say 'no' for me just one more time?" TJ frowned comically and Mare said, "Just do it, okay?"

"No," TJ said, starting the drawl, and soft lips found hers as she completed the word. She entered into the spirit of things and returned the kiss.

"Umm." Mare slipped back under the covers and into TJ's arms. "Now, let's hear the rest of this rescue."

"First time saying 'no' ever got me a reward," TJ said. Then she finished the tale, describing Flag's part in pulling them out between the burning bales. "It was a miracle that Flag didn't panic. Almost as though she sensed we needed her. And she didn't even get burned, just singed a little." TJ touched Mare's nose with a forefinger. "Kind of like you did."

"Yeah, and you, too," Mare said. She moved up and lifted her body over TJ's until she could put her bent arms against the mattress on either side of TJ's head. They looked lovingly at each other. "TJ, you are one fantastic woman, you know that? You risked life and limb to go into a burning building after me. You saved my life."

"You are my life," TJ whispered. "I'd risk anything for you." Her arms closed around Mare, who uttered a small cry and sank against her. Their bodies connected, and their lips met, confirming the union of their souls.

EVEN THOUGH A number of days had passed since Mare was almost lost, TJ found that she still hated to let her out of her sight. She sat at her desk this morning pondering this strange feeling. She knew Mare was just down the hall, in her office. What could hurt her there? TJ might argue logically that her fears were unfounded, but her emotions defied any attempt to quell them.

Sighing, she dragged the tablet closer and willed her thoughts to concentrate on the list in front of her. They had several items in progress at the moment. She ran down the list, going over each project. First, the more immediate ones: new barn being built; barbecue at the ranch being organized by Barry and Berta; Paula and Erin's new home still in the planning stages. Then, the longer term ones: new medical center, including a spinal cord injury wing. And maybe, just maybe, they could manage to finally get a swimming pool when the barn was finished. TJ penciled it in.

She balanced the pencil between her index and middle fingers and drummed its eraser against the desktop. And Tom. Gloria had pretty much agreed to whatever TJ might decide about his contact with the corporation. TJ wanted to get him introduced to some of the people at Meridian—see if they could find something for him to do to learn about the company and fit it around his ranch work. She liked the idea of working up an internship that would mesh with his studies when he entered Harvard. But she needed to talk to him about that first. She didn't want him to think she was pressuring him into anything. She added Tom's name to the list. A tap on the door broke her concentration, and Mare came in, bearing two mugs.

"Is this a good time for a coffee break?"

"Perfect." TJ noticed that the tinge of uneasiness that had been bothering her left as soon as she spied Mare. She watched Mare's graceful movements as she set the mugs on the desk and pulled a chair up next to her.

"Working hard?" Mare saw TJ's admiring look, and she continued with a saucy grin, "Or hardly working?"

"Thinking, mostly, and that's damn hard work." TJ laid the pencil down, leaned an arm on the table, and used it to turn more fully toward Mare. She quieted for a moment, tilted her head a bit, and let her eyes feast on Mare's face.

Responding to TJ's pensive mood, Mare quieted, too. She lifted a hand and softly ran her fingertips across TJ's cheekbone. "What?" she said in a hushed voice.

"You really are beautiful, you know. Your face, your eyes, your hair, the way you move." TJ kissed the fingertips that had stroked their way down her jaw line to her lips. She smiled as Mare brought the fingers to her own lips. "You're beautiful inside, too. I don't ever want to take you for granted. I always want to be aware of how beautiful you are and how much I love you."

A smile spread from Mare's slightly turned lips to her shining eyes. "You know I feel the same way about you, sweetheart. Almost losing each other sure wakes up your awareness, doesn't it?"

"Yes, it does," TJ said huskily.

Mare squeezed TJ's hand. "Hey, we both have stuff to do today, so come on, let's drink our coffee before we get carried away, okay?"

TJ squeezed back and released the smaller hand. "Right." She reached for the coffee and took a drink.

"What are you working on?" Mare tipped her head toward the

tablet. She picked up her mug and drained most of it in one gulp.

TJ pushed the tablet over, and Mare read it. "Whew. When you put it all in one spot, it looks kind of formidable."

"We'll be pretty busy for a while, that's for sure. But we have lots of help. What are you up to today? I could hear some movement going on..." She hesitated at the words "in your office," then chose not to say them.

Mare flexed an arm, showing the muscle. "I've been moving furniture around. I got a new bookcase the other day, and Paula put it together for me. Now I'm trying to figure out where I want to —" She was stopped by the frown emerging on TJ's face. "What's wrong?"

"I'm the one who should be putting bookcases together for you and helping you move furniture around," TJ said, more sharply than she intended. For some reason, her inability to take part in that homey activity disturbed her. She grabbed at the coffee mug and practically threw the brew down her throat.

"TJ." Mare returned the frown. "You know we all help where we can and when we can. Paula was there when the bookcase was delivered, and she put it together for me. Besides..." She hesitated.

"Besides, I'm not physically able to do something like that." TJ's voice sounded rough as she finished the sentence for her. She swung back toward the desk, snatched up the pencil, and mangled it in her grasp.

"Actually, that hadn't occurred to me. I was going to say that since you won't come into the office anyway, how could you do anything?" She paused. "Unless you want to come there now and help me decide how to rearrange it."

TJ's rigidity answered for her. Mare stood up and curled her fingers through the handles of the nearly empty mugs. "I didn't come in here to start a fight. I just wanted to be with you. If you need me, you know where I am." She waited a moment, but when there was no response, she left.

MARE RINSED THE mugs and stuck them in the dishwasher. She went back down the long hall to her office and carefully closed the door behind her. She walked to the nearest chair, plopped into it, and let her eyes roam the entire room. There was no way in hell this room would ever remind TJ of her father's office. But TJ would never know that because she was too damn stubborn to even come through the door.

Now she was upset because Paula had put the bookcase together. Good grief! How was Mare supposed to know that would bother her? Then Mare's fair-minded self stepped forward. She knew TJ was upset because she wanted to be the one Mare looked to for help, yet she knew she wouldn't always be able to give that help. Well, Mare couldn't always help her, either. There were some things only TJ could handle.

TJ WAS MORE hurt than angry. Mare's words tumbled through her head: *"Paula was there...you won't come into the office...how could you do anything?"* The fact that Mare was right— TJ couldn't do anything in the office as long as she refused to enter it—only served to deepen her pain. Tears of frustration moistened her eyes, and she brushed brusquely at her cheeks as a few overflowed. Suddenly, she realized that she was on the brink of allowing herself to wallow in self-pity. She grabbed a tissue from the box on the desk and dried her eyes.

She should stop acting like a damn emotional basket case. She'd been seeing a counselor for close to two years, and she was still allowing her father to dictate her actions. She was letting her hatred of him disappoint the woman she loved—the woman who loved her—the woman she very nearly had lost. Was that hatred stronger than the love she and Mare shared? Never. Nothing was stronger than that. What had Mare said before? *"Our love's too strong to let anything stop it."* Well, it was also too strong to let any obstacle come between them. TJ had waited too long to push this particular obstacle out of the way. Mare's words echoed again. *"If you need me, you know where I am."* If you need me... If you need me...

TJ wheeled out of her office, rolled partway down the hall, and stopped. She looked at the door that stood between her and the woman she knew she would love for eternity. She set her jaw in determination and pushed hard against the handrims, going forward again. *I'll always need you, Mare.* She took a deep breath and reached for the knob.

MARE STOOD IN her office, hands on her hips, seeking a possible spot for the bookcase. She thought she heard a slight noise, and her head swiveled to the office door. Yeah, right. Like TJ was coming down the hall to see her. The impossibility of the thought saddened her, and she winced. Then she saw the doorknob turn. As if in slow motion, she turned her whole body to face the door. She watched speechlessly as the door slowly pushed open, and TJ wheeled into the room. Mare could only stare.

TJ'S BREATH CAUGHT as her eyes darted around the room. Nothing in here looked the same. Nothing. It could be a totally different room...and it was. It was Mare's office. No one else's. She breathed again as her eyes finished their circuit and came to rest on an astonished Mare. TJ's mouth tilted in her lopsided grin as she forced words through her tight throat. "I guess I should have knocked."

The words unfroze Mare, and she hurried forward. She dropped to her knees and buried her head in TJ's lap.

Long fingers stroked through Mare's hair. "I needed you," TJ said in a choked voice, "and, like you said, I knew where to find you."

Half-crying and half-laughing, Mare lifted her head and flung her arms around TJ, and they wept together. After several moments, Mare stood and grabbed some tissues and wiped TJ's face and then her own. She took TJ's hand and pulled her chair toward the couch. "Every time I fantasized about you coming into my office, I pictured you sitting on my couch." She helped a cooperative TJ maneuver into the corner of the couch, then sat next to her and laid her head against the strong shoulder.

TJ bent her head and sought Mare's lips. She kissed her gently. Then they shared a deep, lingering kiss.

When they paused, Mare lifted a palm to caress TJ's cheek. "Welcome home," she whispered.

TJ turned Mare and pulled her even closer. Mare's body eagerly responded to her touch as she slid perfectly against her. "Now it really is our home," TJ said. "No more ghosts." Her mouth began a sensuous exploration of Mare's neck, lingered at her pulse point, and placed small kisses across her flushed cheek.

"Our home," Mare whispered.

Those two small words said everything.

The End

FORTHCOMING TITLES

published by
Yellow Rose Books

Heart Trouble

by Jane Vollbrecht

Heart Trouble chronicles Jackie Frackman's journey through a tumultuous romance with the enigmtic Beth Novatny. The story is told from Jackie's first-person perspective. Lesbians of any age who have ever loved someone so right — who sometimes is someone so wrong — are sure to recognize themselves in the portrayals of Jackie and Beth as they struggle to come to terms with themselves and each other.

Coming August 2006

Learning to Trust

by Jude Morgan

Jace, the director of a college Achievement Center, has a new graduate assistant, Taryn Murphy. Both women cannot avoid spending time with each other, as they are part of an extended family. Both have their secrets and reasons not to trust, but when they find themselves opening up to each other, they realize their problems are very similar. Can a friendship develop between them or will their pasts haunt them forever.

Coming August 2006

OTHER SURTEES AND DUNNE TITLES

published by

Yellow Rose Books

True Colours

TJ Meridian, crippled in an attack on her and her brother, returns to Meridianville, Texas, a small town that her father all but destroyed ten years ago when he closed his ranch and meatpacking plant. Intending to right the wrongs, TJ, with the help of two friends, proposes to bring prosperity back to the area by restocking the ranch and modernizing the packing plant. When TJ's prized horse becomes ill, a local veterinarian is called to treat the animal. The vet, Dr. Mare Gillespie, has lived in Meridianville for the past ten years and has seen the poverty caused by Thomas Meridian's withdrawal from the area. Like most of the native residents, she harbors a great dislike for the family, yet she and TJ are each intrigued by the other woman and a relationship develops. Together they discover love and friendship that endures through personal misunderstandings, a night attack on the ranch, and an ecological disaster that could destroy the town and surrounding lands. Culminating in a life-threatening accident that requires some hard decisions, *True Colours* is the exploration of hope and love and one woman's struggle to clear her name.

ISBN 978-1-932300-52-9

OTHER YELLOW ROSE TITLES
You may also enjoy:

DIVING INTO THE TURN
by Carrie Carr

Diving Into the Turn is set in the fast-paced Texas rodeo world. Riding bulls in the rodeo is the only life Shelby Fisher has ever known. She thinks she's happy drifting from place to place in her tiny trailer, engaging in one night stands, and living from one rodeo paycheck to another – until the day she meets barrel racer Rebecca Starrett. Rebecca comes from a solid, middle-class background and owns her horse. She's had money and support that Shelby has never had. Shelby and Rebecca take an instant dislike to each other, but there's something about Rebecca that draws the silent and angry bull rider to her. Suddenly, Shelby's life feels emptier, and she can't figure out why. Gradually, Rebecca attempts to win Shelby over, and a shaky friendship starts to grow into something more.

Against a backdrop of mysterious accidents that happen at the rodeo grounds, their attraction to one another is tested. When Shelby is implicated as the culprit to what's been happening will Rebecca stand by her side?

ISBN 978- 1-932300-54-3

THE BLUEST EYES IN TEXAS
by Linda Crist

Kennedy Nocona is an out, liberal, driven attorney, living in Austin, the heart of the Texas hill country. Dallasite Carson Garret is a young paralegal overcoming the loss of her parents, and coming to terms with her own sexual orientation.

A chance encounter finds them inexplicably drawn to one another, and they quickly find themselves in a long-distance romance that leaves them both wanting more. Circumstances at Carson's job escalate into a series of mysteries and blackmail that leaves her with more excitement than she ever bargained for. Confused, afraid, and alone, she turns to Kennedy, the one person she knows can help her. As they work together to solve a puzzle, they confront growing feelings that neither woman can deny. Can they overcome the outside forces that threaten to crush them both?

ISBN 978-1-932300-48-2

Other YELLOW ROSE Publications

About the Authors:

Karen is a single 30-something who has served around the world with the Royal Navy as a medic for the past fourteen years. In her spare time she enjoys reading science fiction, especially David Webers Honor Harrington series, watching TV shows, her favourites right now are Battlestar Galactica and Grey's Anatomy, photography and playing golf to a halfway decent standard. She currently resides on the Rock of Gibraltar where she works in the last Royal Naval Hospital.

Nann Dunne lives in Southeastern Pennsylvania and shares her home with family members. She's an author, editor, and online-newsletter publisher, with 30 years of experience in editing. She's been writing fiction since 1998 and has four published books. Her free online newsletter, Just About Write (www.justaboutwrite.com), presents articles on writing, editing, and marketing, while it promotes lesbian authors, poets, book reviews, and publishers. Nann reads excerpts aloud from her books at http://www.nanndunne.com.

Printed in the United States
53485LVS00005B/93